TOOTH *and* NAIL

TOOTH *and* NAIL

jennifer SAFREY

night shade books
san francisco

Cover art by Joseph Corsentino
Cover design by Claudia Noble
Interior layout and design by Amy Popovich

Edited by Ross E. Lockhart

First Edition

ISBN: 978-1-59780-392-2

Night Shade Books
http://www.nightshadebooks.com

For my muse.
I always knew in my heart that if I waited long enough,
you would find me.

CHAPTER 1

Glove slammed into jaw. His glove, my jaw.

Back and forth, back and forth. Evenly matched, this still belonged to both of us. A drop of sweat dripped into my eye but I ignored the salty burn, never breaking away from our locked gaze.

Glove cracked into shoulder. My glove, his shoulder.

Jab, jab, jab. We measured distance by inches, by fractions of inches, pushing in, pulling away. His next punch only brushed the side of my head but it still hurt.

Then I saw it, his twitch of anticipated control. I ducked the confident punch and when I straightened my knees, I brought an uppercut with me.

Glove slammed into chin.

He had nothing, and I came at him again with a left hook.

His head fell to the side with my blow, and over his shoulder, I saw something.

In the fraction of a second it took me to glance at it, my opponent drove into my gut. I exhaled hard and my knees buckled. But I pushed at him again with another uppercut, my momentum tilting me back upright. He swayed but locked his gaze onto mine, and I had to unleash punch after punch to keep him on the defensive, keep my advantage. A shout from below us: "It's over! Let's go!"

Halting my fist halfway to its target, I backed off. And I had to hand it to him—he held his ground until I turned away. I wrestled with my head gear. "You all right?" I called over my shoulder.

"I'm good."

I collapsed on a stool in the closest corner of the ring, and remembered the glimmering distraction. I half stood, searching the spot where I'd seen something. Then I surveyed the dark room, filled thick with sweat and ambition. No sparkles.

My sparring partner, Not-Rocky, walked over to me. A moment ago he was someone I had to take down. But now he was my friend again.

"I'll probably need to suck up my dinner through a straw tonight," I said, moving my lower jaw from side to side.

He grinned around his mouth guard before spitting it out and opening his mouth wide to let go of the hit to his chin. "I'm going to be hunched over for a week if it makes you feel any better."

"It does."

"I knew it would." He slung an arm around me. "Ow," I told him.

"Sorry."

"No, you're not."

"Yeah," he said, "I'm kinda not."

Something shimmered in my periphery. It moved.

I shoved my friend's arm away and spun around, raising gloves to my face. Ready to dodge, and ready to strike—

Nothing.

No, I thought, something. Something alive and formless and there. It hovered around chest-level, then the air seemed to shimmy into wavy watery lines. I put out my fat glove but it only slipped through the apparition. I snatched my hand back and in an instant the waves stilled, the life draining out, and it was nothing.

Of course, it had been nothing.

"What's up?" Not-Rocky asked.

"I saw something. Just now. Out of the corner of my eye."

"You saw stars, is what you saw."

I blinked again, then squinted at still nothing. The air was quiet and empty. I let out a breath. Much as I hated to admit it, he had to be right. But I glanced back once as we walked away.

Nothing.

"Good thing you quit," Mat shouted at Not-Rocky from the free weights at the back wall. "You'se about to get your ass kicked by a girl."

"Bricks isn't a girl," Not-Rocky countered.

I was Gemma Cross to the outside world, the real world, but not here. Here we turned into our own superheroes, and our real-world names weren't appropriate for the transformation. The guys were nicknamed for their quirky personalities, but bewildered by the ways of the female, they did the man thing and zeroed right in on my appearance—christening me the oh-so-not-original Brickhouse. I knew why. I was sort of Amazonian—hard and muscular, but not lacking in curves, thank you very much. Five-foot-ten and often indignant, I was pretty sure I scared a lot of other women. So I liked the company of my boys.

"I'm not a girl?" I asked. "What the hell's that supposed to mean?"

"Ah, you know what I mean."

I did. Every time I stepped into Smiley's Gym, I left my femininity at the door.

Smiley's, nestled in D.C.'s Chinatown, was not your trendy gym with generic dance mixes blaring from speakers on every wall and buzzing blenders mixing up fruity power drinks at members-only snack bars. No girls here in pink sweatpants with "Angel" splashed across a tiny ass—no girls here at all, really. Once in a while, a woman would walk in with a black eye or a split bottom lip, her quiet request for lessons tinged with bitterness and vengeance. These women punched hard but didn't stay long, leaving me, as the representative for my gender, a little bit sadder and angrier on their behalf.

"Not bad for a chick," Not-Rocky said as we walked slowly away from the ring.

"Not bad for a puny little punk."

The usual end to our practice bouts.

My buddy Not-Rocky was about my size, so we were preferred sparring partners. He was our fair and blond Philly boy, and he'd admitted that the one time he tried Rocky's famous run up the steps of the Philadelphia Museum of Art, he'd made it only halfway up before turning an about-face and jogging right back down behind a beautiful redhead. Not-Rocky had a very crooked nose—it tilted slightly to the viewer's left—but he swore that when he was born, it was actually tilted to the right. He claimed there was a two-year period in junior high when it was knocked straight, but he had yet to provide photographic evidence.

He'd been coming to Smiley's for a few years. I'd been coming here pretty much forever.

I'd thrown my duffel bag on a creaky, lopsided folding chair, and now I pulled out the sports section of the *Washington Post* that I'd folded inside this morning. I crumpled a few pages and stuffed them into each of my gloves to absorb my hand sweat, then shoved paper and gloves into the bag. I extracted a hand towel from a side pocket, wiped away the tracks of perspiration sliding down to my jaw line, then patted the back of my neck under my ponytail. There was a TV on an unsteady rolling stand near the free weights, and three guys were slowly lifting while watching with half-open mouths. Keyed up and pacing, I wandered over to the rickety TV stand as the guys simultaneously said, "Ohhh," and winced.

They watched a bit more, then all three boxers exhaled the breath they'd been apparently holding. "Dude, I can't believe he did that," he said.

The others agreed: "That was harsh." "He slept with her sister?

Damn."

I peered at the screen that held them rapt. "Oh, my God," I said. "Soap operas? Really?"

"Shhh," they hissed. Then, "Oh, come *on.*"

Breaking News. The trio threw up hands and turned away. "Always with the breaking news," one said.

"Because," I said, "no actual current event can be more important than what happens to a fictional spurned woman."

Sarcasm did a flyover of three thick heads. One guy muttered, "Now we'll never know what she says to him."

I looked at the TV. A school shooting. Kids dead, teacher hurt, gunman suicide. This was the second school shooting in the D.C. area in six months, the news reminded the viewers. I watched enough to know I didn't want to watch more, and I stepped away from the TV just as Not-Rocky reached my side. I shook my head at him. "The world is really disgusting," I said to him.

He stationed himself in front of the screen and I headed back to my bag and stuffed the damp towel in a side pocket.

"I know that kid," I thought I heard Not-Rocky say.

"What?" I called. "What are you talking about?"

"I remember him. He was here. It was a while ago."

I joined him again and cut him a sideways glance. "You've been knocked around so much, you don't remember what you had for breakfast this morning. How do you remember some kid?"

"I do," he insisted, nodding and squinting to draw it out of his mind. "Maybe about a year ago or something. He came in here, little skinny kid. He wanted lessons. Smiley took one look at him and asked him where he lived, where his parents were. I couldn't hear the kid but he musta told Smiley he lived in a nice house in the suburbs with his mom, because Smiley told him to beat it. He said, come back when you're older and bigger. Chocolate doughnut."

"What?"

"That's what I had for breakfast. Chocolate doughnut."

"Breakfast of champions," I said. "It's no wonder I smacked you around."

He began to protest, but I shushed him to watch a little more. The boy's picture was now stationed at the bottom left corner of the screen while they continued breaking the story.

Yeah, I thought, Not-Rocky's vague testimony made sense. Smiley was a saint, taking care of guys here who had no one and nothing more than a little bit of talent. He wasn't going to train a junior-high kid unless that kid was on welfare or being beaten up at home. He would send a nice suburban kid packing, just like Not-Rocky said. It was the right decision; this place wasn't for a boy like that. This room was full of contenders. It was no place for a lonely child who had anywhere else to go.

Of course, I knew Smiley had made an exception for me, but he'd had his reasons and his promises and he knew who I was.

I'd acted out, I'd been angry, I'd had misplaced aggression, but I was never violent for its own sake, and I was sure that even if this gym hadn't become to me what it did, I still wouldn't have been.

"You know," I said to Not-Rocky, "it feels like this kid violence has become way more frequent."

"Don't know," he said. "I don't watch a lot of news."

"I do. There was that kid a couple of weeks ago who pushed her brother out their second-floor window. He actually survived." I thought a moment. "Wasn't there a boy who took out his grandfather or… yeah, his grandfather. I think that was in Virginia. Right?"

"I told you I don't watch news. This is why. All bad news."

"Maybe I'm just paying closer attention these days."

"Nah. This"—Not-Rocky gestured at the TV—"is nothing new. There's stuff like this all the time."

"I guess." I stood. "It's depressing. Turn it off."

He lifted the remote with his gloves and pressed the power button with his sore chin. I laughed when he winced. "All bad kids don't grab shotguns," he pointed out. "I mean, look at us.

This room is full of fuck-ups."

"Not me." I moved toward the chairs. "I've got my life in order, I think."

"Finally. Only took forty years."

"I'm thirty, moron."

"So that new boyfriend of yours straightened you out, huh?"

"Yes." I slung my bag over my shoulder. "He's a public figure. So I have to behave in public."

"Good luck with that."

"Go home," I told him, moving toward the door. "Lay off the doughnuts."

"What am I supposed to do with the whole box I just bought?"

"Feed them to the pigeons."

"I don't think that's good for them."

"Well, it's not good for you either."

I blew him a kiss and he laughed when my hand shot up to cover my aching mouth. I waved him off and pushed the door open.

Gray clouds fat with threatening rain shifted across the sky, throwing shadowy light tricks onto the street.

The shimmer tickled my periphery.

My body became very still. Wind brushed my hair into my eyes, and caught in my lashes.

I didn't know whether I wanted it to be someone or not. I'd lost fights, and lost them badly, but I'd only suffered humiliation and a few broken bones. Never weird sparkly hallucinations.

I stood in silence. It wasn't hard to do. D.C. was a very quiet city. I was sure there must have been more bustle here than any other city in the country, considering this city ran the country—and was the hotbed of scandal—but I could never hear it. Not even now, when I was actively trying to hear something.

Nothing. But I saw it again.

I whirled, and my bag slammed me in the chest. Standing in front of me was a woman.

She didn't shrink back from my sudden confrontation. I wasn't certain she even blinked. She just looked at me.

Her hair was as blond as mine but far longer and thicker, made even more luxurious by the fact that it framed a tiny little head, attached to a little pixie body that was somewhere around size double-zero. She was smiling, a bright beam piercing the stormy darkness that was falling around us. I placed her at about forty, reconsidered her to be closer to my thirty, then finally gave up guessing. Each of her distinct features was something I'd seen on someone else at some point, but her particular combination was unique in a way I knew I'd never be able to describe.

Under her green-eyed appraisal, I had the uneasy—and unusual—urge to squirm.

"Gemma," she said.

I noticed she didn't raise her voice on the last syllable in a question; rather, it was a statement, as confident as if she'd added, *of course*.

"Do I know you?" I asked. I'd recovered from her apparent materialization from thin air, but I was genuinely puzzled at her assumption of familiarity.

"Not yet," she said, as if it had merely been a matter of time until we'd crossed paths.

I raised a brow, not quite unfriendly, but intending to relay my growing impatience.

If she caught my meaning, she didn't bother to apologize. "I'm Frederica Diamond," she said. "I would like to talk to you about a business opportunity, Gemma."

"A business opportunity," I repeated. O-*kay*. "I'm already employed."

"Not at the moment, I understand."

I thought. "You're a headhunter?"

"In a manner of speaking."

"And you came to find me here? Kind of aggressive recruiting techniques you've got there."

"*You* don't approve?"

Well, at least she'd done her homework and knew the sort of person she was dealing with. Kudos for that. "Still," I told her, "seems extreme to track me down here."

"It's quite an important opportunity. It was my job to find you. I'm very good at it."

"Obviously," I said, trying to process the creepiness of the whole situation. "But I'm currently on hiatus from full-time employment."

"Yes. To avoid conflict with Mr. McCormack's race for Congress," Frederica said.

Okay, I supposed anyone at my office could have mentioned that to her. But my uneasiness was growing. I had about half a foot and forty pounds on this woman—not to mention I was dressed to fight—but not only did I feel completely non-intimidating, Frederica had the cool upper hand in this conversation.

And she'd never stopped smiling.

"It would really be worth your while," she added, "to hear out my proposal."

"This is creepy," I said.

"It isn't."

"No?"

"No." She looked deep into my eyes, down into me, and rattled my core. "We need you, Gemma."

Her delicate emphasis on "you" startled me, almost as much as the door slamming open behind me. Two boxers, now in T-shirts and with perspiration drying along their hairlines, nodded casual goodbyes at me.

"See you tomorrow," I said, forcing a smile. I wasn't sure why I waited until they rounded the corner to turn back around, but I did. And she was gone.

In her place was a shimmer of wavy, liquid energy, and then I blinked it away.

CHAPTER 2

"Hey! I have a dentist's appointment tomorrow." I jabbed a finger into the wall calendar, free with our Peking ravioli from Hun Lee's up the street and depicting a circular parade of Chinese zodiac animals.

"Wow!" Avery exclaimed, matching my incredulous tone. "What a fun day!" He sat on the edge of the bed and took off his socks.

"Shut up," I said. "I didn't mean it like that. I made the appointment months ago for a cleaning and I forgot about it." I nodded. "Cool."

"Should I be worried you're getting excited about the prospect of seeing your dentist?" Avery asked. He stood again, unbuttoned his dress shirt and removed it, draping it on the top corner of our bedroom door. "Most people dread going to the dentist. In fact, some just never even go because they're too scared. But you sound like it's the highlight of your week. Maybe I should go have a chat with this hunky dentist with the magnetic personality."

I watched him slide his black leather belt out of his pants in one smooth motion. "A dentist with a magnetic personality would not fare well in a room full of sharp metal tools," I said.

"Excellent point," he allowed.

"Besides, Dr. Gold is probably about eight years past retirement age. Not my type."

"Good thing. Because I have enough to worry about without my girl running off with the dentist."

"'My girl,' eh? Wouldn't want your voters to hear you talking such blatant possessive objectification."

"You don't like it?"

"It's pretty hot, actually."

I walked over to Avery and wrapped my arms around his now-bare shoulders. I kissed him on the neck and lingered there, breathing in his skin, for—well, not as long as I would have liked. He had a meeting with his campaign manager and some other people in the morning and I knew he ought to turn in early, so I untangled myself.

"An hour in the dentist's chair sounds pretty good compared to the day I have tomorrow," he said, pulling on an old T-shirt. A really old T-shirt. Tour dates for Foreigner fell down the back. "I feel like I'm treading on my own last good nerve. I don't know why I did this to myself."

He crossed to the window and gazed out. I said nothing and let him contemplate. From our brick-front townhouse in the Court House section of Arlington, Virginia, we didn't have a view of the Capitol dome, but its imposing silhouette was out there across the Potomac, representing everything Avery wanted to do.

Although we weren't too far yet into our new domestic arrangement, I'd witnessed his bouts of self-flagellation just enough times to know when to intervene. So I let a couple of well-timed minutes pass, then spoke. "You and I both know why you're doing this," I said. "For truth, justice, the American way, and purple mountain majesties. Plus, you're the best-looking House candidate out there right now, so it doesn't take an experienced pollster to assure you that you have the female 18–35 demographic. Now you just have to reach a few more voters and you're in. So spare me the crap."

A smile played at the corner of his full, sexy bottom lip, and I saw it reflected back at me from the night mirror of a window. "Gemma, you always know the right thing to say. And then you choose to say something else entirely. I can't figure out why."

"Listen, I wasn't in polling for nothing. I know my stuff."

"Doubtless."

"Besides, I already told you I'm happy to do a TV ad where I threaten to beat the hell out of anyone who doesn't vote for you. The boys at Smiley's will back me up."

He pushed the window up a few inches to let in the April air, and drew the curtain before stripping down to his Washington Capitals boxer shorts. "Though I have full confidence that you and your 'Fight Club' buddies could get the job done, I think I might prefer to not run a political campaign in such a—well, Mafia-esque fashion."

"Fear is a powerful motivator," I said, sitting on the bed. "The offer stands when you change your mind."

"You're a scary broad."

I picked up my cup of before-bed chai tea from the nightstand and took a careless gulp. It scalded its way down my throat. I never waited for it to cool. "Seriously," I said with a slightly scratchier voice. "you don't need my help. You have to win. You're the good guy."

"So was my dad," Avery countered.

Avery's father, Johnson McCormack, had been an outspoken, charismatic shoo-in for office—until an ugly campaign money scandal materialized and covered every newspaper's front page from here to the border. Johnson was exonerated, but his career was a casualty that couldn't be revived.

I knew Avery felt the eyes of the nation on him, on each thread of his suits and ties, and on every move he made. To the voting public, the younger McCormack had a dark and handsome appeal, a bright mind, a can-and-will-do attitude and, a small handful of cynical pundits insisted, was a train wreck waiting to happen. How, they asked, could district attorney Avery McCormack be so infallible in his campaign for the House of Representatives when his old man went down like a tower of empty beer cans?

They knew politics, so they thought they knew Avery. But I *knew* Avery. No skeleton had ever taken up residence in any of his closets, and no scandal had ever sniffed its way around any of his ethics. He was good, through and through. He was an idealist, a hard worker, and would be beyond reproach—if politics played honestly with him. And Avery didn't trust that to happen.

"You're not your dad," I said now.

"I'm still the closest thing to it. If I make one wrong turn, no one will give me an inch of leeway."

"Why worry about that when nothing will go wrong? You're perfect. And I'm—well, I'm not, I guess, but I can be low-key."

"Offering to punch people's lights out as they leave the voting booths is your idea of low-key, eh?"

"That was a *joke*, sir. Maybe I do, on occasion, speak without thinking. Once in a while, I *might* have a *small* emotional outburst."

Avery slipped into the bathroom and turned on the tap, but he'd left the door slightly ajar and I could hear his muffled laughter.

"What," I yelled, "is so funny?"

"Nothing," he called over his splashing.

"You lying politician. Or, I'm sorry, is that redundant?"

"Babe," he said, returning with his face in a towel, "occasional outburst? Half the time it's like 'Gemma, Interrupted' around here."

I downed the rest of my chai and flopped back onto the pillows. "I don't know why you continue to mock me when you're fully aware I could crack your head open like a coconut."

"That's my girl. Solving conflicts with brute force." He chuckled. "What I don't understand is how someone so numbers-and-concrete-proof oriented in her career could ignore logic and reason in favor of her emotions the rest of the time."

"I don't do it on purpose," I said. "I don't know why I'm—I mean, I know I should be—"

Avery kneeled on the floor, and I sat back up, swinging my legs around to embrace his shoulders. "You're exactly the way you should be. An unpredictable puzzle, and that's the best part about you. I love you more than anything," he said.

"I know," I said, softening.

When he kissed me, I tasted minty-fresh toothpaste.

When we drew apart, I said, "The original point to this conversation was that I'm happy about my dentist's appointment because it gives me something to actually *do* tomorrow."

"I didn't ask you to leave your job. Go back to work if you're unhappy."

"No," I said. I shook my head with such emphasis, a strand of my hair lodged itself under my contact lens. I rubbed at it, then realized I'd forgotten to take them out. I hopped off the bed and jogged to the bathroom. "We made a decision and I'm sticking to it," I said, filling each compartment of the little case with saline. "It's only until you're Congressman McCormack. I didn't feel right doing polling work during your campaign." I plucked out my left lens and plopped it into the case, then looked at myself in the mirror. Through only one lens, I resembled a blond, blurry Picasso painting.

"Your work doesn't have anything to do with my campaign."

"I don't want even one idiot to insinuate a possible conflict. And," I added, removing my other lens and sealing it up, "I need a break anyhow."

Which was the purest white of all lies. I loved my job. But I didn't feel bad about saying it, because I knew Avery was lying right back at me when he said he thought I should go back to work. It was true that he hadn't *outright* asked me to leave my job, but his protests now were weak and obligatory. I knew full I was relieving him of one less worry.

I also white-lied by omission by not mentioning whatshername who appeared out of thin air today—maybe literally?—with her strange offer for some kind of job. I didn't tell Avery about it mostly because I was suspicious that I went unconscious for a few seconds and dreamed her. I'd never gotten knocked around so hard that it had caused me to hallucinate. I was willing to buy that explanation. But the hallucination had a conversation with me, and that was what worried me. I didn't want Avery to worry too.

But I needed to know: "What is a migraine like?" Avery got them sometimes and had complained about strange swirly light crossing his vision.

"Well, for one, you get a headache like someone beat you over the head with a club quite similar to the kind Captain Caveman carries around," Avery said.

"No. I don't have a headache."

"You've never had a migraine before," he said. "Did you take a few to the head today?"

"A few," I admitted. "I'm getting those swirly light things you said you have when you get a migraine. Not now, not since I got home, but before."

"Maybe it's a concussion."

"No," I said, dismissing it with one hand. "I've had a couple of those." I blinked hard, keeping my eyelids closed until I could feel wetness under my lashes. "When you get those little lights, do they look watery and kind of … alive?"

I heard him pause. "Are we sure it's not a concussion?"

"Positive. And I haven't had it in a few hours." I thought. "Not-Rocky said I was just seeing stars, and he's probably right. It was right after a spar and as I was leaving the gym, the sky was kind of weird so maybe my eyes just did the same thing."

"Maybe," Avery said, "you want to wait a couple of days anyway before you get in the ring again."

"No."

"Okay, maybe I want it."

I sighed. "Fine."

"Gemma?" he asked. "Can we back up a little in this conversation? I need to tell you that I don't want you to think for a moment that I don't realize your sacrifices or that I don't appreciate them."

I stepped out of the bathroom and leaned against the door frame. "Yeah, well, I'm okay with it because now you're my bitch." I grinned.

"Let's keep that between you and me for the time being."

"I plan on it being you and me for a very long time." I took in his smile, then ran both my hands through my short, straight hair, suddenly hot despite the cool spring breeze blowing through the gauzy, raw-edged curtain. "Go to sleep already, before I jump you."

Avery stood and flicked off the bathroom light as I switched off the lamp. He slid into bed beside me, but instead of settling himself into the sheets, he leaned over me.

"What?" I asked, even though I knew very well what.

"Are those my choices? Sleep, or you jump me?"

"Yeah, pretty much."

"I cast my vote for," he said with a grin I couldn't see but could hear, "jump me."

I pushed up and flipped him over on his back, my knees straddling his hips. I yanked my tank top over my head and flung it away. He laughed.

I loved democracy.

>=<

That night, I had the dream again.

The dream that kicked my ass; the dream that was always an omen, a warning to me that life was about to spin into confusion.

I crawl out of bed and stumble, and my hand goes to my mouth, which hurts. It hurts from the inside of my lips to the back of my throat and all around. I press my back teeth together and instead of feeling the comforting close of molars, it's shaky in there, like a city sidewalk moments after an earthquake. I blink hard and grab the door frame, pulling myself into the hallway. I let go of the wall and try to take one step, but setting my bare heel down on the thick carpet is too jarring for my fragile mouth, and a small, smooth tooth drops onto my tongue. It slides around, sticky, salty, metallic, and I spit it out. It hits the carpet with a physically impossible but distinct echoey tinkle, and the sound and horror of looking at my own tooth weakens my knees and I fold down onto the floor. I fall hard and struggle against my fear and fatigue to prop myself onto my forearms.

My jaw is on fire but I can't open my mouth—I won't open my mouth. I don't want another tooth to drop out. I seal my blood-sticky lips together until it fills up, my mouth fills up with it, the pressure building behind my lips until I can't breathe, and I open wide, gasping like a guppy from an overturned bowl.

In a gush of blood and saliva, my teeth fall out. All of them. I press my chin to the scratchy rug fibers and stare at the macabre, wet little pile. My mouth is still hanging open, and as I breathe, I can feel cold air whistling through the new holes in my gums. A warm stickiness trails from my jaw line down my neck and pools hot into my collarbone.

I collapse onto the mess, and my freed teeth push sharp into my skin, biting my cheek.

Then I abruptly scramble to get up and grab at the teeth. I have to get them. I have to put them in my pocket. But every time I get a fistful, they slide from between my fingers and fall away again. No! I have to collect them, save them, keep them, I need them… But now I hear whispers, musical laughing whispers. I can't make out the words, yet I know what they're saying: Grab the teeth, get them all, don't lose them…

I woke up sweaty, blurry, disoriented.

I flailed an arm out and my knuckles thumped a sleeping Avery. He clasped my hand and held it still against his hard chest. I poked my tongue against my front teeth, testing their fortitude, and stopped upon realizing they weren't going to pop out in front of my face.

I slid my hand out from underneath Avery's and went to stand naked by the window. I stared through the transparent curtains as they blew into the room, kissing my forehead, sliding against my nose.

I wondered, and worried.

Stupid dream, stupid nightmare. I hadn't seen this punch coming.

In the boxing ring, I had to know how to land a punch, but to win, I also had to know how to evade one. And I was pretty good at the landing and the evading. Boxing was a dark kind of dance, moving in and out of invisible boundaries, touching while remaining untouchable. When I was fighting evenly matched, I won more than I lost.

But this dream was never my fair opponent.

It waited—sometimes for years—until its chosen night, when I was asleep and vulnerable, when I'd surrendered my physical ability and my mental control. Then it held me down and unleashed one sucker-punch after another. I couldn't fight back and I couldn't pull away. I could only scream into a black void until the dream chose to release me, and I awakened sweaty, blurry, disoriented, and afraid to stand.

Tonight, I hadn't seen it coming.

I knew recurring dreams weren't an unusual phenomenon, and I'd began extensive research on the dream, oh, maybe the third or fourth time I had it, years ago, and I learned teeth-falling-out is one of the most common dreams that people have. I collected all the different interpretations and so-called deep meanings. There were a lot of them: anxiety about outward appearances, fear of embarrassment, feelings of powerlessness, fear of uncontrollable events, fear of getting old.

The one time I told my mother about the dream, she seemed

strangely alarmed for a moment, but then told me that she'd heard the losing-teeth nightmare signifies a loss of childhood innocence. I surmised at the time that she was digging for information the way wily single moms do, so I said nothing further to incriminate myself.

Eventually, I decided I might never narrow down the meaning as it pertained to me personally, but I did pinpoint a pattern to the dream's occurrence—always immediately preceding a significant life- and attitude-altering event.

Example: One week before I graduated high school, I had the dream. It kicked off a week of insomnia, in which I panicked every moment I spent in the dark, wondering how I would eventually pay off my college loans, find a great man, deal with the pain of childbirth—maybe more than once—on top of doing my own grocery shopping and laundry. The prospect of adulthood crushed down on me, pinning me to my bright yellow sheets and daring me to struggle against it. I did finally fall asleep—at the graduation ceremony, during the speeches, my head dropping down. My mortarboard landed on the scuffed gymnasium floor.

Another example: I had the tooth dream, then three days later, my college sweetheart-slash-fiance informed me that he was trading in the previously unbreakable love that we shared for a woman he met on the subway and had sex with within the hour.

And the first time I had the dream was the night before the day my father left us.

So now, I stood shivering in the warmth of the dark. It had rained while I dreamed, and I breathed in blossomy fresh water evaporating off the steaming sidewalks. I worried more, and I wondered more.

Was it possible that this time, this one night, my omen dream simply had the timing wrong? That it was just a little late? Because my life-altering event had just happened last week, when I'd moved in with Avery and taken a leave from my polling job. It marked the first time in my adult life that I wouldn't be working, the first time I'd be a "domestic partner," and the first time I had offered up such a commitment to—anyone.

And I hadn't been scared to do it. I had been confident and sure, even upon leaving the office with my box of desk supplies, even upon collapsing on my end of the sofa after we hefted it into our new living room. Especially when Avery had slammed the door and we both jumped into the sofa to make love, a still-open U-Haul on the street with half our belongings inside.

In my personal history book, this was a life-changing, noteworthy event. I was about to become a full-time stay-at-homer, helping Avery in his campaign for the U.S. House of Representatives. Going to fundraising parties and getting my picture taken. Watching daytime TV and reading magazines. Training at the gym. A temporary life of leisure. Still, a very big change.

He was having a great run. *We* were having a great run.

I shook my head, took a deep breath and pushed the curtains aside to smile at myself. My white teeth grinned at me in the window, my form a darkening shadow against the brightening dawn. I nodded at myself, acknowledging the familiarity of my own face. *That's all*, I told myself, before turning around, peeling back the damp sheets on my side of the bed and sliding back beside Avery's warmth. The dream was just a little late. Maybe even a *good* sign, confirming this important milestone for me—for me *and* Avery.

My worry took a few more minutes to dissipate, minutes in which I allowed the sound of my breath to overtake the lingering sound of those sweet, teasing whispers. They faded away, and I knew I wouldn't be able to clearly recall their laughing entreaties until the next time I heard them, another night.

Tonight had to be a mental blip, an aberration, a break in the pattern. Nothing more.

Convincing myself that I'd just convinced myself, I soon fell asleep again.

>=<

"Gemma."

"Mmmf."

"I'm leaving," Avery said softly into my ear. "I have that early meeting."

I rolled over and got a mouthful of pillow. "Why didn't the alarm go off?" I asked, muffled and confused.

"It did. You were dead to it."

"I had a bad dream." As soon as it was out of my mouth, I wished I'd held it in. It was childish, frightened, wimpy. But my face was still smooshed into the pillow. Maybe he hadn't heard me.

"What was the dream about?" he asked.

I flipped over and looked at him.

I could have told him. I could tell Avery anything. But the timing was no good. I would have had to explain not only the dream but its place in my history—that it was my harbinger of difficult times of change. Given his tendency to worry about his campaign anyway, he might buy into the omen theory, and he didn't need that now.

"I don't remember," I told him. "It's already gone."

"That's the way with dreams," he said, and disappeared out the front door.

I didn't like the sound of that.

I lay staring at the ceiling, then realized after a few minutes that I was actually trying to decide what to wear to the dentist's office, as it was my big outing of the day besides the gym. Pathetic. Yesterday, my highlight had been staring at the TV, hypnotized by Rachael Ray as she manipulated ground turkey for thirty minutes. The day before that, the digital cable telemarketer and I discovered we had a soap opera in common, and after twenty-five minutes of chat, I was kind of obligated to sign up for the deluxe package. I didn't think Avery was yet aware of our new nudie channels, but I thought it safe to assume it wouldn't lead to much of an argument when he did figure it out.

That was the way it was going, day after day. I *did* miss my job. I missed crunching numbers, making phone calls, seeing my work published on our online site, and sometimes cited in newspapers and on TV. More than ninety percent of the polling at the company was market research, but there was a small amount of political polling, and it was enough to worry both Avery and myself when he announced his candidacy.

I would go back soon. But I'd never been out of work, not since I was fourteen and earning paper route cash. In college, I was a scholarship student, but I needed to work during my non-class hours to buy my hefty statistics textbooks for both undergraduate and graduate courses. I worked to pay for my membership at Smiley's. I didn't realize until recently that I really didn't know how to *not* work.

Complaining was pointless because I took the leave from work out of love and support for Avery—the most important reason.

But I had to face it: After three weeks, I was isolated, teetering on the precipice of ennui.

I needed something to do with myself. Soon.

CHAPTER 3

"Go ahead and rinse."

I sat up, reaching an awkward hand for the little Dixie cup as my paper bib swiped my chin. I sipped and spit, watching drops of blood and disgusting bits of God-knows-what slosh into the—I didn't even know what it was. Fountain? Spittoon?

I kept rinsing until my mouth was clean, then I leaned back. My skull hurt from the slightly misplaced headrest, and it didn't help matters when some kind of power tool zoomed to sudden loud life in the adjoining exam room.

"At least I don't have it as bad as the poor patient next door," I remarked.

Denise, the hygienist, laughed, displaying her own shiny teeth. I wondered about hygienists. When they woke up and before they went to bed, did they brush each individual tooth in their mouths to a count of sixty? Or did they figure, "The hell with it, if my teeth go bad, I get a discount at work"?

"No, hon," Denise said now. "We've got contractors renovating in there. Dr. Gold retired last week."

I grinned, remembering last night's banter with Avery. "Finally, huh?"

"You're not kidding. We practically had to shove him out the door and down to Florida. You'd think he'd want some relaxation by now."

"So what are the renovations?"

"New dentist taking over the practice. He wanted to make some changes."

I raised a brow, which I could do really well, by the way. "Dentists' offices generally aren't known for their hip and original interior design. It's usually minimalist. Chair, sink, tray of terrifying sterilized weaponry."

"Yeah, well, I have no idea what he's doing in there, and I don't want to know. I just come in, clean teeth, and leave." She unclipped my bib and scrunched it up before tossing it in the trash can. "You're good to go."

"I can't tell you how much I enjoy our time together," I told her, standing and sliding my tongue over my smoother teeth and sorer gums.

"Me too," Denise said. "I know! Let's do it again in six months."

"Great idea!" Corny as I could be, I still loved it when people went along with humor. It gave me a nice we're-all-in-this-together feeling about humanity. "Thanks for omitting the flossing lecture."

"Please. Everyone's negligence keeps me off the unemployment line." She laughed again. "I guess I shouldn't say that. See you, Gemma."

After I tore out a check for the receptionist and booked my next appointment, I stepped out into the D.C. sun. My overwhelmed eyes immediately teared up, since I'd spent the last hour with my eyes shut so as to avoid staring into the scare-tactic poster of a gaping, rotting grimace on the exam room wall in front of me. I dropped my gym bag at my feet and kneeled down next to it, shoving aside my black sports bra and sweat socks to unearth my sunglasses. Mall shoppers passed me, paper shopping bags bumping against their legs. I watched the 54 bus rumble by, and the rush of dust in its wake kicked up into my face.

Before I could put the glasses on, I saw him.

He was across the street. Just standing there, lazy, leaning against a lamppost as if time was nothing to consider. He was casual blond, and long-legged in beat-up jeans. I'd never seen him before in my life.

And he was watching me.

Not only was he watching me, he wasn't bothering to be covert. But he wasn't flirty or cute, and he wasn't at all creepy. He looked at me like he recognized me.

No, he looked at me like he recognized something *in* me, something that was also in him.

I couldn't break our mutual gaze. I felt like I was drowning in it, my insides turning faster and faster until I was lightheaded. He seemed to exist in his own dimension, one that only I could see, and the cars and buses and people around me faded into silence and stillness.

I wondered how many steps it was between him and myself, and envisioned darting across the street and pressing into his chest.

"Oh!" I exclaimed, as a suited man barged into my left side. I tripped over my gym bag, still on the ground, and put out a forearm, landing flat but uninjured. The man who had crashed into me stepped over me and kept walking without looking back, but rather switching his cell phone to his other ear.

I snapped my head up and waited for a taxi to pass across my vision, and when it did, the lamppost stood alone.

Hoisting myself to my feet, I shook my head—not from my crash-landing but from the sparkly fog that had enveloped me for who-knew-how-long. What was that? Who was that? Who was I?

My still-sore mouth twinged and I put a hand to my jaw before widening my eyes. Teeth. The dream. Oh, this could not be it, could it? A warning not to cheat on Avery? No. Ridiculous. I didn't even know that guy.

But he knew me.

No, he didn't. Of course he didn't. I was obviously delirious from pain. Or the contractors knocked some laughing gas loose in the dentist's office, causing me to visualize a hot man across the street, as well as fantasize about having him.

Much more logical. Because I hadn't even glanced at another man since Avery. Well, sure I had, but only to come to the conclusion that not one would measure up to my man.

I zipped up my duffel, snatched it up in one hand, and walked resolutely down K Street. I would keep walking until I arrived at my haven, my second home, and could pound out my unexpected and unwelcome frustration.

>=<

After my strange street encounter and the shock of sexuality, I was grateful to take refuge at Smiley's Gym.

The door slammed behind me and my eyes watered once again with the reverse adjustment from bright sunlight to dim, sweaty cave. I closed my eyes for a moment to allow seamless assimilation of the rest of me.

Like I said, this was my haven, but certainly not for any kind of sanctuary-like silence. The auditory ambience of Smiley's was multi-layered: Over the top were men shouting, cheering, slapping their palms against the mat in the ring as if the two boxers currently sparring were actually duking it out for a world championship. The second layer was the dull, solid thud-thud of gloves on one or more of the heavy bags, and the relentless cadence of the several small speed bags. Underneath it all was a breathing hum, proof that Smiley's was alive with ambition and pride and pain, punctuated by an occasional strong, huffing exhale when a punch was thrown—or taken.

Smiley had run this place for decades—no one knew exactly how many, but an educated guess could be made by the years etched on his face, and by the yellowing and faded photos of local heroes on the walls. On the rare occasion that he actually did smile at any of us, the irony of his longtime nickname showed through the gaps where several teeth used to be.

Teeth again.

A determined weight barreled into my right side, making my eyes pop open. I stepped away from the shove, and my assailant stumbled through his own momentum, straightening up at the last minute.

"Mat," I said, putting a hand on his bare shoulder to steady his wobbling, "it's sad that the only way you think you can throw me down is with a dirty hit. And you can't even do that."

"Well, what are you doin', sleepin' standin' up?" Mat asked, dodging my verbal jab and returning with his own. "Maybe you too busy at night bouncin' the mattress to get sleep." He grinned.

"Maybe that's all you think about 'cause you're not getting any." I pinched his smooth cheek.

Mat smacked my hand away. "I'm ignorin' that, 'cause it's so wrong, it's funny."

Cuban-American, baby-faced and barely out of high school, Mat had the nerve of men twice his size and his age. Mat was not his real name. I didn't think any of us knew what that was. Since the first day he strutted in here about eight months prior, challenging all comers and going facedown on the mat inside of thirty seconds, he'd been known as Mat. He'd since redeemed himself a bit with hard work, but his more-than-healthy ego never ceased.

I steered Mat toward a heavy bag, and slipped into the bathroom to change from jeans, short black boots and T-shirt to sports bra, black tank and gray sweat shorts. I eyed my reflection in the streaky mirror before pulling my short hair into a baby ponytail at the back of my head. I re-emerged, sat in a creaky metal folding chair, and began to wrap my hands, winding around my wrist and across my palm and between my thumb and forefinger. I opened and closed the hand, then went to work on the other one, glancing around the gym as I did.

The usual suspects were there. Sometimes I wondered whether they ever left. I lifted my chin and nodded to Shirley, who was jumping rope in the corner. He crisscrossed the rope in acknowledgment, and did a quick double-jump before reassuming the rhythm. Shirley was a nice guy. Really nice. Any time you asked for a favor—a ride to the bus stop in the rain, a dime to round out your money for the drink machine—he responded, "Surely," his white smile striking in his dark, chiseled face. It was a good thing the girly moniker didn't bother him, because he'd be real intimidating otherwise. This gallant gentleman was our current local amateur heavyweight champ.

Not-Rocky sat just outside the ropes of one of the two center rings, swigging a Gatorade and sweating off his sparring round. He hopped down and sidled over to me while I tugged on my gloves, and took over my seat after I slid to the floor for sixty knuckle pushups. "Yo, Brickhouse."

Once I brought Avery in to meet the crew and see the place, and when we left, he said, "Brickhouse? You're not—insulted by that?"

"Of course I am," I said. "That's what makes it stick." I never told him that after that day, my gang referred to Avery as The Suit. That's how I knew they approved of him.

Under the eye of Not-Rocky, I finished my pushups and rolled onto my back. He crouched in front of me and grasped my ankles for my sit-ups. "You want to go when you're ready?" he asked.

I considered, but on my next sit-up, I noticed a bit of fresh blood clotting on his chin. Between that and the perspiration still rolling down his jaw, I guessed he was done for the day. I wouldn't have suggested to him, though, or to any of the guys for that matter, that they ever take it easy. This gym was filled with competitors, and they'd knock themselves unconscious to prove their worth. I had competed a little myself, a few years ago, but eventually decided that putting my facial bones at risk every day wouldn't jibe with my career ambition. I boxed now because it was in me, and I didn't think it would ever not be. And, I suspected of myself, I boxed to keep my memories of my father from permanent escape.

But Not-Rocky and the others, they still did it for dreams.

"I'll take a pass today," I said with tact, feeling my stomach muscles tighten and contract with each lift of my torso.

"Get the fuck away from me!"

Not-Rocky abruptly turned and I looked over his shoulder, following his gaze to the other side of the gym.

Within these walls, punching and yelling was expected—but there came rare moments when the athletic crossed into emotional, when aggressive became violent. Maybe it was strange that it didn't happen more, what with the testosterone levels and competing bravados, but when it did happen, we all went on high alert, ready to defend, to fight for real.

But no one would have wanted to be the one to hurt a kid. And that was who was causing this commotion.

"I said, back the *fuck* off!" he screamed again at a boxer easily twice his age and many, many pounds heavier. I raised my brows, marveling at his reckless stupidity.

The kid was Trey Sawyer, a skinny, freckled boy barely into his teens with a myopic squint and uncooperative brown curls. A boy I wouldn't have been surprised to see amassing Boy Scout badges or mathletes trophies. A boy from whose mouth I was damn surprised to hear the word "fuck" emerge. Smiley had taken him in a couple of weeks ago, and he came in after school. Trey couldn't punch a fixed target three feet in front of him, but no one gave him a hard time. He'd been quickly identified as one of Smiley's charity cases: someone he was asked to keep busy or straighten out.

Back when I was his charity case, Smiley did both. I'd mouthed off and I'd acted out, but I'd learned my place, and I'd learned it was a place I wanted to be.

Looked like it was Trey's turn.

His shouts were louder in the new silence around him. "I don't need this!" He put his gloved fists on the bigger fighter's chest, and shoved with all his violent might.

Jackrabbit, the recipient of the shove, put one foot back, the only indication he'd been touched at all. He didn't move from his spot—a calm stone wall. He caught Smiley's eye while Trey stood there breathing heavily, his twiggy arms weighed down with his gloves.

"Dumb kid," Not-Rocky murmured.

I didn't disagree. But something didn't feel right.

No one moved. Trey, maybe sensing he'd gone just far enough, quieted, but his eyes were wildfire.

Smiley moved slowly but deliberately between Trey and Jackrabbit, and his back was to Not-Rocky and me. An innocent, non-boxing bystander might see the delicate skin of the back of Smiley's neck, or the thinned, nearly transparent hair that barely whispered against his head, and assume him to be anyone weaker than he was.

Before he said a word, I caught the irony that though not one fighter in here would want to be the one taking heat, they all wanted to hear someone else taking it.

"You done?" Smiley asked.

"It's my turn!" Trey yelled. "This is my time. There's fifteen minutes left in my lesson and this *asshole* interrupted!"

"Hey, punk, this in't no private school," Jackrabbit said.

"Pipe down." Smiley's tone was mild. He glanced at the big guy before fixing his gaze once more on Trey. "He was letting me know I had a phone call. Jack, go take a number."

The boxer scowled at Trey a moment before walking away to Smiley's office, muttering, "I'm the damn secretary now?"

"He had no right!" Trey yelled again. "This is my time!"

"This is my gym," Smiley said, advancing, and though far less imposing than any of the rest of us, he slowly backed Trey into the wall. "And," Smiley added, "I make the decisions. I run the show. That means I'm interruptible, even if you were actually paying me for this lesson."

Trey screwed up his face again and took a deep breath but Smiley continued. "You heard me. Your brother helped me out a few years ago and you're the way I decided to repay the favor. But I can decide against you at any time. So change your attitude."

"But—"

"*Change* it. Something inside you got to get out? I give you plenty of outlet here. There's no reason for this bullshit. I'm on your side, but I'd just as well not be. I got enough guys to take care of. I don't got to waste my free time. Lesson over. Now get the hell outta here. Come back when you're interested in learning something."

Smiley walked away and Trey glared after him.

The captive audience scattered, and the noise and sweating resumed.

"Well," I said.

Not-Rocky chuckled. "Idiot kid."

"We've been there," I reminded him. "Some more recently than others." I kept my eyes on Trey though, and watched him flatten out. He remained upright, leaning against the wall, but the nasty, hungry thing inside him had perished. He gazed straight ahead at nothing and nodded once or twice, as if now being coached by an invisible mentor. His eyes were familiar. Eerily familiar, dead eyes.

"Sure you don't want to go?" Not-Rocky asked me, and I peeled my stare off Trey to focus on my buddy.

"Nah, thanks. Just the bag for me today. Let off a little steam."

"What steam do you got to let off? Didn't you quit working?"

"No. I took a leave of absence."

"Whatever."

"It's not 'whatever,' it's temporary." I sat up for the last time and reached into my bag, pulling out a Band-Aid and a bacterial wipe. "Sit still," I told him. I cleaned the cut on his chin and smoothed the bandage over it.

"Thanks," he said. "I was just giving you a hard time and everything. It's nice you're here during the day now, not like when you used to be working and we only saw you on weekends."

We grinned at each other, and I almost regretted covertly sticking the pink Hello Kitty Band-Aid on his chin. Almost.

We stood and he punched my upper arm. I retaliated with a light backhand bop to his stomach, then headed to the one available heavy bag.

I walked past Trey and he pushed himself off the wall. His dead stare landed on me, and in the fraction of the second it takes to recognize someone you'd rather not see, his eyes filled with hate and fear.

Hate and fear, aimed at me.

But before I could form another thought, he'd pushed past me and stalked out the front door.

Creepy. Weird. Sort of sad. I turned my attention to the bag.

A heavy bag might be practice for a real bout, but in truth, it was a challenge in itself. It became *the* person in your imagination. The one you just had to beat so you could feel right. You always connected, but who you were hitting, and where, and why, was individual to the moment.

I bounced up and down lightly on my toes, concentrating on keeping my shoulders relaxed. My weakness was my tendency to stiffen my upper body too much, which slowed and hardened my motion, draining my intensity.

Fluidity. I was floating in water. I was water.

I started with some jabs, circling the bag in one direction, then the other, working both arms. Then, still bouncing, I rolled my neck from side to side. Relax, relax, then the one-two punch.

My first power punch of the day never failed to surprise me with the hard reminder of what I had inside, and what I could let out. I connected, and absorbed the shock up my arm, and my sore back teeth clicked together.

I had a flash of that guy against the lamppost, and his easy but purposeful gaze. My next one-two landed harder. I wouldn't have even noticed him, and sure as hell wouldn't have still been thinking about it, if it wasn't for that stupid dream. And *nothing* bad was going to happen. One-*two*. I was in a great place with Avery, with our new condo. His campaign was going as great as we could have planned it. We were masters of our own future. One-*two*. A random man with strangely supernatural sex appeal was not going to mess that up. *I* was certainly not going to mess it up. One-*two*. I had a perfect life right now, and it could only get more perfect, and I would fight with every degree of determination in me to make sure nothing—one-*two*—nothing ruined it.

My father held up a pad in each hand. I hit—crossing my right into his right, my left into his left—with my hands wrapped. Dad hadn't been able to find gloves small enough for me, but he'd promised to keep looking. "Gemma," he said, when I was out of breath and my knees were shaking. "Come on, be tough. It doesn't hurt."

"It does hurt."

"No, it doesn't. When you connect," he said, gently taking my wrist and touching my fist to the pad, "what you feel isn't pain. You're feeling what it is to be human. You're human."

I didn't understand that. But I felt pretty damn human when he left us.

I hit the bag again, envisioning the punch slamming right through it to the other side.

"Easy, Bricks," I heard behind me. Smiley. I kept my fists up, kept up the bounce. "What you after?" he asked me.

"Anything that gets in my way," I answered without turning around. He'd be watching me the way he watched all of us, with the right side of his craggy face cocked forward, and the left side of his head dropping back, left eye squinted. He couldn't afford to tug on the thin gray hair he had left, but he did it anyway when deep in study. He could find the tiniest inch of a hip angle that would double the power of a punch, and he could isolate the exact moment a bout turned a corner, when one boxer's advantage was lost to the other. He knew every one of our bodies better than our primary care doctors, and he chipped away at each of us until our excess fell away and the fighters we were meant to be emerged, tight and strong. Smiley was a scientist and an artist and, if crossed, a force of nature.

I stepped into the bag, bent my right elbow and delivered a right hook, then a left.

"Woman on a mission," he said, and I half-grinned, because the way Smiley said it, I could tell he meant no derision, humor or irony. He was real with me, and always was. He knew my father, when he used to box here. A long time ago. Smiley didn't talk about my dad, and I never asked him to. It worked out best that way.

"Might want to cool out," he added. "You got a visitor."

I dropped my arms to my sides, surprised. The adrenaline slid downward with gravity, and my fingertips tingled with the sudden inactivity. I'd never had a visitor here. The one time Avery came, like I said, I'd accompanied him, and anyway I didn't think he'd have a break in his action until later tonight. My mom never came here, and my pals from work were pretty much my friends only *at* work.

So who was here to see me?

I turned, and what I saw was guys clustered at the door, all talking at once. Testosterone permeated the air even more than usual, and that was saying a big something. I moved toward the group but my approach was ignored. I couldn't see through Shirley's massive back, and I wasn't inclined to hop up and down like a child to get a better view, so I waited.

"You just missed an awesome show, babe," I heard Mat say. "If you'da walked in five minutes ago, you woulda seen me lay out that guy." I had no idea who Mat was indicating but I did know he was full of it. He'd gone over to a bag after our brief chat, and hadn't been laying out anyone except maybe in some daydream. "Feel that," he continued, and I winced, positive he was presenting his bare bicep to a person whom I would have to undoubtedly apologize to later.

"Mat," Shirley said to him. "You're a kid, and what's more, you're a lying kid. Don't pay him no mind," he said to my mystery guest. "Would you like a tour?"

"I suppose you the new tour guide?" Mat asked, surly from the put-down.

"Surely," the heavyweight champ replied.

At least three others joined the shuffle for attention. Then I heard, "Please, ma'am, have a seat," and I watched Not-Rocky step away from the group to shove my duffel bag and black boots off the folding chair onto the ground with an extended clatter. "You can sit right here."

Okay, this nonsense ended now. I understood a female visitor in here was a novelty, but on the rare occasions it happened, the guys generally performed a nonchalant, cool appraisal from their posts while they continued to work out. But this woman had reduced these toughs into a gaggle of ogling junior-high stupidity. I couldn't say I enjoyed this. I mean, I had status in this place, and I intended to keep it.

And I really, really hoped the guest wasn't my mother after all.

I cleared my throat. "Someone wants to see me?"

A group of fat heads swiveled around, still blocking my view of the newcomer. No one said anything to me. I honed in on Not-Rocky, who stared at me kind of glassy-eyed, as if trying to figure out where he'd seen the blond chick in boxing gloves before.

I had another unbidden mental flash of the lamppost dude, and realized I had probably resembled this gang of idiots when I had stood there and stared at him—powerless and drooling. It annoyed the crap out of me anew.

"Everybody get lost," I said now to the group, but no one moved. I put my hands ineffectively on my hips.

"You heard her," Smiley called from behind me. "'Cause I don't see one fighter here who couldn't improve just about everything. Move it."

There was much muttering and shuffling, and there were many longing, over-the-beefy-shoulder glances, but when the pack dispersed, I was left looking at Frederica Diamond.

"Gemma," she said, and again it was a statement, not a question. "Shall we talk? There's a coffee shop across the street."

"Hold it. I mean, seriously." I pushed my sweaty bangs back with my forearm. "You track me down at my gym, magically freak out every male here, make it clear you know all about my extended vacation and my love life, and assume I'll be intrigued enough with your cloak-and-dagger routine to listen to some job pitch. Not to mention that yesterday you pretty much vanished into thin air. If you were me, what could you possibly say?"

The words burst out of me but Frederica didn't flinch. "If I were you," she said, the placid smile still in place, "I probably would think, 'This woman's full of shit.'"

I raised *both* eyebrows then.

"But," she went on, "again, if I were you, I would at least listen after the strange woman told me I'm the only one qualified for this position." I caught it—the smile fading just the tiniest bit around the edges. "I promise I'll explain, but you have to know, we don't just need someone. We need *you*, Gemma Fae."

The use of my middle name startled me. I was sure I never used it professionally—it was a calculated decision. I was hardly faerie-like in appearance or in disposition, and although the middle name had been passed down from my mother and her mother before her, I considered it an unfortunate misnomer that was best left on my birth certificate.

So I could only imagine what else this woman knew about me. And I should have been even more creeped out than I already was.

But it was the other part of her last statement that got me. It had only been about three weeks, but the idea of my professional expertise being so valuable that this woman became my personal biographer in order to recruit me was kind of—flattering. I was needed. And I missed that, I really did.

I twisted my mouth to one side, torn, as Frederica waited, the very picture of patience. Would it really hurt to let her buy me a cup of chai—hmm, and maybe a cookie—and listen to her woo the professional me for twenty minutes before turning her down and going on my way? Besides, headhunters could be, well, tenacious, and she'd proven herself a more-than-adept stalker. Saying no might just drive her to show up in my bathroom some morning to hand me a towel as I stepped from the shower and make her pitch as I dried my hair. Probably best to cut my workout short to let her do her thing now and get it over with.

"What the hell," I told her. "Let me change, and I'll…" I was interrupted by my cell phone. "Call me!" sang rock-star Blondie. I knew it was me she was singing to, because she was coming out of my duffel bag—which was still on the floor, by the way, where Not-Rocky had chucked it. I scowled at him over my shoulder, but out of the two women in the room, I wasn't the one he was looking at. Geez.

I grasped the singing cell phone in my two big gloves and handed it to Frederica. "Press the green button, please?" She did, and held it to my ear as I worked the Velcro off one glove. "Hello?"

"Gemma," my mother said. "I made this huge turkey. I don't know why. It was on sale. Come over for dinner and help me eat it."

"This isn't a good time," I said. "Can I call you back?"

"Are you all right?"

I dropped one glove to the ground and took the phone with my sweaty hand, half turning away from my guest. "Actually, I have a kind of impromptu meeting with a job recruiter."

"I didn't know that."

"No, neither did I. She kind of—" I lowered my voice a few notches "—found me. Something about a business proposal."

My mother began to speak, then cut herself off. "I thought you were taking a break from work."

"Right, I am. I'm just hearing her out," I said, tucking the phone on my shoulder and raising my voice back to normal as I pulled off my other glove. "So, I'll call you later and let you know about dinner."

"What agency does the recruiter work for?"

"I don't, uh, I don't actually know."

"What's her name?"

"Her name's Frederica something. Oh, I suck with names. I'll ask her again."

"Diamond," I heard, and swiveled around. Completely unashamed of eavesdropping, she turned up that smile again. "Frederica Fae Diamond."

"Fae," I repeated, surprised. "Her middle name is Fae," I told my mother. "Now, *that's* random. Maybe we're related."

My mother didn't say anything, and I was about to check our connection when she spoke again. "Gemma," my mother said in my ear, "I wouldn't—"

"I was kidding."

"No, I mean," she said, and her voice rose in pitch. "This isn't a good idea."

"No, probably not," I agreed, "but I'm going to let her state her case since she came all the way down here."

"Listen to me."

"Mom, are you all right?"

"I'm fine," she said, "but you can't…"

A fuzz filled my ear. "You're breaking up," I told her. "The reception in here is terrible. I have to go."

"Gemma!" she called as I was about to disconnect, and I put my ear back to the phone. "Just please," Mom said, and I think what I heard next was, "do the right thing."

"Uh, yeah, thanks. Love you," I said, and hung up. I turned to Frederica. "I'm just going to change."

"Sure. I'll meet you across the street," she said. When she left, every guy in the room watched her leave. Through the window of his tiny office, I even noticed Smiley glance up from his desk to watch the door shut.

I picked up my bag, brushed dust off the bottom, and slipped into the bathroom to change. I pulled out the hair elastic and fit it over my wrist, shaking my hair out. I slung the bag over my back and clunked to the front door in my short boots. I turned to wave at whomever, but everyone had gone back to his business. Jump ropes, as well as fists, were swinging. Speed bags were flapping. The floor in the ring was creaking under two pairs of maneuvering feet.

No one watched *me* leave.

"Schmucks," I muttered, but even I could hear my own grudging fondness. I rolled my eyes at myself and headed outside.

CHAPTER 4

When I stepped into Grounds Floor, Frederica was sitting at the corner window table with two steaming mugs the size of salad bowls in front of her. I slid across from her and peered into my mug. Chai.

"I have to finally confess, you're starting to scare me," I said.

"I assume you mean the drink," she observed, then grinned. "Lucky guess, I assure you. I myself prefer chai to coffee. Sweet over bitter."

Speaking of lucky guess, I made a silent one of my own, then glanced around the café to test its validity. Yup, sure enough, there were four men plus the barista in here and all of their wide-eyed gazes were fixed on the face of my companion. There also were three women who stared, but with far less awe and far more envious animosity.

"Can we switch seats?" I asked, and Frederica obliged without question. When her back was to the restaurant and my back was to the wall, three of the men turned away, and when I scowled at the barista, he turned his embarrassed attention to the pastry case.

"So," I began, "you're here for which company?"

"Not a company," Frederica said, "so much as an organization."

"An organization. And you're a member?"

She nodded. "As are you."

I thought. "Triple A?"

"No," she said with the serene-yet-completely exasperating smile. "Not quite. We're—well, we're collectors. Not trinkets of any kind, antiques or coins. Our collection is far more important, with ramifications for our future."

"Recyclable bottles?" I admit I was now acting deliberately difficult, but I was fed up with the mystery crap and I'd figured out by now that there was no hurrying her presentation.

Maybe I finally struck a nerve in Frederica. A shadow passed across her placid face as she said, "This is difficult because it's clear you haven't the slightest clue what I'm talking about. I was warned, but I was so sure you'd at least recognize me for what I am, if not who I am. But you don't, and I'll really have to start from the beginning—start with what you are."

"Well," I said, "I can help you out with that. What I am is confused, as well as somewhat inclined to cut this short if I don't get some usable information in the next minute or so about a job opportunity, which is the reason I agreed to talk to you."

Frederica sighed and glanced skyward, as if *she* were the one thrown in the middle of this weirdness. Then she clasped her hands together and leaned forward. I concentrated on a spot in the middle of her forehead, instinctively not wanting to look her in the eye.

"It's a family business," she said. "*Your* family business. We're asking you to take a crucial role in keeping this business—and its ultimate goal—alive and thriving."

"My mother is a kindergarten teacher," I replied, "in a public school. My family does not own the school. And even if we did, I'm pretty sure she'd just ask me herself instead of sending a representative. I have no idea what my Dad's up to these days, but I imagine if he were grooming me to take over his job, he might have contacted me in the last two decades or so to say hello. I'm sorry to tell you this after all your meticulous research about me, but you've got the wrong girl."

I bent down to pick up my duffel, but Frederica grasped my wrist, her cool, smooth fingers sure and firm on my skin. I glanced up and was caught in an involuntary—on my part—staredown. Her bright green irises were flecked with gold and ringed with impossible gleaming silver. If eyes truly were the window to the soul, then she'd slammed the window hard on my hands, trapping me at the entrance, with nowhere to look but inside.

When she spoke again, it was in a whisper, but her words echoed and multiplied in my ear until it became a reverent, hushed gospel chorus.

"You're fae, Gemma."

"It's Gemma Fae," I corrected in my own whisper.

"You're fae," she repeated. "And so am I."

She must have interpreted my stunned silence as open-mindedness, because she added, "We, the morning fae, carry an ancient tradition in our shared blood. We have a responsibility to the future."

I tried, and failed, to blink. We stayed that way, gazes locked, for a long time.

"Do you understand?" she eventually asked me.

Did I *understand*?

"Fae?" I choked out. "Fae. What, you mean like faeries? With wings and sparkles and shit?" I waited for a punch line, or at least the clarification of a poor metaphor, but got nothing. "So you're a faerie. And I'm a faerie."

She frowned. There was no furrow between her brows, and the corners of her mouth didn't drop. Her smooth face didn't change in any way, but I saw the frown underneath it. "We don't use the term faerie because that's only a sliver of our ancestry..."

"We're both faeries. Oh, related faeries."

"All fae share—"

"Right, same blood, ancient tradition. I got that part." I sat back in my chair. At some point, Frederica had freed my wrist. She sat back as well.

I watched her for a few moments, then said, "It's funny, but you don't give the overall impression of being crazy. You do it really well, actually. The last crazy person I ran into was a guy on the street hopped up on crack who threw an empty Jack Daniel's bottle at me and screamed that he was cuckoo for Cocoa Puffs. He was pretty obvious. You're more of a sneaky crazy person."

Frederica still said nothing. Maybe—maybe she wasn't crazy? Maybe this was a setup. I examined a couple of corners in the café where the wall met the ceiling, looking for hidden cameras or microphones. I wasn't anyone famous, but Avery was well known, and maybe someone figured they could get his dopey girlfriend with a reality TV practical joke.

"It's not a trick," Frederica assured me as I peered over her shoulder for a video camera. "I'm not crazy. As far as I know, anyhow. Will you let me show you something, if it will help you believe me?"

I sat back and sighed. So much for a job proposal and a little ego-stroking. "Sure, go ahead," I said, gesturing to her and dropping my hand back on the table with a thump. "Blow my mind."

Frederica turned my hand over, palm up, and held it still. Again, her touch disconcerted me. It was like running your finger along the skin of an unusual animal, like a hairless cat, and finding it's not what you expected at all. "I'll give you a glimpse of it," she said. "The best I can right now. Your fae senses have been dormant for so long and only a complete transformation can awaken them, but I still think the beautiful power of the Olde Way can reach you."

"That's olde with an 'e,' isn't it," I said, and wasn't surprised at her nod. The rational part of me demanded to leave this café right now, but the curious side of me won this round. Avery was going to love this later.

"There's a bond within morning fae," she said after a pause. "An attraction, if you will, that goes beyond the molecular."

"You know I'm straight, right? I mean, you know about my boyfriend."

"I'm not talking about sexual attraction," she said, the corner of her lips quirking up a bit. "It's an acknowledgment of an invisible link, an instant recognition. But the first time you feel it, it can be laced with sexual confusion. You can catch the eye of the man across the street and you can see it in him, and he sees it in you. He's merely leaning against a lamppost looking at you, and the mutual gaze can overwhelm your mind with attraction, the need to feel close to one like yourself in this unnatural world that's sprung up around us."

I felt a rush through each ear and it slammed together in the center of my brain. My reason and logic shook and threatened to crumble. I didn't want this weakness. If I hadn't been frozen in shock, I would have put up my fists to ward off this... this...

What *was* this?

"Gemma," Frederica said, "close your eyes."

I did. At that moment, I couldn't disobey.

She placed something tiny in the center of my palm. It tickled a bit and I instinctively curled my fingers in to probe it with my fingertips, but Frederica caught hold, folding my hand over the object so it was snug in my fist. She reached for my other hand and closed it over my first, then wrapped her own two hands around mine.

My eyelids tightened as I tried to crack one open to peek. But the sound stopped me. It was indiscernible at first, fading in and out of my auditory consciousness, then the song began to wrap itself like a gossamer shroud around my mind, cradling my thoughts in its softness, relaxing them into inertia.

Form and substance dissolved, melting into a gentle pool. The hard wooden seat beneath me, the sticky tabletop under my forearms, all fell away, and I felt nothing, nothing, until color and light began to wind around and up my body. Red warmth held me down while white coolness gently tugged at the crown of my head. In between I felt a rainbow of emotion until the white drew down and enveloped me in a radiant glow of peace.

And the scent—like every flower in the world combined, and like crisp brook water, and like sunlight after a week of rain.

The voice came from somewhere, and echoed through me. I heard it in my hands, in my stomach, in my legs. *I lived here. We all came from here, this place of purity. This is where we exist in each other, and the light moves in and out of us. We create our own surprises. Every moment is free of the one preceding it, or the one following it, and every moment is full of genius and wonder, lasting an eternity. It's the Olde Way. It's not gone. It's not gone…*

It *was* gone. It was yanked away and I fell back to here, back into my seat. I couldn't open my eyes. I wouldn't, and perhaps I would return. But the song faded and the warm cushion peeled away from my mind. I heard Frederica, her words coaxing me out of the tunnel. "Come back. Come back."

I think I shook my head, but the motion was slow and cottony.

"That was just a tiny part of it all," she said. "You can pull away."

"I don't want to," I mumbled.

"I know," she said, her reply sounding like a lullaby. "I know. None of us did. We're all going back there, but we can't without your help. Come back, Gemma."

"What is it?" I slurred, then licked my lips and tried again. "What's in my hand?"

"Just one little piece of our growing collection. The innocence, it's deep inside there, but it's not enough to bring the Olde Way back. The morning fae have been extracting the essence for generations—hundreds of years—and storing it, nurturing it, and we're closer than ever before to recreating what we lost when the human world took over."

"What are you talking about?" I asked. My words were clear and my consciousness had returned, but I was breathing hard and I was exhausted, bone-tired. I opened my eyes and stared at Frederica as I repeated my question. "What the hell are you talking about?"

"What have you been dreaming about?" she whispered, and gently opened my hands. I looked down.

A tooth.

Small, smooth and pure white, it was the most frightening thing I had ever seen. And it was moving—but no, that was my cupped hand, trembling.

"We just obtained it last night for the collection," Frederica said. "If I was going to jolt your fae senses, it needed to be fresh, to have as much of its innocence intact as possible."

They—the fae—just obtained it last night? Fresh. Innocence.

Collection.

"*Tooth* faeries?" I shouted.

Frederica blinked.

"Oh, come on," I said, dropping the tooth on the table and abruptly pulling away. "Come *on*. You had me there, okay? You had me, with your hypnotic hocus-pocus whatever, but now I'm supposed to believe I'm a tooth faerie?"

My hands were still shaking. Because honestly, she'd more than had me there. That—vision, or experience, was too much like a memory ingrained in my soul, and even now, I wanted to go back there.

Frederica sighed, appearing far more disappointed than intimidated by my outburst. "This is a first for me," she said.

"You don't say."

"Because," she continued, as if I hadn't interrupted, "the rest of us, we knew who we were from the beginning. They might have chosen to take their part in our quest or not, but we've never had to tell a rational, intelligent fae adult who she is."

"About that job offer," I said then. "You're not recruiting me to break into people's houses in the middle of the night and take their kids' teeth, are you?"

In the silence that followed, I received the answer I'd feared.

"O-*kay*, then," I said. "I'm sorry to let you down, not to mention the rest of your winged buddies, but I think it's time for me to leave now."

"I agree. We'll talk again when you've had a chance to think things over."

"Um, no." I picked up my duffel and stood.

"There's someone I would like you to speak with further, if you don't mind," Frederica said, stirring her chai around twice before reaching into her pants pocket for a slightly bent card. I noticed her pants were diaphanous ivory linen, belted with a filmy pink scarf. Her clothes, her manner, were all faerie.

Okay, she probably could convince a stupid person into believing she was fae. But what kind of person could be convinced that they were born fae as well? *Fae*, for crying out loud. It was like some geek live-action roleplaying game gone way too far.

But even my own mind was failing in its effort to be indignant. I was *there* just now, while I was holding the tooth. I was there.

I'll take her card, I thought. *I'll take it and get the hell out of here.*

Frederica produced a pen from her little handbag and wrote something on the card. Then she held it up. "My number's on the front of this card, as well as information about our local community gatherings. There are three every month, and you should come, Gemma. We get together to reconnect, to re-experience our history. You'll be welcomed, and you'll get to know your family."

"I know my family."

"Do you?" she asked, and the challenge was genuine but not unkind. "You won't be alone. I guide this particular gathering and I'll be there tonight. I know it will help you understand. But your mind won't open to it until you hear all this, all that I've told you, from someone you trust."

"How could you know who I trust?"

"I believe I got this one right." She held the card out to me, and I grabbed it so hard that it bent nearly in half, but my eyes didn't leave her face. "Talk to her," she said. "She's our only hope to getting through to you, if she tells you the truth. I think now, she finally will. I didn't write her number down. I assume you have it."

I glanced at the card, and what I read, what she'd written, caused a theatrical double-take before I dropped it on the floor. Then I looked back at Frederica. Her satisfied smile held only kindness and understanding. She reached down and retrieved the card, then slid it gently into the thumb crease of my now tightly fisted hand.

"*What*?" I managed, shaking my head. The one word emerged as an ineffective squeak.

"Like I said," she said, "it's a family business."

>=<

For the first time in my life, I knocked on the door. After so many years of banging in and out, the entitlement had suddenly disintegrated. Perhaps I didn't know this house—and the other person who'd lived in it—as well as I thought I did.

When she opened the door and I saw her face, the first face I ever saw, I felt a flash of that moment when I held the tooth—that overwhelming strength of innocence and purity, that childhood sensory perfection—but it passed before I could hang on to it.

"So, where do you hide your wings, Mom?" I asked.

Please, my mind cried. *Please, Mom, ask me what I'm talking about, look at me like I'm nuts, tell me I'm hungry and overtired, and that everything is the same as it's been my whole life.*

"I think you should come in and sit down, Gemma," she said.

Unfortunately, I didn't wait until there was a chair under me before I took her advice.

CHAPTER 5

Ignoring Mom's offer of assistance, I somehow dragged my beaten self up onto the blue sofa. Mom watched me collapse against the cushions, then closed the door and stood in front of it. She fidgeted, then wrapped her arms across her chest—not defiantly, but defensively.

Any other day, she'd be pushing a glass of wine into my hand, giving me a chunk of fresh bread from the bakery up the street, and chattering about the day's antics of one of the naughtier children in her class.

But this wasn't any other normal day. At least, not normal as I'd always defined it. When normal changed this much this fast, what could be the meaning of strange?

"I made a turkey," my mother finally ventured in a small, weak voice.

"Oh, you made a turkey, all right. About thirty years ago," I said. "And here I am."

"Gemma, don't…"

"Do *not* 'Gemma' me that way. Don't imply that I'm the unreasonable one. However," I amended, "I'm okay with you saying my name as in, 'Gemma, I can explain why for your entire life, I withheld a crucial and bizarre detail of your existence.'"

Rather than taking the cue I provided, Mom remained silent. I regarded her the way a detached scientist might regard a newly impaled butterfly on a cardboard display. Women walked into the homes they grew up in and expected comfort and familiarity, but what I found in the living room this time was Bethany Fae Cross, a woman with a collection of secrets and complications so enormous, yet so invisible to me up until today.

Perhaps not just because she was fae, but also because she was a mother.

She moved to the sofa and sat beside me. I scooched a few stubborn inches away from her, but she reached her hand across those inches and brushed a few errant strands of hair off my cheek. I was almost surprised to notice it was the same hand I knew. It hadn't suddenly morphed into Frederica's dainty long-fingered hand. Mom's fingers were short and strong. I'd more than once felt her grip on my upper arm to restrain me from crossing the street without looking both ways. The skin of her fingertips was tight and tough, cultivated in a dishwasher-free domicile. Her nails were ragged from scraping between bathroom tiles and digging deep and gloveless into the backyard garden.

"What did Frederica Diamond tell you?" she asked softly.

"Everything you didn't."

She gracefully dodged the hurt I hurled, continuing, "How did she get you to believe?"

I searched my mind for another surly-daughter comeback, but I'd depleted my usually bottomless arsenal. I was too tired to reload. So I went for the truth. "She showed me. She showed me the place, or time, or whatever it was..."

"The Olde Way," Mom said, and in her familiar, sure voice, it wasn't crazy. It was a bedtime story under a pile of warm blankets.

I wanted to weep.

"Were you there?" I asked her. "Ever?"

"I've glimpsed it, like you," she said, looking past me at something in her mind.

"Where is it? *When* is it?"

"The Olde Way predates you, me, Christopher Columbus, Moses, King Tut. The fae didn't record our world. They didn't feel the need to preserve their history because they never anticipated its extinction. They couldn't predict an existence where it's necessary to learn from mistakes. All that's left is the memory, passing down through our lineage, but that memory weakens with each generation."

She sighed and refocused her gaze on my face. "My few glimpses were as brief as yours," she said, "but they were a tiny bit more vivid. It's harder for you to access the memory, but it's still there."

"When you called me on my cell earlier," I said, "did you know who Frederica was?"

"Not right away. There aren't just a few of us, Gemma. There are so many, everywhere." She paused. "But when you told me you were meeting unexpectedly with a job recruiter, and when you told me her middle name was Fae, I knew. Some fae families, ours included, continued the tradition of giving children the name, even though we couldn't any longer give them the valuable inheritance that went with it."

And here I'd thought it was just tradition on my mother's side because it was a pretty name.

"You didn't want me to talk to her," I said. "Maybe you didn't want me to talk to any of them, and that's why you never told me who—what—we are?"

"I couldn't stop this, Gemma. I did try, but it's impossible to leave your destiny behind. I knew that. I'd just hoped that by now, you'd stayed under the radar long enough so that you wouldn't be pressed into service."

"As a…" I struggled to remember the words Frederica had used. "A collector? Were you a collector?"

"Yes," she said. "I collected because it helped me to continue the definition of who I am, who we were and what we had. The morning fae are split into lineages, and each lineage carries on a tradition and a specific role and responsibility in bringing back our world, our way. My lineage—our lineage—are collectors."

"Morning fae?"

She paused.

"Are there afternoon fae?" I asked.

"Midnight fae," Mom said, then, "The dark fae. They're not us."

She stopped, chewing her lip. "I should get dinner on the table," she said faintly.

"Let's hear it," I said. "I just found out today I'm a tooth faerie, so if you're wondering about my capability to handle what you're about to say, we're way past that. I want answers. I don't even know the right questions to ask, but I want the answers."

I realized my fists were clenched tightly, and I stretched all of my fingers out, in the space between Mom and me, and maybe the fact that she couldn't fully see my expression let her continue.

"My parents are dead," she said quietly.

"I know," I said, softening my tone.

"But not for as long as you thought," she said at the same low volume. "Your grandfather died when you were ten. Your grandmother died seven years after that."

I blinked, startled, but considering the fact that I'd never known my grandparents to miss them—and considering everything else I had learned today—I waited to hear my mother out.

"I cut myself off from my fae family. I kept up infrequent contact with my parents because I couldn't bear to—oh, but you were too important to me, and I knew you'd be too important to all of them."

"What do you mean?"

She sighed and her shoulders melted down deeper into her pink cotton cardigan. "Fae marry fae. We're barely hanging on to our existence as it is. But rare mixed marriages do happen."

Dad. George Cross's presence was in every room of this

house even still, like old rugs you couldn't unload at a garage sale because the strangers who stopped into your yard knew—despite the fact that you'd scrubbed the rugs clean—that they were covered with ghosts. Since he left, Mom hadn't talked about him ever, not to me, even when I asked her over and over, "Why?" Then somewhere along the line I had become an adult, and I had realized his leaving had hurt her more than it had hurt me, and that maybe she didn't tell me why because she didn't know why. And I stopped asking.

But I had more questions now. "Your family didn't want you to marry Dad?"

I saw her flinch, and I felt awful.

"The fae do tolerate a mixed marriage," she said, "and it's only because of what—who—they produce."

Produce? Would that be me?

"What did you see, Gemma?" Mom asked before I could take my conversational turn. "When Frederica showed you a glimpse?"

I didn't have to struggle to remember that. Brief as it was, it had embedded itself into my permanent heart's memory. But putting it into words was difficult. "I didn't see," I said, "as much as I *felt*." I slid from the sofa cushions onto the carpet, and lay on my back staring at the ceiling. I tried to will it back to me, that sense of falling into soft nothing, that certain joy. "I felt light, and air, and music, and water, and peace."

"You felt peace," Mom repeated. "So you understand the true essence of the Olde Way is peace and innocence. War doesn't exist there, or chaos, or violence in any form. It can't. So when the Olde Way crumbled, the fae had no means of resistance. The fae have no physical fighting instinct, so there was nothing to draw upon—and humans simply took over without conflict, most likely without even knowing our ancestors were there."

From my spot on the floor, I just looked at her feet, one curled over the other, in thick blue socks. None of that made sense, at least as far as the individual me was concerned. "How could I not have the fighting instinct?" I asked. I nudged my duffel on the floor where I'd tossed it when I came in. It was zipped, but only partway, and a few inches of the stretchy wrap I used under my gloves snaked out. "I'm a fighter."

"The half-human side of you is the fighter," Mom said. "And that's why you're a precious gem to the fae, and that's why, before I was even pregnant, I knew I had to get you away."

I waited. I didn't get it. I needed her to explain it to me. She'd taught me how to read, how to tie my shoes, and how to safely cross a busy intersection. I had to trust she could reach and illuminate the confused part of me, because if she couldn't, I wasn't sure anyone could.

But she sat there, looking not at me but at the spot I'd occupied on the sofa a few moments earlier.

"You didn't want me to be part of this?" I finally asked. "You didn't want me to be a collector? You didn't want me to be"—*oh*, I thought, *God help me*—"a tooth faerie?"

She winced. "'Faerie' is not the right word. It's a human word for the ideas they have of us. And no," she said quickly, her voice rising on the last syllable. "It wasn't that I didn't want you to embrace this. My reason for leaving had nothing to do with escaping the fae dream. Not at all."

"You grew up in Connecticut."

Her brows drew together. "Yes?"

"So is that like faer-" I checked myself—"fae headquarters or something?"

She smiled a bittersweet smile. "They're everywhere," she said. "We're everywhere, although many cluster in communities. Frederica recruits for the D.C. fae."

"So not only is tooth collection real," I said, "but there's a whole network?"

"It's a global operation," she said, reflecting my wryness back at me through her grin.

"Yet still retaining that homey family business feel."

I paused, remembering the crumpled card in my pocket. "Frederica said there are local meetings. What are they, like AA?"

Mom laughed. "Maybe, in terms of the confidentiality and locations. They're gatherings where fae—can be herself. Or himself. Shed the human guise and just be fae for a while." Her smile remained, but changed. "I told you the memory is fading with each generation."

I nodded.

"Well, when you go past the beginning of human time, that's a lot of generations. When you touch the tooth, come in contact with the essence, a tiny sliver of that memory is sliced off so you can taste it. It's intoxicating, but fleeting. When the fae gather, there's power in the group, and they use that power to channel the Olde Way. It's a little stronger, and they can hold it a little longer. They renew the connection to the dream, and to one another."

"To remember why they're—we're—doing all this."

"Yes," she said. "The different lineages all have a role. There are morning fae who gather innocence from animals, in zoos and shelters and the wild. There are fae who manipulate the environment—the best that they're able. Humans would have destroyed the Earth we share long ago if not for the fae efforts, and we need the Earth intact to bring about our, well, our heaven." She sighed. "When you're a tooth collector, every tiny bit of innocence you obtain becomes a piece of that whole dream that we're striving to get back. It's our purpose. I loved doing it. I would have done it for as long as I was allowed to, if not for…"

"Dad?"

She fell silent, the word hitting her again. I hated with all my heart to be the one delivering the painful blows, but I needed to know what was at the center of this powerful secret. "Did you not say anything all those years and leave your family because of Dad? You didn't want him to find out what you were?"

Her eyes watered a bit, and I squeezed my own eyes shut so I wouldn't have to see it, but in my personal darkness I saw Dad again, saw him holding up the pads for my tiny fists to punch. One-two. One-two.

"It hurts."

"No, Gemma, that isn't pain. You're feeling what it is to be human. You're human."

You're human…

"Dad knew," I said, and snapped my eyes open. I jumped to my feet. "Dad knew what you are. What we are."

She nodded. "I told him right before we got married. He had a right to know me. He had a right to know why he could never truly be a part of my family. And he had a right to know what your destiny could be if I didn't break away."

"He had a right to know," I echoed. "But I didn't?" I began to pace around the room. Emotions swirled and gathered heat in the center of my chest, and I felt my fists ball up, tightening and stretching the muscles on the insides of my wrists.

"Your father agreed," she said, and despite my anger, I hated to hear her plead with me.

"Maybe I…" I pressed the heels of my fists against my eyes hard enough to see red and yellow streaks before I dropped my hands again. "Maybe I would have *wanted* to be a part of it. Maybe I want to be a part of it now. What Frederica showed me…" I shook my head. "You shouldn't have kept me from that. I would have wanted to do my part." *I still can*, I thought. I still could. I didn't lose my chance. Frederica was offering it back to me. She was only waiting for me to believe in what I was.

And looking at my mother curled up in the corner of the sofa I had spent so many hours on, in the living room I had lived in, I believed.

"It was never my intention to take you off the fae path to peace." Mom got up. Standing, she was tall enough to look me straight in the eye. "I left so you would have peace in *this* world. I couldn't give you over to fight their battles."

A thousand more questions crowded my head and I opened my

mouth to let the next one spill out, but the doorbell rang before I could make a sound.

Mom and I both looked at the door, then at each other. “Avery,” she said, her tone dissolving from that of Scheherazade storyteller and re-solidifying as mother. “He called earlier and said he’d meet you here for dinner.”

I actually felt my shoulder blades quiver with tension. “You didn’t tell me that.”

“Seems like keeping information to myself is my character flaw,” she said. “Go open the door.”

I stood rooted to my spot on the carpet, completely unnerved. I wasn’t ready to see Avery. Since he’d left the house this morning I’d met a faerie, been told that my mother was a faerie, been informed that I was half-faerie, and melted into a sensual puddle at a guy leaning against a lamppost who I was now relatively certain also was a faerie.

Not faeries. Fae.

Yeah, that distinction really just wasn’t sinking in.

“Open the door,” Mom repeated gently, and placed her hands on my shoulders. “Go on. You’re no different than you were before now. Your self-awareness is the only thing that’s changed.” She kissed my forehead, but I saw her crease her own before she left for the kitchen. Somehow I got to the door and opened it.

I didn’t remember what the three of us talked about over roast turkey, or how many glasses of white wine I had, or how Avery must have kissed me and said, “No problem,” when I told him I wanted to stay overnight with my mother and I’d be back in the morning.

When my mother and I were finally alone again, we made a mutual silent pact to not resume our discussion, and I retreated to my old bedroom. She knew I had questions, and I knew she had answers, but I needed to own this for a while, to turn this new information around and around and inspect it from every angle, the way I would spin and examine each row of a Rubik's Cube.

Although my glow-in-the-dark stars on the ceiling had been scratched off years ago and my golden throw rug had flattened into a roughened scrap, this room was still mine. I pushed against the wooden window frame, throwing my whole body behind it once, twice, before it rose, creaking with resistance, the chilly breeze lifting the hem of my T-shirt. I was grateful for it, and for my room, and for the momentary normalcy.

Sinking cross-legged to the floor, I pulled out Frederica's card and my cell phone, flung both onto the threadbare rug in front of me, and thought.

I thought for a long, long time.

I thought about destiny—*my* destiny. Mom hid me from it. Dad ran away from it. Frederica invited me to accept it. Avery didn't know a thing about it.

"We need you, Gemma Fae."

I was half innocence and peace, and half chaos and conflict. Had I always known that, deep down?

My emotions had taken hold of me and shaken me senseless for the last few hours, so I let my brain take over for a while, cooling my core with logic and analysis. My mind only had to turn everything around a few times before it told me what Mom hadn't yet: That the morning fae, knowing I was out there in the world, had chosen to leave me alone, biding their time. Tracking me down now meant they had a reason, a strong reason.

If there were fae everywhere and they had a large recruiting pool, they could have asked any local fae to join the D.C.-area collection. So this wasn't just a help-wanted plea. They bridged a three-decade communication gap to find *me*, the hybrid, and I knew why.

There was a threat to the fae again, and they needed a warrior. They needed me to fight.

I could say no. I could tell them to flap their filmy little wings and get the hell away from me. I could resist their twinkly entreaties, no problem. I was no wimp.

I had to make a decision, and my room had been the location of many decisions I'd made in my life. In here, I'd decided to call Tim Saporino and ask him to the prom because I knew he was too much of a lame-o to ask me first. In here, I'd decided whether to do my math homework before bed, or save it until the morning and do it in the hurry time before homeroom, with my back against the lockers and my books balanced on my knees. In here, I decided to color the sky green-blue instead of blue-green, and my silver horses soared between the clouds, close to the crayon sun, with huge feathered wings that took up half the page. I decided to draw wings even though horses didn't really have wings. Faeries had wings. But faeries weren't real.

I had to make a decision, and my room was too full of memories of the me I was until this morning.

Think, I told myself. *Think rationally. Think the way you would have at work.* When would I make a decision at work? When would I present my findings and make a recommendation?

When I knew for sure that I'd covered every angle, gotten every opinion.

I'd listened to Frederica's plea, I'd heard Mom's story, I'd felt the Olde Way imprint my soul. But if I was to deny my so-called destiny, then it was only fair for me to face a roomful of the people—the fae—I was saying no to.

I dialed the phone, and no sooner had I placed it against my ear than I heard Frederica say simply, "Gemma."

She was wide awake. Why wouldn't she be? After all, it only made sense that tooth fae worked night shifts, and it wasn't even eleven o'clock.

"So," I asked. "You busy tonight?"

"You know I am." I heard her soothing smile.

I paused, then swallowed. "Mind if I tag along?"

"I thought you'd never ask," she said. "But I hoped—we hoped—you would."

CHAPTER 6

From a key on a huge jangling set, Frederica let us into a side street bakery at ten minutes to midnight. It wasn't open yet, but a gritty sugary scent lingered. The counters were wiped clean, the display cases empty.

We went back through the kitchen, where the floor was very recently wiped clean, and stopped at the back wall.

I thought I was looking at nothing but a wall, but Frederica nudged me a little closer until I found, at eye level, a small but intricately carved wrought iron pair of wings. Like the faerie wings in children's books. I traced the grooves with my fingernail, and a tingle of fear—or something else?—shivered through my hand.

Frederica stepped forward and discreetly licked the tips of her index and middle finger, then put one finger on each wing.

Suddenly there was a door.

That had *not* been there a moment before.

I would have known I was looking at a door if the large frame and golden knob had been there. But it *hadn't*. And now it was, with the iron wings square in the middle.

I turned wide eyes at Frederica. She had to be expecting me to flip out, run through the kitchen to the front of the store, crash through the bakery window, and flee, never to be seen again. But she merely turned the knob and opened the door to wave me in.

I'd slipped out of Mom's house earlier tonight—well, no, I didn't. I'd walked through the front door, trying to keep quiet not because I didn't want her to catch me but because she might have fallen asleep. If she noticed my absence for the next couple of hours, she'd know where I was.

Frederica and I had traveled in silence. I resisted the urge to joke that she was driving the hybrid *in* a hybrid, but I let it go even though I was pretty sure she would have gotten a laugh. She was content in our silence, leaving me to percolate my fresh information in my own mind. After sneaking a few glances at her profile—the portrait of serenity—I had pressed my forehead against the window and watched without seeing the D.C. streets. As the familiar scenery blew by, my eyes rested on nothing. Instead it served as a moving backdrop for my thoughts.

Now, I glanced around in a near panic. We were only a few blocks from Smiley's Gym. I could easily break free from this surreal living dream, run from Frederica and whoever else waited for me inside, kick open a window at Smiley's and lie across the hard row of chairs until morning. That was me, that was where I belonged: in there. Not where I was going.

But I didn't run away. Probably because I knew that if I did, Frederica wouldn't make the slightest move to stop me. I was here on my own volition, and now I had a responsibility to myself to see this through.

So now, I entered through a magical door and allowed Frederica to usher me down a very tight, spooky stairwell. Dark stairwells were generally spooky, and at best, made me wonder why I didn't take an elevator, and at worst, gave me the feeling of fleeing from fire or gunmen. I looked over my shoulder as we descended, flexing my hands and ready to spring if I needed to, but Frederica didn't so much as glance around her. Her ballet-slippered toes made no sound, and I clunked behind her in the platform sneakers I'd dug up from my last stay at Mom's.

We emerged on the underground floor and stopped at a red door at the bottom. I didn't know what I expected—a sign that said, "Welcome Tooth Faeries" or something—but it was just a door—one I could see—and my heart started to pound. On instinct, I tried to take mental note of possible escape routes. To my left was an impenetrable silver steel wall, but on my right was a hallway with doors, ending in another steel wall.

Closed in and suddenly short of breath, I grabbed Frederica's shoulder but immediately loosened my rough grip. She was a living porcelain doll and I wouldn't want to hurt her. But she looked at me, seeming to understand my bout of claustrophobia.

"Where are we?" I asked her. "What was that illusion of a door?" *What was I getting myself into?*

Ever patient, she smiled. "We're in a fae safe house."

"Safe house?" I repeated stupidly. "Safe from what? What's after us?"

"We're vulnerable, Gemma," she said. "All the time. Innocence is delicate, and the collection is fragile, even though most humans have stopped speaking of fae as real and mischievous or evil, and instead relegated us to Disney movies."

Her gentle teasing didn't ease my discomfort. "Then why a safe house?"

"They're for fae to come together, like for tonight's moon gathering, or just to be able to talk freely to other local fae. It's a community center. Of course," she added, "as a safe house, it's properly equipped as a shelter in case of natural or human disaster. We have rooms to sleep in down there." She gestured down the hallway. "Well-stocked, brand-new kitchens, and rec rooms with virtual games. Locked vaults. Emergency headquarters with all the technology we need."

"Survival," I said.

"Yes. Everything we fae do is about survival."

"The carved wings?"

"A marker for a safe house, but also a bit of an inside joke by a fae around the eighteenth century. It was human folklore for a long time that faerie could be killed or frightened off by cold iron. So these simple people would create weapons from iron, and put iron objects outside their homes to keep faeries out."

"We live in a major city," I pointed out. "We're surrounded with iron and steel."

"Exactly. And the Earth's inner core is made up of iron. We live on iron, and have done far longer than humans did." She laughed. "Silly. And ironic, isn't it, that now our safe houses are protected with iron, to keep the humans out?"

"The bakery's a front."

"A fae-owned front, yes. Like at all our locations. All over the world. We know at all times who goes in and out."

"The magic door?"

"We're fae," she said. "What did you expect?"

Good point.

She pushed the red door open, and we walked into a room of bright, smiling, laughing people. Or, rather, fae. But they looked like people. Two long tables were set up against one wall, with plates of brownies and cookies, a coffee machine, and a few bottles of soda with stacks of plastic cups. Fae milled around the food, laughing and chatting with each other, and hugging as they noticed one another, happy as friends.

"I didn't bring anything," I said to Frederica, mostly because I didn't know what else to say.

She laughed, a birdsong of a sound. "I didn't bring any food either. But I brought you." She lowered her voice and took hold of my arm. "Maybe you could contribute some orange soda next time? It's my favorite, but no one ever thinks to bring it."

"Is this everyone?" I asked, nodding my head to the group. "Every one of us in D.C.?"

"Oh, no," she said. "Not even close. There are several meetings like this in the city tonight, in other safe houses. We gather at every new moon, half moon and full moon. And there are a lot of fae who only come once in a while."

I opened my mouth to ask another question but realized the group had gotten very quiet as, one by one, they turned to us. To me.

"Hello, everyone," Frederica said. "It's wonderful to see you all again."

Her greeting was warm, familiar, but rather than acknowledging her, they continued to watch me. Some moved in closer and squinted as if I was an exotic plant. Others leaned back, wide eyed, as if I was a meteor shower.

"Oh," one breathed. "Welcome."

"This is Gemma," Frederica said, and they sighed, a breeze winding through a forest of rustling, soft spring leaves.

I eyed the wide circle of folding chairs in the center of the room, and had the frightening thought that I might be made to sit in the center with everyone around me, ringside for a show they expected me to provide.

"Gemma," a young woman said. She had a tiny, emerald-green nose stud, and bright eyes to match. "You can sit next to me, if you want."

"Or sit with me," a startlingly handsome black man in an azure blue dress shirt said. "It's so nice to meet you. Gemma," he said, shaking his head with wonder.

"Mom," said a little girl. I couldn't even see her through everyone's knees. "Is she—"

Someone shushed her.

A few people stepped closer and I didn't know if I actually edged away to the door or if I just wished I could without seeming rude. I started to lift my fists to my face, ready to defend against the soft smiles and beatific gazes, but Frederica beat me to it. She held up a slender hand. The fae retreated a bit, and the room grew silent again.

"Gemma is new tonight," she said to them and in those four words, she made it very clear that I was new not just to the group, but to everything. She then turned to me, continuing to hold my elbow and although it was nothing but a feather on my skin, it held me steady and standing and I hoped she wouldn't let go just yet. "Gemma," she said to me, but clearly wanting all to hear, "we will leave you be. Leave you to be quiet if that's what you need. Feel it out, ask questions if you like."

I nodded, not trusting myself to speak. The group must have sensed my inner panic, because one by one, they moved to the circle of chairs, respectfully obeying Frederica's unspoken command but peeking over their shoulders at me.

Frederica guided me to the circle, where there were two empty seats together. We sat and there was silence. Not a shuffle, not a cough. I looked into my lap, picked a fuzz off my jeans and let it go. It didn't fall, but rather hovered in the air beside me, swaying in one direction, then the other, as if trying to decide which path to take to the floor.

I looked around again and now that fae were hushed and seating themselves, I could see the walls were covered with paintings. Paintings that glowed with colors my eyes weren't accustomed to distinguishing, and I could taste them. The art leaped off the wall and came in close.

And the music—gentle swaying notes I've never heard but have heard a thousand times. I could see the music dancing before my eyes.

I leaned into Frederica. "The music," I said. "The paintings."

She knew right away the source of my confusion. "It mixes your senses," she said. "Synesthesia, and fae art draws it out of you, of us."

It was beautiful.

"Welcome," Frederica said to everyone then. "Welcome to our moon gathering. Tonight we meet on a new moon, heralding new beginnings and reaffirmations of what already is."

No kidding.

"I am Frederica Diamond," she said, "and to those visiting us tonight from other communities, I am the guide here and we extend the hand of kinship. We are all bound by fae blood and history, and we come here tonight to experience anew the wordless joy of our long ago, to commit once more to the task of its re-creation, and to celebrate its hopeful rebirth with our descendants."

I ventured a look around the circle but I wasn't the main attraction anymore and I began to feel a tingling at my tailbone that slid up my spine and bloomed at the crown of my head. There was something powerful here, strong and supple. They felt it.

I felt it.

"Let's join hands," Frederica said, and she took my right hand in her cool, comforting one. I turned to my left and found a woman with auburn hair pulled into a ponytail with a perfect curly bounce. She was maybe around my age, wearing an orange cashmere sweater and jeans. She was a soccer mom. She was fae? She was *normal.* She smiled at me and took my left hand, then closed her eyes, as did everyone else, I noticed.

After a minute of indecision, I did the same.

When Frederica spoke again, her voice vibrated down her arm and into my hand, and somehow, I felt it in my left hand too, even though the soccer mom hadn't said a thing. It was being passed around, a continuous electrical current.

I tried to recall what Mom had said. This gathering was to reconnect to the Olde Way, and to hold it—hold it for longer, I imagined, than the few moments I'd held it in my palm in the coffee shop today. It felt like a million years ago, which now seemed appropriate, because we were about to channel a million years ago. Or more?

I became aware of a humming that was nothing at first, just a gnat passing by my ear, but the humming grew and lengthened and grew and lengthened, and in that split second before I let it take over my mind, I let go of everything, willing to give myself over to the colorful, musical formlessness, the peace and perfection, the place of nothing important and everything beautiful.

Then I hurtled forward into a black void, shoved down into endless darkness, pushed farther and farther as the space around me narrowed. I gasped and choked with fear but I couldn't hear myself. I was deafened, and I was going to get stuck.

Until I hit a wall—not hard, but a blockade that bounced me off and sent me down, down, down. I couldn't see myself. But then there was light and pictures rushing by me on both sides, fire and stars and water and people. Then came the sounds: laughter, cannon blasts, sobbing, ice cream truck tinkling, crickets chirping, dishes breaking, snow falling off a branch onto the ground. Every sound I'd ever heard twisted into one hard, bright knot and filled my brain to bursting and maybe it did, because I hit bottom, and there was nothing.

Only my breathing. But I when I checked myself for broken bones, I wasn't there.

My nonexistent fingers brushed the pine-needled ground, and I pushed myself to standing on my nonexistent feet. I turned my invisible head and saw I was standing beside a woman.

Her hair was pulled under a dirty white headwrap, and the few dark strands of her hair that had escaped were tangled. She stared at me…

And then I was her.

I took a deep breath, and broke into a run.

I wasn't sure my leather-shod feet could keep up with my intention. I weaved through trees, over rocks and logs I should have tripped over. I pushed away branches, but missed one, and it scraped my cheek and warm blood pushed to the surface. The russet wool of my long tunic should have slowed my running, shortened my stride, but it didn't.

I knew where I was going.

A house, solitary and still. Slits for windows. I blinked and I was at the door. I blinked again and I was inside.

I saw, I smelled, I felt in flashes.

Cold, packed dirt floor.

Single candle, burned halfway down.

Bowls and bowls of powders and liquid.

Dried animal heads dangling from the ceiling, a fox, a squirrel.

Dust in my nostrils, body odor.

A table. Half-filled bowls of foul-colored mixtures.

Malice staining the air.

Witch, my mind screamed. *Dark witch. Evil.*

I won't let her…

A bowl on the shelf, then in my hand.

Emptying it into my apron. Little tiny teeth.

Grab them, I silently ordered myself. *Get them all, don't lose them.*

I paused. Someone coming…

I bundled my apron into a little sack, twisting the top. Then I whirled and caught my own face in a dirty, cracked mirror.

I saw me. *I saw her.*

Peasant girl. White witch. Fae.

Warrior.

I lashed out an arm, upending the candle into a potion bowl.

Flames whooshed to bright life. I looked up at the macabre heads.

Thank you, the fox said into her brain, into mine. *Go*, said the squirrel. *Go now.*

I fled through the door, took cover behind trees. I wrapped my fingers around bark and splinters pierced my fingernails.

A violent scream ripped behind us, a long, hard howl of anger, defeat, surrender.

Clutching at the apron, my relief flowed through my blood. Innocence stolen back, nefarious plans now going up in smoke.

I laughed, and my soul pulled away, and I was looking at the woman again from my Gemma eyes.

The fire's golden glow lit up my companion's smile of triumph. She lifted her apron to her nose, inhaled, and threw her head back, eyes and mouth wide open, one arm extended, embracing the sky. Wings, wet and glistening, burst from her back and wrapped around her.

Then they unfurled, and she was gone.

Everything grew silent. I exhaled slowly, and my breath was loud, air puffing and dissolving in front of my lips.

Only one still, cold breath.

Then I was yanked back. I groped at my neck, but I was tossed once again into darkness.

Down, down, and this time I anticipated my crash landing, but my jaws snapped painfully shut when I hit earth.

Eerie, blank landscape, like the surface of the moon, desolate, dry, horizon splitting into sky.

I looked down at my hands again to find no me where I should have been. I wasn't alone, and the presence with me was solid, confident. I turned to find a man, a young man, dark-haired with sharp eyes, in khaki with a name label over his breast pocket: Brown. He looked into me…

And I was him.

Dark Arizona desert, he thought, I thought. *A dust storm hides the prisoners from view better than we can.*

I wiped at my gritty lashes and rubbed at my stubbled jaw, then turned and entered the barrack.

I smelled, I felt, I saw in flashes.

Heaviness of hundreds of sleeping people.

Flashlight shining into gray desolation.

Sweet, sweet penny candy store air. *Where is it…*

Next door, no. Next door, no. Next door, no.

Final door, inhaling confectionary sugar into my brain. Hesitating.

Mr. Ishikawa. Pear farmer, driven inside four walls. The only pear trees now, drawn in poetry, Japanese letters of swirling black beauty.

Smiling wife. Son Kevin, born here but trapped by 1942 ethnic misfortune.

Not so many innocents here, not so many innocents anywhere now.

I blinked and I was inside. I blinked and I knelt at the boy's side. Handkerchief out, I swept the little tooth off the shaky table.

A hitch of breath.

A sudden light.

A yell of terror.

Kind man. Pain in my heart. My own face in the small, streaky mirror.

I saw me. *I saw him.*

Soldier. Night watchman. Fae.

Warrior.

"I'm sorry," I gasped. Fled out the door, ran down the hallway, burst outside.

Dust blurring my eyes, coating my lungs, crunching in my mouth.

Cry behind me. "Herman!" *They know, they know… no escape.* "Herman!" A bullet powered past my ear, then another.

Blinding pain, my back split open, pulling off the ground and whirling around.

"Herman?" Uncertain, frightened.

I hovered before him. My fellow watchman. My friend. He fired. I fired.

Heat blasted Gemma out my open back, and I was thrown face first into sand. Two bodies before me, still. One wide-eyed forever, one crumpled among transparent, gossamer silk that shimmered and dissolved.

Grab the tooth. I pushed my formless hand through sand, grains sharp under my nails, fingers barely brushing tooth before I was pulled away into the darkness.

Down, down, longer, deeper.

No crash landing—only a roll to a stop on softer earth.

Fae all around me but different, Different from what I knew, different from each other.

Bright eyes, long ropes of shiny hair. Dewy skin in colors I'd experienced and colors I haven't.

Fae in groups, two groups. Somber expressions seemed out of place on every face. All their faces looking at her.

Beside me, a fae but human, a woman who could gaze in a mirror and find herself looking back at someone like me.

Nervous. Serious. Half and half, and torn in half.

Gemma pushed out the back of my neck, and I was her.

A whisper surrounds me, repeating, echoing, "Choose, choose, choose."

I—she—shakes our head.

The fae. Light and dark. Shadow and sun.

Midnight and morning.

Choose...

On opposite sides they sit.

Divided in purpose, dividing the future.

On opposite sides they wait.

Choose...

Come with us. The dark seduces with silver words on the wind. *We are closer to what you are. We will make this world ours, recover what humans took. Be with us, fight for us. Become our legacy, our warrior.*

Come with us. The light beckons with golden words on the wind. *You are closer to what we are. We will bring our world back, recover what humans lost. Be with us, fight for us. Become our legacy, our warrior.*

I am the warrior. Decision is mine. Destiny of warriors to come is mine.

Moving to light. Choosing innocence. Choosing love.

A scream splits the purple sky. "It is midnight," the dark fae cry. "The first moment of the divide."

Dissolved into the night. Midnight fae, gone.

A hum, a song closes the yellow sky. Hands join. The morning fae will welcome the day together.

A hand reached for me, my hand reached for them. Gemma me tore away and even though I was aware that I had to leave for who knew where, and even though they couldn't see me anymore, I reached out my own hand.

Falling…

The rush of light and shapes. The rewind of sound: the machines, the screams, the laughter. Wind rustling through trees in a whisper.

Silence. Silence. One bird's song. I raised my eyes to open sky. One drifting cloud.

Then I gasped, and fell to the hard floor.

When I looked up, the florescent lights hurt. A few dozen fae were stretching out hands. I bowed and covered my head with my forearms, wrapping myself into a ball.

"Gemma," Frederica said, her voice a healing balm on my soul rubbed raw. "She's all right," she says to the room. "We need to be alone. Enjoy the rest of your evening, be together. We'll all meet again soon."

She helped me to my feet, feet I could see again. My body was intact, and my mind felt like my own. She wrapped an arm around me and I leaned on her. I should have collapsed her willowy frame with my weight but she was my brick house for the moment.

She led me to the door, and the soccer mom fae gave Frederica a cup of water. There were murmurs of soft goodbyes behind me. I thought I heard one man's voice say gently, "We love you" before we were in the blank hallway and I slid to the ground.

She handed me the water and sat beside me, tucking her legs under her. She smoothed her thick hair behind each of her tiny ears. "I take it," she said, "that you weren't with us, Gemma. You were somewhere else."

I downed the water in three gulps and gasped with the last swallow. I was sweating like I'd just gone four rounds. I guessed I'd really gone about three—three rounds in time. Was it real?

"Warriors," I said. "I saw them."

Frederica's placid barely-there smile didn't waver. "I didn't know that would happen. I didn't know it could. I've never worked directly with… someone like you. Are you all right?"

"Yeah. I mean, I think so."

"Do you want to tell me about it?"

"I don't think so," I said. "I know—I think I know what I saw. Did you ever see them?"

"See the warriors?"

"Did you ever communicate with them? Feel what it was like to be them? Be there when they…" My voice trailed off.

"No, Gemma," she said. "We have great reverence for the warriors and we try to keep their stories alive the best we can, but that's all. They spoke to you?"

"No, not really. But I was there when they—I saw them but I didn't just see them. I *was* them. I was in their fight."

"Our energy brought you there, it seems," she murmured. "We went to our past, and you went to yours."

I brought my knees up to my chin and dropped my head in my crossed arms. "I saw the midnight fae," I said, muffled. "I saw them split, leave the morning fae. I was the warrior who had to choose one side."

Frederica said nothing for a long moment. Then, "You were at the summit. The summit we only know about from oral tradition. The fae split that day into light and dark."

I squeezed my eyes shut, and mercifully, no pictures or colors invaded my space. Just black.

"Some of the fae wanted to focus our existence on the Olde Way, bringing it back to Earth, sharing it with humans. The rest of the fae didn't want to share. They were bitter, thought the fae had been shoved aside, and they wanted to focus our goal on replacing humans completely. Then the warrior had to choose one side, and that would become the dominant fae, the fae with power on its side, and the warrior chose us. At the stroke of midnight, one half of the fae split into darkness, the midnight fae. The remaining fae joined hands and waited until morning, taking the night to mourn our lost ones before beginning anew with dawn."

"I was there."

"You were there," she said, and her voice echoed my own amazement.

I shook my head and lifted it again, opening my eyes to painful light.

"Let me take you home," she said. "You have a lot to think about. You are being asked by so many to be so much. But you do have a choice," she added. "I can't promise that any other recruiters won't try to change your mind in the future, but I'll respect your wishes. I respect you now. You walked right into what you couldn't believe, faced it head on." She smoothed a hand over my hair. "That's the courage of a warrior."

Take me home, my mind begged. *This can be one day in my life and I can try to forget it and just continue to be what I was.*

But what I was for thirty years hadn't been truly me.

How could I know those warriors' souls and turn away from the destiny they'd embraced, fearless or not, victorious—or not?

The Olde Way shimmered inside me now, and I couldn't turn my back on it. It was the meaning of life that each ordinary individual searched for. It was nirvana, heaven, enlightenment, the ultimate goal, and after one brief shining moment inside of it, I couldn't pretend this world was all there was. I needed to bring it here, and give it to Mom, and to Avery.

That was the fae in me, I was sure.

But I had another half. And that half remembered waking up one morning to find my father gone. That human half never stopped hoping he would come home, and that human half recognized now that he'd rejected me. That human half wanted to fight against the force that would take away my happiness, because I could now.

"You're human," Dad said. "You're human."

I lifted my head.

"I'm in," I said to Frederica.

She looked deep into my eyes. "You were always in," she replied. "We never let you go."

And with that, I slammed the door behind Dad, and returned to my real family.

>=<

Frederica dropped me off at Mom's, but only for the time it took me to write her a note, letting her know I was going home. Then Frederica drove me home.

I shed my clothes piece by piece from the door to the bedroom, and I slipped into bed in my underwear, wrapping myself around Avery. He sighed and rubbed my arm, then asked sleepily, "I thought you were at your mom's."

"I was," I whispered. "I was a lot of places. Now I'm here."

"Good."

"Good," I repeated.

There, in bed, I remained the Gemma I knew, with the man I loved. I fell asleep wishing I wouldn't have to wake up, and wondering who I'd be when I did.

CHAPTER 7

It was a door. One I could see. An inch-long iron pair of wings hung above the doorbell I pressed twice.

A woman opened the door—a delicate-boned woman who would rival Frederica in a Thumbelina contest. Her dark hair was braided and roped around her head, and there was so much hair and so little head, I found myself readying to catch her when she toppled like a Jenga pile. She wore a dark purple tank top and khaki cargo pants that she had to have purchased in a children's department.

I found myself wondering if my new role as fae warrior had more to do with my weight class than with my breeding.

"I'm Reese," she said. "You're Gemma."

That was easy.

"We're *so* excited you're here," she said. "We've heard just *everything* about you. And about fae like you who came before you, and—well, just come in!"

Far from flattered, I instead felt uncomfortable that my legend had preceded me. Especially since I was informed of that legend only yesterday.

Oblivious to my hesitation, Reese took my hand and tugged me inside, closing the door behind me. "I asked especially to be the one to show you around."

Although she appeared as ageless as Frederica—and, I realized last night as I couldn't sleep, my mother, who hadn't really significantly aged all that much over the years—Reese's demeanor was that of an overly eager office intern. I relaxed just a bit, managing a thin smile.

Reese didn't seem to mind my lesser enthusiasm. Still holding my hand, she led me down a long hallway.

I wasn't sure what I expected at the D.C. Collections Headquarters on the H Street Corridor. Well, that's not true, actually. I'm ashamed to admit it now, but I pictured it as looking a bit like the Soho apartment of one of my NYU college friends: nag champa incense burning, long bead curtains separating each room, a marble Buddha sitting in one corner like an unobtrusive roommate, posters depicting yoga asanas and rainbow chakra centers, groovy tunes heavy with tabla drums and sitar emanating from an invisible sound system. Maybe I was hoping for that somewhat familiar feeling here, or a more generic but similar atmosphere, like a touristy New Age store.

I confess that at the very least, I *did* expect sparkles.

This place, with its bare walls, utilitarian track lighting and carpets that smelled fresh from the factory, seemed anything *but* magical. It could have been any office in America. My polling office was smaller and cluttered, but otherwise retained the same 9-to-5 feel.

"What does the landlord think it is that you—we do here?" I couldn't help asking.

Reese blasted a ray of that bright cheerleader smile over her bony shoulder. "The landlord is fae," she said.

Right. I did wish Reese would let go of my hand but it wasn't hard to guess that her feelings would be super-hurt if I made that request.

We turned a corner and she slid the ID card on a lanyard around her neck into a slot next to a windowless door. "You'll get your own card soon," she said, and I pretended to be reassured. She dropped my hand so she could push the heavy door open with both of hers.

I stepped into the room after her, and my jaw dropped at what this average office façade had kept hidden.

The room was enormous, much like the NASA mission control rooms I'd seen on late-night cable TV. I was technology challenged, so I wasn't one hundred percent sure, but I was at least fairly confident that even the most advanced ordinary humans generally didn't work on holographic screens. Seriously, holograms. A few dozen people—well, fae—stood between desks and sat on rolling chairs monitoring the hovering images in front of them, occasionally poking a finger in the air to pull up different iridescent images or change screens. It freaked me out.

The entire room around them was sleek and spotless and silent, with silver gleaming desks and high-polished floor. Each fae had wore a small earpiece though none seemed to be talking to anyone. They just listened.

Every fae in the complicated, intimidating room turned to stare at me, ID tags dangling from lanyards around their necks.

"Uh, hi," I mumbled, though no one but Reese could have heard me. They watched me for a moment, turning around to glance at screens every few seconds before their work consumed them again and they turned away. Reluctantly.

The air was charged here with something I couldn't identify. Urgency, certainly. But there was a sense of pride, as if the workers weren't just toiling for a paycheck. They worked as one efficient machine with age-old coordinates set to one common goal.

The common goal was the Olde Way, I understood, and I suddenly itched to take my part.

"Welcome to The Root," Reese said with that pride. "Our monitoring center. I work at that pod over there, and my job is routine confirmation of the location of all the tracking bugs, and to intercept signals. It's a big city, and it's important to keep track of what's going on in all the homes."

I couldn't be hearing that correctly. "Hold up," I said. "You have bugging devices in every house in D.C.?"

"Not every house," Reese said. "Just the houses with one or more children between 6 and 11, the age range for exfoliation of primary teeth."

She must have confused my stunned expression for lack of basic understanding, because she clarified, "Baby teeth falling out. Kids grow and lose 20 primary teeth, and we can't catch them all, but I still say we have a pretty good track record. Approximately 87 percent. Well," she faltered, "more like 70 percent right now. But you'll be working on that."

"Sorry," I cut in, "I'm still stuck on the bug thing. How do you know what houses to bug?"

"Public records like birth certificates," she said. "School records, Registry of Deeds. Information is pretty easy to find."

"What is it you're tracking, exactly?"

"Innocence."

"I don't follow."

"When a tooth falls out, it exposes the innocence essence we need. The bug can sense it, and emits a signal. We intercept the signal, but we have to do it fast, because the bug has a time limit. It can only sense it when it's strongest, when the tooth first falls out. We lose the signal quickly, so The Root is staffed around the clock."

Despite my amazement at what I was hearing, I was impressed with Reese. I usually considered perkiness a personality flaw, but in her element, she knew her stuff. "How do people not find tracking devices in their own homes?" I asked.

"Oh, they find them," Reese said. "When a bug gets squooshed, the Research and Retrieval Department has to ask a collector who's not on assignment to go in and replace it. It's a real inconvenience but it happens all the time."

"People *squoosh* the bugs?" I asked.

"Exactly," Reese said, then, "oh, you haven't seen them?"

"I haven't seen much," I told her. "I'm about twenty-four hours into this whole thing."

"Be right back," she said and dashed out a different door than the one we entered through. I waited, and I caught several people assessing me. They were obvious but I gave them credit for at least trying to be polite about it by glancing up and down and up again, or smiling.

"We got one!" a man shouted. He put his hand up, and I spotted him two desks away from the door. I edged closer as a woman briskly acknowledged him and joined him at his station. Heads close together, they examined his holographic screen, tapped a few invisible air keys, and a signal screamed out of a speaker. I plugged one ear with my finger. The man pointed to the screen. "Target. Who's on tonight?"

"Give it to Nilsen," his supervisor—I guessed—told him, and he nodded. While she made a note on a wall chart, he pulled a phone out of his pocket and awkwardly text-messaged with his thumbs, squinting at the much smaller screen.

"Hold out your hand," I heard, and almost jumped. I swirled and there was Reese. She raised her brows. "Go on."

I did, and she placed something small in my palm. Something small with legs. Many legs. It moved.

I yanked my hand away with a shriek. Yes, a shriek. It didn't often happen that I shrieked, but spiders had a way of bringing out the girl in me.

"What the…" I yelled, and took two steps back, colliding into a tall, broad someone.

I felt hands take hold of my upper arms. The whisper was like a sweep of silk across my ear. "I can never resist the call of a damsel in distress."

Ire—and not the warm breath on my neck—made my hair stand on end, the spider momentarily forgotten. Damsel in distress? Someone was about to take a walk on the wild side of me. I set my jaw and turned.

My knees buckled slightly and my balance suffered.

Lamppost guy. The well-built, painfully sexy blond man whom I'd really wanted to forget about. From this short distance, new details hit me: his black, silver-ringed irises; his fresh, warm scent; his flop of naughty hair that hid one cheekbone; his long pale eyelashes.

I longed to feel those lashes brush against my neck, fall into the dark velvet of his gaze, inhale his skin until his scent came out my own pores—

A whoosh filled my ears and I couldn't hear much. I took a step closer. Just to touch him, just once…

"Knock it off," I heard, and I tried to shake off the intrusion as I reached out my hand.

But I heard it again. "Svein, I said knock it off. Leave her *alone*."

In an instant, something like a light in me snapped on. The blur was gone, like someone had swiped my lenses clean with a dishrag, and my thoughts were my own again. I lowered my hand. The man remained standing before me, but suddenly he was just an incredible-looking man who had called me a damsel.

"What's the matter with you?" Reese demanded, and I realized she was the one who had cut into my embarrassing reverie. She walked right up to him and jabbed a finger hard into his solar plexus. "Don't you know who she is?"

Despite the determined little fae getting into his personal space, his eyes never left mine. But now that I had returned to my logical self, I met his even gaze with one of my own. I crossed my arms and arched a brow.

He wore a black T-shirt which stretched enticingly over a rock-solid chest, and a pair of jeans that probably stretched enticingly over places I absolutely would not look at.

"Yeah, I know who she is," he drawled impressively for a man who didn't have a Southern accent. And when he arched a brow back at me, it became clear that he'd also known who I was yesterday afternoon, from across a busy street. "What's wrong?" he asked now. "Scared of little creepy-crawlies?"

I glanced down at the ground where I'd dropped the spider. "They're not my favorites," I muttered. It was right next to the chunky heel of my boot, but I refused to edge out of its way.

Reese bent and scooped it up. She flipped it over and squeezed it. Its back popped open on a miniscule hinge. "It's electronic," she said. "It's not a real bug. It's a *bug*."

"These are your bugs? These are in people's houses?"

"Yup," Reese confirmed as the man with the phone approached us.

"Nilsen," he said, "I just sent you a dispatch. You've got one tonight in Georgetown."

"Send the address."

"Already did," said the man, moving back to his station.

"So, Svein Nilsen," I said. "Nice to meet you."

"Is it?"

He laughed at me. Not out loud, but I saw his chest contract.

"No, it really isn't," I said. "Why don't you scamper off now and do your googly magic act on a woman who can't kick the shit out of you?"

"That's not very ladylike."

"Take a step closer and you'll feel me change your definition of a lady."

I sensed the room had grown very quiet. Key-tapping ceased, the creak of chairs silenced. Everyone was frozen, leaning forward in anticipation.

"People always want to see a fight," I remarked.

"No," Reese said quietly. "They don't. Fae don't fight. Svein won't fight you. He can't."

Svein cut her a vicious look but she ignored it. "Fae can't do conflict," she said.

"My new pal Svein here seemed pretty bent on raising conflict," I said.

"No," she said. "He was honest. You were the one who raised the possibility of a fight."

I twisted my mouth with the realization that she was quite right.

"We're curious about you, you know?" she said. "We knew Frederica found you a while ago. She didn't want to bring you here until we identified the threat. And," she added, her voice chirpy again, "you're, well, you're like a miracle to us. You're the first warrior to come out of our lineage, the collector lineage, so not only are you a fae star, you're *our* star."

She grinned, and I tried to grin back, but I had a feeling my face conveyed nothing but bewilderment—bewilderment that these brilliantly ahead-of-any-human's-time fae could consider *me* any kind of hero.

"That's enough," Svein said. Apparently I didn't hold the same appeal to him. "I'll explain the rest to her. She's mine now."

"I beg your pardon," I told him.

"That's right. See, sweetheart, I'm your new mentor."

"My mentor," I repeated, hoping I'd misheard.

"That's right."

"Yeah," I said, "I don't think so. Where's Frederica?"

"In bed, I imagine," Svein said. "She works nights."

"Don't you?"

"I don't sleep."

Mr. Enigma. "I'll stay up tonight," I said, "and wait for Frederica."

"Frederica's a recruiter and a guide," he said. "Not a trainer. I'm not looking forward to this any more than you are, if it makes you feel any better."

"It does."

"Because not only do I have to train you," he went on, "I have to oversee your transformation." He turned to the small fae woman I'd quickly come to respect as an ally of mine. "Reese, we'll need the Butterfly Room," he said.

"I prepared it this morning," she said. "Gemma's all set."

"Wait a minute," I cut in. "What transformation?"

"Yours," Svein said, "so you can become one of us instead of what you are now."

"Svein," Reese warned.

"What's your problem?" I demanded of Svein. "For a mentor, you have a hell of a snarky attitude."

"And for someone who knows zero about us and what you'll have to be, you have one hell of a cocky attitude."

Agreed. But I wouldn't apologize for it, because it was how I got by. Clearly, this was how Svein got by, but I didn't see why he had to resort to it at the moment. I was on his turf, and I'd be playing by his rules.

I turned to Reese. "You said you identified the threat. What is it? That's why I'm here."

"It's not a what, it's a who," Reese said. "We found…"

"*I* found," Svein interrupted her. And, to me, "You don't get to hear one more thing until the transformation and some training. I'll see whether you are what they say you are."

I wished I could retort that I was, but truth was, I didn't really know myself yet.

"Whenever you're ready." He stalked out one of several side doors. I glanced at Reese.

"I've met plenty of people who have issues with me," I said, "but I'd known them at least a half-hour or so."

Reese sighed with her slight shoulders. "You didn't like him right away either," she pointed out.

I didn't, but I didn't want to tell her why. He'd made me feel vulnerable for those first few seconds, when he'd drawn me into him and made me forget everything else in my life. "What did he do to me?"

Reese smiled. "It's a fae glamour. You'll get that. You'll be immune to it yourself when you do."

I remembered Smiley's, and the guys' reaction to Frederica, and then the same thing at the coffee shop.

"Svein's in Archives," Reese said. "He's the chief archivist, and he knows a lot. His trainees are among the best." She bit her lip. "He's—well, he's a little hard to figure out. But I know Frederica was right to assign him to work with you. I'm sure he'll be a good mentor."

"I thought he was a collector."

"We're all collectors. Most of our collectors are freelance but all of us at Headquarters work rotating shifts as collectors."

"Who pays you? I mean, who's paying for all this?"

"Fae landlords, fae philanthropists, fae scientists and specialists," she said. "You've met lots of fae in your lifetime and you don't even know it."

"That's what my mother said."

She nodded. "They donate time, money, resources, manpower. Fae intelligence is greater than human, and they achieve more as an average group than any average group of humans. Gives us an edge, financially and socially. And we age a little more slowly, giving us more time. Go down to Budget sometime and they can give you more details if you're interested, although I do know most of the backers remain anonymous even to us because of their high status in human society."

"I'll get paid?" Yeah, I was ready to collect innocence and fight for fae survival because it was my destiny and I believed in the Olde Way, but let's face it, a little something every Friday was *always* a plus.

"Ask Frederica, but I think you'll pull a collector's paycheck for the time being," Reese said. "We recruit a bunch of fae from unemployment lines, because they're free to work nights. Some fae seek us out if they want a break from their full-time jobs. And they never stay to retirement age. The average collector does a few years and that's it. So we have to keep recruiting."

"Got one!" This time it was a woman who put her hand up, and the supervisor approached her in a hurry.

"What's next?" I asked Reese. "For me, I mean."

Reese squeezed my arm with a smile. "Your transformation. Don't be scared."

"Should I be?"

"No, no," Reese hurriedly assured me. "Svein will take care of you, and then you'll get acquainted with your new collector job."

"I'm here for something else," I said. "You said it when I came in. The ones like me who came before me? The threat?"

"Ask Svein," she said. "That's his—well, it's his investigation. You'll work with him. But I'm here to help you with anything else." She snatched a pen and Post-It off a nearby table, and scratched a phone number on it. "Me," she said, "if you need anything. Oh, and I almost forgot." She disappeared for a quick moment and returned with a metal ring that held about two pounds' worth of keys. "For the D.C. area safe houses. If you're planning to go out of town, let us know and we can supply you with key access wherever you're going, if you like."

The shape of her grin told me it would be an honor for her to help me. The fae had found me, had brought me here and, I suspected, gotten hopes up about my abilities. I worried about letting Reese down, about letting down everyone in this room, and the tradition we all came from.

However, I really didn't give a rat's ass if I let Svein Nilsen down. That rebelliousness pushed me forward.

>=<

I walked down the long hallway, turned my first left as Reese had instructed me and, sure enough, a small purple butterfly was carved into the wood of the first door I came to. The Butterfly Room.

I entered a room that could have been called cozy, but only as a default characteristic of its cramped space. I myself wouldn't have gone so far as to call it cozy because Svein was draped over the only chair in the room—an armchair that looked as though it had seen better-stuffed days.

He didn't bother with a verbal acknowledgement, and I tried to interpret his expression, but I got lost somewhere between seductive and hostile.

"Now what?" I asked him.

"Transformation," he said.

"Right, into something more or less acceptable to you."

"It has nothing to do with me. It has so little to do with me that I wasn't even consulted before they brought you in."

"Ha," I said. "I knew it. You had a beef with me the minute I walked in the door."

"I have a problem with everyone behaving as though you're some kind of fae messiah when the truth is you have no idea what you are and what you're supposed to be doing."

"I'm a tooth faerie," I told him.

He winced.

"Yeah, yeah, yeah, not 'faerie.' I'm tooth *fae*, okay? I'm supposed to be collecting teeth, with a side assignment of butt-kicking."

"It's the butt-kicking that's the issue. You're even more volatile than I thought you'd be, and I don't want you kicking and screaming your way through my investigation."

"I'm a boxer, actually."

"Point is," he said, unfolding himself from his chair and standing, "the situation is delicate. I don't need some half-cocked half-human going in swinging."

"Identifying the threat, that was your job, wasn't it?" I asked, trying to keep up my end of the conversation so I didn't prove him right by clocking him on the side of the head. "You know who it is. You figured it out."

"I narrowed it down and narrowed it down until I pinpointed the location. I know what needs to be done, and who needs to be taken out, and they brought *you* in to do it. You."

"You think you can do better? Then be my guest." I waited a beat. "Oh, that's right. You can't. You can't fight."

He only had to take one step closer for our faces to be less than an inch apart. I felt his breath on my cheek. His shoulder twitched, and I dodged the punch I saw coming.

I didn't really believe he'd intended to connect, but I wasn't taking any chances. I bounced on my toes, fists up. I feinted left, and grinned.

Then he fell back into the chair cushion, swept his leg into the backs of my knees, and sent me crashing to the carpet.

Pain flared in my elbow where I broke my fall, and in my new vulnerability, I put my forearm up to block whatever he'd hit me with next.

But he grasped my arm and hauled me to my feet. "Don't ever," he growled, "say I can't fight. I'm a black belt in taekwondo, with a little muay thai and Krav Maga in the mix. I'm a proficient fighter, when I'm in a sparring match. Or when I'm teaching a bigmouthed half-breed a lesson."

I rolled my shoulders back and forth, circled my neck.

"As soon as you perceived me as a real threat," he said, "and I sensed it, I couldn't make another offensive attack. I can go through the motions as long as the emotion stays neutral. When it becomes violence, I have no choice but to stop."

So he'd smoked out the fae's enemy but couldn't fight the battle. Might make me a little edgy too. I rubbed my elbow.

"I signed on for this," I said. "I understand your frustration, but I chose this because I *do* know who I am, and I *do* know what I'm supposed to be doing. I'm the front line for all of us against a threat. The only thing I'm missing is the how and the who. Frederica didn't bring me in to finish your job. She brought me in to help you see it through. So you might want to let me in on it sometime soon."

He said nothing for a long time. Then he nodded, imperceptibly at first, but I saw it, even before his nods became heavier and true.

"Let's get you to the room," he said. "No sense prolonging this."

He grabbed a clipboard from off a small, shaky desk and opened a door that I'd assumed was a closet. He ushered me into an antiseptic-like anteroom. The walls were painted eggshell, and a sign on the door instructed to make sure the first door was closed before opening the next. Svein obeyed, and ushered me into the Butterfly Room.

The *padded* Butterfly Room.

Floor to ceiling pads, in case someone was inclined to flip out at any moment. I turned to ask Svein what the hell was going on, but he'd slipped out and closed me in. I heard a lock turn.

I banged on the door with a fist. "Svein! Open the door!" I opened my fist and whacked on the door with my two open palms. "What the hell am I doing in here? Open up!"

"Gemma." His voice echoed above me and all around me. I stopped banging.

"Svein?"

"That's me. I can hear and see you. Speakers are in the four corners. See them?"

I did, but it didn't quell my fast-growing anxiety.

"Camera's in the upper corner to the left of the door. See it?"

I did, but again, no reassurance whatsoever. "Why am I in a padded cell?"

"Everyone reacts differently to a transformation."

"Who else transforms?" I asked. "Aren't I the only half-fae around?"

"There are partial transformations, for those who need to bind a certain ability for whatever reason."

I wanted to ask him whether I was going to look any different, but remembered that I lived with my mother all those years and she looked perfectly normal—perfectly human. "What's going to happen here, exactly?"

"Your physical fae traits have been dormant your whole life. We're going to awaken them. You'll still be you—God help me."

"Hey!"

"Your fae side will physically manifest. But Gemma, you have to go with it. Your human side will fight this. You have to let up, and let go. Whatever you feel, you have to go with it. Do you understand?"

"Not exactly." I was starting to panic, though.

"The process of transformation will bring out everything underneath, including any emotions you've been hiding, fears you have, feelings you don't express every day."

"In case you hadn't noticed, I'm not the type to hold things inside."

"Yeah, I'd noticed." I think he smiled, and I caught myself regretting I wasn't able to see it. "But we're all deeper than our surfaces. You have to ride the wave. It won't take too long."

While we'd been talking, the lights had dimmed, and the air was starting to feel thick around me, like a blanket being wrapped around my head. I sat down on the floor, and the padded surface squished under me. "Will it hurt?" I asked, softly enough for Svein to possibly not hear me, because I wasn't sure I wanted the answer.

My mind was melting. I rolled over, tucking my legs under me and curling my fingers.

"You'll be fine," he said more gently than I thought he could, "I'm right here."

"Promise?" I couldn't make my lips form the word properly, and it came out in a mumble. A part of me was mortified that I even asked him that, but that part was fading away with the rest of me. I closed my eyes.

"How could it hurt?" he said, his voice a lullaby. "You're returning to yourself.

"Gemma," he said, "You'll emerge with wings."

A burst of indigo surfaced in the middle of my mind, and spilled like dark, cool ink into every corner. It filled my ears, my eyes, my mouth, and dripped down the rest of me. My fingers moved in it, and my toes. I smiled, because it was a dream, a good one.

My mother tucked me in. My head pressed against the cool cotton of my pillow and my mother's hands laced through my hair. She bent to kiss my forehead and I caught a whiff of her perfume and my nose tickled and twitched. My father was silhouetted in the doorway behind her, and he said, "I love you." I couldn't hear him but I didn't have to. I was safe.

The inky fluid in and around me dissolved as a sunburst exploded in the center of my chest, sending powerful rays down my arms and legs. I walked across the stage to receive my college degree. I arrived for my first day at the polling office and walked straight through my cubicle wall to get to my desk. I won an amateur bout and threw my gloves up with pride. I punched a heavy bag and my fist blew through canvas and stuffing and came out the other side.

I pulled my arm back to strike again, but a ribbon of pink wound its way around my heart and squeezed softly. I dropped back into Avery's embrace. I breathed with him. I inhaled his breath and his love and my love radiated out of my face in sparkles that danced in the air between us. I closed my eyes again but I still saw him smiling; I basked in the rosy warmth.

But the warmth turned hotter and hotter and suddenly it was bright red and it wasn't in me—it was outside of me, jabbing at me, burning me. Avery's loving gaze grew hard. "No," I said, and he turned and walked away. "Avery, don't go!" I cried, and when he looked back at me, his face was my father's. "No!" I screamed, in a voice that tore out of my gut. Ripples ran up and down my back, pain blossoming from my shoulder blades. "Dad!" I clawed at my own skin, tearing at my shirt to get hold of my own anguish. "Dad!"

He didn't see me, or he didn't care. He left me and the red followed him out, giving way to black.

I collapsed, weak and spent.

Eventually, the green came in and carried me on soothing waves back into my body. I knew I was back, but I stayed there consciously in that moment, letting my heart beat my own way again.

When I opened my eyes, I discovered my head was cradled in Svein's lap. And when I tried to sit up, I discovered I was without my shirt.

CHAPTER 8

"I think I should be outraged," I said, my tongue thick in my mouth, "but I don't have the energy." I pushed myself onto my knees and sat on my feet, wrapping an arm around my front.

"I was sure you'd have at least a couple of tattoos," Svein commented. "A fire-breathing dragon, or a tiger in mid-leap."

"Just give me my shirt."

He handed it to me and it didn't look like my black long-sleeved cotton shirt as much as a tattered scrap left over from a pissed-off pit bull's tirade. "Turn around."

He pushed himself to his feet and obeyed. "You ripped it off," he said. "And you had a hard time coming back into reality, so I came in to pull you back. You needed an anchor of security."

"I'm not sure you would have been my first choice for that job," I said, trying to figure out which hole was for my head.

"I was your last connection with reality."

"I think my last connection with reality was sometime yesterday," I told him. "And anyway, I have a headache like someone slammed me with a two-by-four. I hope you knew what you were doing in that room."

"I was only there to keep an eye on your emotional reactions. There was a team of people for the physical stuff."

I stared daggers into his strong, broad back. "A team of people watched me rip off my shirt?"

"Butterfly agents. Up until now," he said, "the Butterfly Room's only been used by fae who need to bind one of their abilities for some personal reason, and then eventually to regain it. You were the first to ever undergo a complete awakening. We needed a team in case something went wrong."

I wriggled into the tattered remains of my shirt, and realized I was still mostly out of it. I huffed with aggravation. "Well, then I hope *they* knew what they were doing."

"All indications are normal," he said and yanked his own black T-shirt off. He tossed it over his shoulder. I caught it and stared at it a moment, fighting the urge to hold it up to my nose before I pulled it over my head. As I pushed my left arm through, I caught a glimpse of my watch, and swore.

"I have to get out of here," I said, hoisting myself to my feet. I swayed a little but managed to stay upright.

"Not a good idea," Svein said, turning and hooking a thumb through his belt loop. Now that he was the one without a shirt, I nearly reconsidered his words, maybe just to linger a few minutes more...

"Are you doing that thing on me again?" I demanded, trying to remember what Reese said. "Glamour?"

"No," he said, the corner of his mouth quirking up a bit. "I'm not. And what's more, even if I was, you're immune to it now. So whatever you're thinking, it's all you, sweetheart."

I shook my head in disgust, but I wasn't sure whether it was at him or at myself. "I have to leave," I repeated.

"Again, not a good idea. You're still weak, and you need to have your first training, to begin to learn control over your new capabilities."

"I'm sure it can wait until tomorrow," I said. I'd been here long enough, and I was emotionally wrung out. And Avery was actually going to make it home tonight early for a rare dinner together. I needed to pick up Thai food, head home, and put it on nice plates. Avery would know full well that I didn't cook it, but neither one of us let that get in the way of a good meal.

"It can't wait."

"Well, it's going to have to." The door to the padded cell of the Butterfly Room was open now, so I went through it, pushed open the second door, and leaned against the armchair in the office. Svein followed me.

"Letting you leave now would be like handing you a loaded gun and sending you home without telling you how to not use it."

"I know, I know. I have *powers* now." I wiggled my fingers in front of my face. "Whatever they are, I'll keep a lid on them until tomorrow."

"You need to stay on an even keel," he said. "No matter what your boyfriend says or does in the next twenty-four hours, you need to stay completely neutral."

"Won't be too hard. He doesn't get on my nerves in an entire year as much as you have in the past two hours," I told him. "And what do you know about my boyfriend anyway?"

"It's my job to find things out," he reminded me. "And I'm completely against you leaving right now."

"Well, you're not the boss of me."

I put my hand on the doorknob and he grabbed my wrist. I glared at him.

"No extreme emotion tonight," he said. "Good or bad. Just take it easy. Don't watch a sad movie on TV, don't argue with your mother on the phone, don't talk or even think about anyone or anything that will affect you on any deep level. Just eat your dinner and go to sleep."

"You told me in the Butterfly Room to go with my emotions, and now you're telling me to squash them?" I tried to wrench my wrist out of his grip but Svein only tightened his fingers. "In case you've forgotten—and based on your nasty comments thus far, I'm sure you haven't—I'm supposed to catch a bad guy. I need my anger to do that."

"You'll battle our threat out of necessity, not anger," he said. "But that remains to be seen. Tonight, no emotion."

I opened my mouth to speak but he interjected. "If you can't do that," he said, very softly, "then Avery McCormack will find out the hard way who Gemma Fae Cross really is. And your recklessness will not only have consequences on your love life, but it will have consequences for *all* of us."

He released his hold on me but I didn't move, a wave of fear rippling through my body, settling in my shoulder blades and heating up.

My secrets were piling one on top of another. Secrets that I needed to keep from everyone. Including Avery.

What had I done?

I spent my life emoting all over everyone I met. I held nothing in, and I was comfortable letting everyone know my opinions. Now I found that everything for me and for all the fae depended on my emotional control?

I had no idea how to control what I was now. But Svein had just said I had to. I had just become a different being physically, and I had to become a different being emotionally, and somehow this was supposed to be my destiny?

"What have I done?" I whispered.

My back itched and burned.

Oh, God. Avery. What could this to do his career? What would this do to us? What would this do to *me*?

"Fear," Svein said quietly, "is the hardest to control. Fear and anger."

Why couldn't have I thought this through a little longer? My mother had asked me to wait before making any decisions. For thirty years I didn't know I was fae. I couldn't even think it over for a *day*? Two days? Gemma, going in swinging. As usual.

My shoulder blades spasmed and contracted back, once, twice.

"What's happening to me?" I demanded.

"You're tough, Gemma," he said, putting his hands on both my shoulders. "Control the fear. Don't fight it. Accept it."

I tried, I really did. But I could only grit my teeth and tighten my jaw and push against my frightening thoughts. Fighting was the only way I knew to suppress an emotion, and this time, I realized I was going to lose.

My shoulders stretched back, as if someone pulled me hard from behind, and I hit the wall.

This time, Svein was the one who swore. He pushed the desk up against one wall and the armchair against another wall and stood on it, giving me all the floor space the tiny room would allow.

I had no time to turn and see what pulled me. My back ripped open. I screamed at the excruciating pain, but by the end of my scream, it was over. I was heavier, leaning back, standing on my toes in an effort to stay upright, and I twisted my head to look behind me.

Wings.

Huge, gossamer wings. Silky and pale pink and as delicate as spider webs. Yet they were powerful, still threatening to topple me.

I didn't pass out. I wanted to. I wanted to think this should have shocked me but apparently my mind *had* transformed along with my body.

In the Butterfly Room. *You'll emerge with wings...*

Could I move them? I wiggled my fingers first. How did I wiggle my fingers? With intention, and my brain understood, and my fingers wiggled.

Intention. *I'll just move my wings*, I thought. Close them, and open them.

I *did*.

In the cramped room, my right wing brushed the wall when it reopened, and I felt it. I *felt* it.

Wings!

"Looks like both of us have lost our shirts now," Svein said, but he didn't appear angry to see the back of his T-shirt, on me, torn completely through. Instead, he grinned.

I laughed out a sob, and drew in a breath. I closed my wings. I opened them. And I couldn't stop laughing.

:>=<

I stumbled into the kitchen, my hands full of takeout cartons. Maybe I went a little overboard on the food, but in my tardiness and my guilt, I figured the more food I bought, the more Avery and I could linger over eating and increase our time together.

"Sorry I'm late," I said, dumping everything on the counter. I considered making up an excuse, but the thing about Avery was that he wouldn't ask for one.

Which, I realized, was going to make it a lot easier to lie to him.

I felt sick inside.

"How was your day?" I asked, opening the overhead cabinet to find our "good" dishes. The good dishes were the ones with a black-and-purple flowered border. The "regular" dishes were plain white. Both sets cost about the same.

"My day," Avery said. He took silverware out of its drawer and the dishes out of my hands, kissed my lips, and began to set the table. "Today was a door-to-door day. I drank a cup of tea at each of the first twenty homes, and had to use the bathroom at the next twenty. I had an informal chat with the League of Women Voters that went pretty well, and I worked on a Rotary Club luncheon speech for next week. Then, while I was waiting for you, I updated my blog to answer voters' questions. I'm not completely sure why it's important to some voters if I have a pet and what my astrological sign is, but I did answer everything."

He folded two napkins and slid them under our silverware. I liked how he did that, as if the moment I put this food down on the table, we weren't going to crunch our napkins in one hand

and shovel rice into our mouths with forks in our other hand.

Avery had changed into jeans and an ancient American University sweatshirt, and his feet were bare. I always thought he had nice toes. Who was I kidding? He had nice everything. My heart melted a little.

"And you?" he asked, pouring Diet Coke into two tall glasses. "Busy day?"

I didn't want to lie. I didn't want to lie.

"Well, yes, now that you ask. My new mentor Svein, a mostly unpleasant fae who I may or may not be physically attracted to, needed to teach me how to control my wing burst and retraction by controlling my anger and fear. Then I had to borrow a hoodie from a nice guy in The Root Center of Collection Headquarters and run to the Gap to buy a shirt to wear home since I destroyed mine during my transformation. Then I had to stash a five-inch-thick training manual under the stairs in the hallway of our building, and shove my new bells-and-whistles super-smart holographic Fae Phone into a zippered pocket of my cargo pants so you won't find them."

That wasn't what I said. What I said was this: "I stayed late at the gym."

It was only the first lie, but knowing how many more were lined up behind it, I felt sick again.

Maybe—maybe I *could* just tell him? I glanced over my shoulder at him. Still standing, he took a few gulps of his soda, then winked at me. He did love me. I was sure of that.

But this whole thing, my new life mission, was too freaky for anyone. His campaign was the most important thing in the world to him—and it was important to me too, really, to not deprive Congress and the American people of his intelligence, ideas and vision. He was poised on the brink of becoming someone in a position to make a real and lasting mark on history, and he'd worked a long time to get there. His father had been in the same position but, through no fault of his own, had become entangled in a scandal that the public might have been able to forgive but just couldn't quite forget.

Avery saw with his own eyes how one wrong move could kill the most promising campaign. So I was pretty damn sure he wouldn't want to be publicly involved with a woman claiming to be a tooth faerie. *Fae.* His ambition wouldn't survive that.

Would our relationship survive? My father left his fae wife and his half-fae daughter. Sure, he stuck it out for a few years, but he clearly hadn't been up to the task of spending his life with us. He'd bolted.

What made Avery any different?

After all, he was human.

I was an adult engaged in a mature relationship. I knew relationships sometimes had to end, and I'd been on both sides of that scenario. It hurt, but that was life, and love.

But if Avery ever left me, I could *not* let it be for the same reason why my father left me.

What had Reese said? Most fae don't do the collection thing for long. I could put in my time, catch a bad guy for them, transform my fae side back into dormancy, and be normal again in no time.

"Dinner's up," I said, and carried two serving dishes to the table. Avery wasted no time digging into the chicken satay, piling it on his plate.

"Hey, you could leave some for the rest of us," I said.

"Or you could quit dawdling and take some."

Or, I thought, *I can get you to give me yours.* Svein told me the glamour was the easiest fae talent—just pick a target, and intend the glamour in their direction. It was possible to exude the glamour in a way that would enrapture an entire room of people, which is clearly what Frederica had done to get my attention at Smiley's, but that required considerable practice. Doing it on one person, Svein had said, came naturally.

I worked up a little mojo, and the skin on my face tingled. I stared at Avery, willing him to look up, but his plate of food was commanding his full attention—which was my fault, wasn't it, for being late and causing his stomach to cry out in distress.

I cleared my throat with authority—twice—and he finally looked up.

"Can I," I asked quietly, "have one of your chicken skewers?"

He blinked once. "Take them all," he said, and put his three on my plate. "Do you need anything else?"

"No," I said. "Not at the moment."

"Gemma," he said, dropping his fork and dragging his chair until it hit mine, "I want you."

I raised a brow.

He crushed me to him, kissing me, pushing his hands through my hair. He broke off the kiss, and held my face in his hands. "Right now," he said.

"Don't you want to finish eating?"

He pushed our dishes aside and lifted me onto the table. He pushed his body between my legs and kissed my neck. "No," he said. "Please."

He tugged at the button of my cargo pants, and I lifted my behind to let him slide them down my legs.

I considered the morality of seducing my man with magical powers. But when Avery's fingers slid inside my panties and across my skin, I decided morality was overrated.

>=<

That was on Friday night. Sunday afternoon, Avery and I were still in bed.

Well, "still" was overstating it a bit. We did leave the bed to shower and eat, but every time we left to satisfy a basic need, we returned to satisfy our favorite need.

As for the morality conundrum, I had cast it aside. I only used the glamour on Avery at dinner that first night. Everything that came after was a byproduct of the realization that it had been a very long time since we had spent a few days together in bed.

Okay, okay, I did use the glamour *one* more time, when he looked as if he was getting sleepy, and believe me, I heard no complaints.

Avery had cleared his calendar for the weekend, and he was more relaxed than I'd seen him since he'd announced to me that he was running for Congress, so I didn't feel one bit guilty for prompting his spontaneous time off.

He dozed, surrounded with various Sunday sections of *The Washington Post* and *The New York Times*, so I slid out of bed and headed for the bathroom, intending a nice, long shower.

I scrutinized my face in the mirror. It was true. I really didn't look any different. Judging from the number of times Avery had very recently run his hands and tongue over every inch of my back, it was clear that my wings were folded up in there nice and tight and completely invisible to anyone.

Right now, what I looked like with wings was my secret. Mine and Svein's.

I scowled. Stupid Svein had popped up unbidden in my mind a few times this weekend—maybe just once or twice at totally inappropriate times—but also because he'd instructed me to call yesterday morning and I kind of hadn't. Because I was kind of busy.

But we could start training tomorrow, as far as I was concerned. We all needed a weekend off. Sure, I was off all the time because I was jobless, but Svein didn't know that. I was pretty sure he didn't know that. Anyway, I was doing all right on my own with controlling these wings. Hard to feel afraid or angry when you were doing the wild thing for forty-eight hours. Waiting until Monday morning to call seemed reasonable.

Svein had also told me to read the manual immediately. Since I wasn't inclined to drag that massive binder into bed with Avery and start highlighting, that too would have to wait until tomorrow.

I stared at myself in the mirror. If I aimed my glamour at my reflection, would I fall in love with myself? Certainly worth a try.

I intended—and though I wasn't overwhelmed by a sudden urge to kiss the glass, I did notice the glow coming through my skin. It was subtle. I was sparkling from within. Thin but distinct rings of silver circled my brown irises, brightening my eyes. Very cool.

Busy examining my face, I was startled to hear chimes coming from the kitchen. I followed the sound, padding down the hallway. The chimes rang scales, up and down, and I discovered it was coming from my cargo pants, abandoned on the tile floor the other evening. But my cell was turned off, and I realized it was my new cell phone, which I'd dubbed my Fae Phone.

I flipped it open and hit *OK* to read the new message.

It was an address. Just a street address. No explanation.

Was this some kind of code? Was I being summoned for training?

Or …

I remembered Svein talking to the agent at The Root, and asking him to send him an address to his Fae Phone for tooth collection that evening. So clearly, this was an address for collection.

For me.

With no training.

I scrolled through the phone's preprogrammed numbers and found one for The Root switchboard. When it began to ring on the other end, I quietly slipped out onto the porch and pulled the door mostly closed. The late-morning air was warmer than I'd expected; April in Virginia was unpredictable.

"Root, Jason speaking."

"Jason," I said. "Um, hi. This is Gemma Cross. I haven't met you yet, but …"

"Right, Gemma. I've heard all about you."

Of course.

"I just sent you an assignment for tonight," he said. "Do you need any clarification?"

"Well, it's just that I haven't gotten around to talking to Svein, and…"

"I just talked to Svein this morning," Jason told me. "He said you were all set, and we could put you on shift tonight."

I closed my eyes and jammed my back teeth together. I would not get angry. Angry meant big wings. I would accept. I would accept and not fight.

I accepted—barely—that Svein, in retaliation for not hearing from me, had put me on assignment with no training, setting me up to look like an idiot in front of Root agents.

"Gemma?" Jason asked. "Is there something you need?"

Svein wanted to play games, fine. I would tell Avery I was going to the gym, and instead I'd find a coffee shop, settle in with the training binder—there was bound to be some sort of Quick Start guide in there—and cram. Then tonight, sometime after midnight, I'd head on out, cross the river, and grab a tooth.

What I would *not* do was call Svein and ask for help. He didn't deserve the satisfaction. Let him see how well I could handle this on my own.

I accepted my destiny. For tonight.

And I accepted that tomorrow, Svein and I would have words. Mostly my words.

"No," I told Jason. "I'm good."

I disconnected and pressed a few buttons again, returning to the screen with the address. I squinted at it. Virginia Avenue. Wait, I knew where that was…

Oh, for crying out loud.

I closed my eyes and bumped my forehead against the wall once, twice. I cursed Svein for his twisted sense of humor in doing this to me, and I cursed myself for insisting on following through.

Breathe. Accept the reality.

Here was the reality: In order to retrieve a newly exfoliated tooth, I was going to have to do a little breaking and entering.

Into Watergate.

CHAPTER 9

Foggy Bottom was an interesting and silly name for the D.C. neighborhood, but I wished it was more literal. A thick, watery, dense fog dropping over the city would have been the perfect night cover for me.

Instead, I found myself in the courtyard on a clear, starlit night, straddling my bicycle, staring up at one of the buildings in the Watergate complex. I was positive that the secretary of state was watching me from a bedroom window while sipping a nightcap.

I had read as much of the manual as I could today in my very limited time alone. I'd convinced Avery that he might want to catch up on work, what with spending the last two days and nights in bed, and he had retreated into his home office for a short while. I'd slipped into the bathroom, locked the door and read what I could for about an hour. I was never a fast reader, so what I read probably amounted to only about twenty percent of the information, and what I committed to memory was far less than that. I had tried to absorb a small portion of each chapter to get a workable mental outline of the job ahead of me, but when I set out on my bike to cross the Potomac, I knew I was flying blind.

No faerie pun intended. *Fae* pun.

There was one sentence I did remember, because it was hard to forget. *For your first collection, you'll probably be a bit nervous.* No, really? A bit nervous? Standing in shadows outside Watergate East with a jacket pocket full of makeshift lockpicking implements, I was way beyond nervous and almost into terrified.

Almost. Because uncontrolled fear would pull out my wings in two seconds flat. And if a stranger lurking around private property didn't arouse any suspicion, a stranger lurking around shirtless with a giant pair of glittery wings would no doubt give a casual passerby a coronary.

As for lurking, I decided now it wasn't the best approach. Yes, it was 1:30 in the morning and yes, I didn't live here, but any random resident out with his dog didn't know that. As far as they knew, I had every right to be here. I could just walk into the building as if I were visiting someone. Which I was. Just without their knowledge.

Getting into the apartment itself would be another story, but that was why I programmed Reese's number into my Fae Phone. I knew I'd need an SOS, and it was *not* going to be Svein. He wanted to play games? Well, I was going to win this one.

My gaze wandered up the side of the building. Balconies jutted out with the trademark railings that looked like, I realized with a sigh, teeth.

Come on, you wuss, I chastised myself. *Just get in there, do your thing, and get out again.* Fae had been doing this forever without a problem. As far as I knew, anyway.

Luckily for me, Avery was a sound sleeper, but I didn't want to be gone long. I didn't want to be here long. I didn't want to be here at all.

I'd managed to sneak a phone call in to my mother today, whispering to her in the bathroom that I'd accepted my destiny. She was upset—upset that I hadn't finished our talk before I made my decision, but I told her I knew was I was getting into and

I'd be fine. I left out the part about an imminent threat to the fae, and let her believe collecting was my only priority for the moment. The easy part.

Right.

Breathe, I said to myself sternly. *Breathe and accept. Breathe and accept. Please, wings, stay folded up nicely.*

My lower lip trembled, and my shoulder blades quivered, and I had to do something.

The Olde Way. That's why you're doing this.

I squeezed my eyes shut and tried to conjure up the vision that Frederica had given me. I couldn't see it, but after a moment, I felt a warmth beginning in my solar plexus and extending to my heart, a glow that radiated through my limbs to my fingers and toes. It was inside me now, I realized. When I transformed, the Olde Way became a physical part of me—and I became part of the Olde Way, a piece of the puzzle that needed to fit to recreate the Olde Way on Earth. To come alive, it needed me. To stay alive, I needed it.

I walked to the main door of Watergate East, and leaned my bike against the building. Assured and calm, I went inside.

My sneakers squeaked as I walked, and when I looked down, I noticed the watery, icicle-like black and gray design on the marble floor. It was pretty, and a little bit magical, and I took it as a sign that I was going to be okay.

But I heard a throat clear, and I slowly turned my head to find a large, wooden, marble-topped desk. A reception desk.

A manned reception desk.

Security man. He was sitting down, so it was hard to gauge his height, but his circumference was substantial. His glasses were oversized and a bit crooked. He was around my age. In front of him was a refillable cup that I'd have to use two hands to lift. I had no idea what it was filled with but I couldn't imagine liking any beverage so much that I would drink that much of it in one day. If it was anything containing caffeine, he might give me a run for my money.

"Hi," I said, and attempted a casual stroll past him, as if he had no reason at all to question my presence. Clearly, he didn't agree.

"Who are you here to see?" he asked.

"Ninth floor," I said, though after only six words out of him, I knew that wouldn't be enough.

"Which resident?" he asked.

I did *not* read a section in the manual about how to get past a security guard. What would it have said?

Then, I realized, it wouldn't have said anything at all. The manual was written for fae who were fully cognizant of their abilities. It would be assumed that they would know how to use them in a situation like this.

And so did I.

I half-smiled. Slowly. As if caught between amusement and attraction.

He blinked.

"Listen," I said, ambling over to his desk and leaning over him. I tucked my hair behind my ear. "I'm surprising my friend upstairs. I don't want him to know I'm here." My voice, my words, were honey. "You don't mind if I just slip into the elevator, do you?"

He licked his lips. His eyes were magnified about eighty times with the glasses, and they were glazed over. "Uh-huh," he said.

"Thanks," I said, walking past his desk.

"Uh-huh."

"See you later!"

"Uh-huh."

I had to go down a glass hallway to get to an elevator and, feeling as though I was being watched from all sides, I pressed the button again and again until the elevator doors opened and I was snug inside. I studied my reflection while I ascended. My hair was in fifty directions from riding my bike from Court House to here. Faced with myself in ratty brown hoodie, tattered sweatpants and worn-down Velcro-ed sneakers, I could only marvel once again at what a little fae glamour could do.

I emerged at the upper floor, checked the number on the nearest apartment, turned right, and headed down the curved, carpeted hallway until I found the apartment I wanted on my left.

I stood there, unmoving, in front of the door. A sweet scent like glazed doughnuts oozed into the hall. There was no light coming from under the door, but I had no way of being sure that one half of the parental unit in this apartment wasn't in a back room, watching TV or reading a book. I stuffed my hands inside my hoodie pockets, fingering the "tools" I'd gathered together before stealing away—a screwdriver, a credit card, and a bunch of paper clips and safety pins. I hadn't had time to browse the Internet for novice lockpicking advice, but I'd seen enough heist movies in my life to figure I could just jam different things in there and something should work.

But the moment I grasped the doorknob, it would be breaking and entering. I might have been half-fae, but the half-human me was still obliged to obey the law.

Laughter floated from around the corner, and I dashed ahead to the stairwell and pushed in. I sat on a top step, pulled out my phone, and speed-dialed Reese.

She answered immediately. "Yes?"

"It's Gemma," I said, lowering my voice because it echoed all around me. "I'm about to break into a Watergate apartment and thought maybe you could help me out with that."

"What time is it?" she asked, and I could hear her blankets rustle. The late hour had tempered her perkiness, and I realized I was disappointed. That perkiness would have given me a little more confidence, but she was more on the perplexed side. "Why are you on the collection schedule tonight? Are you done with training?"

"It seems," I said, grimacing, "that I made a real impression on my so-called mentor."

She sighed. "Okay. Did you read the manual?"

"Yes," I said, then, "no. Well, some."

If she was passing judgment on me, she wasn't doing it out loud, and I appreciated it. "Are you in the building?" she asked.

"Yes, I'm in. I made it to the apartment, and I was getting ready to pick the lock when I heard someone and I ducked into the stairwell."

"Pick the lock?" she shrieked. "You picked the lock?"

"Not yet."

"Gemma. Do. Not. Pick. Any. Locks."

"How the hell else am I supposed to get in?"

"You have fae abilities now."

"And?"

"Why hasn't Svein told you anything?"

"I kind of haven't gotten around to starting our training. I know about the wings. And the glamour—which worked, by the way."

"It always does." I heard a smile in her voice, and it reassured me. Somewhat. "Listen to me," she said. "You can walk right in. Right through the wall."

"*What*?"

"Just think about it, and do it."

"How do I know no one's awake in there? It smelled like doughnuts. Maybe someone's in the kitchen baking."

"That's not doughnuts. You smell the tooth. It's the essence inside. The innocence smells sweet to us. The scent will be stronger when you get inside, so just follow your nose so you won't have to search the whole place for the tooth."

"But…"

"Gemma," she said. "You don't have time for me to explain the physiology of it all. I'm just telling you the information you need to do the collection. Stand outside the apartment door. Close your eyes. You should be able to detect humans inside as dark shadows. If they're moving, they're awake. If not, go in. Intend to go in and keep up the intention the entire time you're inside."

She cleared her throat. "You're kind of rearranging your

molecules to get in, and if you keep it up, your appearance will retain a blinking effect. So if a human sees you, it will startle them, but then they'll believe it was only a trick of the light. Which of course doesn't mean you shouldn't get out of there fast if someone does see you."

My breathing grew shallow, and Reese heard it.

"Go," she said. "Do it now. Don't be scared. You're one of us, and you're one of them. That makes you the safest of all."

I didn't know whether I believed her, but I decided I had to.

"Do it for me," she said, that cheerfulness returning to her voice. "You're my hero."

"No," I told her, "you're mine, believe me."

"Go."

"One more thing," I said. "Don't tell Svein I called you tonight. Please."

She laughed. "Understood," she said. "But Svein's never thrown anyone in the field like this. Even trainees who've really pissed him off. He knows you can do it."

I doubted *that* very much, but this was hardly the time to assess Svein's motives.

I disconnected and stood, but when I tried to leave the stairwell, I found the door had locked. Either I'd have to run all the way downstairs and come back up via elevator, or…

I intended. *I will walk through this door. No, I will just walk. There's no obstacle here.*

I stepped into the door and out the other side.

It didn't even hurt. One would think my cells splitting and reassembling in a fraction of a second would render me unconscious, but no.

I squinted into the hallway ahead, searching for anyone who might report me as a loiterer but, finding no one, I returned to the apartment. I stared at the door and inhaled a noseful of the sticky-sweet scent. I closed my eyes.

At first, I saw nothing but the usual streaky light patterns that

I assume all normal people see on the backs of their eyelids. But then, smoky shadows began to take shape, outlined in black. Two together, pulsating but not moving in any direction. A couple in bed? And one smaller shadow, unmoving, alone. That was the child, I decided, with one tooth less than this morning.

As sure as I was ever going to be—meaning totally and completely *un*sure—I opened my eyes, intended, and stepped through the door into a living room straight out of *Home and Garden*. Or what I thought the pages of *Home and Garden* looked like—the closest I had ever come to the magazine was staring at the cover in a doctor's waiting room.

I held my breath and waited one minute, two. No one screamed or burst out wielding a golf club. I relaxed my shoulders an inch. Keep up the intention, Reese had instructed me. *I am invisible*, I thought. *I am invisible*. I raised my hand and it looked, well, there. I wiggled my fingers in front of my face, and that was when I noticed they appeared kind of dreamy and formless.

A deep cough emanated from another room and I almost jumped out of my now-transparent skin. I froze my fingers along with the rest of me, but I heard nothing further.

In, I told myself. *I'm in. Now, find the tooth.*

I did remember this part from the manual: *You can usually locate the tooth in one of three locations: Underneath the child's pillow if the parents haven't exchanged it out yet, in a nearby trash can, or in some sort of keepsake box belonging to a sentimental parent. Leave an appropriately sized decoy enamel replacement from the kit provided by your local Root.*

Unwilling to stick my hand under a pillow, and hoping to hell that I didn't have to rummage through a woman's belongings, the trash can was my obvious first choice, so I tiptoed into the kitchen and poked around. The room was high-shine chrome, and there was no trash can to be seen. I opened a few bottom cabinets, willing none of them to squeak, and found the can under the sink. I rolled it out, wrinkled my nose, and hovered close to the open can for a perfunctory search.

Someone had macaroni and cheese for dinner, and didn't finish it. I supposed it was the kid, because I remember from my own childhood days that tooth loss meant an empty, sore gap in my gums, requiring a mushy dinner.

But the doughnut smell was less prevalent here, and I eliminated the kitchen trash as the location. I shoved it back into the cabinet and slid it closed, slowly and silently. Then, heart pounding and shoulder blades twitching, I crept down the hall.

Breathe and accept. Keep intending. Keep sniffing. Keep moving.

The bathroom was next. I crept into a dark corner and lifted the wastebasket, which was completely empty. I replaced it and caught a glimpse of the mirror over the sink—not a glimpse of my reflection, because there was none. I removed my hoodie—interestingly, my clothes blinked with me—and tied it around my waist. The T-shirt underneath allowed me better movement.

Unsettled by my lack of physicality but definitely more confident I wouldn't be seen, I continued down the hall. Through a half-open door, I peered into the next room, the master bedroom. I wasn't going in there, I decided. That would be my absolute last resort. A woman's thin, bare arm hung over the side of the bed. I backed away and kept moving.

On the next door across the hall, a crayoned sign ordered me to "Keep Out!" Unfortunately for both myself and the small occupant, I was going to have to ignore that directive. I took a breath, intended, and passed through the door.

Posters plastered on the walls depicted baseball heroes and cartoon characters. The low placement of the posters and their crooked edges suggested the decorator was the sleeping boy in the bed. He was sprawled on his side in the sort of unusual contortion that kids eventually grew out of. He wore only one sock, and one side of his dark hair was sticking up and out.

I stood there for a few precious minutes, and it wasn't because of any sudden maternal instincts, believe me. I just didn't want to approach this kid's bed and betray the trust he undoubtedly nurtured that his parents were the only adults with access to his room. I didn't want to wake him, but I didn't want to do this without his knowledge either.

I had a flash of the warrior I'd seen, the warrior I'd been for a frightening few moments—in the internment camp. He'd done this duty. He'd died for this duty.

To do less would dishonor what I was.

The sugary, cavity-inducing scent was fierce in here, beckoning me closer to his sleepy head, closer to his pillow.

I moved closer, closer, and tripped over a toy truck in the center of the room. Catching myself before I collapsed on top of bed and kid, I froze again as the truck rolled into a corner. I waited for the rustle of someone waking up and deciding to investigate, but somehow I remained the lone conscious person in the apartment. When I was arm-distance from the bed, I reached across the space and slid my hand under the pillow.

And closed my fingers around the tooth.

Instantly wrapped in a thin, lacy blanket of peace, I fell into the rainbow void. Emotion surged through me and I swayed on my feet as a single voice, made up of millions, sang a tuneless melody meant just for me, made up of my own shimmering soul. I smiled through the light that surrounded me, the white purity that I never wanted to leave. We all come from here. It's not gone…

I slowly came back and realized I was on my knees on the ropey rug. Standing, I looked again at the boy in the bed, and gratitude overwhelmed me, almost sending me to my knees again. "Thank you," I whispered. This child, all these children, had no idea of the gift they gave us, but one day we'd repay them with our gift, the one we spent so long re-creating.

I didn't have a decoy to leave, since I hadn't gotten my fake-tooth kit yet, but I was less than concerned. His parents would assume the tooth dropped onto the floor and rolled somewhere, and wouldn't worry about it when they went to exchange it for money. In fact, since the tooth was still here and the parents were already asleep, this one might have been yanked out by its owner and pushed under the pillow without parental notification. In which case, a little someone was going to be disappointed in the morning. I considered leaving him a few bills but being childfree myself, I had no idea of the going rate.

I stuffed the tooth in my pants pocket, then moved back into the hall. *I did it,* I thought. *I'm almost out. I can't believe I pulled this off.* My pride swelled from the inside out.

When I reached the kitchen, moving from thick shag carpet to tile floor, I heard distinct footsteps on the tile behind me.

My heart jumped into my throat. Oh, shit.

Wait! My mind screamed. *Breathe!* But as I whirled around, my body's instincts won the battle for supremacy and I had a flash of unbearable pain before my wings crashed out, noiseless but heavy.

I closed my eyes a moment, trying to keep my balance and, at the same time, hold on to the certain last moment of my normal life before I was discovered as a freak show.

When I opened my eyes, there was no one. But when I looked down, there was a little girl—and I mean little, three years old, tops—clutching a battered stuffed Piglet in both hands.

I kept my intention going. It hummed through all the cells in my body and I knew it was working and that I should be formless and blinking. But as this tiny girl stood there calmly returning my gaze with serious brown eyes, I realized she could *see* me.

She was still innocent enough to see me.

I struggled to recall whether the manual mentioned what to do in this kind of Grinch-meets-Cindy-Lou-Who situation, but obviously I'd skipped that chapter. Her blond hair hung around her adorable face in rumpled ringlets. Her yellow ruffled nightgown fell to the floor, hiding her toes.

Somehow, she seemed to understand this was a moment meant only for the two of us. To her, it made complete sense that I should be standing in her kitchen in the middle of the night. She was unsurprised, and pleased. She smiled at me. Uncertain, I smiled back.

"You should be in bed," I whispered.

"I heard you in Mike's room." Her whisper was more exaggerated. She understood this was a game and she was eager to play. "You're the tooth faerie."

I slipped my hand into my pocket and grasped Mike's tooth. I held it out for Cindy Lou to see. "I need to take this back to"—uh—"back to my castle."

"I know," she said. "Want to play Barbie with me?"

"I'm sorry, honey," I said, "but I have to go home. And it's time for you to go back to bed. This is just a dream."

She giggled. "No, it's not."

So much for trying to outsmart her. "This is our secret, okay?"

"Okay." She smiled again. I knew full well she'd tell her parents she saw the tooth faerie, but I also knew full well they'd tell her to stop making up silly stories. She was a tiny little thing with an incomplete memory system. She would forget all about me.

As I repocketed the tooth, Cindy Lou stretched out her arms. I knelt down and let her hug me. Calm washed over me, and my wings retracted. The skin on my back sealed over. I wrapped my arms around her, emotion swirling in my throat and chest.

"I'm Juliette," she said sleepily into my ear.

"Juliette," I said, "when you get bigger, and your first tooth falls out, I'll come back to visit you."

"Okay," she said. We let go of each other, and I turned her around and patted her on the behind. She trotted back down the hall, turning once to wave at me.

I waited until she disappeared into her little room at the very end of the hallway, then untied my hoodie and tugged it on to cover my now-backless T-shirt. I backed out of the apartment, ran down the hall, slammed down nine flights of stairs and scooted out of the lobby without a glance at the security guard.

My bike was where I'd left it, leaning outside the lobby door. I yanked it upright and straddled it, walking it awkwardly toward the street, then slid my hand in my pocket and drew out the tooth. I held it in the middle of my palm, breathing the sweet essence in for just one moment more before my job was complete.

The sound of a throat clearing spooked me, and I dropped the tooth. It landed next to my sneaker, and I snatched it up. When it was safely in my pocket, I looked up.

I found myself in front of one of the property's round fountains, but in the dark, I hadn't seen the man until now.

He held a cigarette and didn't appear to be waiting for anyone or anything. He was just passing time, blowing smoke—smoke that my nose hadn't detected around the tooth's overwhelming sweetness. He looked me up and down—not lecherous, merely observing. He wore black-rimmed glasses balanced on a small nose, and a faded Pac-Man T-shirt which had seen better decades. One of his sneakers was untied. He was young, late twenties, tops. Headphones snaked up to his ears from an mp3 player attached to his belt loop. He was just anyone.

But something about him turned my senses on high alert—something about the way his gaze seemed to record my features for later use. His half-smile was untrustworthy.

I acknowledged him with a nod, because not to would imply some kind of guilt.

"Late night at the Watergate," he said. "We can't be up to any good, eh?"

I stopped my bike and looked him square in the eye. "Guess you can only speak for yourself."

He took a long, leisurely drag, and turned his head to blow out. "I won't tell if you won't."

"Deal," I replied, then pushed off. If he said anything further, the sudden rush of wind in my ears drowned it out.

CHAPTER 10

Avery was buried under the covers in deep slumber when I'd left. Good thing I hadn't tried to intend my fae butt through this door, because now Avery was awake. Awake and sitting at the kitchen table, phone pressed to his ear, his forehead cradled in his hand.

The note I'd left for him was there on the table—"Couldn't sleep, went for a bike ride"—so I figured the distress on his face hadn't been caused by my unexpected disappearance. I listened to just enough of his conversation to gather he was speaking with one of his campaign aides, so I slipped back into the bedroom to allow him privacy. My sweats were comfortable enough to sleep in, but I didn't want to wear them anymore, so I tossed them into the corner and pulled on a white tank top and striped cotton lounge pants. The blankets were rumpled where Avery had no doubt jumped up and sprinted for his phone, and when I slipped into the space he'd vacated, I found the sheets had completely cooled. He'd been on the phone for some time.

I didn't want to even think about my activities of the past hour, insanely paranoid that somehow my secret excursion would show on my face, but I couldn't help it. I was psyched that it was now mission accomplished. After I'd left Watergate, I'd followed the directions on my Fae Phone to a drop box hidden in the side wall of a small hair salon on 24th Street. I'd unfolded the perforated envelope I'd torn out of the manual, sealed the tooth inside, and dropped it in like it was going back to Netflix. In fact, it would be picked up and sent to Headquarters for identification and testing. I'd seen the fae in the Root packing up the little teeth, and they'd ship this one and others to one of several shrines around the world, where it would be stored under controlled conditions.

Every tooth counted toward the dream, and I had done my part tonight.

It hadn't been easy, by any means. But it hadn't been impossible. And next time I would do it better. I vowed to read the manual tomorrow. Cover to cover.

If I'd survived tonight with zero training, I could only imagine it would get easier from here. I would study like crazy. I would be a tooth fae ninja. Get in, get the tooth, get out. And as long as Avery didn't doubt my perpetual insomnia, I could do this.

Avery came into the bedroom and tossed the phone on the dresser. A few papers slid in its wake and landed on the floor. I tended to deposit anything without a home onto the dresser, and it was covered with junk mail, matchless socks and ponytail holders. He covered his face with both hands and rubbed.

"What's wrong?" I asked.

"I had to fire Tim."

"Tim…"

"One of my researchers."

"Oh, right. Why?"

He shook his head, his mouth hanging open. "He was at a Waterfront bar some night last week, telling everyone who would listen that I was a terrible candidate. He went on about my lack of experience, and said he couldn't stand to work for me but he was waiting it out until another opportunity came along."

I was surprised, to say the least. "Probably just some drunken ramblings of an idiot who'd had a bad day."

"Well, he rambled to the wrong person, and the D.C. Digger broke it on his blog a couple of hours ago."

I knew the D.C. Digger. Well, not personally. His identity had been guessed at, maybe correctly, but never confirmed. The notorious political blogger had a knack for finding out little ugly things and getting them out there in the public. He had yet to break anything major, but no doubt he someday would. And tonight, it seemed he had his sights trained on Avery.

Avery sat on the edge of the bed, his back to me, staring out the window. Although all he probably could see was the reflection of me in the bed, staring at his back.

"So you fired Tim. You did the right thing," I told him.

"Of *course* I did the right thing, Gemma," he said sharply. "I know that, and you know that, but the press doesn't know that. When they pick up this story, all they'll care about is one of my aides was disloyal. I bet they won't even print his name. It will just be 'Avery McCormack's aide.'"

"Former aide," I said, "as of now. When did you find out about this?"

"Half-hour ago."

"You fired him as soon as you found out. That's your answer if the press gives you a hard time, and I don't think they will. You had no idea that he felt the way he did."

"But it was my judgment to bring him on to my team."

"And it was your judgment to can him."

"You don't get it," he said, but his voice had lost the edge. "My judgment is my best thing going, and now one of the people I brought close to me just stabbed me in the back."

I swallowed hard. "You haven't come so far in politics and law by being naïve. Don't start doubting your own judgment because of the people around you."

He raked his fingers through his hair. "But it's the people around me that I *need* to trust."

I fell against the headboard and turned my gaze to the ceiling. I couldn't look at his vulnerable back. Guilt wrapped itself around my midsection and squeezed tight.

"Come over here," I said.

He crawled up to the pillows and I switched off the bedside lamp. He turned on his side and I wrapped my arms around him, tucking my knees into the crooks of his. I pressed against his back, trying to warm it, protect it.

We stayed that way, quiet but awake, for a while. Eventually I said, "We met two years ago, almost exactly."

He shifted. "You're right."

"You were taking pictures of the cherry blossoms," I recalled.

"And you rode by on your bike, right through my picture."

"I apologized."

"You did. But then you asked me if I was a tourist, and I said no, that I was just a local hobbyist photographer. And you said…"

"I said, 'Cherry blossoms. Why are you taking pictures of something so touristy and completely unoriginal? They're beautiful but you see them every year. How can any one be special and unique?'"

"And I said, 'Well, I see a lot of beautiful blondes too. How can any one be special and unique?'"

"And I said…"

"You said nothing," Avery said. "I shut your belligerence right down. There was no possible reply to my flawless logic."

I looked over his shoulder. My eyes had adjusted enough in the dark to see the vertical line of small framed cherry blossom photos beside the window.

"Why did you talk to me that day?" Avery asked. "Why didn't you ride on by?"

I ran my hand down his arm. "I don't know. I saw the way you looked at those flowers. Maybe I wanted to see how it felt to have someone—you—look at me like that."

"I look at you like that every day. Sometimes when you don't even notice." He lifted my hand and kissed my palm. "When did you go out?"

"Probably right before your phone call."

"You couldn't sleep? Are you all right?"

"I'm fine."

"I love you, Gemma," he whispered. "I'm sorry I snapped at you."

"You didn't."

"The stress, it's really getting to me."

"I know. But it'll be okay, really. You're doing great."

"I'm doing great with you," he said. "This moment—us, right here—no matter what else happens, this is what I can trust."

He inhaled deeply, and when he breathed out, I felt his body relax against my newly stiffened one.

"Try to get some sleep," he whispered.

No chance of that.

>=<

When I walked into The Root Center, each pair of eyes landed on me. I was still a celebrity sighting, and it still made me very, very uncomfortable. "Archives?" I asked the nearest fae young man.

"It's upstairs, then the end of the hall," he said. "Would you like me to bring you there?"

"No," I said, happy for the chance for some solo exploring in a headquarters of my heritage. "Just point the way."

He nodded at a side door and I jogged up the steps.

A little ways down, I came to a windowed door and I peeked in. Children, lots of them. Fae children listening to a teacher, watching maps slide across a holographic screen like the ones in The Root. They scribbled in notebooks and, I was amused to notice, surreptitiously passed notes and chewed gum. Fae or human, kids were kids.

A little boy in the front row glanced up at me and I was reluctant to wave and disrupt the lesson, but there was no need. His eyes widened in recognition, but then he dropped his gaze, only to peek back at me with a sly smile. I returned it. I'd be his secret today.

I backed away from the door and moved on.

Near the end of the hallway, I found a black door which I might have ignored, but I was intrigued by the white flickering light that slid out the gaps under and around the door. I pushed it open and stumbled into blackness.

Blackness for just a moment before bright light burst to life—below me.

I was in a projection room, with a man beside me manipulating a control board. "Hi, Gemma," he said, and again I had that strange sensation of unwanted celebrity, but I was grateful his greeting wasn't accompanied by an amazed stare. He was too busy.

I went to the glassed-in window and looked down at one woman seated cross-legged on the floor in a planetarium-like room. All around her and above her was a rainforest—large, wet, green leaves close enough to brush from her face; gentle raindrops soft enough to cover her shoulders in a mist; airy cries of exotic birds behind the music of a breathy flute. I saw her seeing it—and hearing it and breathing it like it was real. The lush splendor would have been real to me too, I knew, if I were in her place and not where I was, looking down at her like God.

Slowly, so slowly, the image faded and changed. The blue-green wet sky dried out to a sandy red, and the fresh trees dissolved into heated dirt. I resisted the urge to wipe grit from my eyes before I turned and asked the projectionist, "What *is* this?"

"The Morning Shrines," he said, then clarified, "our sacred places."

"Sacred places?"

"Where our artifacts are stored," he said reverently. "Our remains of history. And our storing place."

He didn't have to clarify that. The storing place for all those teeth, all that innocence.

"The old holds onto the new," he added.

"Where?" I asked. "Where are these places?"

"One on each continent."

I raised a brow. "The one on this continent…?"

"Sedona. Would you like to go?"

"Yes. But I can't. Serious business here."

"You don't need to fly there. You can visit it here." He gestured to the room.

I was tempted. "No," I finally said.

"Soon, then?"

I nodded and he opened the door for me. I stepped back into the hallway, back onto solid, real ground.

Following the hallway down two steps and another hundred feet, I came to the Archives office. Despite the happy children and despite the sweet perfection of the Morning Shrines, I narrowed my eyes, remembering why I'd come.

Svein and I were going to have words.

I kicked the door open without knocking, but he wasn't there to appreciate or fear my theatrical entrance. The one desk in the room was piled so high with folders and papers that I did worry for a moment that the occupant might be buried under a recent landslide, but, hearing no moaning of desperation or pain, I left it alone.

I was in no hurry. I would wait.

Like the office in the Butterfly Room, this décor eschewed high-tech for comfort. Bookshelves were crammed with folders filed with colored alphabetical tabs sticking out. Happy that the records here were preserved in old-fashioned hard copy, I stuck my fingers into the tight squeeze under "C" to see if I could find a file on myself. A file that would probably list my name, address, age, and temperament: volatile when heated.

Nothing, so I checked under "G"—and "W" for warrior—to be sure. Maybe I was somewhere in the mess on Svein's desk but I wasn't willing to go spelunking through there.

Across from the bookshelves was a long file cabinet, with binders lined up on top. I recognized the binder for collection training, which I had yet to finish studying. Not that I'd had much time between last night's Watergate adventure and this morning. Next to it was a set of about a dozen binders in volumes with one common label of *Lineages*, and despite my curiosity about my fellow fae and their role in the Olde Way's recreation, I was more intrigued by the set of binders beside it: *History*.

I pulled the first one out and flipped through it. Yup, a history book, made mostly of handwritten and typed notes. Some looked very old; some could have been done yesterday. Mom had told me that the fae before humans hadn't kept records, so this must have been what was been discovered or found since, a compendium created partly by Svein, and partly by many fae before him.

It could take days to read everything carefully and fill in all the historical gaps, but I skimmed what I could, trying to get a basic feel for what came before them. Before *me*.

I already knew the fae had existed in their idyllic world—now called the Olde Way—before humans came and took over the Earth when the fae couldn't put up a fight. For years, the fae desperately searched for a way to obtain innocence, which would bring their world back. The only pure human innocence came from young children and some fae somewhere figured out that children's first sets of teeth must hold some key. But he or she didn't know what it was.

So they began to collect the teeth as relics, keeping them in safe underground reliquaries. They were certain the teeth might have the answer but they had yet to unlock it.

Meanwhile, the fae evolved to co-exist with humans—uneasily—out in the open.

I flipped some more pages.

In the eighteenth century, the Industrial Revolution took hold. No longer living off the land, hunting and gathering, humans very quickly mechanized the world, their population boomed, and they unwittingly set the Earth on a path to destruction. Not only was the Olde Way gone, but now the physical planet was in peril, the fae realized.

So much for the modern movement toward green and recycling, I thought. Fae understood it right from the start. I skipped ahead in the binder.

Around the same time, dentistry began to emerge as a serious discipline, and several curious fae entered the field. They discovered the innocence essence in milk teeth and devised a way to extract it, and suddenly the fae had a plan.

A really, really, really slow plan, but a plan nonetheless. When that plan was threatened, a warrior was called to duty.

There was a tabbed section a couple of inches thick that appeared to contain case studies on warriors past. I was tempted to read them, but I had seen enough, experienced enough, at the moon gathering. I'd felt victory and tasted death. I didn't need to know more than that, nor did I want to.

"There'll be a test on that later."

I gasped and looked over my shoulder at Svein. I jumped up and brushed floor dust off my jeans, then slammed the binder shut and shoved it crookedly back into its spot on the file cabinet. "Doing a little light reading," I said.

"Ah."

"Is this what those kids down the hall are learning?"

He nodded. "They attend regular schools but a few days a week they also come here. They're not going to experience their fae history in a public—human—school."

I glanced at Svein and realized he was feeling sorry too—sorry for me and what I missed, although as a child, I hadn't known it to miss. Back then, I was already missing enough.

We stood there, looking at one another. Electricity cut the air between us, but I wouldn't be the one to acknowledge it. Finally he said, "Here for a lesson?"

Remembering that I was there to rip him a new one, and mindfully trying to keep my wings under control despite my frustration and anger, I said, "Well, I had a memorable first lesson."

He smirked.

"Watergate?" I asked. "Really?"

"The daughter of the House Speaker also lost a tooth that night. I'd say I let you off easy."

I opened my mouth to tell him what he could do with himself in seventeen different ways when he pre-empted me. "I've got to hand it to you, Gemma. You came through. For all your bluster, I honestly didn't think you had it in you. You're not what I thought you were."

Thrown, I hesitated before I said, "You didn't know me."

"You're not," he amended, "what I thought you'd be."

"You tried to sabotage me."

"Because you didn't hold up your end of the bargain. You were supposed to call me and schedule your lessons."

"I was busy all weekend," I said, and I added for good measure, "having sex. A lot of it."

"So was I," he said, "but I still have a job to do. And like it or not, as your mentor, you're my job at the moment."

I refused to look at his face, and found myself looking at his chest instead, so I tried some middle ground around his shoulders. He smelled good. He was pissing me off. I wondered for a moment who he'd been having sex with, then I wondered why I was wondering.

Then for an instant—short, really short, but definite—I forgot who *I'd* been having sex with.

Damn this guy.

"Well, as a mentor," I said, "you're doing a crappy job. Throwing someone into the deep end who can't swim usually doesn't end well."

"Your hubris last time I saw you encouraged me to give it a shot."

"You got lucky."

"Did I? Or did you step up to the challenge?"

I said nothing. How had this conversation veered so far off my intention?

"I admit," he said then, "that I wasn't willing to give you an inch when I first heard they'd found you and were bringing you in to work. But you've actually managed to earn a modicum of my respect."

I set my jaw. "I didn't do it for your respect. I don't *need* your respect."

"Then why are you here?"

I said nothing for a long moment.

"You're a jerk," I finally said, because I had nothing else.

He chuckled.

"Schedule me in for tomorrow at noon," I said. "How long do these lessons take?"

"We can work for about an hour at a time. More than that will tire you out. We're working on your new physical abilities and your emotional control over them, and it's not easy."

"I'll be fine," I said. "I'll see you then. In the meantime, piss off."

I stalked out of his office, slammed the door behind me, and leaned against the wall to breathe, breathe, and calm down. Then I headed to the stairwell, pushed open the door, and instead of going down, I sat on the top step.

Jerk, I thought. Then I thought some worse words I should have used.

I didn't need Svein's respect. Who did he think he was? Who did he think *I* thought he was?

I pulled out my non-Fae cell phone and hit a speed dial.

"Gemma," Avery said. "What's up? I'm about to go into a meeting."

"Do you respect me?" I asked.

"I love you more than anything," he said.

"But do you respect me?"

"I couldn't love anyone I didn't respect. Gemma, what's wrong?"

"Nothing," I said. I hoped.

"Listen," he said, lowering his voice, and I pictured him slipping behind the others heading into some meeting room. "Is this because you miss your job?"

"No," I said. "Certainly not."

"Because I can imagine what it must feel like for you to take a back seat to all of this."

"No, it's not you," I said weakly.

"I'm going to clear my calendar tonight and take you out for a nice dinner. You pick the place."

"Oh, you don't have to do that."

"I do," he said. "I don't want my girl feeling bad. Or disrespected."

"'My girl,' huh?"

"Yeah," he said, "and I don't care who hears me say it. I'll pick you up at home around six. Gemma?"

"Hm?"

"If you're feeling disrespected, go over to Smiley's. It'll only take thirty seconds in the ring for you to get your respect."

"True."

We hung up and I dangled the phone between my knees.

I didn't know why I'd called him. I sounded needy, silly: two adjectives that were not me. Avery's respect for me was a sure thing. I didn't have to fight for it.

But Gemma Fae Cross was always up for a good fight. And Svein already knew it.

I ran down the stairs.

CHAPTER 11

Glove connected with chin.

I shook my head once to clear it, and a lock of sweaty hair fell into my eye. I stuck out my lower lip and tried to blow the strand away, my gaze locked with Not-Rocky's.

I saw the next one coming, and ducked it, countering with a one-two punch.

Avery didn't like to dance, and my height had intimidated all the boys looking for partners at my high school mixers. The only guys I danced with were the ones in here. Not-Rocky was my most frequent partner, but he didn't always lead. I stepped into his space for an uppercut. He pushed into my space with a left hook.

I was slow today. Maybe not to a casual observer, but I felt it, and Not-Rocky sensed it. He was holding back, and I hated that. My self-frustration sent my right cross a little harder than I would have allowed in a quick afternoon workout, and he met the challenge. He feinted with a jab, I fell for it, and I took a body blow that sent me staggering back. My opponent switched from him to myself as I fought not to fall to my knees.

Not-Rocky dropped his gloves. "Geez, Bricks."

His sincere concern—lisped through his mouth guard—wasn't intended as an insult, but I interpreted it as such. All the guys in here knew that on my best day, I could take on all comers in my weight class. But this wasn't my best day. I was exhausted, and the corners of my eyes ached. My neck felt weak, and my limbs were molasses. I collapsed into a wooden stool in the corner of the ring, trying to breathe into the pain.

Not-Rocky spit out his guard into the opposite corner and came over to me. "Sorry."

"Only thing you should be sorry about," I told him, "is that you couldn't drop me with that lame hit."

He lowered his gaze to the mat and didn't respond. At Smiley's, we all understood the language of hurt pride.

"I could tell you was having a bad day," he finally said. "Weren't all there, right from the start. It's okay. No one's watching."

I looked around me to confirm. Just a couple of guys here on a Thursday afternoon, working the heavy bags. Shirley having a one-on-one with Smiley.

And Svein sitting on a folding chair, looking right back at me.

"Crap," I muttered, and Not-Rocky thought I was still in conversation.

"Next time," he said, "ain't letting you off so easy."

"Next time, I'll be the one apologizing," I told him. "But I'm not going to mean it."

He nodded gamely, tapped me on the shoulder, lifted the ropes, and hopped out of the ring.

I glared at Svein, who didn't move a muscle to acknowledge it. I pushed the ropes down and hopped over them, slid off the mat to the floor, and walked slowly over to him. I would have liked to say the slow walk was deliberate, but it was really all my sore gut would allow.

I sat beside him and slumped, my butt sliding down and my legs straightening out. He said nothing. We shared the silence for a few minutes before I stretched out my right hand to him.

"Make yourself useful," I said.

He began to unlace my glove. We'd met daily for more training sessions every day this week, but we'd kept the lessons under an hour each, and limited our dialogue to the training manual, Root operations, and emotional control of my new abilities. I didn't trust myself with the last one yet, and frankly I didn't think Svein trusted me either, but if we waited until I became still water and Zen, we would be old and gray and I'd be in no shape to war against anyone, except maybe a nursing home attendant. But I was better with control than a week ago, if only in theory. Svein assured me—and himself—that control would come with practice.

"What are you doing here?" I asked him now. "Thought I had a day off."

"Curiosity," he said. "I'm impressed. Although not as impressed as your bravado had led me to believe I'd be."

He'd loosened the laces enough for me to tug my wrapped hand out, and I did, going to work on my left glove myself. "I'm freaking tired," I told him quietly. "I'm not getting any sleep at night."

"Why not?" He lowered his voice as well. "You haven't been out on assignments. I took you out of the rotation until we're done with basic training. Flying's your last lesson. Easy."

Between him *and* Not-Rocky saying they were letting me off easy, I snapped. "First of all," I said, keeping my voice down but not bothering to mask the anger in my face, "I told you during training that flying is *out.* So if that's the only lesson left, then I'm done. And the reason I'm not getting any sleep is because I'm lying to Avery. Guilt isn't much of a sleep medicine."

"What do you suggest?"

"I have a lot at stake here. I need more of a reason for this."

I watched Shirley and Smiley talking in the corner of the room. Smiley demonstrated a punch in slow-motion, pushing his shoulder and hip into it, then stopped to explain something as Shirley nodded. I tugged off my left glove, and let my sweaty hands dangle between my knees.

"I'm sorry," Svein said. "I didn't realize that the Olde Way quest, hundreds of years in the making, a legacy that will restore our world of innocence and ensure everlasting peace for our species and every species with whom we share it, was not enough of a reason for you to be involved in this."

"That *is* why I'm here," I said, still quietly but now through gritted teeth. "However, I could do that at any time of my life. I could have waited a couple of years to pick up my part on the path. I didn't need to choose the most inconvenient time for me, professionally and personally. But you and I both know the reason I'm here *now*—the reason the fae searched me out *now*—is because there's a threat, and they—*you*—need me to fight it."

I tossed my gloves onto the floor, and one bounced off my foot. "If I'm going to jeopardize everything that's important to the human side of me," I said, turning my head to look at him, "then I deserve the respect of not having that time wasted. You need to tell me about the threat, and you need to do it pretty damn soon, while I still believe this is worth it."

"Bricks," I heard above me. Not-Rocky had approached us, and cast a wary eye on Svein while he spoke to me. "You okay?"

"Yeah."

"This guy's not bothering you, is he?"

"This guy," I said, jerking a thumb toward my fellow fae, "bothers me like you wouldn't believe. But it's under control. Thanks."

So funny. I was always treated like an equal at Smiley's, even from my first day. Of course, I was treated like an equal that first day because Smiley threatened to toss anyone out who gave me a hard time, but they treated me like an equal now because I was one of them. Still, deep, deep down, they felt obliged to protect me. Deep down, Brickhouse was still Gemma, the woman in the room. I tried not to smile as Not-Rocky narrowed his eyes at Svein.

“I’d be crazy to mess with her,” Svein said, standing and putting out his hand. “Svein Nilsen. I’m a friend of Gemma’s.”

“Don’t be throwing that term around too loosely,” I muttered as Not-Rocky put out a glove. I didn’t assist in introductions, and maybe it was rude, but I couldn’t help wanting to keep my normal life and my weird life separate.

The door banged open and Trey stomped inside. He didn’t close the door. He just never stopped moving forward, as if he were on the grill of a Mack truck in the fast lane. He didn’t stop until he was in front of Smiley. Then he started screaming.

I didn’t know what he was screaming about, exactly. It was the kind of screaming that didn’t come out in sentences, just venomous words flung out one after another. He was shaking, and his shoulders suddenly tensed. I knew that body language. I knew what was coming.

I launched myself out of my chair and ran. I pushed in front of Smiley just as Trey pulled his arm back, and I took it hard on my cheekbone.

My vision went glassy for a minute. It was a wild, unskilled punch, but he’d hit me with his bare knuckles. It hurt like a son of a bitch. I shook off the daze and saw that Shirley had stepped behind Trey and pinned his elbows behind his back. Shirley *is* a Mack truck, so it was interesting to see the surprise on his face when he realized he actually had to use two hands to restrain this child-turned-thrashing hellion.

Trey’s fiery gaze locked onto mine and he stopped moving, just for a second. In his eyes I saw rage, but as he looked at me, it was as if recognition had dawned and behind that rage emerged a black fear. “You,” he said.

I blinked.

Then he kicked.

I managed to evade with a small slide to the right. My right fist curled, but I was not going to hit a skinny teenager, even a crazed, combative one. But Not-Rocky, who’d also run over, didn’t have that restraint. He reached forward and thrust a glove into Trey's gut. It wasn't the kind of hit that would drop anyone else here, but Trey blew a hard breath out of his mouth and stopped struggling.

"Stop," Smiley said. "Everyone knock it the hell off. You," he said, pointing at Not-Rocky. "We don't hit kids here."

"Sorry, sir." Not-Rocky did look sorry. It wasn't a hard hit, and I didn't really blame him for stopping the fight in the only way most of us here knew how.

"You," Smiley said to me. "Go in my office for ice. Take care of your face."

"Okay," I said, and I moved aside, but I didn't go anywhere.

"You're done," Smiley said to Trey, who was doubled over, not looking at him. "Everyone in here has got a second chance at some point, but they don't get a third, and neither do you. You leave this gym and do not come back. Ever. If you do, I'm tossing you in the ring and letting one of these guys have at you. Just see if I'm joking."

No answer.

"Do you understand me?"

Trey raised his head, and despite his obvious pain, and despite being restrained by a heavyweight champion, and despite being outnumbered, he narrowed his eyes and said, "Go fuck yourself."

Shirley gave him a threatening shake but Smiley said mildly, "Let him go. He's leaving."

Shirley shoved Trey in the direction of the door. He shuffled a few steps, but then he stopped, turned and glared at me. "It's you. I know."

"I don't see you leaving," Smiley said. "And the ring's free."

What happened to this boy? Did he think I was someone else, someone who'd hurt him? I didn't remember ever saying anything more than hello to him. I hadn't done anything to offend him.

Troubled child. Maybe mentally ill. He seemed to be waiting for a response but I just shook my head at him. He backed away, then ran out the door.

"What the freaking hell?" Not-Rocky said. Shirley rubbed my shoulder, then shrugged and went over to the heavy bag as if this had all been nothing more than a blip in his schedule. Smiley did the same, slipping into his office.

I turned and saw Svein. I'd forgotten he was there, because he'd only watched the events unfold. A fae, unable to jump in and fight. I twisted my mouth. "Weird."

"That it was," he replied, and didn't seem to want or need to say anything more about it.

I stuffed my own gloves into my gym bag, and zipped a purple fleece sweatshirt over my tank top. It was warm enough to get away with my black shorts, but I changed into street sneakers while Svein and Not-Rocky chatted. "See you tomorrow," I told my sparring partner.

Svein bent over and lifted my bag onto his shoulder. I let him, and we emerged into the city sun.

He turned left on 9th Street rather than right, away from the Gallery Place-Chinatown Metro station I usually used to go home, and toward Mt. Vernon Square. I decided to let him have his way, for the time being. We walked along in silence for a while.

"His name is Dr. Riley Clayton," Svein finally said. "D.M.D."

D.M.D.? "A *dentist.*" I stopped short. "The threat is a dentist."

"That's right."

"You're kidding, right?"

"No, I'm not."

One dry, silent laugh escaped from my open mouth, and my chest heaved to expel it. I shook my head and looked at the sky. "That's what this is? That's why I've been called to action?"

"A threat is a threat," Svein said.

"No," I said. "It's not. This is bullshit." I pressed my palms to the sides of my head. "I went to a fae meeting the night I discovered my—who—what I am. We all joined hands and I didn't connect to the Olde Way and groove with peace and nature like everyone else. Instead, *I* had some kind of acid trip that blew me back in time, into the bodies of warriors past. A warrior who burned down the house of a dark witch. A warrior in a *prison* camp, who *died*. And the warrior who chose, forever, morning over midnight."

I laughed again, hard and mirthless. "And *this* is what I'm risking everything I care about for? A dentist with a bad attitude?"

"Gemma..."

I stepped closer to him and set my jaw. "This isn't a destiny. This is a joke, and an insult, not only to me but to those who came before me. If this were a movie, this would be the point where I leave the theater." I threw up my hands and turned away from him.

I was supposed to walk away now. Why wasn't I?

Behind me, Svein said, "This is where we live. In the twenty-first century in a safe, democratic civilization. We don't kill people to take their land, and we don't have to take down woolly mammoths to eat. There's no war on our soil, at least for now. You are the warrior of *this* time and place, and to help us, you won't have to run through a forest with a spear. You might not *need* to do anything violent at all, and I'm sorry if that disappoints you. We don't know what we're up against. But it's something, and it's getting worse every day, and we can't get to it without you."

I opened my mouth and before I could speak, he said, "It's the dark fae. It's always the dark fae, always with a different weapon. This guy, he's the weapon this time."

It embarrassed me to have been disappointed that my fight didn't seem to be a major one.

"Besides," Svein added, "I haven't told you everything yet."

I turned back to him. "Fine, let's go. Wherever we're going."

We walked in silence. I was grateful to be left alone to smooth out my thoughts, but after about a block, I said, "Wouldn't all dentists be our natural enemies?"

"No," Svein said, amused. "In fact, they're unwittingly useful to us if they can get kids to brush and floss their teeth."

"So why's this Clayton guy a threat? And how could he even *be* a threat unless he knows the fae exist and what we're up to? I thought humans weren't on to us as anything other than bedtime stories."

"That's the thing," Svein said. "Clayton is fae."

I stopped short. "A fae dentist?" I thought of both instances where I'd touched a tooth—with Frederica and at Watergate—and I'd lapsed into an Olde Way mini-coma. "How can he be around kids' teeth all day and not be passed out on the floor every second?"

"A fae dentist isn't unheard of," Svein said, steering me gently by my shoulder to the curb after a woman, encumbered with supermarket bags, huffed angrily around us. "But most of them treat adults. There are a few fae specializing in pediatric dentistry who do their part by donating teeth from routine extractions. They also help kids keep their teeth healthy for us. They bind some of their abilities in the Butterfly Room so they can work *without* passing out on the floor all day."

"So if Dr. Clayton is one of those fae…"

"He's not. He has nothing to do with our collection process."

"But he's fae. Can't you *make* him give you teeth if he has them?"

"We operate on free will," Svein said. "Even you—as much of a pain in the ass as you are—*chose* this."

"What fae wouldn't?" Again, I tried to remember the light and colors and purity of the visions I had when I held the teeth, and instead felt it humming inside me, moving with my blood, pumping in and out of my heart. I slowed to a stop and breathed with it.

"It's a rush," Svein said, moving to stand in front of me.

"It's more than a rush. It's alive in me."

Even standing inches apart, it seemed we were locked in an embrace stronger and warmer than if we'd used our arms. The city I'd always thought silent fell away, and I realized I didn't know what silence was until I truly heard it—actually heard *nothing*. My gaze locked with Svein's and I saw it in him, and I knew he saw it in me, an eternity of peace and love. He blinked slowly and deliberately, his lashes sweeping the tender skin below his silvery eyes.

He reached out and stroked my hair, his fingers coming to rest on my chin.

A dog's snappy bark snapped me into reality—into human reality. As the little dachshund and his harried-looking female walker dashed past, I blinked myself back into the Mt. Vernon neighborhood, its grittier townhouses and Section Eight housing a world away from where I'd just been in my mind. I stepped back. Afraid that if I looked at his face again I'd be pulled back into the daze, and afraid that I wanted to, I began to walk again, and he fell into quiet step beside me.

We turned onto K Street and the moment was, thankfully, gone.

"The Olde Way," he said, softly, "is the reason we all do it. So—"

I finished his question. "Why wouldn't Dr. Clayton?"

"That, my Gemma," he said, "was the million-dollar question."

"Was?"

"I found out he renounced his identity and upbringing. He's got nothing to do with fae any longer."

I thought for a minute. "Did he bind his abilities to masquerade as a full human?"

"There's no record at any of our headquarters, here or abroad, of a transformation."

"Well, then," I said, a candy bar wrapper crackling under my sneaker, "all you know is that he doesn't want to have anything to do with us. Doesn't mean he's actively working against us."

"Some months ago," Svein said, "it was discovered at The Root that we had an inordinate number of collected teeth that were depleted."

"Depleted?"

"Depleted of essence. They're dead teeth, useless to us. When collections realized they were getting only the shells, I began an investigation."

We turned again, and I headed toward Metro Center, but Svein steered me away from the station and further down the street. I didn't bother to interrupt his story with a protest.

"Using school health reports and other records we happen to have access to, I found the common denominator. Every single D.C.-area child who yielded one or more dead teeth is a patient of Dr. Riley Clayton."

I wrinkled my brow and twisted my mouth. "He's killing their teeth?"

"In a manner of speaking. He's draining them of essence somehow. He's renounced his fae heritage. So something tells me he's got a big grudge against us, so big that he's draining the teeth deliberately to thwart the goal we all work toward."

"But how could he physically do that?" I asked. "I thought fae had no capability for violence, and I would say that killing the essence in baby teeth is an act of violence. It puts him on the offensive, and fae can't do that."

"Unless he's a fallen fae."

"Meaning what?"

"Meaning he aligned with midnight fae to turn him into a demon, a being with some fae abilities—and the capacity to indulge in violence."

"So midnight fae *are* evil."

"The midnight fae depend on our existence, as we do on theirs," Svein said. "Without us, they don't survive. For our light, we need their darkness. Both sides recognize the necessary symbiosis. But our side has warriors, and some dark fae in power see this as an imbalance that they need to set right. So they strike where we are the strongest, and the most vulnerable: the Olde Way collection."

"Any chance Clayton is acting alone?"

"I don't see why he would, though I would prefer that to be the case. We're hoping to not cross the midnight fae," Svein said, his mouth tightening into a thin line. "We can't afford to stir up suspicion in the underworld since we can't fight whomever might take umbrage. I'm not saying this to insult you, but you're not enough to do that for us."

"So instead, you brought me in to deal with Doc Clayton alone. What's the assurance that he won't figure me out and call on the midnight fae to annihilate my ass?"

"There is none. But look at the bright side. Fighting a demon—that changes things, doesn't it? You might be in it as deep as your ancestors were after all."

My mother's deepest fear, the reason she had hidden me from my destiny, was because my destiny might just include a fight I couldn't win.

Now that it was reality, it was *my* deepest fear. It sparked inside my gut and shook me to my core. Breathe and accept just wasn't going to do it.

Svein sensed it and pushed me down a narrow alley. He pinned both my shoulders to the side of a building. "Breathe," he ordered.

"Can't."

"Accept."

"No."

He kissed me.

It was hot and hard and insistent, and I surrendered to it almost immediately, sliding my hands inside his jacket to grab two fistfuls of his T-shirt. My shoulders relaxed, my back muscles released, and then I had to pull away but couldn't, so I pushed him with all my force.

He stumbled back but caught himself quickly. His breathing was shallow, and I realized it was the first time I'd seen him rattled. Which was some kind of victory, I supposed.

I bent over, propping my hands on my knees. "That can't happen," I said to the sidewalk. "That—*can't* happen."

He didn't respond, but his breathing quieted. After a few minutes, he said, "Fight or flight."

"Excuse me?"

"Seems that as a warrior, those are your two options. When

you sense danger, you can literally go into fight or flight mode. Human or fae."

"I don't want to fly."

"You do have wings."

"I'm keeping them decorative," I said, staying bent over but lifting my head.

"You can fly right now, if you feel like you need to."

At first, I thought he meant I could fly away from this coiled and heated-up tension between us, but then I realized he meant the threat. My new enemy. Riley Clayton, fallen fae. Demon.

Svein was giving me permission to back out.

I didn't want to get hurt, or die. If I backed out now, I'd get my life back. I could take a visit to the Butterfly Room and shed my wings for good, go home and live happily ever after with hopefully-soon-to-be U.S. Rep. Avery McCormack.

And Dr. Clayton would continue to poison the D.C. collection, and for all I knew, he had other people helping him, or a grander plan. He endangered the Olde Way's return, and the morning fae, after generations and generations of labor, would be set back again.

"You're human, Gemma," my dad said, as I slammed a tiny fist into a pad, into the center of his palm. "You're human."

He couldn't take it. He couldn't deal with the fae life, and he had left.

That was why I would *not* back out.

"Where are we going, anyway?" I asked Svein, straightening up and stretching my spine. He'd sat on the curb while I was in thinking mode, and he squinted up at me.

"Knew you hadn't lost your fight."

"I panicked," I said, "but that isn't the same as quitting. And next time I panic, try to find some other way of chilling me out. This was—was—inappropriate."

"Yes, sir," he said, standing.

"Stop laughing at me."

"Believe me, I'm not laughing."

It was true, he wasn't, but I needed to beat this into the ground for the last time. Svein couldn't think we could just manhandle one another and it would be okay. It was *un*-okay. Avery and I were okay, and I intended for it to stay okay.

Despite all my recent lying and sneaking around.

We headed around the corner and Svein said, "Stop."

"What?" I asked.

He casually leaned against the lamppost and surveyed the landscape, which consisted of dense late-day traffic. I thought about how the first time I'd seen him, he was leaning against a lamppost.

Wait. *This* lamppost.

I looked across Franklin Square, its new greenery a urban oasis. Yup, that's where I had been standing. Just after my tooth cleaning. I pointed at the medical building.

"That's where my dentist's office is."

"That's why I was here, doing a little surveillance."

"On me?"

"No, but you were quite the distraction." He smirked and I wanted to slap it off his face. "I was trying to get a glimpse of Clayton."

"And you thought he'd be here?"

"Dr. Gold just retired, didn't he?"

"Yeah, and—" Light dawned. "Dr. Clayton's the one taking over?"

"His practice was across town but he wanted something bigger for more patients or more whatever the hell he's doing. Coincidentally, you're now his patient."

"Coincidentally? No way. There are a lot of dentists' offices in a city this size. He must have known…"

He cut me off. "I agree, but we can't afford to waste time looking for the connection. You need to get in there."

"Too bad we didn't have this conversation last week. My next cleaning's not for six months."

"Funny. Make an appointment, get in there and see what's going on."

"*You* make an appointment," I said. "One of your front teeth is a little crooked anyway. Might as well kill two birds."

"Fae know fae," he said. "If I get within twenty feet of him, he'll know I'm fae, and he'll know I became a new patient to scope him out."

"Then he'll sniff me out too, won't he?"

"Probably not," he said. "You're half-human, and your scent is different. You should fly right under the radar, so to speak."

I started to ask him why, if the dentist wouldn't recognize me for what I was, the fae at the group meeting did, but I mentally answered my own question. I'd arrived with Frederica, and humans didn't attend those meetings, and if I smelled like something other than a true fae, then they instantly knew what I was.

"You might not even need to see him," Svein added. "You could see one of his assistants. Just get in there and get a good look around, and see if you can figure out what he's up to. It's a longshot that it would be obvious, but I'm hoping you can get a few clues, at least."

"Here's one clue," I said. "Denise told me the new guy was renovating big-time."

"Denise?"

"The hygienist. She's worked for Dr. Gold for years. She's got nothing to do with Doc Clayton."

"You wanted to know about the threat, Gemma. This is it. Get in there as soon as you can. I've been watching him from way over here almost every single day. I've followed him home. But I can't confront him. I can't go near him. I know he's messing with teeth, messing with us, but I can't—" He cut himself off and tightened his jaw, looking across the street again.

I thought, not for the first time, how incapable he must feel, how frustrated to not be able to finish the job he started.

"Wouldn't you know," I said, poking my tongue around my mouth and talking around it, "I think I'm getting a toothache." I prodded a back bottom molar with the tip of my tongue. "Ow. Yup, no doubt about it."

The corners of Svein's lips quirked up.

"I'm going to have to make an appointment," I said, "and get this thing examined. Yup, this cavity's getting deeper by the second. It feels like the Grand Canyon in there. Hey," I said, leaning into him. "Yell into my mouth, see if you hear an echo." I opened wide.

He chuckled and shoved me gently away. "All right, already."

"I'll let you know when my appointment is," I said. "I want you as backup out here."

He nodded and looked at the building again. The door opened and a woman stepped out, holding the hand of a little girl. The child skipped as they walked down the street, swinging a plastic goody bag.

"You got it," Svein said. His jaw relaxed.

So, I was going to face an evil dentist with power drills, scalpels and possibly a hell minion.

But, I realized, the kiss still hot in my memory and on my lips, I also was in another kind of danger, the kind that was right in front of me, leaning on a lamppost.

CHAPTER 12

"Gemma Cross," I told the receptionist. "I have an appointment with"—gulp—"Dr. Clayton."

"Are you a patient of Dr. Clayton's?" she asked. She was new. I wasn't sure where Brenda, Dr. Gold's longtime receptionist, was. Probably retired when he did. Brenda always had a sugar-free candy at the ready and a piece of celebrity gossip she was willing to dissect with anyone interested. I always pretended I was, because she made me laugh and I would have hated to disappoint her by telling her I had no idea who she was talking about.

"I was Dr. Gold's patient," I told the new woman behind the desk. "I called yesterday, about a toothache?"

"That's right," she said, but her tone indicated she didn't remember at all, and she flipped through pages. Pages, I noticed, that were crammed full of appointments. Clayton certainly wasn't hurting for business, having likely brought all his patients across town with him and gaining Dr. Gold's as well.

"You can have a seat," the receptionist told me. "The doctor will be with you in a moment."

I sat, and realized I was shaking a little bit. The air conditioner was humming, but I was pretty sure that wasn't affecting me nearly as much as the prospect of getting into the chair and opening my vulnerable mouth for the supposedly evil Dr. Clayton to peer into, or wrench all my teeth from. At least with my mouth open, I wouldn't say anything stupid to give myself away.

Svein was only across the street, sitting in the picture window of a coffee shop. I'd suggested the more low-key surveillance, surprised that no one had noticed him before this. Life in the big city, I supposed, but I still insisted we be more subtle. I touched my zippered jacket pocket where I'd stuffed my Fae Phone, knowing I could summon him in an emergency one-button speed dial. I reminded myself I was going to be okay, for the time being anyway. The office was full of people. Even Dr. Clayton would probably agree that opening up a hellmouth at high noon wouldn't be a smart way to do business.

Remembering I was here to uncover clues, I looked around. The waiting room didn't have much in the way of renovations, not the kind of renovations I'd heard going on in the back when I was last here. Obviously, I'd have to investigate back there, but I was five minutes late to this appointment thanks to the Metro, and I didn't want to risk having the doctor call my name as I was snooping around.

I refocused my attention on my immediate surroundings. Again, there were no actual structural changes here, but the atmosphere was distinctly different from my last visit. It had been transformed into a children's playroom. The chairs were upholstered in various circus colors with fat cushions. The rug was long and shaggy, an invitation to sit. Blocks and Legos were stacked in one corner, a dollhouse in another. Picture books were piled on all the end tables, without a *Time* magazine or newspaper in sight. It was a waiting room designed for children, and it would have been perfect, but for one thing.

It *was* perfect. And by that, I mean immaculate.

The books should have been scattered, the blocks should have been plowed through, the Legos snapped together to form a half-something. The miniature dolls should have been in their tiny beds, or lounging in the shrunken living room. But everything was in its place, and it shouldn't have been because I was sharing the waiting room with three children.

Three children, all younger than seven, who sat calmly, hands folded in laps, their facial features arranged in far-too-mature serene expressions.

Surrounded with toys and books beckoning them to play and make a joyful ruckus, they merely sat without the slightest fidget. One mother had one boy and girl on either side of her, and the other mother had her daughter in her lap, and neither of them seemed to notice their kids' lack of normal enthusiasm. It was probably because they needed a respite from their parental weariness, and this seemed like what they needed, and so in their relief they didn't notice what I did.

It was very, very creepy.

These kids should have been jumping, crawling, laughing, whining, and generally disregarding all good manners. Acting like kids.

Instead, these three were acting like weird, stunted little adults.

"Mindy?" the receptionist called. The mother slid her child off her knees and onto the ground, and held her hand as she obediently ambled behind. They both disappeared around the corner.

A man's voice reached my ears. "Mindy," he said, "you're even prettier than last time I saw you. Tell me, how do you like my toothpaste?"

I imagined Mindy nodding, and her mother said, "She loves it. She never misses a night brushing her teeth. I can't believe it. I don't know what you put in it, but it's great."

"Go on in," he responded. "Denise will be with you in a moment."

A man and his son emerged from the examining room area, and I immediately noticed the little boy. He bounced with exuberance, and said, "You said pizza. Dad, you said pizza."

"I did say pizza if you were good, Brian," his father answered, "and you were good, so we're on our way."

Brian balled up his fists tightly with barely contained joy, and hopped up and down. His father pulled a checkbook out of the pocket of his denim jacket and leaned over the desk to settle the bill. Brian wandered into the waiting room, surveyed the landscape, and made a beeline for the Legos. He sat, pulled out some bricks and snapped them together, studying them before adding a few more. He looked up at me. I smiled at him, but he turned his attention to the other boy in the room, who appeared to be about his age. Then Brian looked down, snapped on another piece and looked up again, trying hard to get the attention of a potential new friend.

Not only did the creepy little adult-child not acknowledge Brian, he never even glanced his way. He wasn't being rude. He just had no interest whatsoever.

I heard the father make an appointment for Brian's sister next Wednesday at 3:30. "Come on, Brian," he called. "You can play some more when we bring Jamie in next week." Brian hopped up, breaking up the perfection of the room by tossing aside two handfuls of Legos. His dad zipped him into a similar denim jacket and they turned to go, but were stopped by a "Wait!"

A man in a white coat strode into the room, but I saw only his back as he opened a deep drawer in a file cabinet and rifled through it. "Brian," he said, "you can't go without your special goody bag." He withdrew a plastic bag filled with the usual dentist treats of a toothbrush and floss, no doubt. "There's some very special toothpaste in here that I want you to try, and when you come back with your sister next week, I want you to tell me what you think."

He closed the drawer, turned around, and for the first time, I saw Dr. Riley Clayton.

He was a beautiful man. I guessed he was around my mother's age, but his youth had remained prominent, like a heartthrob movie actor you last saw onscreen years ago and now, in a prime-time guest appearance, you knew him instantly, because he'd aged just the way he should have. His bright blue eyes crinkled at the corners as he smiled at his young patient, and his own teeth were white and straight. Brian grabbed for his goody bag and Dr. Clayton said, "Do you remember what we talked about?"

"Brush morning and night," Brian recited.

"And then?"

"My teeth won't fall out."

"They won't fall out before they're supposed to," Clayton corrected. "Have a great day," he said, winking at Brian's father, and picked up a file folder as the man and his son left. I turned my head so I was facing away from Clayton, but I kept my sidelong gaze on him. He flipped through a couple of papers, one bearing a drawing of an open mouth with some penned-in remarks. He abruptly shut the folder and called, "Gemma?"

Tentative, I approached the desk, then, to cover up my nervousness, gestured to the waiting mother and her two Children of the Corn and said, "They were here before me."

"They're waiting for the hygienist," he said, holding out his hand for me to shake. I did, almost surprised to find his palm didn't burn mine. "Don't worry," he said, reading my expression. "I get lots of fearful patients, but I promise to be as gentle as a man can possibly be."

I squinted slightly at him. His smile held as his face brightened, and I watched as silver shot around his irises and gleamed from under long, blond eyelashes. Glamour.

Well, he could glamour me from now until the sun went down, and it wasn't going to have the slightest effect. A human would have been affected—affected to the point of cloud-floating to the dentist's chair and agreeing enthusiastically to a root canal.

And if I didn't do the same, he'd get the big hint that I was no human.

I blinked once to feign disbelief, then batted my eyelashes several times. Unaccustomed to stupid flirtatious tactics, I immediately felt dizzy, but it worked to make me seem disoriented by desire. "I'm not afraid," I told him, and ran my tongue over my bottom lip.

"That's my girl," he said, and led me into an exam room. It was standard—a desk, a rolling stool, two backlit wall units to view X-rays. And the dentist's chair, leather with a plastic protector at the bottom and around the headrest. My teeth did start to ache then. I didn't like this ordeal on a good day. I certainly didn't like the idea of Dr. Clayton approaching my face with a metal clamp in one hand and a gas mask in another.

I did notice, however, that this room looked mostly as it did when Dr. Gold was here. Which meant all those renovations went on elsewhere—further back down the hall.

"What's going on?" he asked.

"What?"

"With your teeth," he said. "I assume that's why you're here. Most people don't visit the dentist for fun."

He'd dropped the glamour, likely so he could do his job. I imagined it would be hard to get close enough to treat a patient when she was likely to pull you in for a long, slow kiss.

"I took a good crack to the jaw," I said. I touched the left side of my face. "I'm a boxer. This tends to happen."

"Your chart says you were just here for your cleaning," he said. "Too bad you had to come back so soon. Let's have a look."

I opened my mouth and he eased my shoulder into the chair. He didn't know what I was, I was sure. He rolled his stool over to me and poked and pressed a few metal things into my gums. I almost wished I didn't know he was fae so I could test out my own ability to sniff out my own. But perhaps my prior knowledge was screwing up my radar, because I got nothing.

Tightening my grip on the armrests, I prepared to scream if he made one wrong move, but with dentists, it was hard to tell what a wrong move was, since it all felt invasive and sore.

"You're good on the bottom," he said. "Open a little wider and

I'll check the top."

"Dr. Clayton?" I heard. I was unable to turn, but I knew it was Denise by her nasally Boston accent. "Could you come in and take a look at Mindy for a second?"

Clayton dropped his instruments on the paper-towel covered tray over my knees. "Bear with me," he said, and rose.

I didn't have more than a moment to contemplate a next move before he returned. "I'm going to take a couple of X-rays, so I can check below the gumline and make sure nothing's going on under there."

He angled the X-ray machine in front of my face, had me bite down on a couple of nasty little slides, and said, "I'm going to go have a look at these. I'll be a few minutes."

"No problem."

As soon as I heard his footsteps fade, I slid off the chair, my sneakers noiselessly hit the floor. I tiptoed out of the exam room and moved in the other direction, down the back hallway. *Just trying to find the bathroom*, I lied to myself.

With my fingertips, I pushed open the first door I came to. Bathroom.

I crept ahead quickly to the next and last door, straight ahead. This door was shut tight, but when I turned the knob, it clicked open. No lights were on, but the afternoon sun beamed straight in, illuminating everything in front of me.

A laboratory.

In my heart, I supposed I should have expected this. A villain always has a secret lab. By the papers and test tubes and little flat Petri dishes covering one of the counters, and water droplets still clinging to the sides of the metal sink, it was easy to surmise someone had worked in here recently.

No kids in cages, so that was a positive start. And, I noticed, no teeth. There was a powerful microscope, far beyond anything I remembered from high school biology, and there was an emergency eye wash box on the wall. No teeth.

Padding silently into the room, I slipped two fingers into my folded-up sweatshirt cuff and pulled out a spider. Ick. Just didn't matter that they weren't real and breathing—they were still disgusting to look at and touch. I reached around behind the open door and pressed it onto the freshly painted wall. As if with a mind of its own, it skittered toward the ceiling and nestled into the corner crack. Ew. Upon giving me the bug earlier this morning, Reese and Svein had informed me it wasn't the usual essence-sniffer. This one was more state of the art, with a teeny, tiny video surveillance camera. They couldn't control this spider's movements—it followed heat and motion—so they just had to kind of hope it would capture something, but at least in a room like this, the chances were pretty good.

I saw two cylindrical machines against the wall whose function I couldn't identify. They looked like big mixing vats and thermometers protruded from each. All the wall cabinets were shut but had glass doors, and by stepping into the room a little further, I could read some of the labels on the containers inside: hydrated silica, glycerin, sodium lauryl sulfate, peppermint oil, p-hydrozybenzoate.

I tried to memorize the alphabet soup of chemical names so I could investigate on the Internet later. I turned my attention to the worktables, and realized what I'd thought was a rack of test tubes wasn't actually holding test tubes. They were plastic, triangular tubes. The empty tubes were lined up cap down, their top ends gaping open. There were about a half-dozen filled racks, and beside them on the table was a sealed, finished tube. I picked it up.

Toothpaste.

He was making toothpaste.

My mind reeled to put all the pieces together. Robot children. Lab-created toothpaste in goody bags. Dead teeth.

I thrust the tube into the front waistband of my jeans, feeling it squash against my stomach, and ran to the door. I pushed it open and doubled back toward the exam room I'd vacated—as Dr. Clayton rounded the corner. And made eye contact with me. And raised an eyebrow.

"Um, bathroom," I mumbled, and ducked into the bathroom. I closed the door and pressed my back against it, holding my breath. Shit.

Thoughts were shoving each other around in my brain, and I couldn't catch any one of them and hold it long enough to make sense of it. Toothpaste lab. Kids sucked of innocence. Wings must stay in. I dropped my face into my hands and raked my fingers hard through my hair. Reaching over to flush the toilet to at least maintain very shaky appearances, I got a look at myself in the clean, clear mirror over the sink. My eyes had the hollowed, haunted look of an insomniac. My jaw was set hard in the look of a criminal. My mouth was a taut straight line, the look of someone who facing a grim, no-way-out situation.

If I were Clayton—hell, if I were anyone but me—I might keep a distance from someone like me. Because he didn't know what I was. He *didn't*. To him, I was probably no more than a crazy, sleep-deprived trespasser.

Of course, my wings could still give me away. I had gotten the information I needed. Now I just had to get out.

Turning on the faucet, I thrust my hands under the water and splashed my face with very cold water. I waved my hand in front of the paper towel dispenser, wiped my face and with a deep, renewed breath, left the bathroom for the exam room.

Dr. Clayton was there already and didn't look up as I came in. I re-positioned myself in the squeaky plasticky chair again and lay back as if nothing were amiss. He rolled his stool to my side. He looked down into my face and we stayed that way for about five very uncomfortable seconds until I realized I'd forgotten to open wide. "Did you see anything?" I asked, using just my tongue and vocal cords to form the unintelligible words.

He picked up his metal instruments and peered inside again,

but rather than earnestly examining, he lifted his chin and looked down his nose, as if this time suspecting that I was not quite here as a patient after all. I jammed my hands into my pocket and fingered the Fae Phone, ready to call for my backup if he did or said one threatening thing.

But he merely sat back and dropped the instruments onto the table. "I found nothing that might be causing you pain."

"Huh," I said. "Well, that's strange."

"Not so much," he answered. "Your jaw's probably just sore from getting a pounding. Next time, you might want to duck."

"Roger that."

He rolled out of the way and stood, lifting my armrest as he did so, and I slid off the chair and to my feet. He made a few notes on my file. I was almost out of there, and I couldn't be more relieved.

"I'm always happy to see a patient," he continued without looking up, "but I'm afraid you're not going to be happy."

His glamour was gone, and so was his smile. I steadied myself against the counter behind me, groping one hand for something I could use as a weapon, but my fingers only found a pen. I grasped it tightly.

"I'm sorry," he said.

I took a breath, prepared to lunge.

"But I'm going to have to charge you a full office visit fee."

What? "What?" I dropped the pen.

"I don't really have a choice," he said. "You can see Rebecca at the desk on the way out to settle up."

"Right," I said.

He held out his hand. "Nice to meet you, Gemma. You have a cleaning scheduled in a few months. I'm looking forward to seeing you then."

He squeezed my hand. Hard. I lifted my chin, and did the same.

Then I practically ran out to the reception desk.

Rebecca quoted the fee and I gave her my credit card as Denise walked out. “Gemma!” she said. “I thought I heard your name.”

“You did. Hey,” I asked, “do I get a goody bag?”

“Silly rabbit,” she said, “those are for kids. Why are you in today, anyhow?”

Oh, well. “I had a toothache,” I said. “Or, what I thought was a toothache. Dr. Clayton assured me my teeth are still perfect.”

“Isn’t he wonderful?” she asked, and her eyes glazed over as she stared over my shoulder. Rebecca had frozen as her eyes caught whatever Denise’s had. I turned to find Dr. Clayton leaning in the doorway of the exam room I had exited, smiling at the three of us.

I wanted to lunge at him again, this time on the offense. Messing around with his glamour, luring Denise under his spell, turning kids into jaded, far-too-mature small adults, screwing with the Olde Way. My fists balled and I itched to close the distance between us and land a hard uppercut to his chin, banging his teeth together hard enough to pulverize them into enamel dust.

Turning back, I saw the two women were still zombies. The corner of Denise’s lip-glossed mouth was so slack, she was almost drooling. Rebecca’s eye-blinks were slower than I thought possible. I swiveled my head around, and realized too late that I’d forgotten to pretend to fall under the glamour spell, like an obedient human.

Avoiding his direct gaze, I nodded a calm acknowledgment at him, then forced myself to take slow, deliberate steps when I walked out the door.

>=<

“He’s making toothpaste.”

After I’d fled Dr. Clayton’s office of doom, I’d managed to keep my wings under control in the few more seconds it had taken to sign my credit card slip and get the hell out. With every step I’d taken away from that place was an increased sense of security and calm.

Svein had caught up with me quickly, which meant he’d seen

me leave, which meant he'd been watching the door to the office building every second. He walked along with me, matching my pace, and didn't badger me for details. He knew I'd give them, and he was waiting until I was ready to speak. And when I was ready, the first thing I said was, "He's making toothpaste."

"Toothpaste," Svein repeated.

"Toothpaste that I think is wrecking kids' teeth. It's sucking the innocence right out of them. And by them, I don't just mean the teeth."

I described the children I'd seen in the waiting room, children completely uninterested in playing and having fun. I told him how Mindy's mother had said she loved the toothpaste and never missed a brushing. "There was one boy who was normal," I added. "This kid Brian. I think it was his first visit. But Clayton made sure he got goody bag toothpaste, and made him promise to use it every day."

"You're sure about all this?"

"I'm sure of everything I saw, but I want to make sure my theory is correct. I want to go back. Just one more time."

"Why? What else do you think you're going to find?"

"Brian's sister has an appointment next Wednesday. If Brian shows up also, I'll want to get a good look at him. If he's undergone a personality change, I'll know I'm right."

"Why aren't parents noticing?"

"Well, I figure first of all, how can parents be expected to make the slightest connection between toothpaste and personality? Besides, I was thinking when I was in there that for the most part, parents want nicer, quieter, better-behaved kids. If they suddenly have them, they'll consider themselves lucky, or think they did something right in raising them. They're not going to take a son or daughter to a therapist and say, 'Hey, my kid's not acting up enough. Can you do something to make him more disruptive?'"

"Excellent point."

"And I found his evil laboratory." I yanked up my shirt and, while Svein unapologetically checked out my abs, I pulled out the squashed toothpaste tube and handed it to him. "You might want to have the guys at The Root run some tests on this. I'm no chemist, and even if I were, I doubt I would have learned anything in college about innocence essence."

Svein took the tube and peered at the label. "Seem like pretty straightforward ingredients."

"Yeah, well, I'm pretty sure Clayton would not list 'innocence essence demolisher' on there."

"Good work, Gemma," Svein said, drawing a Ziploc bag out of his pocket and sealing the toothpaste inside. "Great information, great evidence score. You're going back next week?"

"Yeah. Problem is..." My voice trailed off.

"What?"

"He's kind of on to me."

He stopped short. "How?"

"It was nothing he did and everything I did." Filling him in on my not-quite *Charlie's Angels* performance, I caught myself feeling disappointed in myself for possibly not impressing him. Which was very stupid, because I didn't give a crap what Svein thought of me.

"He caught you in the lab?" Svein interrupted.

"Well, he caught me leaving the lab. I said I was looking for the bathroom."

"Imaginative."

"Look," I told him, "if you don't like the job I'm doing, you can always do it yourself. Oh, no, I forgot. You can't."

As the words fell out of my mouth, I knew they'd bounce hard against a nerve, but Svein managed not to let it show, even when I forged ahead with my story and ended at the part where I forgot to pretend the glamour affected me and Clayton was well tipped off that I wasn't a fully gullible human.

"So, mission accomplished," he said. "You don't need to get back in there. The next time you go in there is after we outline a plan for you to take care of Clayton and his lab."

"But I'm not done," I argued. "The toothpaste thing is only speculative until I make a better connection. I need to see Brian again, and see if he's changed after getting the goody bag toothpaste. Once I do that..."

"Clayton won't stand for that. You already faked one toothache. You have no record of being a dental hypochondriac, and even if he didn't think you were up to something—which he clearly does—you'll never get away with faking another toothache. Even if you ate nothing but candy bars and didn't brush or floss at all, I'm not sure you can induce a cavity in less than a week."

"I've got this part figured out," I told him. "I have a plan."

"What can you possibly do? Make an appointment for Mr. Avery McCormack and go in with him?"

As if I'd consider, even for a half-second, tossing my adorable and determined but essentially helpless boyfriend in front of a hell spawn. "No," I said, disgusted. "This is better. It's not a great plan. I mean, Clayton will still know I'm up to something. But I'll have a legitimate reason to be in a dentist's office, and I don't think it will make matters any worse. Just be available next week to back me up."

"Lot of good I did you today."

I remembered my shaking hands in the waiting room, and my terrified stint in the bathroom, and my angry reaction at reception, and realized I got out of there unscathed and armed with information because I knew Svein was out here all along, watching my wingless back. But, unwilling to acknowledge it, or how I was glad that he was the one out here for me, I just said, "Yeah, lot of good you did."

CHAPTER 13

The kiss on my neck was butterfly soft, and the scent of aftershave floated under my nose. "You look beautiful," Avery said, brushing my hair back to kiss me again.

"I look ridiculous," I replied, rummaging through a blue satin-lined jewelry box for my other faux-diamond stud earring. "Aha," I said, lifting it only to have it promptly slip from my fingers and roll under the bed. "Crap," I said, just a little louder than necessary, as I hiked up my calf-length violet linen sheath dress to kneel and grope the dusty floor with the other hand. "I hate dress-ups," I said. "I hate high heels, and I hate earrings. You're lucky I'm even going."

"I am," he said. "And you're getting a free meal."

"It'd better be good. I'm talking caviar." My fingers found the earring and I stuck it in my ear before standing.

"You've never eaten caviar in your life," Avery said.

"Well, I'm just saying it had better be an option."

Avery pulled me to my feet and held me close. "I will demand the caterer find caviar for you if that's your wish," he said, bending to kiss my lips.

Grasping at T-shirt to find bare skin, brick wall rough against my back, surrendering just for a moment...

I abruptly pulled back.

"Are you okay?" Avery asked, dropping his hands and releasing me. "You've been jumpy since you got back from the gym."

"I took a bit of a beating today," I told him, grabbing a pink freshwater-pearl necklace from the top of the dresser and looping it around my neck. "I was tired and not all there, and I just didn't have it." I fumbled with the clasp, and Avery turned me around and took over.

"Why can't you take it easy? You didn't leave work so you could work yourself silly at Smiley's and develop insomnia."

"No," I agreed. "I left work for a full-time arm-candy gig."

Avery didn't respond, but fastened the clasp at my neck, and I instantly regretted my meanness. I didn't handle guilt well.

"I'm sorry," I said. "I'm a jerk and I didn't mean it. I've actually been looking forward to tonight."

In reality, I'd forgotten about this fund-raising dinner, and the last thing I needed was to totter around in black patent three-inch pumps and shake a bunch of wealthy hands. Not to mention, I could have used a few hours alone, lying in bed, maybe reading a book or watching a DVD. For almost two weeks, my waking life—and, in the instance of my first collection, my sleeping life—had been interrupted by my new obligations and self-discoveries. I may have been supernatural, but I still needed some time off.

But I needed, and I wanted, to stand by Avery tonight. I suspected there'd be a lot of check-writing potential, and Avery's campaign deserved as many extra zeroes in his war chest as he could ask for. Besides, he was still reeling from his former aide's betrayal, and although it hadn't come close to a real public scandal, both CNN and MSNBC had made a couple of offhanded references to the D.C. Digger's blog. I would have loved to wring that writer's scrawny little neck—if I had any idea who he or she was.

"I'm looking forward to this," I repeated, putting my hands on either side of Avery's face and squishing it before kissing him.

"You can't get rid of me that easily. Now, hand me my wrap."

That made him grin. "You don't own a wrap. Do you even know what a wrap is?"

"Just grab me a hoodie."

"Very stylish. Which one?"

"The black one, of course. You said this was a formal event."

>=<

Under the Maple was a restaurant dedicated to Americana, just like any good politician.

A live tree trunk rose up in the center of the dining room. From its branches hung glass balls, each one depicting a scene of American life. When we'd arrived earlier in the evening, I'd ventured over to look closely. On a ball hanging at eye level, I saw a horse-drawn sleigh gliding along a snowy New England road. I stood on my tiptoes to examine a ball showing a car rolling along on the Pacific Coast Highway.

The tables had been moved out, clearing the wooden floor for mingling, and a bar was set up in one corner where bicoastal wines were being poured. When guests began to arrive, waiters and waitresses circulated with trays of ham laced with maple sugar, assorted Wisconsin cheeses, bite-sized crab cakes, and fried chicken bits dipped in gravy. Drinks included mint juleps, Manhattans, martinis and, for the non-drinkers, lime rickeys.

I tried to make a good impression on everyone, and it was a snap. I met women with rocks around their necks that I was certain would win the war with gravity and pull them crashing down on the high-polished floor. I met men with unlit cigars protruding from designer jacket pockets. I shook a lot of hands, loosening my firm grip for some of the slighter women and a couple of men, so as to appear more warm than overwhelming.

And they were all charmed. Women complimented my dress and hair, which I knew were both nice but much less remarkable than they claimed. Men fetched me drinks and hors d'oeuvres, and offered to escort me across the room, and listened with rapt attention when I said, "Avery McCormack needs *your* support."

My glamour was on.

I'd practiced a lot, but I still couldn't hold a whole room captive at once. Turned out, it was unnecessary. The two hundred or so people here mingled and laughed with each other. But every person got their turn to meet Avery, and I concentrated my glamour on each person in that crucial time when they were deciding on a financial contribution.

Unfair? Manipulative? No, not really, I rationalized. These people were here because they'd already made up their minds to support Avery. I only nudged them to support him a bit more.

The gentleman Avery and I were entertaining at the moment, Mr. Someone-or-Other of Really Important Company, clapped Avery twice on the shoulder, beamed a lingering smile at me, and let his bejeweled wife drag him away.

"This is going well," Avery said. "Looks like you're my secret weapon tonight."

"You have no idea," I told him. "Now, you'll have to excuse me. The fifteen or so lime rickeys I scored have gone right through me."

I slipped around through people and perfumes and escaped the main room. I spotted a door proclaiming "Women" in curly script and headed for it, only to bump shoulders with a man pushing out of the opposite door.

"Pardon," I said, then froze.

"No problem," he said, pushing his glasses up on his nose. His hair was still messy but mousse had made it artfully so. The T-shirt had been replaced by a navy suit, but I was close enough to him to notice some fabric pilling at the shoulder. His tie was a little wider than was fashionable. He smelled faintly of cigarettes, and his smile was unmistakable.

"We meet again," he said, using the smooth words of a Marvel comic book villain despite the cracking, wavery voice of a social outcast.

At the moment, though, I couldn't appreciate the irony.

"Wouldn't have thought this would be your scene," he went on. "Thought you were more of a loner, a fellow night prowler. But you're a regular Miss Congeniality this evening, Gemma Cross."

It was hard to believe I was so unnerved by this twentysomething punk, but I was. When I last saw him, perched on a fountain in the middle of the night, smoking and idly watching me, I had just completed an evening of activities that most normal people would consider illegal.

"Who are you?" I asked. "What were you doing at Watergate?"

"The question is," he countered, "what were *you* doing at Watergate?"

Swallowing my fear—breathe and accept—I beckoned him even closer and whispered into his ear, "That's between me and Mr. Nixon."

He chuckled and I took a big step back. I mustered up my glamour mojo, and I felt my face grow warm, my skin tingling, but his expression didn't change into that of someone under a spell. In fact, his expression didn't change at all. I felt my back quivering insistently. I struggled to control it, contracting every muscle in my body, and I succeeded except for my shaking hands, and I nearly dropped my little black beaded purse.

"What's wrong, Gemma?" he asked. "You seem jumpy."

"I have to pee," I said. "If you'll excuse me."

"McCormack's a good guy," he said, as if he hadn't heard me. "I mean, he's a *really* good guy. He's got nothing to hide, nothing to answer for, nothing to suggest he's not the stand-up guy he claims to be."

He removed his glasses, slid a handkerchief out of his breast pocket, shook it out and rubbed at the lenses, squinting as he did so. His show of being cool and casual was kind of funny, considering his king-geek appearance. "It's interesting," he said, "and I wouldn't have thought it possible. Because see, it's the ones like McCormack who have the trouble, the ones who appear earnest in public but are sneaking around in private."

He put slight but obvious emphasis on the word "sneaking."

"What's your point?" I asked curtly, shifting my weight from one foot to the other and nearly rolling my ankle in on my stupid pumps.

"Just observing. It's my job to observe."

"Then you won't mind observing my back as I leave."

"Campaign's a success, so far," he said, replacing his glasses on his face and pushing them up the bridge of his nose with his middle finger. "Only thing that could bring him down now is something, or someone, he has no control over."

He grinned. "Sure wouldn't want to be the one trying to control you."

My yellow alert of fear quickly smoldered into bright red anger. Earlier today, I'd faced down a living, breathing, evil threat to everything good and innocent, on his own turf. This little peon was barely a blip on my radar. He certainly didn't look or act like a campaign contributor, so I was willing to bet he was one of the many journalists that showed up tonight. "Observe," my ass.

I quickly closed the distance between us and breathed right into his face. I had about two inches on him, a flared-up temper, and a strong urge to slap his stupid grin right off his face. "What's your name?"

He didn't blink, but when I cracked two knuckles on my right hand with my thumb, he did swallow. "Greg Mahoney."

"Mahoney, you're pissing me off. If you've got something of any real importance to say, I suggest you say it now."

He looked me right in the eye. "Intimidation. I know you're a boxer, but is that how you do things outside the ring? Knock people's teeth out and carry them around as souvenirs?"

My eye twitched.

"That's right," he said. "That was a tooth you dropped that night."

A wave built and crashed in my brain, drowning my thought

process. My ears clogged with it, and my hearing narrowed down to a little tunnel. I wanted to speak, to ask him what he was talking about, but I couldn't. We both knew what he was talking about. I glanced toward the dining room, hoping and not hoping that Avery might emerge and interrupt.

"Gemma," Mahoney said, lowering his voice as two women passed us in a swish of skirts to enter the ladies' room. "I went to Watergate to have a smoke and do some thinking. I do my best thinking outside in the middle of the night. Scandal happens at night." His words spilled out faster. "Then I saw you."

I blinked, not breathing.

"I write the political stuff for fun," he said. "Dirt's not hard to come by in this town. Do I want to write bigger, more important, life-changing things? Sure. But when it comes right down to it, I'm a hack. For now. And when a hack like me sees the nice girlfriend of the perfect candidate skulking around in the dead of night where she's got no friends or family that I can determine, I sense chum in the water."

My shoulder twitched and realizing I'd regained the power of movement, I backed up a step, but Mahoney reached over and clasped his fingers around my wrist. They were warm, and that surprised me.

"If you've got anything else to feed a hungry shark," he said, "you might want to toss it in. Otherwise, you'd better throw a life preserver to your boy McCormack and tell him to start swimming." He let go of me and straightened his tie. "I'll find something to nail him eventually. But there's a bigger story out there, one I'd rather have, and I have a feeling you know which one I'm referring to. If you want to chat, you'll know where to find me."

He headed toward the dining room but stopped and turned back. "Might I say, you look radiant tonight, Gemma."

As Mahoney left the room I stood there, shaking with anger and fear, the two emotions which, left unchecked, would draw out my wings and send me running for the nearest balcony. I turned my head this way and that way, desperately searching for an alternative exit or a place to hide. I dashed to the restroom but it was crowded with women with rustling dresses, so I rushed past the coatroom and found a small open room on the end. I leaped in and tried to slam the door shut, but the door was in two halves and only the top half slammed. I pushed the bottom half tight and backed up against the rack of hangers in this secondary coatroom.

My Fae Phone was in my tiny, useless beaded bag and I clawed at it, tearing loose black and silver beads with my fingernails. They hit the floor, rolling and scattering, as I grabbed the phone and punched the number I still had on speed dial.

"Yeah."

"Svein," I said. My muscles wanted to release with relief, but my brain was still acting as if under attack. "Svein, listen to me. I'm at Under the Maple on Pennsylvania Ave. I'm at a fundraiser with Avery. I need help."

"Is it Clayton?"

I'd never even thought about Dr. Clayton being out in the real world with the rest of us. I guess I'd figured once I escaped his lair, the only way I'd see him again was if I went back. I never gave much thought to where he lived, what he ate. Who he voted for.

"No," I said, as much to push my own horrible thought away as to clarify to Svein what I meant. "No. It's this reporter named something Mahoney. Greg Mahoney. I saw him the night I collected at Watergate. He's here, he recognized me, he saw me with the tooth..."

Rage and fear twisted up again from my core, and my breath grew shallower. I crawled over to the door and pushed a hand against it so I could feel if anyone tried to enter. "Svein, he knows."

"What," Svein asked, "does he know, exactly?"

"He knows something," I said. "He's out to ruin Avery. He says if I don't give him something, he'll—he'll..."

"Easy," Svein said. "Relax."

See, the thing about me was that whenever I was agitated and my mother or Avery or someone told me to relax, somehow that made the situation worse. So right after Svein advised me to relax, I dropped the phone and reached a hand behind me to unzip my strapless dress, tugging it to the bottom. The material fell away from my breasts just as my wings burst out. I cried out in momentary pain, then sank to the floor and banged my fist on the ground in frustration. My wingtips brushed against the wire hangers, which cling-clanged together like wind chimes.

I snatched up the phone and pressed it to my face. "You have to get here," I whispered with clenched teeth. "I'm with Avery. I can't just leave. Well, at the moment I can't leave this coatroom until I look human, but when I do, I can't just leave without Avery. I have to get out there and behave like a normal person." My last few words were a hiss. "You've got to get here so you can follow him. Follow him home and see where he lives, or follow him back to whatever paper or TV station he works for. He's a threat."

"Doesn't sound like much of a threat," Svein said. "He saw you with a tooth. Could have been yours. Could have been a shiny pebble."

"He knew there was a bigger story. He said I knew what he was talking about."

"Journalist horseshit. I'll look him up and we'll keep an eye on him, but it's not worth tailing him tonight."

"You didn't talk to him," I said. "I did. He knows something. He's danger."

"To McCormack, maybe," Svein said. "Not to us."

I pressed the material against my front, and the satin slipped against my sweaty skin. "If I hadn't been on assignment that night," I said slowly, "he wouldn't have seen me. And I was on assignment that night because of you. Maybe Mahoney's not a threat to the fae at large. Maybe he's only a threat to Avery's career, and to my love life. But *I'm* fae. Doesn't that merit a little friendly concern? I need help." I drew in a long, shuddering breath. "And I need to get out of this freaking coatroom and back to where I'm supposed to be."

"Open the door."

"Right now?"

"Yes, right now."

"Bad idea. I'm winged and indecent. I need to calm down and get normal again. Are you coming or not?"

"I'm there."

"What?"

We lost our connection, and I dropped the phone into my lap and swore. But then, again, I heard, "Gemma, open the door."

His voice was soft and floated through the crack between the door and the wall. "Svein?"

"Open."

I turned the knob, pulled the door open a centimeter and peered out into Svein's black eyes.

"Holy shit," I whispered. "Did you fly here?"

He pushed both halves of the door open enough to squeeze through and closed it behind him, crouching beside me. I pressed my open dress tighter against my front. "I didn't fly here," he said. "I was already here."

He was dressed in a charcoal suit and a crisp white shirt and dark crimson tie. He looked good. I mean, he *really* looked good. "What do you mean you were already here?"

"It may surprise you," he said with a half-smile, "but I happen to be registered to vote, and I've been known to donate to a candidate if I deem him or her worthy of that vote."

Sifting through my jumbled emotions for a proper response, all I came up with was a wry laugh. "I'm glad you think Avery's worthy."

"Only of my vote," he said. He reached out and trailed a finger down my cheek, tracing my jawline to my bottom lip. I felt a rush of blood to my face, and a swirling moist heat inside my panties before I jerked away.

We stared at each other across the charged space until my wings retracted and folded into my back. My skin sealed over and I hurriedly zippered myself into my dress.

"You loved those wings," Svein said.

"What?" I asked, smoothing my hair back.

"When you first got them. You were ecstatic. You loved them."

I reached around my waist to touch the middle of my spine. "They're beautiful," I said. "They're like something out of a storybook. But I can't *use* them. I can't fly."

"You mean you *won't* fly."

"Why should I? When do *you* fly? This city has an effective public transportation system, and you have two good feet."

"You need to be able to master every ability, Gemma. They're given to you for a reason. If you have to fight, you'll need everything you've got."

"No," I said, and held up my hand when he opened his mouth again. "No. I want to stay myself. At least with the walking-through-walls thing, and sniffing essence, and glamour, I can still be me. The wings," I gestured behind me, "make me feel like a different creature. I know I'm not fully human anymore but I have to keep what I can. I don't want to be a freak, a flying Mothra freak. I've got plenty of frequent flier miles, should I need them."

He wanted to smile. I thought so, anyway. "Meantime," I added, "I *am* trying to master my wings as far as keeping them inside my body. As you can see, I still have some work to do. So just lay off the flying thing. Please."

What I didn't tell him was that I remembered my journey back in time, my occupation of the night watchman's body, and how his wings had come out, and how they hadn't saved him in time. They were useless to him then, and I had no use for them now.

Svein caught my gaze again, and I had a harder time pulling

away this time. "I have to get back," I said, fumbling to stand. He put out his hand to help me but I didn't take it, propping my hand instead against the wall to propel myself to my feet, one of which was asleep and tingling. "Avery's going to think I took off."

"He's busy talking up the crowd," Svein assured me. "You're all right."

"No, I'm not," I said, and it was the truth. Between Mahoney and Svein, I was incapable of rational thought.

"Go out there and do your thing," he said. "I'll track this guy Mahoney."

"But you don't know who he is. I'll point him out for you, and..."

"No, you have a job to do. I'll take care of it."

My shoulders relaxed, dropping down and away from my ears. "He's wearing glasses," I said, "and a really stupid-looking tie." I rubbed my face with both hands, and took a deep breath. "Thank you."

"Don't," he said. "Just walk out this door like it made sense for you to be in here."

I pushed on the door and both halves swung open. I stepped into the carpeted hallway with faked dignity and poise, but no one was there to notice. I felt Svein's hand on my elbow, and he fell into step beside me.

"What are you doing?" I hissed.

"Escorting you back to the main room."

"Bad idea."

"I think not."

Avery picked that moment to emerge from the dining room back to the hallway, and he smiled at me. I smiled back. "Go away," I said through my clenched teeth, but Svein didn't, and I approached the love of my life on the arm of a man I wasn't even sure I liked but had made out with in broad daylight against a brick building.

No idea how to start *this* conversation.

But apparently, Svein did. He released my elbow and put out his hand. "Avery McCormack," he said. "You have my vote."

"That was easy," Avery said, somewhat taken aback, but he recovered quickly, shaking Svein's hand.

I looked at their clasped hands and realized both my worlds had collided.

"I'm sorry, have we met?" Avery asked.

"Svein Nilsen." That was surprising. I'd thought for a moment he was going to go with an alias. "You and I haven't met," Svein continued smoothly, "but I met Gemma at Smiley's Gym recently. I'm thinking of joining and went there to have a look around, and I watched Gemma spar before talking to her for a while about the gym. I just ran into her by the restrooms and realized it was her. She's hard to forget."

"She is," Avery said, pulling me close to his side. I liked how he did it. Avery wasn't a jealous thug. In fact, he loved it anytime we were out together and a random man gave me the once-over.

Of course, now I felt like a worm.

"So you're a boxer?" Avery asked.

"Martial arts, at the moment," Svein said, and the two of them chatted as I gritted my teeth and willed Svein away. To be sure, he'd done quite a good job covering for me—fae couldn't be violent, but apparently they were fine with a few fibs here and there—but I was having a hard time standing there listening to their small talk.

Avery and Svein weren't supposed to be in the same place, ever. They needed to be in separate places. Even if I was growing more and more unsure every day about which man belonged in which place.

Avery asked Svein about his business and Svein gave him some story about financing and investigations or something, and I kept smiling and nodding, mentally vowing to kill Svein if this conversation ended with a golf date.

"It's been a pleasure to meet you, but I'm going to let you get back to winning people over," Svein said. Speaking of winning people over. "I apologize for monopolizing Gemma earlier."

"I'm sure you'll be seeing her soon," Avery said. "Though for your sake, I hope it's not on the unfortunate end of her right hook."

I smiled.

"If you'll excuse me," Svein said. "I see someone I need to catch up with." He cut me a look, and I knew which someone he was referring to.

"Thank you," I said. "For, uh, for your support."

Svein nodded at both of us and I watched him disappear into the dining room crowd. When he was out of sight, I kept my eyes on the spot.

He'd help me. Despite his balking, I knew he would.

"I was getting worried about you," Avery said, breaking into my reverie. "I thought you fell in."

"There was a line in the ladies' room," I said, "and then I ran into him."

"Nice guy," Avery commented. "And I'm secure enough in my manhood to say that he's a really good-looking guy."

I wondered how glamour worked between heterosexual members of the same gender. Probably just worked to charm them. "Maybe," I said. "But after a few days at Smiley's, he'll have the same facial imperfections as the rest of us."

"You are perfect," he said.

"In here," I said, "where the light's dim, I look pretty good. In daylight, anyone can tell my nose has been broken. But the other guy was worse off that day."

"I never doubted it."

He put his arms around me and I leaned into him for a moment. I rested my cheek on his navy blue tie and breathed him in. I held him, and thought about all the things I loved about him, then realized there were many things I hadn't seen in a while. "Are you tired of this yet?" I asked. "You've been working this thing day and night. You haven't taken your bike out in weeks. You haven't played your guitar, you haven't seen much of your real friends, and you used to spend so much time with your camera. Maybe that's what you should do. The cherry blossoms are almost gone. Take some pictures before they go."

"The cherry blossoms come out every year," Avery said into my hair. "An election is every two."

"I understand it's your priority, but it shouldn't be all you do. Avery McCormack is more than that."

"Just hang on," he said. "Just hang on, babe. It will be over in a few months, and I'll win or lose, and I'll get back to being me."

"I'm not saying it for me," I said. "I'm saying it for you. I love you, and I don't want you to get lost." *I don't want to get lost*, I thought. When it was Gemma and Avery, it was fantastic. Now that it was Avery the political candidate and Gemma the top-secret tooth faerie—*fae*—it was confusing and scary. We were working this relationship part time.

"How could I get lost?" he asked. "I can always ask you for directions. You know exactly where we're going."

In my memory, Svein trailed his finger down my face again, pushed me up against a building again. And deeper down in the same stack of memories, Avery kissed me for the first time.

"We'd better get back to your adoring constituents," I said.

⪢=⪡

I rose from bed and stumbled into the carpeted hallway. I looked down and saw them, tiny and white, scattered all over the ground. My hands flew to my face and I pushed against the skin around my mouth. Then I clamped my jaws shut and heard a click. My own teeth were intact.

I didn't know whose teeth were on the ground but the whispers had started, laughing and musical: Get them, grab them all, don't lose them…

Dropping to my knees, I pushed along the rug, gathering two handfuls of teeth, but when I lifted my hands to examine them, they slid between my fingers like sugar and fell away. No! I had to get them, keep them. Each was a gem, containing a fragment of the whole, and I couldn't lose even one. I clutched at the teeth again and closed my fists around them, but a flare of pain in my mouth made me cry out. I sealed my lips shut and tried to hold it in, but it throbbed and ached. I pressed my fists into my face, but the pain pulsed stronger and I opened my hands, releasing all the teeth again as my own teeth dropped from my gums, falling in a mess onto my tongue.

I felt them all sitting there, rattling against each other, and I couldn't, wouldn't open my mouth and lose them. But the pressure against my lips was unbearable, so I cupped my hands in front of my mouth and prepared to catch them. But as I opened my fingers, they were sticky and crimson with blood. I looked up to see Svein at the end of the hall, standing calm, watching me. Whose blood? *I tried to ask him, but I didn't want to open my mouth.* Whose blood? *I projected the thought at him. He still didn't move, didn't speak, didn't blink. I opened my mouth and my teeth fell out in a gush and I screamed,* I can't do this…

I jerked awake, sweating and breathing hard.

⁂

I dragged myself to the table where Avery was already eating an English muffin, his mug of black coffee steaming beside his humming laptop. I collapsed into a chair.

Avery looked up and did a double-take. "Are you okay?"

Choosing to go for the understatement, I said, "I didn't sleep all that well."

"Yeah, you don't look too good."

"Thanks a lot."

"Don't worry," he said, smirking. "You've got another admirer besides me."

"Can we not be cryptic so early in the morning? I can hardly see straight."

He swiveled his laptop around. “Take a read.”

I squinted at the screen. The D.C. Digger’s site featured a little cartoon of a guy in thick glasses with a shovel, pushing deep into the ground in front of the Capitol. His top blog entry was dated this morning at 2:23 a.m., and detailed Avery’s fundraiser.

“Guess he was there last night,” Avery said. “But he must have had a good time, because he didn’t have it out for me.”

He was right about that. The blog copy was complimentary for the most part, and the few catty digs were not at Avery himself but at several mucky-muck guests in attendance.

But it was the last item in the entry that woke me up: “McCormack’s sweetheart, ex-pollster and local amateur boxer Gemma Cross, enraptured guests with her witty banter and bright smile. She was nothing short of radiant.”

Might I say, you look radiant tonight, Gemma…

My eyes darted again to the little cartoon man and his black-rimmed glasses. Then I let out a long, quiet sigh.

Mahoney, that little shit, was the D.C. Digger.

CHAPTER 14

I evaded a flailing jab and countered with a hook that didn't land.

Mat laughed.

Mat considered laughing and taunting to be his brilliant key strategy. His form had improved considerably and he was in far better physical shape than the day he'd first arrived at Smiley's, but he still had the patience of a child. Convinced he had the psychological game down, however, he continued to laugh at and taunt every opponent he faced.

Everyone in the gym was biding time. Mat was a clown, but we weren't going to teach him his most important lesson until he was ready. In the meantime, he didn't throw any of the rest of us off, but he was very, very annoying.

Especially to me, especially today, because I had a plan, and it involved Mat emerging superior.

Smiley leaned into the ring from the floor, one hand gripping the rope above him. "Easy," he said to Mat. "Take it easy."

"I'm takin' it easy," Mat said. "This ain't nothin'. Why'm I sparring Bricks, anyway? She's too little for me."

"'Cause I don't want you just swinging useless. I want you to pay attention to your opponent's mind game, and Gemma plays a good one."

Ironic he should say that.

"All right, stop a minute," Smiley said, and climbed into the ring. I backed into the corner and let them confer. It was Mat's time with Smiley, after all, and I had been volunteered for the lesson. I squeezed my plastic water bottle and only half the water made it into my mouth, with the rest splashing my cheeks and dribbling down my chin. I glanced over my shoulder and saw the two of them in deep discussion. I crouched and spit my mouth guard onto the wooden stool. With my gloved fists, I pushed my sweatshirt over it, then walked back to the center of the ring just as Smiley slid back down to the floor.

While his back was still to us, Mat laid a sharp jab into my chest, despite Smiley's instructing us earlier to engage in light contact only. I exhaled hard and Mat chuckled with glee.

I hoped with all my heart that when it came time to wipe that cocky grin off Mat's face permanently, the guys would let me be the one to do it.

I stared him in the eye, and let him try to figure out my next move. When I knew he didn't expect it, I caught him sharp on the chin.

"Easy!" Smiley reprimanded me.

I snorted, barely containing a contemptuous smile, and Mat, taking the bait, scowled at my arrogance. Back and forth, back and forth, and I laid another one on him. Same spot. Just a hair harder.

"Bricks!" Smiley warned.

Openly smirking, I barely had time to recover when Mat retaliated with a cross that caught me square in the mouth. And I didn't duck.

His hit lacked in style, and was only a fraction of his full force, but he'd made his point. Blood oozed from my split upper lip.

I backed off and covered my face with my gloves. I outlined my front tooth with the tip of my tongue, and felt a piece of it had chipped away. Good. This had worked out well. The only hope I'd had of getting back into Clayton's office so soon under minimal suspicion was with a dental emergency, and this was as minor an incident as I could have orchestrated.

"Who's laughin' now?" Mat taunted. "That's right, that's right. Not Bricks."

"Shut up!" Smiley yelled, and his voice was near me.

He pulled my gloves away from my face and tilted my head back to look at my messy mouth in the glare of the bare light bulb overhead. "Nice job," he said, low into my ear. "Get your sorry ass out of this ring. *Now.* You," he said, louder, to Mat. "Shut your stupid mouth. Only reason you got to her is because she was crazy enough to let you. Get out of my sight."

"What about my lesson?" Mat asked.

"Lesson over."

I went to retrieve my shirt and water bottle. I pulled the sweatshirt over my head and pushed my mouth guard into the kangaroo pocket. I climbed through the ropes and hopped onto the floor, and Not-Rocky was by my side in an instant. "What's the matter with you?" he asked. "Why you playing games with Mat? He's an idiot."

"I know. I don't know."

"You okay?"

Before I could respond, Smiley pushed past both of us. "You and I are having a talk," he said, and I nodded wearily.

"You're in trouble," Not-Rocky said as Smiley stormed into his office ahead of me.

"Yeah, well, must be a day ending in 'Y'." I followed Smiley at a safe distance and entered the office after him.

"Close the door."

I obeyed, and squeezed into the tiny folding chair across from his desk. He handed me a ragged but clean white towel wrapped around a handful of ice. I pressed the towel to my upper lip, which throbbed against the cold.

The room wasn't designed for two people. I didn't actually think it was designed for one—I had a feeling that in the original floor plans, this was a janitor's closet. But here I was, close enough to Smiley to feel the waves of anger evaporating off him. I began to pull the towel away from my lip but the sticky, clotting blood resisted my effort. I winced.

Smiley sat, and the chair cushion squeaked and hissed underneath him. He crossed his arms over his chest. "What's up with you?"

"I'm sorry," I began. "Mat was…"

"Not talking about Mat. Talking about you. What's up with you?"

I didn't answer.

"All week you're coming in here exhausted and half-dead on your feet, a target for anyone with half your speed and a quarter of your concentration. Starting shit with that fool kid just now. Getting in the ring without a *mouth guard*, for crissakes."

He slapped his palms on his desk and leaned forward. "You got a death wish? You don't bring it in here. You leave it at the door. You *know* that."

I nodded. "Yes, sir."

"I got you coming in here day after day since you was a teenager. Always a stubborn pain in my behind. But now, now you're an old lady."

I glared at him. "Thank you."

"Your best boxing years, you can count more of them behind you now than ahead of you. That's a fact. So if you want to keep coming day after day, you need to be an example around here, and not act worse than when you were a crazy kid."

Chastised, I cleared my throat. "Yes, sir."

He leaned back again and scrutinized my face, or what he could see of it over the bloody towel. "You in some kind of trouble?"

I furrowed my brow. "Like what kind of trouble?"

"Don't answer a question with a question. How should I know what kind? All I know is you're acting like a mad dog. And suddenly you've got strangers coming by to see you."

Frederica and Svein.

"Don't know if I can help you," he said, "but if you got a problem, go ahead and tell me."

"There's no problem," I said around a now-numb pair of lips. "Everything's fine. I've got a few old friends in town to visit me, and we've been doing some late nights. The campaign keeps me busy with social things. Look, I'm fine. I don't need you to keep tabs on me."

"Don't tell me that now. I been keeping tabs on you since he left."

I narrowed my eyes. "No one asked you to."

"*He* did."

I held my breath for several seconds, hoping I misunderstood. "My father asked you to keep tabs on me?"

"Right before he left."

"I was a *kid*."

"You were a kid he knew would grow up to be a fighter, and he wanted you to learn here."

The cogs in my mind creaked backward, and I remembered. A guy named Jim Paolo had run afoul of me in tenth grade. The offense was too minor to recall the details but, at the time, I rewarded him with an punch that sent him sprawling. I spent unhappy time in the vice principal's office and, shortly afterward, Mom had re-introduced me to Smiley, the guy who owned the gym where my father used to go. That day, Smiley was quick to tell me that my father didn't have half the talent he thought he had. After an hour of working with me, Smiley assured me I'd be a far better student. That was all I'd needed to hear to feel like I was rebelling against my dad.

Now I wondered: had my mother been biding her time, knowing she'd eventually bring me to Smiley for years of male influence?

Did she bring me here so I could be close to Dad?

"What made him think *you* could take care of me?" I asked now.

"I think it was more of a hope," Smiley said.

"Why didn't you tell me? I've been here forever and you never *told* me?"

"What was the point? You woulda never wanted to hear it. You don't want to hear it now, even."

"Why did he go?" The words burst out of me before I could think to stop them. "Why?"

"Don't know his reasons," he said. "He didn't tell me. Wasn't like I was his best friend. But he saw the way I keep an eye on guys around here. Lonely guys, angry guys, guys with no place else to go. Guess your daddy thought I had enough experience to handle the job."

I closed my eyes for a few seconds, then reopened them. My lip throbbed hard. "Did you?"

He raised his brows. "You'd try the patience of a saint of God. You had problems, you had talent, and you had brains, and that doesn't add up to nothing but trouble."

"Must have been what he thought," I said with a half-smile to try to mask the bitterness.

"No."

Smiley rose from his chair, rolled it a few inches away, and opened the tiny freezer box on the floor. He pulled another towel off the clean pile on the wall shelf and filled it with ice chips. He held out his hand and I peeled my towel away from my face and exchanged it for the new one. He sat down and watched while I gingerly pressed it to my face, the fresher cold shocking my nerve endings.

"Bricks," he said. Then, "Gemma. I don't know why your daddy left, but I know why he didn't want to leave, and that was you. When he asked me to keep an eye on you, he was desperate, nervous, like something was coming after you and he couldn't stop it. You were the most important thing to him. He looked at you and saw himself. Hell, *I* looked at you and saw him. For a while. Now, you're all you and you've gotten this far. He's proud of you."

"And how would you know that?"

"I know what I know. Quit asking me questions. There's nothing else to say."

My emotions were mashed up together into a hard lump that sat on my chest. "Well, you waited too long to say *that* much to me," I said. "Way too long."

"Go ahead, take it out on me," he said. "I've gotten used to being the punching bag around here. But think about this. Only reason you're angry now is because you're finding out you don't got as much to be angry about as you thought all this time."

I stood and my knees banged into his desk. "Anything else?"

One corner of his lips tugged upward. "Big, bad Brickhouse," he said. "But you've got a few cracks. Yeah, we're done."

"I'll see you tomorrow." I turned and reached for the doorknob.

"No, you won't."

I slumped my shoulders and looked at the ceiling.

"Take your stuff," he said, "and don't come back for a week. And when you walk back in, I want to see you awake and alert and able to knock the crap out of the first person you see—but you won't, because you'll be under control. Are you hearing me?"

"Yeah."

"Cool out, Bricks," he said to my back. "Get some sleep. Send your friends home. Tell your boy no more late nights. Tell him my vote depends on it."

"Okay." I walked out of his office without looking back, grabbed my bag off a folding chair, and left the gym with my head down. I didn't want to make eye contact or start a conversation with anyone just then.

The afternoon was gray with ineffectual raindrops spitting down, just enough to frizz my hair, but not enough to make me regret not having an umbrella. I walked—almost stomped—for about half a block before realizing I didn't even really have a destination, so I turned back. I planned on crashing Dr. Clayton's office again and asking for an emergency tooth repair, but I couldn't do it until tomorrow afternoon, when that little boy Brian would hopefully be back and I could get a good look at him.

I'd have to give Svein a call, and—

And what?

This was ridiculous. Svein couldn't take care of me. I had asked him to be my backup when I went into Clayton's office the first time, but it was more to soothe his feelings of inadequacies and to keep my own nervousness at bay. If it came right down to it, fae Svein couldn't do a thing to defend me. He'd only be able to stand around and take notes while Clayton beat the crap out of me or set me on fire. He'd taught me all he could about using my abilities, and even still, it was an effort for me. It was going to take a lot of practice to be able to master them, even with flying out of the picture. I wasn't having any of that. Point was, Svein couldn't do anything more for me.

I trotted across the street and into Grounds Floor. I bought a chai from the same barista whom Frederica inadvertently charmed last time I was here. He did stare at me now, but it was my bruised and bloody lip that captured his attention. I took my cup and slid into a booth at the window. I watched cars, watched the rain fall heavier, drop by drop.

Turning, I noticed a powwow in the corner—lots of binders and legal pads and papers and general busyness. At the center of the executive circle was a senator—from New Jersey. I had a pretty good memory for faces and I recognized him from my polling office work. He looked very young for the age he probably had to be. He was a pillar of calm within his aides' chaos.

Fae?

I knew the fae were everywhere, in all walks of life, in all locales exotic and mundane. But this city—I had subconsciously convinced myself that we fae were a very small minority. When I thought of magic, and the Olde Way, and the idealism of the morning fae, the last place I thought of, frankly, was Washington D.C. It was so serious, so corrupt, so *real.*

But fae governing human society? Making and enforcing and upholding the laws by which we lived? That was power, and if the fae had that kind of power, why not throw humanity under the bus? Humans were the cause of the Olde Way's demise, after all.

Because they couldn't perpetrate physical violence.

But in my heart, I knew there was more to it than that. The fae remained separate and secret, but not angry or hostile. That was not the way of the morning fae.

I turned away and tried not to think about the big picture for the moment. I needed to sort out my thoughts.

I sighed.

I loved Smiley and I knew he had his reasons for making his decisions, but I was angry all the same. I wouldn't have wanted to hear about my father back then, but he still should have said something. Maybe something would have shifted in me, maybe my resentment would have faded a bit more or changed shape. Or maybe I would have been more bitter, and developed a bigger chip on my shoulder.

He's proud of you, Smiley had said.

Well, my father didn't know me anymore, but if he did, what was there to be proud of? I spoke without thinking, easily flew off the handle, and hated to compromise. And now I was lying to my boyfriend, breaking laws, manipulating people I didn't know with glamour and picking fights with the people I did know. I was running after a dentist, running from a journalist, and running out of reasons to do all of it. I was alternately ignoring and acting on my attraction to Svein, which, if I was being honest for a change, amounted to nearly cheating on the only man I'd ever loved.

Not much to be proud of, eh, Dad?

But really, why did I give a damn what he would have thought? He didn't know me anymore.

I was the one who had to live with myself the rest of my life. What should have mattered most was what *I* thought.

I sipped my chai, keeping my damaged upper lip from touching the cardboard cup, but the drink stung me anyway.

What would make me proud of myself? What would I have to do to become the person I thought I should be?

The fae instinctively trusted me. They didn't know me personally. They only knew who I was—the legendary half-breed, the warrior born to defend the Olde Way. They didn't look at me and see Gemma Cross, mixed-up basket case. They looked at me and saw Gemma Fae Cross, the one who would fight for them, the descendant of the warriors I saw—became—in my dream journey, and all the warriors whose pasts I hadn't seen.

The morning fae trusted me.

Earning that trust—that was what would make me proud of me. Fulfilling that destiny I was born for, despite my mother's efforts to hide me from it.

If I stayed on this path I chose, I knew full well that I was going to screw things up. The D.C. Digger would find me out, or Avery would, or both. Or Dr. Riley Clayton would kill me with his rubber-gloved hands. But this was what I was now, and no matter how often Svein insisted on standing by my side, I was in this alone. I needed to stick it out so I could live with myself, or die with self-absolution.

I would make myself proud. I would do this on my own, the way my *worthy* ancestors did. And if I ever saw my unworthy father again, I wouldn't be the one looking for approval. It would be him. And he wouldn't get it from me.

I drained my chai and stood, half-expecting to draw the kind of attention a hero should, but I was only a would-be hero right now, and the few customers in the room didn't glance up from their newspapers or conversations to acknowledge me.

Except for the senator from New Jersey.

He looked at me, and I looked at him.

I hoped I'd wiped all the blood off my face. But I had a feeling that he recognized me as the warrior, and that bruises and bleeding were part of what I was.

He smiled a faint smile. A smile that said, *we both have work to do.*

I wanted to smile back, to acknowledge my fellow creature. But I backed out the door and clung to it as I tore myself away from our eye lock. I tried not to run down the street.

>=<

I pushed the door open and walked into the waiting room of Dr. Clayton. I hadn't called ahead because I didn't want the receptionist to insist on an appointment at a different day and time. I needed to be there when I knew little Brian would be there, and so I walked in off the street as a tooth-chip emergency case.

Svein didn't know I was here. I had expected I would be as frightened as the first time but I was strangely calm. Maybe I was counting on Dr. Clayton not executing me during business hours. I hoped I'd get away with this today, especially with my very real tooth problem, but I knew if I entered this office after today, it would be to carry out whatever plan Svein and I would come up with to foil the toothpaste scam.

I checked my watch. 3:27.

He might suspect me as fae by now, but he had to have fae patients who were completely innocent and had no business with him except tooth care. He'd caught me leaving his lab, but I was pretty sure I'd succeeded in looking stupid enough that he wouldn't suspect I was really on to anything. And if he didn't want anyone to know he was making evil toothpaste, he should have locked the door.

What would stop Dr. Clayton from coming for me after hours?

Nothing, except I really hoped he wouldn't. Every time I thought this through and attempted to visualize the eventual outcome, I tried to fool myself that this was going to be easy, that I could smash the villain's evil plans and walk away victorious and unscathed. I had to believe that, because I'd never be able to do this if I didn't. And I had to do this.

Rebecca was parked behind the reception desk, and I approached her. "Hi, um, any chance I could get in to see Dr. Clayton today? I chipped my front tooth."

She looked up at me. I smiled, and she took in my chipped tooth. "Are you a regular patient?"

"I was just here last week."

No sign that I'd jogged her memory at all. "Oh," she said. "Name?"

As she searched in a drawer for my file, I asked, "What happened to Brenda, by the way?"

"Who?"

"Brenda, the receptionist who used to be here."

She pulled my file and glanced at it. "She retired when Dr. Gold did."

It was what I had originally surmised, but now I wondered if Rebecca was the midnight fae with whom Dr. Clayton might be working. It would be a pretty good disguise for a demon—an inattentive, humorless woman with hair so short and pale she seemed bald.

No, I remembered, Clayton had had her under his glamour spell last time. She was merely a replacement receptionist. And anyway, she wasn't physically alerting me in any way that she was fae.

The door opened behind me and Brian's family walked in, much to my relief. The little girl, Jamie, barreled through and plopped in front of the dollhouse. Brian came next, more sedate than his sister, and far more sedate than the last time I saw him. Their father brought up the rear, nudging a plodding Brian along. They took seats in the waiting room.

"Gemma?"

I turned back to Rebecca. "Is this an emergency?" she asked.

"No," I said. "It was such a nice day outside that I thought I'd come by for a visit."

She blinked. "Huh?"

I smiled widely at her. "Have a seat," she said. "I'll see if the doctor can fit you in."

I thanked her and sat in the closest chair, where I could watch the family—the only people in the waiting room besides me.

The kids' father went to speak to Rebecca. Jamie, who looked about four, sat engrossed with the dollhouse, her legs sprawled in careless-kid fashion. She floated a doll up the dollhouse stairs and placed her face down in the tiny bed. She hummed a little song that could have been a lullaby, or just her mind working out loud.

Brian watched her, uninterested. He blew out an annoyed breath and slumped further into his chair. Last week, he'd been eager to keep playing here. Today, he looked like a sullen, world-weary teenager. In a six-year-old's body.

It was the toothpaste. It had to be.

His sulky face hypnotized me until I realized with a start where I'd seen it before—the boy who'd shot up his school the other week, the one I saw on television in the gym. His picture had made every newscast, the front page of every paper.

Brian's expression was only a weak, hollow echo of the now-dead teenager's, but it was well on its way to belying a mind that was dark, dull. Dead.

I heard Dr. Clayton behind me, giving instructions to a woman who'd just had some kind of procedure.

"Brian," Jamie said from the floor. Rather than answering, he rolled his eyes and stared at the ceiling. "Briiiii-aaaaaan," she sang, pulling herself up into a crouch and rocking with impatience. She arched her neck back and projected her voice into the air as though her brother were on the opposite side of a mountain. "Briiii-aaan!"

"Brian," their father said. "Your sister's talking to you."

"I don't give a shit," Brian answered.

My eyes widened and my mouth dropped open.

"Gemma?" Dr. Clayton called.

Standing quickly, I glanced at Brian's father. The expression on his face was a combination of angry and completely baffled at this child's nonchalant and unexpected swearing. Then I looked at Brian.

He was looking straight at me, no longer indifferent but instead—scary. His lips parted to bare his tiny teeth in miniature fury. His eyes narrowed, barely containing the rage within. He pulled his legs up beneath him, and twisted his little hands into fists, coiling himself up like a snake before a deadly strike.

He was scary.

"Gemma?" Dr. Clayton repeated, his voice giving away nothing—not even a normal impatience.

Despite my undercover mission, I just couldn't help flashing a disgusted look at Dr. Riley Clayton as he ushered me into his exam room.

When I realized it, I hastily rearranged my facial features into something more resembling neutral. For his part, Clayton seemed unaffected. "Have a seat, Gemma," he said, and I sank again into the leather chair, which was starting to seem too familiar. "I didn't expect you back here so soon."

I pulled back my lips in a toothy grimace.

He pulled on rubber gloves while he leaned over me and peered into my mouth. "Ah," he said, "I see. I thought we agreed last time that you were going to duck."

I shrugged, my mind racing. The toothpaste *was* draining the innocence of the kids who used it. What were the permanent repercussions? Was that teen gunman a former patient, a good child who never had to be told to brush his teeth?

What if the kids just stopped using it? To stop using it, they'd have to no longer have access to it. And I couldn't exactly firebomb a dentist's lab and get away with it.

Open-mouthed, I stared into the face of the fae who was making it his mission to mess up kids, even kill them. Why? Some kind of vendetta against the fae? Was it personal? A political opposition to the Olde Way?

As Clayton tied a paper bib around my neck, I reminded myself that although these were all legitimate questions to ponder, they could wait until I was safe at home. In the meantime, I had to permit him to treat me with sharp instruments.

I'll be okay, I reminded myself. *There's nothing he can do to me here.*

"This is something I can certainly do right now," he said, "since I have a background in cosmetic dentistry, and the tooth chip is small. I'm going to roughen up that area a little bit, apply a primer, then use a composite that matches your tooth color..."

He continued but I was distracted with my own thoughts of his nefarious plan and my own hopes that he wasn't going to kill me in the next half-hour. I wondered how he could live with himself, and what went wrong in his life that turned him into such a hateful bastard.

"...requires no anesthetic," I heard him say, but at that moment a thought struck. Maybe he didn't even know he was doing something wrong. Maybe he was making toothpaste for kids, hoping to make a few bucks or whatever, and maybe he mixed a few lab chemicals wrong and inadvertently created a compound that sucked out innocence essence. Maybe he didn't even know it was happening. And the fact that he was fae? Well, I didn't know, but Svein hadn't provided me any concrete evidence to suggest past or present conflict between him and the rest of the fae community. I'd called Reese this morning and she had told me the spider video feed from Clayton's office was showing nothing but dental work and lab tinkering. Not so much as a maniacal cackle.

And Clayton was acting normally with me, as if I were any

other patient, which led me to believe I might be right—that he might have smoked me out as fae, but didn't connect me to any investigation into his activities.

"If it's all right with you, we can go ahead and proceed," he said, and I nodded. *I'm okay*, I thought. *I'm going to be okay. He'll fix my tooth and I'll get out of here and I'll come up with a plan.*

He scrounged around for some instruments, pulled on a pale blue surgical mask and wheeled his stool beside me again. "Open," he said, "and we'll get this all squared away. You'll be just as pretty as when you first woke up this morning."

He didn't know about me. Possibly he didn't even know about the toothpaste effects. Certainly he hadn't aligned with a hell minion.

Before he could touch my tooth, he sat up again and rolled to the countertop next to his sink to check my chart.

And I saw the spider.

It was crawling up the edge of the countertop. What the heck? Weren't these things supposed to be unobtrusive, unnoticeable? It was tiny but obvious. No wonder people squooshed them.

I looked at the spider, and wondered whether the camera was still working, and if someone was at the Root monitoring the feed and could see me now, paper-bibbed and vulnerable.

Clayton's eyes flicked to the bug.

I held my breath.

But he only watched it for a moment. As if aware it had been discovered, the spider scooted down to the floor and into a corner.

Clayton raised a brow and adjusted the surgical mark elastics behind his ears. He rolled back to his spot beside me and asked me to "open." His eyes caught mine, and held them.

He knew exactly why I was there.

I swallowed. Hard.

CHAPTER 15

I thought about bolting. I still could. I could push up the armrest and crash out of this office and run for my life.

And, I thought, I might very well regret not doing that. Because when I shoved aside my very real fear of being assaulted by his weapons of oral destruction, a small, still-sane part of my brain realized that by continuing to remain cool and calm, I could gain more helpful information that I could use to stop him—if I got out of here alive.

"Don't be nervous," Clayton said, smiling.

"Huh?"

"Don't be nervous," he repeated. "I see you clenching your jaw. This procedure isn't painful. At worst, it will just be uncomfortable."

I nodded, hoping he was referring only to the tooth bonding.

He worked, scraping and smoothing, spraying and rinsing, and I began to lose track of time. With each minute, the edge to my alertness became sharper. He hummed as he worked.

He was biding his time.

Eventually, he said, "I'm going to apply the composite now," and I heard Rebecca's voice behind me. "Dr. Clayton, I'm just going to catch up on some accounts payable. Denise just left and

Gemma's the last. Let me know if you need anything."

"Go on home," Clayton said. "Paperwork can wait. Take a walk. It's a nice afternoon."

"I don't know. I really should stay. There's still a lot to do."

Clayton looked up at her. "Go on, I insist," he said, and when Rebecca stammered, "Oh, um, yes, okay," I knew he'd turned on the glamour.

"Don't worry about anything. When I'm done with Gemma," he said, "I'll close up shop."

Crap. Oh, crap.

"Bye, doctor," she said, but her footsteps didn't retreat, and I knew she was lingering in the doorway, hoping for a smile, a secret wink, anything, but he'd already turned his attention back to my open mouth. The silver rings around his pupils dissolved. "Goodbye, Rebecca."

The handle of whatever instrument he used next pressed into my upper lip, and I tried not to wince as the still bruised and torn skin throbbed.

"So," he said conversationally, his voice muffled from behind his mask, "I'm going to be on TV this week."

I wasn't exactly in a position to answer, but I would have said, *TV?*

"I created a toothpaste," he said, and though I couldn't see his smile, I heard it. "I wanted to come up with a special toothpaste that kids who still have baby teeth would love. I see a lot of kids whose teeth are just not healthy. Parents try to get their kids to brush, but they don't try hard enough, or kids fake them out by rinsing. They can only do so much, right? They're human."

"Ow," I said, as metal hit my fragile lip again.

"I'm sorry, Gemma," he said. He paused for a moment and squinted at his work on my tooth, but he soon spoke again. "There are a lot of toothpaste brands out there, but I wanted to mix it up a little, see if I could come up with a formula that would make kids *look forward* to brushing their teeth." He chuckled. "I'll tell you, I came up with some duds, but I kept at it because by that time, I realized this was something I *had* to do. You understand."

His voice was even and conversational, as if I were a morning show host and he was telling his success story to a studio audience.

"And I did it. I came up with this terrific combination of flavors—with a secret ingredient tossed in—and Smile Wide was born. Can I get you to tilt your chin up just a tiny bit?"

Shifting in my seat, I complied. I was a captive audience, literally and otherwise.

"After I got FDA approval," Clayton continued, "I started giving it out to kids in goody bags, and the kids loved it. I mean, they loved it. Parents started asking me for more samples, telling me I should get it in chain stores, or start selling online. I realized they were right. I mean, my patients were having such success with it, so why shouldn't I think even bigger?"

My subconscious managed to notice that the hinges of my jaw were starting to ache, but I couldn't move for fear of interrupting his story. And maybe also for fear that he would jab something in my eye.

"The more I thought about it," he said, "the more I realized I just *had* to do this. You understand."

Um.

"So I contacted TV-Spree. You've heard of them, haven't you?"

TV-Spree was a national home-shopping station based in D.C. It sprang into being only a couple of years ago, but it was now one of the big ones. The last time I had channel-surfed, I found TV-Spree selling self-cleaning toasters. I paused a moment, watching the number counter ding higher and higher as thousands leaped on the chance to update their kitchens with an appliance they suddenly couldn't live without.

"I pitched the toothpaste to them," Clayton said. "They don't have any other products to compete with it, and a few executives took it home. When their kids refused to go back to their old toothpaste, they signed me on. So if you tune in, you can see me on TV. I'm going to expose your tooth to a curing light so this can set, okay?"

He rolled away from me and left the room. I stared at the ceiling, trying to process what he'd just told me. TV-Spree meant millions of people. Millions. I saw, in my mind's eye, the TV number counter going up and up and up. I saw mountains of brown cardboard boxes filled with orders being loaded onto idling trucks. Then I saw Juliette, my little Cindy Lou Who, eagerly holding out a pink toothbrush for her mother to squeeze on a blob of Smile Wide.

I clenched my hands into fists, and my back itched and burned and quivered violently. No, no, breathe and—oh, the hell with it. I sat up, pushed the table of instruments away from my lap and swung my legs over to the side.

"Good idea, go ahead and stretch your legs," Clayton said as he returned holding something that looked disturbingly like a ray gun. "That chair's not the most comfortable thing. It's particularly hard on the back."

My back was shaking so hard, my shoulders hunched up. Anticipating a confrontation, I'd practiced all morning with wing control. I was much better now than I was when they burst out at the fundraiser, but this anger, laced with sticky fear, was so potent that I had to let it out somehow, and the vehicle I went with was my mouth. "I know what you're doing," I said.

"Good," he said. "Then you know this will beep every ten seconds. When you hear it beep four times, we'll be done. Sit down and you'll be out of here before you know it."

"That's not what I meant," I said. "I know what you're doing with the toothpaste, and what you're doing to kids' teeth. I *know*."

"This is forty seconds of light," he said. "Almost done."

I sat. It was insane, but I did. If he assaulted me, I could fight back, because I'd expect it.

He leaned over me and the machine went *beep*.

Beep.

Beep.

Beep.

Clayton squinted and rubbed at the tooth one last time. "That," he said, "is good work."

He handed me a mirror, but I didn't even need to look. He was right.

Then I dropped the mirror in my lap. "I know," I repeated.

"And I know," he said, rolling his chair back and resting an elbow on his countertop, "that you were sent to stop me." He peeled off his gloves and tossed them into the wastebasket. One caught on the rim and hung there. "The fabled and supposedly rare half-breed, right in front of me."

"Listen," I said. "This is harming kids. I can't imagine what your reasons are to interfere with the Olde Way mission, but you're taking innocence away from kids."

"I knew they would send you to stop me," he said.

I pushed the armrest up and stood over him for a bit of advantage, but he continued as if I were a no bigger threat than a squashable spider. "I tried to get to you first."

"What?"

"I knew you'd come, so I came up with all different ways to stop *you*," he said. "I had a list of plans and defensive schemes to keep you from ruining what I was doing. In fact, when I decided to switch offices, I came here, where you were a patient, so I would have you in plain sight. But I didn't have to do anything."

He stood and leaned into me. I willed myself not to move. "Because," he said, "you're too late."

I hissed in a breath.

"Maybe it took them a while to find you?" he asked, smiling gently. "The morning fae always do find who they're looking for. They're an incredible network of resourceful beings. But I kept a low profile, and it took them just as long to find *me*, and now I'm sorry to say you're just too late."

"I'm here now," I said, and set my jaw.

"And what are you going to do?" he asked. "Smile Wide is being mass manufactured and shipped to TV-Spree warehouses all over this country. On Monday night, I'll be making my television debut. With express overnight shipping, kids all over the country will be using Smile Wide before bedtime Tuesday. It's a done deal, Gemma."

My gaze darted around the room, as if anything in here could prove him wrong.

"Kids, their innocence doesn't last very long anyway," he said, his tone as soothing as if he were talking to a fussy toddler. "No big deal."

"That's why they deserve to keep their innocence!" I cried. "Because it doesn't last long."

"So what?" Clayton took a step toward me. "I lost mine earlier than I should have. I turned out okay."

"This is okay?"

"Wouldn't you say *you* turned out okay?"

"What do you mean by that?"

He stood and turned on the faucet to wash his hands. I watched every move he made. I'd trained for years on how to watch an opponent, every twitch and every blink.

As he dried his hands, he asked, "How's your dad?"

My breathing stopped.

"Oh," he said. "I'm sorry, I forgot. He left when you were what? Seven? Eight? Must have been a real innocence-killer for you."

He smiled. "Are you coming after me for all those children who won't even miss what they'll lose? Or are you coming after me so you can reconcile with yourself that your own innocence was lost too soon?"

His words crawled under my skin like roaches and made me want to scream and tear them off me. I wanted to hit him hard, do damage that I didn't even think I was capable of. I didn't know how he knew anything about me, and I wanted to demand answers. But I steeled myself. It was an inner struggle against my nature to instinctively act, but I won. He didn't deserve to see how deep he'd cut. "You're a threat to the Olde Way," I said, willing the muscles in my face to not betray me. "It's my job to take care of it."

"I'll have Rebecca bill you," he said. "Your tooth might be sensitive to heat and cold for a couple of weeks, and I wouldn't go tearing into any hard foods for a while. Just use the teeth on the side."

"Do you think I'll just go away forever?" I asked. "This *isn't* done."

"Go home," he said. "Go home to your mother so she's not lonely."

I didn't think about it. I just swung. I leaned into the punch and my fist crashed into his jaw. He doubled over, then the power of his wing burst pulled him upright. Momentarily transfixed by his change, I was startled when he grabbed the neck of my T-shirt, pushed me into the wall and held me there, his face close to mine.

"Gemma," he whispered, "I'm a fair man. You aren't my problem. You can't help who you are or where you came from any more than I can, and you and I are *exactly* the same."

"I'm nothing like you," I spat. I felt my wingtips break from my back and shove hard against the wall, desperate to open, but Clayton had me pinned so tight that they jammed up, stretching the open flesh of my back. I was being crushed from the front and the back, like I was in a panini press. His white coat had risen to accommodate his wings, which had torn through the shirt underneath.

"This isn't between you and me," he said in that same whisper.

"If not you," I asked, "then who? Your midnight fae hell spawn pals?"

He furrowed his brow, bemused for a moment, but he tightened his grip even more on me as he did so. My toes lifted off the floor. Then he laughed. "Is that what your stupid fool fae think? That I'm a *demon*?" He laughed harder, but didn't loosen his hold.

"They haven't figured me out at all. I guarantee you, Gemma, I work alone. I wouldn't be surprised, though, if the dark fae decide to pick up where I leave off. Go home."

I lifted my closed fist but he slammed it against the wall next to my head, my knuckles clacking hard. He held my wrist there. His strength was indomitable. If he backed off, allowed my wings to emerge, I would have my own power. I had learned from Svein that body strength nearly doubled when winged. I would equal Clayton. But he didn't let me go, and I remained trapped and squirming.

"You had all this time, your whole life," he said. "You had your chance."

Then before I could hiss a vitriolic reply, he punched me hard in the gut. I was a boxer, and I knew how to steel my stomach, but his supernatural strength brought hot tears to my eyes. He dropped me and I collapsed on the floor, clutching at myself, breathing hard and ragged. My back quickly sealed over.

"Get out," he said. "And don't come back until it's time for your six-month cleaning."

I crawled toward the doorway and hoisted myself up. My air was coming shallow, from my chest, because if I ventured to draw in a deeper breath, it would send me smashing back to the floor in agony.

When I was in the waiting room, I paused to lean on the reception desk, slowly trying to straighten up enough to walk out the front door.

I stumbled out and gulped in the fresh air so hard, I choked. I coughed twice and the spasms tightened my brutalized muscles. I wrapped an arm around myself. I wanted to sit somewhere and not move. But I didn't want the good dentist to find me still here when he left for home.

A sheet of *Washington Post* blew up the street and wrapped itself around my calves. I was grateful—pulling the paper off me would allow me an excuse to double over without necessarily looking like I was battling ripping pain. I bent my knees to drop a hand closer to my lower legs, and pinched a corner of the damp paper. I was about to release it back into the D.C. wind when I saw it.

A black-and-white, crinkled mug shot. There were words too, but I didn't have the mental wherewithal to string them together properly: arrest, arson, damage, one woman dead. Trey Sawyer stared up at me.

I gasped, and it hurt.

From Trey's eyes, the child school shooter stared up at me. From Trey's eyes, little Brian stared up at me.

In that cold, dead gaze, dark fae stared up at me.

CHAPTER 16

The bakery was closed when I arrived, so I flipped through my key ring to find the right one. I let myself in and locked it behind me, and walked, wincing, with one arm around my torso.

Licking two fingers and placing them on the iron wings, I opened the door that materialized.

When I got to the bottom of the stairs, I turned right and wandered down the corridor, squinting into dark-windowed doors, until one opened and a fae guy came out. He stopped short when he saw me, then approached me.

"Gemma," he said, alarmed at my hunched-over posture. "Do you need help?"

At this moment, I wasn't creeped out by the fact that I was an instantly recognizable fae star. Instead, I was relieved to have found a friendly face. "Is there a bathroom?" I asked.

"Of course. Follow me."

I walked behind him down one hallway, then we turned right and headed down one more. The hallways and doors were dark but not a scary, abandoned dark—it was the companionable, familiar dark of a room where kids are playing hide and seek.

Each of our footsteps seemed to echo with distant music. The music and magic of a fae house.

The man stopped in front of a door and opened it a crack, flipping on a light. "Let me or anyone here know if there's anything we can do."

"I'll be fine," I assured him. "It's nothing that ibuprofen and some water can't fix."

"Try a hot bath," he suggested, and left me to my privacy.

Flipping the light on, I widened my eyes. I'd been expecting a kind of bunker bathroom, strictly utility. But this was a four-star luxury. A bathtub with whirlpool jets gleamed invitingly. A plush white bath mat lay beside it, and when I flipped a switch on another wall, red heat lamps came to life overhead. Wooden racks offered soft pink towels. A gold-edged mirror reflected my pale face back at me.

I'd almost gone straight home but I didn't want to risk running into Avery. A bad day at the gym would explain this to him, but I didn't feel like lying again. A safe house by its very name had seemed like the best place to go.

I rummaged behind the bathroom mirror, finding lots of shampoos and body lotions and mouthwashes until I located some single-dose packets of ibuprofens.

"Take two for temporary relief of headache, cramps, muscle aches"—yep—"and toothache." Oh, the irony.

I swallowed two tablets back with some water, then after a moment's hesitation, ripped open a second packet and tossed back one more pill. The dosage instructions didn't include "relief of pain from crazed winged superhuman beating the shit out of you," but I considered this self-prescribed off-label use. I doubted it would help.

Crumpling the Dixie cup and leaning against the sink, I breathed in and out through my nose. I thought it might be a good idea to hang around near the toilet until my nausea passed.

I bared my teeth in the mirror, ran my tongue around the

previously damaged, now-perfect one. Damn. He *was* a good dentist.

What had Svein said to me? Living in this day and age, my fight would naturally be different than those who came before. Less bloody, less romantic. But modern-day technology and industry offered an enormous base for Clayton's poison. TV-Spree coupled with inevitable online ordering suddenly made Clayton possibly the fae's most dangerous, most far-reaching essence adversary of all time.

Well, at least I'd cemented my place in morning fae folklore. I sincerely hoped it wasn't the tale of my violent death that kept my descendants riveted.

My Fae Phone vibrated, and I fished it out of my khaki cargo pants pocket. "Hello?" I said, but the buzzing continued to tickle my other hip. I threw the Fae Phone onto the bath rug and pulled out my regular cell. This was ridiculous. As a warrior of historical legend, I should have had, at the very least, merited a personal assistant to deal with this crap while I was busy getting smacked around. "Hello?"

"Got anything for me?"

I let out a breath. Great. Here came the two of the one-two, and I stood right in its way.

"No," I said. "How the hell did you get my cell phone number?"

"I'm just good," Greg Mahoney said into my ear, his voice cracking on the suave word choice.

Along with the bile, I tasted fear in my mouth. I still didn't know what or how much Mahoney knew about me. "Well, to answer your question, the only thing I've 'got' for you is a hang-up."

"Why won't you work with me?" he coaxed.

"What makes you think I have any information about anything? I don't even have a job right now. I'm the least interesting person you ever met."

"You know what I'm looking for," he said. "You know what I'm after. We can break the story together," he added in a rush. "If you want to share the spotlight, I'm willing to consider it, work out a deal. But if you don't want to go public, at least give me whatever evidence you've got so I can."

He kept asking the same thing. *Tell me something, give me something, talk to me.* He was on to me, but not completely. What piece was he missing?

"For the last time," I said, "I don't know what you're talking about, weirdo. Leave me alone and go away."

"Give me something." Mahoney's voice turned hard and angry, as if *I* were the instigator in this back-and-forth. "Give me something or I'll find something on McCormack, I swear. I'll be in touch."

He hung up, and I threw the phone down hard. It bounced off the other one on the floor. Then I screamed as loud as I could.

Hot pain in my back overpowered the sharp pain in front, and my wings burst out, hitting and dropping a framed watercolor of peaceful lilacs.

I'd already removed my shirt to assess my deranged-dentist damage, so at least I didn't ruin another shirt. I stepped into the dry tub, and lowered myself onto the cold porcelain. I leaned over with a groan, grabbed the Fae Phone off the floor, and pressed a few buttons.

"Nilsen."

I didn't bother with niceties. Not that we ever exchanged any. "What did you get on Greg Mahoney?"

"Who wants to know?"

"Listen," I said, "I've not had a good day."

"What happened?"

"Some other time. Right now, I need to know what you learned about him."

Svein paused, and I was about to scream a second time when I realized he hadn't hung up. I heard him shuffling papers. "Greg Mahoney is the D.C. Digger."

"Old news."

"Home schooled until eighteen, Boston University grad, bookkeeping day job. He doesn't live far from you. He's over by Rosslyn station. He does his writing from home, but he takes to the streets to find his dirt. He's got regular hangouts. Bars popular with politicians, fundraisers, press conferences. He goes out walking at night to smoke and walk his dog. And he's spent more than one late night in the past week watching your building."

"Are you kidding?"

"If you weren't already off the collection rotation," Svein said, "I'd have recommended it after finding that out. Political blog or not, I'm pretty sure it's not Avery he's watching for at one a.m."

"He knows *something* about me. He told me at the fundraiser that he saw me with a tooth." I paused. My heartbeat was slowing, as rationalization and reason took over to calm me. "He called me."

"Just now?"

"Yes."

"What did he say?"

"The same. I didn't let on that I had any idea what he was talking about. Then when he realized I wasn't caving, he threatened again to slander Avery and hung up on me."

"He's certainly charming," Svein observed. "Online and in person."

"I just can't figure out why he hasn't confronted me directly. Blackmailed *me*. Why say, 'tell me something and I won't go after Avery' when he could instead say, 'tell me you're a tooth faerie and I won't expose your sparkly ass'?"

"Because the D.C. Digger hasn't dug up the full story. I'm sure when he's got it, he will."

"You know," I said, "Avery caused me to rethink my previously cynical view of politicians. But I haven't met a journalist yet that I liked."

"Ditto."

Something quickly occurred to me, and I couldn't believe I didn't remember it sooner. "I couldn't glamour him."

"Who?" Svein asked.

"Mahoney," I said. "That night at the fundraiser. I glamoured everyone at the party. But it didn't affect him at all."

"Interesting," Svein said, and he did sound like he thought it was.

I sighed. I wished the tub was filled with warm water, but it seemed too much effort to lean over and turn on the water. I propped one elbow on the tub rim and dropped my forehead into my hand. "Listen," I said. "I have something that I think is actually something."

"I'm listening."

"You know that school shooting not too long ago?"

"Right."

"There's a kid who was just in the paper for arson and a bunch of other stuff. Trey Sawyer. Can you find out if those two kids went to the same dentist when they were of tooth-losing age?"

"You're kidding," Svein said, but I didn't need to say I wasn't. "That would mean Clayton's been at this a while."

"And that the kids are getting more and more messed up as they grow up. This is more than losing innocence early and missing out on a nicer childhood. You saw Trey in the gym the other day. He got kicked out of the gym the other day for acting violent."

"That would mean whatever's in that toothpaste is having long-term effects."

"Or..." I thought about Trey's cold, dark fae eyes. I refused to say that out loud because I hoped I wasn't right.

"Or what?" Svein asked.

"Nothing. But could you find out?"

"Yes, but that would be quite the coincidence," Svein said. "Every kid in this city can't be going to this dentist."

"I could be wrong."

"Probably, but I'll look into it," he said, sounding unconvinced. Again, I hoped his skepticism was justified.

"So," I said. "What was Mahoney's address again?"

"I didn't give it to you."

"Really? I'm sure you did," I said. I stretched both legs out in front of me.

"No. Why would I?"

"Why wouldn't you?"

"I'll give it to you," he offered, "if you'll agree to one very short flying lesson."

"No."

"Well, then…"

"Well, then, *nothing*," I said. "Look. I have a job to do and I don't need your permission or your trust to do it. I could find Mahoney myself but let's not waste time. Just fork over the address."

He sighed. "Don't do anything stupid."

I decided to not bring up the events of my day so far. I *would* tell him. Later.

When I disconnected, I had the information I needed.

My wings retracted, so I lay back against the puffy bath spa pillow and thought about what I had to do next.

I leaned over one more time, dropping the Fae Phone and picking up my regular cell phone again. This technology was out of control. Couldn't anything be normal anymore?

"Hi," I said when my mother answered. "I think I might have met a blast from your past. Do you know anything about a man named Riley Clayton?"

Her intake of breath, then silence, was all the confirmation I needed.

I arranged to meet her in the morning at a bistro near the museum, then hung up. I'd invite Svein and Frederica to sit in on that summit as well. I felt like the answers were out of reach. Together, maybe we could clear some of the dust. I chucked the phone on the floor and lay back again.

But I needed something now. After what had just happened with Clayton, I was afraid that if I just gave up and went to bed tonight, I would wake up with a changed mind, ready to get out of this whole thing. For that to not happen, I needed to end this day in control, with some kind of victory.

I turned on the water jets and waited both for the tub to fill up and for the pain reliever to work.

I'd just gotten beaten up by a big bully. So I was about to do what any attacked kid in a playground would do to save face—find someone smaller than me, and become *his* bully.

Greg Mahoney, I thought, *hand over your lunch money.*

Or I'll knock your teeth out.

>=<

Lingering among the trees lining the huge parking lot and monitoring the brick apartment complex, I thought about how very little time it had taken for me to transform from a law-abiding citizen to a person with an undocumented record of assault and battery, breaking and entering, petty larceny, loitering and stalking.

Should I have waited until the next workday? Yes. Because then I could get in there knowing for sure Mahoney wasn't home. But I was dead set on tonight. I knew what I was up against on one side with Clayton. I needed to know, right now, what I was up against on the other side. Besides, every day that Greg Mahoney was left alone at his computer was a day he drew another bull's eye on a politician's back.

As twilight darkened, I thought, *I've got Avery's back.*

Well, the only way to tell if Mahoney was in his hideaway was to lure him out. I pulled out my cell, and scrolled on the screen to find the last number that called me. I would tell him to meet me somewhere with a promise I would talk. Of course, when he got there and realized I'd stood him up he'd be pissed, but it wasn't as if he wasn't already after me. If he really had anything scandalous on me or Avery, I was quite sure he'd have published it by now. He was slick, but shock journalists like him didn't tend to sit on a story they could verify, however tenuous the source.

I was mentally rehearsing my invitation when the front door to the right apartment tower opened and Mahoney stepped out. He paused, looking into the distance, and I pulled in tighter behind the tree. My gut ached and I cursed the pharmaceutical company for their inferior over-the-counter pain reliever, but I kept my eyes tracking Mahoney. He was wearing a long-sleeved gray T-shirt, jeans with ripped shreds at the knees, and thick-soled black shoes. From this distance, he looked almost cool. It was probably just his nemesis status that made him so, because the first time I saw him he just looked like a dweeb.

He pulled out a pack of cigarettes, lit one, puffed a few times, shoved his hands in his pockets, and took off down the street.

Well, I was due a little luck, and here it was. I waited until he rounded the corner before I jogged to the door. It was open, and I slipped into the vestibule with three long rows of mailboxes. I already knew his apartment number, and thankfully it was on the first floor because cardiovascular step exercise was not high on my list of things I wanted to do right now. After a quick glance around to make sure I was alone, I intended and walked through the main door.

I turned right and traversed the carpeted hallway, passing a few doors. I smelled simmering tomato sauce and I heard a woman yelling at someone who clearly had no inclination to yell back. Maybe she was on the phone.

When I reached apartment A-16, I nearly stepped through the door when I stopped myself short. Presumptuous, was I not? Mahoney could have a roommate, or more than one. Or a woman masochistic enough to be his girlfriend. Either way, someone could be in there, waiting for him to return.

I closed my eyes, and watched for gray shadows pulsing, indicating breathing life.

Nothing. Blank.

I hesitated again, but I summoned up the courage of my

ancestor warrior fearlessly entering the home of her enemy. I opened my eyes.

I stepped through the closed door.

And a bomb hurled itself onto me.

A furry, spotted beagle bomb.

Barking, barking, barking.

Learn a new thing every day, I thought. Seemed the shadow trick was only to detect humans. I intended, and blinked into formlessness. He kept barking, jumping around me, wiggling his tail, stepping on my toes. I wasn't fooling him. He saw me; he wanted to play with me. Animals must have fallen into the category of those who could see me—the innocent.

So I bent down and stroked his head. He stopped barking, and instead panted happily. I crouched and rubbed both his sides vigorously and he fell on me in ecstasy, licking my hand. I reached for the tag on his collar and turned it over to find Mahoney's phone number and the dog's name. "Canine."

As in dog. Or, I supposed, as in canine teeth. Maybe I'd find a hamster named Molar.

Having become Canine's best friend in less than fifteen seconds, I took a look around. The living room was nothing special. Standard beige apartment rug. Affordable couch. Cheap, self-assembled coffee table.

Keeping up my blinking, and with Canine trotting after me, I moved past a bathroom—very male, with shaving cream and a bath mat and little else—and entered Mahoney's bedroom.

D.C. Digger Central.

The computer was humming with several different windows open: news sites, blog sites, weather. A Word document was minimized on the screen—probably his current Digger draft. Two televisions sat side by side on an arm's-reach shelf, one turned to CNN and the other to the baseball game (Nationals up by four). An iPod cooked in its charger on the desk. A pack of matches sat in a glass ashtray. An oscillating fan blew dusty air around my head. Books and newspapers were open and scattered all over every surface of the tiny room.

Mahoney had created his own Situation Room. He was a current events junkie. He was plugged in.

I instantly realized two things about him. One, with all his equipment on, he wasn't planning on being gone long.

And two, he knew full well about tooth faeries. *Fae.*

Over his bed, on the wall, were sketches. Dozens of sketches, in charcoals and colored pencils, of faeries.

Or, I noticed, inching closer, one fae. Drawn over and over and over.

Lithe and toned, she wore a halter top—a red one, I realized from the color pictures. Her jeans were skintight and encircled with an embroidered belt. Her feathered black hair fell around her neck, and her eyes were wide and blue. A stack of gold bangle bracelets ran halfway to one elbow.

Her wings were blown out behind her, large and—if my personal experience was what I went by—realistic. He'd drawn them delicately, with fine lines.

Each picture caught her from a different angle: head on, from the back—wings blooming out the skin left bare by the halter top—and from each side. But from every angle, she was looking at me—in distress. And in every angle, her hand was outstretched, holding a small, white tooth.

She wasn't the product of an idle mind, or a fantastical one. She didn't have comical, golden round breastplates, and she didn't have the creepy eyes of manga heroines. This fae wasn't an exploration of the imagination.

She was a memory, rendered over and over again.

A few of the pictures were fresh and crisp, but most of the paper was yellowing and curled. I didn't know who she was, and I knew I was looking at trouble, but I couldn't help my relief that this fae's face was most definitely not mine.

I scanned rows and rows of bookshelves, finding classic

literature, political history books, a big book of notorious newspaper headlines—and many, many books about faeries: faerie tales, faerie folklore, faerie art.

Turning back to his computer, I noticed it had fallen into screensaver mode: a strange geometric swirl of primary colors. I wanted to look through his files, but I'd never put much faith in the validity of the TV and movie spies who sat down at the enemy's personal computer, tapped a few keys, discovered the blueprint to destroy the world, downloaded it and ran off. I'd never be able to pull it off; it had taken me at least ten minutes to figure out how to play online sudoku a month ago. Besides, I didn't want to touch a thing in this apartment. I didn't put it past Mahoney to have a cereal prize spy kit lying around with fingerprint-dusting materials.

It wasn't necessary, anyway. I had some answers.

I bent and rubbed Canine's head again. "Thanks for the tour," I whispered. "I gotta go."

And I would have, the same way I came in, if I didn't hear Mahoney's key in the lock.

The front door creaked open and Canine sped off to greet his human, barking with crazed joy.

I stood, frozen, as Mahoney chuckled. "Honey, I'm home," he said to his pet. "You always act like you thought I left forever. It was just a smoke. Okay, maybe more like three."

His heavy shoes approached and my heart throbbed in my pained body. He detoured into his bathroom, leaving me a moment to remember what I was, and that I could get out of here.

Breathe. Breathe and accept. Relax.

Now, blink.

I intended, and edged toward the bedroom door. I didn't need to hold my breath when Mahoney entered the room, almost touching where I should have been, but I did anyway.

He clunked in and fell into his desk chair, kicking his shoes off and away from him. He glanced at the game and jiggled his computer mouse.

Canine tore into the room and stopped in front of me. He wagged his tail, awaiting a pat, and not getting one, he offered one short bark. Then another, and another, and he jumped around me, trying desperately to command the attention of his new friend. He looked back over his doggie shoulder once at Mahoney—*don't you see her?* he seemed to say—then yapped at me some more.

Mahoney looked at me.

My blood stopped running for a few painful seconds before I realized he was actually looking through me. I chanced lifting a hand to be certain I was blinking but my movement made Mahoney start. I was a trick of the light.

I backed against the wall and the window behind me. I didn't know if I could go through brick. Or glass. But I didn't know that I couldn't.

Canine continued to bark, and Mahoney stilled him with a hand on his collar. "Are you here?" Mahoney asked the air I was in. "Are you?"

He couldn't be crazy, because I *was* there, but I wasn't who he thought I was. Was I?

"I'm still looking for you," he said.

A shiver ran through my transparent being.

"It's not just me anymore," he added. "I found someone else. She's looking too. I'm not the only one anymore." He stood, his chair scraping the hardwood floor. "Let me see you again. It's okay, it really is."

Mahoney's gentle, respectful, almost reverent tone disconcerted me, and I was suddenly afraid my mixed emotions would erase my cloak, give me away.

"Please," he said.

I stepped back, and fell out onto a small patch of grass under his bedroom window. I stayed blinking as I pressed myself to the brick building, edged toward the parking lot, then ran.

⋙

Nodding at the Root desk operators in the monitoring room, I weaved in and out of desk space until I found Reese staring at her screen.

"Gemma!" she said, standing and giving me an enthusiastic hug. Her arms barely made it around me. I felt, as always with her and Frederica, like the Un-incredible Hulk. I tried not to gasp as she pressed against my banged-up midsection. "I haven't talked to you since the night you were on assignment," she said.

"I owe you dinner for that," I told her. "More like dinner every night for a month. You saved my life."

"You would have figured it out," she said modestly.

"Uh, no," I said. "But thanks for your blind, unwavering faith."

"You can count on me."

"Svein around?"

"He came in with his duffel bag, so try gym one or two. Down past the Butterfly Room. I'll show you."

"It's okay, I'll find it," I said. She might have insisted on the walk, but she turned and touched the screen I hadn't realized was behind her and suddenly called out, "I've got one!"

The supervisor headed over, and I squeezed Reese's shoulder before going in search of Svein, leaving the squeal of the newly found spider signal.

I peered into gym one, where a couple of men and one woman were working weight machines. And indeed, in gym two I found Svein, wearing sweatpants and not much else. The room was Spartan—mostly rubber-mat flooring. I slipped in and sat on the floor next to the door and watched him as he moved in intricate patterns around the room, punching and kicking the air. He was sweating, but his movements weren't accompanied by the determined grunts of Smiley's guys. His fists cut the air—powerful, but relaxed and graceful. He lunged and blocked, and his bare feet never slipped. I imagined his mind must have been calm white because his muscles instinctively knew where to go without hesitation, and I was mesmerized by the beauty of the human body in fight.

Or maybe by his particular bare-chested human body in fight, a trickle of perspiration running down the center to his navel. His arms were carved by his art, and his stomach was tight. He could take a hit, and doubtless he could throw one, but only in the purest form of sport. Not in a bar fight, or a street fight, or a fae fight.

My own stomach throbbed and I realized I should have been taking some more painkillers right about now.

Svein saw me as he moved around the room, but I stretched out my legs and relaxed, willing to wait, respecting his work.

When he was done, he walked over to me. I had to really try not to stare below his neck. I'd seen a lot of athletic men in prime shape who were shirtless. But with Svein, there was a magnetic pull that I had to brace my feet on the floor to resist.

If he was surprised to see me, he didn't let on. "I'm impressed," I told him, echoing his criticism of me at Smiley's. "Though not as impressed as your bravado had led me to believe I'd be."

"*Touche*," he said.

"Didn't expect The Root to have fitness facilities."

"Employee benefits."

"Ah," I said, nodding. "I should have known. This is a massive culture, a massive operation. What were you doing?"

"Taekwondo *poomse*. Forms," he clarified.

"Nice."

"You should try it. Martial arts would be good training for you."

"I'm lacking in grace," I said, "in case you haven't noticed."

"I've noticed quite a bit."

I ignored his implication, which was easier than it could have been since I *had* come here for a reason. "Mahoney saw a fae, a tooth collector," I said, "and he's trying to find her."

Svein sat down on the floor in front of me and leaned back on his forearms. "Before you explain what you know, would you mind explaining how you know?"

"I went to his place."

"Uninvited, I assume."

"He might have invited me in," I said, "had he been there."

He sighed and leaned over on one arm so he could rub his eyes with his other hand. "Now, who's doing whose job?" he asked. "You need to let me do this kind of thing."

"You would have just done the same thing I did. Besides, I wanted to do it myself. He pissed me off."

"All the more reason," he said.

"For your information, I was Miss Calm, Cool and Collected. Until he came home."

He closed his eyes and didn't open them.

"He's got pictures," I said. "Drawings of a tooth faerie. One very specific tooth faerie. I don't know when or how, but he saw her, and it was a long time ago."

"Only children too young to have a fully developed memory can see us," he said, opening his eyes again and leaning forward, crossing his arms on his knees. "How could he remember?"

"I don't know, but he did, and does, and he's still looking for her. In the pictures, she had wings, and her hair and clothes were kind of 1980s."

"He was born in 1980," Svein said. "I remember that from the file."

"Huh," I said. "I thought he was much younger than me."

"Even you must realize how intimidating you are to the average man, human or fae."

"I don't intimidate you."

"I'm not average."

No argument there. "Well, Mahoney saw a damn fae," I said, "and he's still looking for her. Judging by the literature in his den of iniquity, he's as obsessed with fae as with politicians, if not more. He wants to find her, and show the world the tooth faeries exist."

"The tooth *faerie*," Svein corrected me. "The folklore in this country is that there's one Santa Claus, one Easter bunny, and one tooth faerie. I'm betting he thinks the one he saw is *the* one."

"Still doesn't explain how he was able to see her at all. What can we get from his background? Can I see his file?"

"I remember most of it," Svein said. "I only did it recently and there wasn't much on his childhood. He was an only child, like you. Two parents, average home. We caught all his teeth. He must have seen the faerie at his home, as nearly impossible as that is."

"Maybe she wasn't blinking. Maybe she was careless and screwed up. Should we look her up, pay her a visit and ask her?"

"I don't see the point," Svein said. "Fae are supposed to report in when they've been compromised, and they would, because the greater good is more important than one fae's screw-up. It isn't in his collection file, and frankly, if it was, it would make his file a historical one. There hasn't been a time in recent history that any of us have been seen. We're well trained and our abilities are natural—more natural than yours, since you're half fae. It would have been as instinctive as breathing for the fae to have been blinking at little Mahoney's home that night."

"Yet he was old enough to lose a tooth, so his memory was developed, and he shouldn't have seen her," I said. "Unless..."

"What?"

"Didn't you tell me he was home schooled?"

"So?"

"So he wasn't out in the world with his peers as early as other kids. So maybe he stayed innocent...just a little longer than other kids."

"And he saw her," Svein said, nodding. "And he could remember her."

I thought again of Cindy Lou Who. Little Juliette's parents probably assured her she'd seen only a dream and she had believed them, the thin memory of me dissolving into her vast imagination. "I wonder who he told," I said. "I wonder who told him he was crazy, told him to stop making things up. But he held on to his conviction."

"This might also explain why you can't glamour him," Svein said. "He saw a fae when not only was he old enough to see her in the first place, but old enough to recognize her as a faerie of some kind. Sounds like after seeing her face in person, he's immune to glamour."

"Like if you're exposed to mononucleosis early, and you develop immunity," I said. "Which would have been nice for me. Having mono sucked."

"The question is," Svein said, "how are you in the picture?"

"He saw me that night at Watergate. I dropped a tooth and he saw it. He thinks I'm him. He thinks I'm a fellow hunter, that I saw a faerie also as a child. He thinks I'm closer than he is to the answer." *Give me something, tell me something.*

"That puts you in the clear," Svein said, standing. "Excellent work. Now we can go back to dealing with Dr. Clayton full time and put the D.C. Digger behind us."

"How can I?" I looked up at him. "He's after Avery."

"Is there something on Avery to find?"

I didn't like his tone. Not one bit. "Absolutely not."

"Then you've got nothing to worry about."

"But Avery's father was a good politician too, a good man, and the media tore him apart on something he had nothing to do with. Even when it came out he'd done nothing, his career was ruined. Mahoney could do that to Avery."

"Other journalists could do that to Avery."

"Most of them have quit trying by now," I said. "But if Mahoney thinks I'm holding out, for all I know, he could make something up."

"So *you* make something up," Svein said. "Tell him you saw the tooth faerie when you were a kid and she did the hokey pokey with you and took you to her ice-cream castle. That ought to shut him up."

"Tell him a lie?"

"Well, you're saying the Digger could lie, so beat him to it.

Counter his punch with one of your own. You're good at that."

I let my head drop. "Ouch," I said.

"What?"

"Nothing. My stomach hurts."

He put out his hand, and I took it so he could haul me upright. Too close to him, I took a step back.

"Don't worry about Mahoney," Svein assured me as he reached for his crumpled T-shirt on a nearby chair and tugged it on. "He's nothing. Clayton's the problem. I have a few ideas, and we need to make a plan."

"Yeah, that," I said. "I've got some interesting things to say on the topic of the good dentist."

"What?" he said, and it was clear in his voice that he knew he wouldn't like what came next.

"Tomorrow," I said, opening the door. "I'm inviting you to a powwow. Someone's holding out on me."

I paused and watched Svein tug on his sneakers. "If no tooth collector in recent history has given us away," I asked, "how come you sent me to Watergate? Teaching me a lesson couldn't be worth the risk."

"I followed you."

My mouth hung open. "I hate you," I finally said, letting the door slam in his face. I heard him laughing as I headed back down the hall.

CHAPTER 17

When I got home, I was a half dozen different emotions by then: confused, defeated, jumpy. Angry at Riley Clayton. Strangely sympathetic to Greg Mahoney.

Surprised to see Avery at the kitchen table, cell phone at his ear, yellow legal pad in front of him.

Not that I should have been surprised. It wasn't like I didn't live there. But I was afraid that all the happenings of the day were on open display on my face, and I didn't have the energy to create a careful mask. And I didn't want to add guilt to my simmering emotion pot—the low, quiet, slow guilt that comes with lying by omission.

He nodded at me to acknowledge my presence but he didn't lift his eyes from his notepad. I moved around him and opened the cabinet over the sink. I filled a mug with hot water and put it in the microwave. Then I tuned in to Avery's half of the conversation.

I wished I didn't. I heard, "kids," "arson," "shooting," "underage," "violence."

I didn't know if it was the scorching pain in my gut from the beating I took or the bruised tailbone I got from falling through a brick wall, but whatever it was that was preoccupying my mind was keeping it from processing full sentences. The isolated words in Avery's calm, assuring voice twisted in an out-of-control cyclone in my head.

The microwave beeped several annoyed times and I didn't make a move to get my mug. I was grounding a chai teabag in my fist into sweet-smelling shreds. Avery clicked off, placed his phone next to him on the table, and wrote down some notes.

"Who was that?" I asked.

"The office."

"Not the campaign office."

"No, my office."

"Why?"

Avery still didn't look up, and his pen kept on moving. "Consulting on a few cases."

"Why?" I asked. "You're on leave. You're kind of busy. What, they can't do their jobs without you?"

Avery quirked a brow. "There are a few cases right now that are delicate. They wanted my opinion on how to proceed."

"Well, tell them you don't have time."

He finally looked at me. "Why would I do that?"

I backtracked, because I really didn't have a reason that I could tell him. "You've got a lot going on. You don't need this too."

"This has nothing to do with what I need," he said. "But I appreciate what sounds like concern. So let me tell you what's going on."

Please don't, I thought.

"Have you noticed an increase in violence in this area that's perpetrated by kids?"

Yes. "No."

"It's all over the news," he said. "That school shooting. Some kid just set a vacant building on fire. A girl tried to kill her brother. These are little kids, Gemma. Only in the last couple of weeks."

Brian's dead eyes drifted in front of my own. "So..."

"So, these cases are landing on the desks of my associates. These should be isolated, unusual cases that we could put senior people on. But they're piling up, and the less experienced attorneys are having to handle these scenarios. What caused the violence? Should they be tried as adults?"

"Should they?" I asked, not knowing myself.

"It's a case-by-case decision."

"And so everyone needs your help?"

"I'm senior," Avery said. "I've had a few instances in my career when I've had to prosecute underage felons. So they're looking for my advice."

"I thought you said you were leaving this behind to campaign," I said. "That's what you said you were doing."

I heard desperation in my voice. But it was too late, because he'd heard it too. His expression hardened into a stone wall of determination. "What's the matter with you?" he asked. "There's a problem in this city. I don't know where it's coming from, or even if it's coming from the same place for every one of these messed-up kids, but this is my job. You want me to walk away from that?"

"You already did," I pointed out. I stepped on the trash can pedal. The lid flipped up, hit the wall behind it, and slapped down. My tossed teabag bounced off onto the floor. "Let your office handle it. They're capable, and you have enough right now. You have more than enough. You're exhausted. Why are you adding more grief?"

"Because when I see a problem," he said, his voice tight, "and especially when I see a tragedy, I do what I can to stop it. I do everything. I have to. That's my mentality, and that's what it has been my whole life. What I'm always thinking is, if I don't do it, who will?"

I will, I thought.

But then I thought, I wouldn't have, if I hadn't been talked into it. Frederica, Reese, Svein. They'd had to explain, demonstrate, even guilt me into accepting my destiny of birth.

Avery had no destiny, no responsibility other than to himself. He was free to make his own choices, and faced with a choice, he always went with—without advice or compulsion or even a second thought—what he thought was the right way.

I was a promise to the fae to protect them. But Avery was a protector of humanity, and that included me.

"You're not the only fighter in this house, Gemma," Avery said. "Unfortunately, the opponent isn't limited to rules of a game. This is reality and it's dark and disgusting and I'm not going to watch it float by me like a parade. It's my responsibility."

Suddenly, I wished it was him and not me. If my battle was his to fight, he'd win. He wouldn't have the conflicts I had, or mess up the way I did. He'd have a better plan than me. He'd more clearly see the victory in front of him. He was what I needed to be. And I wished I could ask him how.

His jaw was set stiff, and his shoulders were squared back, and I felt bad for the fae, who didn't have Avery on their side.

Avery abruptly rose, shoved the chair back so hard that it momentarily teetered on one leg, crossed the room to where I was standing, grasped my shoulders and kissed me.

Hard. Edging on rough.

I could do rough. I smiled beneath his lips. He didn't have anything to prove to me, didn't need to show me he was any kind of hero.

But, I thought as he tugged my shirt over my head and tossed it over my shoulder, that didn't mean I couldn't let him show me. Over and over again.

"Thank you for meeting me today."

I was holding very small court in a back booth at a little bistro at 10th and Constitution. I got there twenty minutes before any of them so I could watch them as they arrived. My mother arrived with a perfumed kiss, a tote bag, and a puzzled expression when

I informed her that two others would be joining us. Frederica had swept in wearing a pale green floaty top, lightweight beige gauchos and brown ballerina flats, serene and content to wait for the last of the guests. Svein had strode in, frowned at the crowded table, and slid in beside Frederica and across from me, the bench creaking under him.

I'd introduced both Frederica and Svein to my mother, and by their mutual nods, they all silently acknowledged each other as fae. Then I'd taken orders and gotten our sandwiches, but when I returned to the table, there'd been no indication they'd said one word to one another in my absence.

Frederica smiled. My mother raised her brows. Svein leaned back, his foot in its engineer boot protruding into the aisle.

"Riley Clayton," I said.

"I knew Riley Clayton," my mother said.

"Okay," I said. "Good start," even though it wasn't good at all. I had been hoping, despite her reaction on the phone, that my mother couldn't confirm a connection to Clayton, but at the same time, I was hoping that with a little cooperation, I could glue together the broken pieces of Clayton's story.

"I don't understand," my mother said. "Do you know him?"

"Yes," I answered. "He's my new dentist. And he's a fae threat."

My mother put a hand to her forehead. "A threat." She took a deep breath. "I knew they hadn't just recruited you to collect. I *knew* this would happen."

"With Clayton?" I asked.

"Yes, I worried about Clayton for a while," she said. "But to me, it didn't matter who a threat would be and what form it would take. All I know is that you're in danger now, and I abandoned my family and my heritage thirty years ago to make sure this wouldn't happen. So that you," she said, pointing a finger at Frederica, "wouldn't get her and put her on the front line as our race's only weapon." My mother's shaking voice rose in pitch, but dropped in volume, mindful of fellow diners. "I respect what we are and

I respect the dream but I will *not* let my daughter die for you."

"Bethany," Frederica said, and stopped, letting my mother's name float there in the air, as if its magical vibrations could soothe my mother's soul. After a few moments, when my mother's tremors had subsided a bit, she continued. "Gemma is a smart, brave, wily human, and a cunning and strong fae. She is not the warrior of an earlier time. We're not tossing her in the middle of an uncivilized and violent fray. We have faith in her to neutralize the threat without bloodshed on either side."

My bruised gut hurt with my every inhalation.

"You think modern day is more civilized?" my mother asked Frederica. "You're delusional. This world is more unpredictable and more perilous than ever. You know that as well as I do. Earth is on a well-worn path to self-destruction, and you know that means the Olde Way, more than ever, is the savior. My daughter, as bright and strong as she is, can't be alone out there. No one can."

I'd never heard my mother talk this way, and I suddenly realized my fighter's instinct hadn't just come from my father. "It's done, Mom," I said quietly, leaning into her. "I'm doing this now. I have to do this. No one is making me. The fae gave me a choice, and I accepted. I'm on this. I'll be okay. I love you," I said. "I'll be okay. But I need to hear about Clayton. I need to learn how to stop him."

My mother put her arm around me and hugged me, glaring at Frederica, then at Svein. "What do you need to know?" she asked, kissing me on the cheek like I was a child. After the batterings of the last few days, it felt good. When Avery had hugged me last night upon his return home, the pain in my bruised abs had made me squeak. I'd told him I had a stomachache, and he'd put me to bed with chicken soup and crackers.

"Anything and everything," I said. "He said some things yesterday that…"

"Stop right there," Svein said, leaning across the table. "Yesterday? You went there yesterday?"

"Yes."

"Before you came to see me?"

"Yes."

"How come I didn't know about this?"

"It didn't come up, specifically."

He glared.

"It was an emergency," I said. "I chipped my front tooth in the ring."

"Well," he drawled, leaning back. His foot hit mine under the table before snaking out into the aisle again. "That was rather convenient."

"Wasn't it," I replied, matching his sarcasm.

"I dated Riley," my mother said, and my sarcasm melted away in a hurry as I stared at her. "It wasn't serious," she clarified, after taking in my expression. "It was just casual dating. To me, anyway."

"Mom." I took a deep breath. "This isn't going to be a 'Luke, I am your father' moment, is it? I'm not—" I swallowed—"his daughter?"

"No!" She actually laughed, and I was glad for it, because if she thought it was that funny even in this charged conversation, there really was no chance. But then she stopped laughing and searched my face. "You," she said, "whether you want to hear it or not, are your father's daughter, inside and out. I would know. As far as Riley is concerned, our relationship never got that far. We had a few dates, and that was it."

"Are you sure?"

She eyed the others at the table. "Sweetie, I do remember who I have and have not been intimate with."

"Sorry, I just meant …"

She waved off my apology. "It's all right. I understand why you would ask. But how is he a threat now?"

"He's a dentist," I told her, "and he's making toothpaste for kids that's draining the essence from their teeth, so the teeth are useless and the kids are suddenly little jaded zombie adults."

Mom looked shocked. Then she shook her head slowly. "Why?"

"We don't know why," Svein said, though I knew he was thinking of midnight fae.

"Honestly," my mother insisted, "it was just a handful of dates. I would have broken it off anyway, even if I hadn't met your father."

In the sudden silence, I could almost hear the others mentally processing what she'd just said. I had a feeling that Svein and Frederica were hoping I would take the lead. "You broke up with Clayton for Dad?" I finally asked.

"That's right," she said. "I fell away from the fae community, married your father. I think you can fill in the rest."

"Was he upset?" I asked. "When you broke up with him?"

"I wouldn't even say we broke up, because it wasn't involved enough for that. I just told him I didn't want to keep seeing him." She took a deep breath. "But yes, he *was* upset. I remember thinking it was odd, because I'd done nothing to make him believe our relationship was serious. He told me I was making a big mistake, that he knew I was the one for him, all the kinds of things you say when you're being dumped, I suppose. He said he loved me, which was close to preposterous, considering our short relationship. But I told him if I was making a mistake, it was mine to make. Because the moment I met your father, I realized he would become the biggest part of my life."

She grew quiet, and I couldn't pretend to know what she was thinking, but I knew if I were her, I would be wondering at the surety with which I'd made that long-ago decision.

Finally, she said, "I didn't even think about Riley again, until after your father… left. Riley wrote me a letter, asking me to give him another chance."

"How did he know Dad was gone?" I asked.

"I don't know. I wondered at the time, but things were too—well, too raw for me to care, and so I just threw the letter away."

"Without responding?" Svein asked.

"That's right."

She twisted her hands together until Frederica said, "Any woman would have done the same. I would have."

Mom looked at all of us in turn, her gaze settling finally on me. "About a year later, a package came in the mail for Gemma. You were only nine years old," she said to me, "and there was no one I could think of who would send you a package with no return address. So I opened it."

She didn't say anything for a moment. Despite my impatience for answers, I didn't prompt her. Then she reached down into the large leather bag at her feet, pulled out a thick manila envelope and dropped it on the table.

We all stared at it, plain and brown with one word scrawled across it: *Gemma.*

"Inside here are three more envelopes," Mom said. "They all arrived together like this. I opened them all and read them right away, then I panicked. When I left the fae community with my husband George, no one followed or us, and we had no contact with anyone other than Gemma's grandparents, so I didn't know how—I didn't know *why*—he would care, or try to talk to my daughter."

"Riley," I said.

"Yes," she said, and pushed the envelope toward me. It was torn open and taped back together, so I ripped through the tape and emptied the contents in front of me. Three letters, all addressed to me. The first read: *Gemma, Open Now.* The second read: *Gemma, Open When You're 18.* The third: *Gemma, Open When You're 21.*

"I read them all," my mother repeated, "and each of those years I was extra careful with you. When I got the letters, I practically didn't let you out of my sight for a year, not even to your friends' houses to play. When you were eighteen, I sent you to Amsterdam for that study-abroad program."

"Yeah," I murmured. "I wondered why you didn't give me much of an argument when I asked."

"I couldn't lock you in the house at that age, and I trusted that you'd be supervised there, surrounded with friends and instructors. When you turned twenty-one," she said, "I couldn't be your guardian. But you were old enough to handle strangers, ask questions, and physically fight someone twice your size. I knew that if Riley contacted you again, you'd tell me and I could give you these letters to explain. But you'd said nothing until now. I thought he was gone."

"I'm sorry you couldn't come to us," Frederica said.

"I'm sorry you didn't go to the police," Svein added.

"I couldn't," Mom said. "Not one of those letters is an overt threat. Only I could read between the lines, and how was I to explain that to humans?"

"I'm going to read them now," I said.

"Yes, please," Frederica said. "Do you want some privacy?"

"No, stay," I said as I tore the tape off the first letter: *Gemma, Open Now.*

Dear Gemma,

Hello. You don't know me, but I thought perhaps you could use a new friend. I understand that you lost someone very important recently, and I think when you lose someone, it's good to know you have a friend out there, a friend who understands you just as you are.

My name is Riley. When I was about your age, I lost my mother. I loved her a lot. Whenever I was sad, she would tell me a story to make me feel better. Maybe a story would make you feel better now. I'll tell you my favorite one.

Once upon a time, there were fae. Like the faeries you read about, with wings, who were so happy living in their beautiful land, dancing and laughing and flying, where nothing was sad and everything was as it should be.

Eventually, humans took over the Earth, and the fae lost their world. They were sad, for years and years. They tried to bring back their world, bit by tiny bit.

One day a little girl was born. She was special, and she was different, and the fae rejoiced, because she was their golden hope.

But her parents hid her away. They were afraid of how special she was, so they didn't let her embrace her great future for herself. She grew up without realizing she was only living half of her true self.

Do you know who you are, Gemma? Do you know you're a very special girl? I hope your Mom told you. You shouldn't allow her to make you into something you aren't, because sometimes that happens.

Go, ask questions, learn who you are. Don't feel alone. I'm your friend and I'm out here. Don't open the next letter until you're 18. Promise you won't peek ahead. You must become what you are before you can do what needs to be done.

Your friend,

Riley

I dropped the letter, then passed it to Svein and he moved close to Frederica so they could read it together.

When they finished, I addressed my mother. "Why didn't you give these to me the other day, when I learned I was fae?"

"I thought—I hoped—that there was no threat, and that the fae found you and just wanted you on call, and to collect. And you know full well that if I had just handed these over to you that day, you would have followed up on them out of curiosity. You would have gone looking for trouble."

I opened my mouth to deny it and caught Svein's raised eyebrow, then Frederica's wry smile. Okay, yes, I would have.

"Let's interpret these letters one at a time," Frederica suggested. "What do we get from this one? He reached out to Gemma as soon as her father left. So he knew where and what she was. Probably because he was still so in love with you," she said to my mother. "He had a vested interest. The rest of the fae community didn't have a reason to follow you because lots of fae choose to live as masqueraded humans, but he did, and he knew you married, and he knew you had Gemma."

"He tried to establish a link with you, Gemma, by telling you he lost his mother," Svein said. "When I identified Clayton as our tooth threat, I did background checks. Clayton's father, Carl, didn't emerge in the active fae community until he was a widower with a school-age son. Which isn't unusual. When a fae loses a spouse, they tend to find comfort with their fae family."

"I'm sorry you felt you couldn't do that, Mom," I said. "Maybe it would have been easier."

"Keeping you safe was the most important thing," she said, but I still felt guilty by blood.

"Who was Clayton's mother?" I asked.

"Clayton's school records don't show the mother's name. They list Carl as the father and sole guardian."

"None of this explains why he cared about me in the slightest," I said. "He had reason to hate me—however misguided that hate was—because he'd loved Mom more than she cared about him and left him for Dad. But why try to be *my* friend?"

"Maybe the next letter will tell us," Svein said, so I ripped it open and read.

Dear Gemma,

Do you remember me? I wrote to you when you were a little girl. I wonder if you asked your mother about what you are. I wonder if she ever gave you that letter. I wonder if you're reading this one.

If your mother still hasn't told you who you are, and why you're special, she should, because eventually the fae will come for you. You, Gemma Fae Cross, are their highest hope. They'll want you to fight for them, and you'll become part of their history if you die for them.

I let part of myself die because of them, but they don't know it.

Humans and fae have been at silent war for all time. How could that war exist in one person? Do you feel the fight inside you—both sides battling to emerge?

The humans have failed you from the start. Where did your father go?

The fae will fail you too: the Olde Way is a promise they can't bring to life for you.

I have a better plan, one to bulldoze the impossible ideal and steal from those who stole it.

They ripped me in half. But you can help me, and help yourself. You can still choose another destiny, and start a better and stronger world.

Find me. I'm easy to find.

Yours,

Riley Clayton

Again, I let Svein and Frederica read the letter when I was through, and I put my head in my hands.

My mother shook her head. "I still don't understand. When I left him, he was angry, but harmless. He was"—she shrugged at Frederica and Svein—"fae. He couldn't intentionally hurt so much as a mosquito. How can he be doing this?"

"The question is, why?" Svein said. "We might have figured out the how."

"No, you haven't," I told him. "He hasn't aligned with dark fae. He's not a demon. He's working alone. He told me."

"What do you mean, he told you?" Svein asked.

"My visit yesterday developed into a, uh, an interesting conversation."

"You did this on your own? Why didn't you call me?"

"What the hell were you going to do?" I yelled at him. The closest diner was three tables away, and she turned from her newspaper and eyed me. I glared at her until she looked away, then continued in a furiously low whisper. "You couldn't save me. You couldn't help me. I did this on my own because I *am* on my own, Svein. If you could have done anything, you would have by now, instead of sit around on your ass waiting for *me* to come save the day."

Svein took a deep breath in, but Frederica laid a claming hand on his arm. "Gemma," she said, "what did Dr. Clayton say yesterday?"

"He knew who I was. He knows I'm after him. He said he'd tried to get to me first. I asked him who he's working with and he laughed in my face and said the fae were too stupid to figure him out, that he's working alone. And he said I'm too late."

"Why too late?" my mother asked.

"Because Monday night is his premiere on TV-Spree, where he'll be selling his Smile Wide toothpaste to millions of parents of millions of children."

"Oh," Frederica said, and her one word was a sigh. No one said anything for a long time.

"So why didn't he just kill you?" Svein asked. My mother sucked in a breath.

"No point," I said. "Like he said, I'm too late. Besides, he said it wasn't between him and me, that I'm not his problem. He asked about Mom. He knew Dad left. He knows about me." But did he really know *me*?

He'd said yesterday, *You can't help who you are or where you came from any more than I can...*

"If he's acknowledging who you are and your purpose," Frederica said, "maybe he still wants your help? Or maybe he *wants* you to stop him?"

You still have no idea just how much you and I have in common...

"If he's working alone," Svein said, "then how? How could he be doing harm?"

You and I are exactly the same...

Then again, in the letter: *They ripped me in half.*

"Because," I said, my mouth blurting out the answer even before it fully cemented in my mind, "Riley Clayton is a half-fae." I closed my eyes a moment, and when I opened them, the room was so much clearer, it was as if I'd put on magic glasses. I looked into Svein's black eyes and spoke directly to him what I now knew to be the truth. "Clayton's half-fae, half-human. Just like me."

CHAPTER 18

A long, contemplative silence at the table followed my epiphany. My mother looked at her hands. Frederica gazed at a wall painting of a poppy field. Svein stared at me, so I looked out the window.

The National Museum of Natural History was across the street, and I thought about how I hadn't been there since I was in high school. Theoretically, it shouldn't have changed, since the history before me hadn't changed. But I didn't become fae this month. I was fae all my life, and suddenly my perspective and my purpose had changed with the knowledge. If history changed so easily, shouldn't every exhibit in the museum seem brand-new to me if I returned?

I ate my last potato chip, staring at that museum, filled with artifacts that at one time, no one believed could exist—except for the few tenacious people who found them. I suddenly had a vision of myself in wax, with sightless eyes watching crowds of tourists and junior high field trips, molded wings spread out behind me, a placard in English and in Braille explaining my discovery.

Who'd be the one to put me there? Mahoney? Avery? Myself?

"Anyone have insight to share?" I asked, in a strong effort to return to what I could control.

Frederica interlaced her delicate fingers together. "Only that you're probably right about Dr. Clayton."

"I know I am," I said. "It's the only explanation as to how he's capable of doing harm. And he's hurting both fae and humans—fae by attacking the Olde Way, and humans by robbing kids of innocence. It makes sense, right? He was spurned by a fae." I nodded at Mom. "And he was beaten out by a human, when Dad came between them."

Frederica said, "But it has to be more than love gone sour. Why didn't he kill Bethany or George Cross if it was merely personal?" She reached over and touched my mother's hand. "I'm sorry," she said, and held my mother's gaze. When my mother turned her hand over to clasp Frederica's, I realized she was forgiving Frederica not only for the harsh comment, but for searching me out and handing my destiny back to me.

"Which brings me to my next question," I said. "Why didn't we *know* Clayton is a half-and-half? I assume the research was thorough."

Although I addressed everyone, the last comment was aimed at Svein and I avoided his eyes as he responded. "I didn't look for his mother. I was looking for Clayton's methods, not his motivation. There was no reason to believe he was anything but full fae. What I did look for, as you know, was a record of a Butterfly Room transformation, and there was none."

"Now we know why," I said.

"I didn't even think," he said, clearly unsettled, "that his mother could have been human."

"That's how rare you are," Frederica said to me. "So rare that Clayton's being a half-fae wouldn't even have occurred to Svein, or me, or any of us. There are only two other living half-fae on record. One was born three years ago in Czechoslovakia. The other is in South America, and in his lifetime, we only needed to call him in for very minor threats. He still does research for us now."

"Why didn't you ask *him* to deal with Riley?" my mother asked.

"He's 106," Frederica said.

"He's 106 and he's still working for the fae?" I kind of hoped that wasn't my destiny. At 106, I expected to deserve a rest.

"We live longer," Frederica reminded me, "and our bodies age slower. Not by much, or we'd be far too noticeable, but the people with milestone birthdays who you read about in the newspapers are usually fae."

"Just FYI, I plan to retire at sixty-five," I told her, "so don't make any long-term plans for me."

"My point is," she said, smiling gently at me, "that we keep what we believe are accurate records about those like you. We knew you existed and we knew where you were all this time, but we kept a respectful distance. Your mother's family was insistent on that, and we complied until you became an adult and a deliberate threat materialized. And now," she said, half to herself, "it's worse than we all thought. TV-Spree."

My mother looked out the window as she said, "Riley was awkward and shy, and a gentleman. But that anger when I broke it off," she added, looking back at us, "it felt long in coming, like something he'd held back for years. I remember thinking maybe it wasn't about me, but it was something else in him."

"I don't think you're the reason for this," I told her. "I think your breakup was only the trigger for something else that was brewing in him for a long time. Some kind of hatred against one or both sides of his heritage. In his letter, he says"—I grabbed the letter back and skimmed with my finger—"*I died for them, and they don't know it.* Then later, *They ripped me in half.*"

"The 'they' isn't you and George," Frederica said. "Although it seems he wanted the thrill of recruiting your daughter to his side, I think it's bigger. I think it's all fae, all humans."

"It's something sad," I said, and we all fell silent for a moment.

I didn't want to understand Dr. Riley Clayton. I didn't want to think he'd reached out to me not just to help him, but to be his only friend.

Svein cleared his throat. "I'm wondering what part you play in this scenario now," he said to me. "You're the celebrated half-fae while he—deliberately or not—lives in shadow. And while he didn't manage to make an ally of you all those years ago, he also didn't kill you, today or before now. It could mean he's waiting for a more convenient moment, or that he wants you to witness his success."

"What about what Frederica said?" I asked. "What if he originally *wanted* me to stop him, and that's why he said yesterday that he'd given me all this time, that I'd had my whole life to get to him, and now I'm too late?"

"I'll talk to Clayton," Mom said.

"Mom, no," I said, just as Svein said, "Absolutely not."

"I agree," Frederica said. "It's a bad idea. His war is bigger than you now, and it will only be the cherry on top for him if you get involved."

"Let me handle it," I said.

My mother looked at me, and her eyes were cloudy and sad. "You're going to handle this alone?"

"She's not alone," Svein said.

He and I locked gazes.

"What about Avery?" my mother asked.

I tore away from Svein's eyes. "What?"

"I said, what about Avery? Does he know any of this? Does he know you're in danger?"

"No," I said, "and he doesn't know what I am, and it's going to stay that way."

"He deserves to know," my mother insisted, and I suspected she was insisting because she wanted to assure herself that other people were taking care of me in this, people who weren't fae, who only had my interests at heart and not those of the Olde Way.

"That may be," I said, "but I'm still not going to tell him."

She cut a sideways glance at Svein before continuing. "You're in love with Avery," she said to me. "He should know."

"Why?" I asked. "So he can walk out on me?"

No one said anything. My instinct was to apologize but if I did, I felt my point would be lost. Finally my mother spoke again. "He might walk out on you anyway. You might never tell him, and he'll walk out on Gemma the human for completely different reasons. If you think not telling him the truth will guarantee you security, you're telling yourself a lie." She took hold of my wrist. "Gemma, it's better to be honest."

"I will be honest," I said. "If Avery ever asks me, 'Hey, are you a tooth faerie, by any chance?' I'll definitely say yes."

"You need him now," my mother said. "And he's here now. That's all I'm saying."

I glanced at Svein again. He'd listened to the whole exchange, expressionless.

"There's one more letter," I said, and they all nodded. I tore open the rattling envelope that read: *Gemma, Open When You're 21* and found one sheet of unlined paper, along with a teardrop ruby on a gold chain.

Dear Gemma,

There are two things that could have happened: Either you never received my letters, or you chose not to come to me.

I regret both of those possibilities.

We may yet meet.

Accept this token as a respectful acknowledgment.

Riley Clayton

I folded this final letter and put it back in the envelope without sharing its message with the others. I held up the necklace and watched it sway and sparkle. It looked like a drop of blood. I fastened it around my neck.

"Gemma," my mother began.

"Acknowledgment," I said.

After a moment, Frederica said, "I should be getting back. I start my shift in a couple of hours and I'd like to get a nap in."

I got a look at the clock and realized just how long we'd been sitting here. "I'm sorry," I said, but she touched my cheek.

"Don't be sorry," she said. "You do whatever you need to do. You know how to reach me, or any of us." We all got up from the table and Frederica put her arms—pale and fragile—around my mother's shoulders. My mother, to my surprise, hugged her back and rested her head on Frederica's shoulder for a brief moment. Bethany Cross, always so strong and sure, looked as vulnerable as a dragonfly, and my heart hurt to think that it was because of me. Frederica murmured into her ear and my mother nodded before disentangling herself and enfolding me in a bigger, warmer embrace.

"As much as it is your destiny to do this," she said, "it is my destiny to be your mother. I want to do that forever. Do you understand?"

"Yes." My stomach still ached from the brief beating I'd suffered from Clayton, and I rested into my mother's embrace more than I would have in the middle of an urban bistro.

I remained standing beside the table as my mother and Frederica left, parting in opposite directions. I heaved a sigh, still looking at the door where they'd exited.

"Let's get out of here," Svein said, steering me out into the street. "I'll give you a lift home."

"What, on your back?"

The air had grown cooler, reminding me that the warm days of spring didn't necessarily mean balmy nights.

"In my car."

I scoffed. "City people don't bother with cars."

"Maybe I'm not city people."

It occurred to me that I didn't know anything about Svein except for what role he played in my life—mentor, pain in my behind and something more I didn't want to think about. I wasn't sure whether he expected me to ask about him, about his life. We walked only a half-block before curiosity took over. "Where are you from, anyway?"

"Originally? Iceland."

"Really?"

"Yes, a town called Akranes."

"What's there?"

"Fishing," he said, then smiled a little. "Football. Or, to Americans, soccer."

"Did you play?"

"I was only a child. We moved to New York, eastern Long Island, when I was ten. Then I did play, in high school and in college."

"Were you any good?" I asked, knowing the answer.

His smile grew. "Yeah, I was good."

"Were your parents collectors?"

"For a while. My mother collected until she got pregnant with my older brother, and then she became a full-time mother. My father was in finance, but he'd collected when he was in college."

"So the whole tooth-under-the-pillow thing isn't just an American tradition."

Svein shook his head, and drew out his keys. He pressed a button, and a spotless, shiny black car at the curb beep-beeped a greeting. "Some countries are similar, like Canada and Australia, with leaving the tooth under a pillow." He opened the passenger door for me and closed me in. He came around the other side and slid in behind the wheel, turning the key in the ignition. "In France and Spain, the kids believe a mouse comes to collect the tooth and leaves them candy or money, and in South Africa, it's also a mouse, but the kids leave the tooth in a slipper. In some countries in South America, it's a rat." He maneuvered the car into a quick, smooth, illegal U-turn. "Just be glad you're not in Sri Lanka or India. Those kids fling their teeth on the roof for squirrels and birds. You'd actually have to use those wings to get airborne and grab them."

"No, thanks."

"How can someone who deliberately breaks her own tooth be afraid of heights?"

"I'm not afraid of heights," I told him. "I'm afraid of being more of a freak than I already am. And don't make this conversation about me. We were talking about you, for a change. Are your parents still on Long Island?"

"Yes," he said. "In a cemetery."

"Oh," I said, feeling like an insensitive jerk even though there was no way I could have known. "Oh. I'm—I'm sorry."

He waved off my apology. "They died when I was in college."

"What happened?" The question was rude and implied my prurient interest, but maybe there was a bigger part of me than I'd realized that wanted to know where Svein had come from, and how he became who he was.

"My father worked in Manhattan," he said evenly, his eyes never leaving the road. "My mother went in one evening and they were going to see a play. With my brother and myself both out of the house, they were dating again."

We crossed the river in silence. I felt bad for requesting the story, and I opened my mouth to change the subject when he spoke again.

"They had gone down to one of the subway platforms after the play, to head back to Penn Station, and they were mugged." He tightened his mouth. "I don't know what happened. No one saw what happened. Apparently, a train had just left and they were the only ones on the platform. The police didn't even know if it was only one guy, or a group, and they didn't know why they didn't just take the money and leave instead of knifing them both." His hands curled around the steering wheel, his knuckles whitening. "The thing is, they couldn't fight back."

My heart broke for the fae couple who couldn't defend themselves in the face of danger, and my heart broke for the two sons they left behind. I swallowed the lump I realized had risen in my throat. "I'm sorry."

He nodded.

"Where's your brother now?"

"At the L.A. Root Center, working as a technician. He's part time there and part time at a more legitimate job he can list on his tax forms. I see him a few times a year. You'd like him. He's a lot like me, only nicer and with a better sense of humor."

"I probably would like him, in that case." I rubbed my forehead.

We had been headed toward my condo when Svein suddenly veered right and parked on a small dead-end street. I sat and waited, and wondered whether he was going to kiss me again. I wasn't going to let him, I thought, and then I wondered if that was true.

He turned the car off, reached into the inside pocket of his open jacket, then reached out his hand low and covert to pass me something underneath the dashboard.

I looked down at his hand hovering over my lap and yelped. "What the fuck? A *gun*? Are you out of your *mind*?"

"We need to deal with Clayton."

I stared at him, but he didn't so much as blink, just calmly gazed at me while probably every emotion I ever had showed on my own face.

"Get that away from me," I said. "I mean it. Get it out of my sight."

"Then how do you plan to kill him? With your bare hands?"

"I'm not killing anyone. I said put the gun away, now, or I'm out of here." I gripped the door handle and prepared to push out and start running toward home.

He slid it back into his jacket's inside pocket. "I'll teach you how to use it, if that's the problem," he said.

"Uh, no. The problem is I'm not touching that thing, and I'm not killing anyone."

"Listen to me. I have a plan," he said. "No detail has been overlooked. No one will know, he'll disappear, and…"

I covered my ears with my hands. "La, la, la, I'm not listening to a murder plan, la, la, la."

He peeled my left hand down. "I'm telling you I have a plan that, if pulled off correctly, will not land you in jail, nor will it touch Avery in any way."

I dropped the other hand. "Although it's comforting to know you care enough to come up with an elaborate scheme, it's got one glitch: I'm not going to murder Clayton."

"This is your *job*, Gemma."

My mouth dropped open. "My job," I said, "is to stop the threat."

"He'll be on TV in four days, hawking his weapon at some low, low price. You need to stop him, and this is the way. He's harming kids, he attacked you. The Root scientists identified a compound in the toothpaste that's rotting essence." He raked his fingers hard through his blond hair. "And by the way, that school shooter? And that kid Trey? You were right. Clayton patients, both of them. Also, a little girl who pushed her brother out a window, and a boy who killed his grandfather."

I blinked.

"That's right," he said. "How can he have treated so many kids? I wondered. Well, here's what else I learned. Dr. Riley Clayton, out of the goodness of his charitable heart, ran a clinic for poor families about eight years ago. Other dentists helped him out. And I'm sure they gave out those freebie toothpaste tubes also."

I felt my mouth drop open. More of them were out there? More hurt, possessed kids. Older kids, who had gotten worse, sicker. How many…?

"So what else do you need so you can *understand*?" Svein demanded. "Do you need me to spell it out? *Clayton's the bad guy*."

I breathed in deeply, out hard. "Frederica just said we can do this without bloodshed," I pointed out.

"She said that before she knew TV-Spree is his new weapon of choice."

"Don't you think she can come up with a better idea than execution?"

"No," he said bluntly. "She would be against this solution, but she wouldn't be able to come up with a better one because there is none. I have nothing but the highest admiration for Frederica, but she's an idealist."

"I thought the Olde Way *was* an ideal."

"We live here now," he said. "We need to adapt a little better to reality."

"But..."

"*This* is reality," he repeated, "and this is what *you* were *born* to do."

I froze, and the anger rose up my spine and radiated out to every finger and toe until I curled them tightly. I forced myself to breathe, and I braced my sneakered feet on the floorboard, pressing my back against the passenger seat in an effort to hold in my offended wings. My back teeth jammed together, and when I spoke, I didn't unclench them. "That's what you think? That I was born a warrior, born to blindly fight our battles without question? I *chose* this," I reminded him. "And do you actually think that because I'm half human, I'm half violent and reckless, and I'll be *okay* with killing someone?"

My fingernails dug into the heels of both hands. "Maybe humans aren't perfect. Maybe the fae are. Maybe a fae father wouldn't leave a fae child forever in the middle of the night without saying goodbye. Maybe he wouldn't leave the fae mother to cry herself to sleep for a year. I don't know. I do know that humans aren't perfect, but they're not the polar opposite. They're somewhere in between fae and something I never hope to see. And maybe as a consequence of that limbo, humans *can* swing between good and bad."

I twisted in my seat so I was facing Svein. "But I'm not going to kill anyone. I'm not that angry, or that hopeless. I'm not the person on the subway platform who killed your parents. I'm a fighter, but only to defend my way, and to defend the Olde Way. I'm not a fighter who's out to kill someone else's way. That's not my place. My place, what I was *born* to do, is to make it right. I don't happen to think murder makes anything right."

I stopped for a moment, my breath hiccuppy and shallow. "I'm going to figure out how to stop Clayton without killing him, because when you morning fae finally do bring back the Olde Way, *I*—" I jabbed my thumb into my sternum "—am going to be worthy of it."

I grabbed the door handle and pushed, and the cool evening air, mixed with the scent of sidewalk and new leaves, brushed in. "Thanks for all your help," I said, stepping out, "but I think that due to creative differences, we've come to the end of our professional relationship. I'm going to take it from here." I bent down to look at him one last time. "I'm sorry to disappoint you, but I can live with that. I can't live with disappointing myself."

I slammed the car door and walked home. Halfway there, I realized I was cold, but I swung my arms by my sides, refusing to wrap them around myself for warmth.

CHAPTER 19

When I got home, Avery and his father were sitting in the living room. "Here she is," Avery said.

Johnson McCormack stood and kissed me on the cheek. "Lovely to see you, Gemma."

"Did I know you were coming tonight?" I asked him, smoothing a hand through my hair and tugging the wrinkles out of my shirt. "I'm sorry. When I worked full time, I kept flawless track of time. Now that I'm leisurely, I never know what day it is."

Johnson was as tall as Avery, with completely white hair. I've seen pictures of him younger, with dark hair, but the pictures didn't make any sense to me, because the white hair was a true manifestation of his personality—strikingly distinguished and utterly original. His smile was wide and frequent. I didn't know Avery when his father had run for office, so I couldn't tell whether Johnson's good humor was a coping strategy he'd cultivated to deal with the loss of his career or whether it was just the way he'd always been. He was nice to be around. Avery had told him at some point about my father, and Johnson never brought it up; rather, he quietly assumed the role when he felt the situation warranted it. Nearly a year ago, I had confided to him about a co-worker at the polling office whom I'd been clashing with, and Johnson had listened, asked me questions, and offered sound, serious advice accompanied by a pat on the shoulder and an assurance that he knew I could handle it. He was generous, smart and sharp, and I wanted to take a pickaxe to the anonymous jerk who'd embroiled him in needless—and ultimately career-crushing—scandal.

"Dad just dropped by," Avery said. He'd shed suit and tie for jeans and a T-shirt. "I'm going to run out and grab a couple of pizzas. Ball game's about to start."

"Are you sure you don't have work to do?" Johnson asked him. "I really just stopped by to say hello."

"I always have work," Avery said, "but it's nothing that can't wait until tomorrow. I need a night off. Want anything special, Gemma?"

"Whatever you're getting is fine."

Avery tugged on a baseball cap and left. I grinned at Johnson and plopped down on the rug in front of him. I grabbed the remote off the coffee table and flicked on the flatscreen. As happy as I always was to see Avery's father, the timing wasn't ideal. I was planning to spend the evening coming up with some kind of perfect plan to stop Clayton. I could always escape to the bedroom after I ate, and do some thinking. I was still insanely angry at Svein, but knew that anger was useless if I couldn't figure out a non-murderous plot. And I only had four days to get it all done.

For the moment, I was obligated to be a gracious hostess. "How's Avery's mom?"

"She's fine," Johnson said, "thanks for asking. She's volunteering a little late at the hospital, and then it's poker night with the girls. Left me to fend for myself."

"Guess she figured you could handle it."

"I think she knew I'd head over here for some guy time."

I laughed. "Sorry to interfere."

"You know you're one of the guys," he said, and winked.

"Yeah, I get that a lot."

"How's your right hook?"

"Maybe not quite what it was," I said, grimacing as I recalled Smiley calling me an old lady. "But I still wouldn't advise you to stand in front of it."

"I'm not that kind of fool, my dear."

We both looked at the screen as I surfed through channels. When I found the Nationals' pre-game commentary, I glanced at Johnson. His eyes were still on the screen, but he didn't seem to be seeing it. He was thinking hard, seeing something only in his mind. "Are you okay?" I asked.

"I'm fine," he said, but suddenly his smile was thinner, and more tired. "Gemma," he said, "I want to ask you something, but please don't tell Avery I was asking."

"Of course not."

"Is he all right?"

I dropped the remote on the rug beside me, leaned back on my hands, and frowned. "What do you mean? Why wouldn't he be?"

He sighed. "It's tough, doing what he's doing."

"It's been tough," I admitted. "He's working even longer hours than he did as a DA. Sometimes he's fatigued, but then he pulls himself right back up. He's going on Graham Wright's late-night talk show this weekend, which is pretty cool. I'm sure he's glad to have a night off to watch the game and hang out with his dad."

"I'm really proud of him," Johnson said. "Really very proud. He knows why I stay out of the public eye instead of campaigning for him. But I hate that I have to stand back. I want everyone to know how proud I am, and what a good son he is, and how committed he is to doing good things for Virginia, and the country."

I shifted a little, slightly uncomfortable. He and I never talked about his past career, and it was certainly not a topic I would have broached. "Avery knows," I said. "He's your greatest admirer. And don't worry about the public support. I've got that covered for both of us."

He nodded slowly. "I have no doubt. But he witnessed what can happen to a career if—and I don't want him to be thinking only about that."

"He's vigilant," I said. "I'm not going to lie to you. He thinks about it, worries about it."

"I'm sure there are plenty of talking heads out there who say the apple doesn't fall far from the tree."

I sat up straight. "But you didn't do anything wrong. Why would anyone still be implying you were guilty when you proved you weren't?"

"People don't remember I wasn't guilty," he said gently. "They only remember a scandal with my name on it. My exoneration wasn't interesting enough to make headlines. And Gemma, it's all about headlines. Facts don't mean anything where public opinion is concerned. If you want to ruin someone, go to the media with a rumor or some allegations. Once it hits the streets and public opinion takes an ugly shape, that person's life will become nothing but a series of defense tactics. It won't matter if, in the end, they've done nothing wrong."

"That's not true," I insisted, but I did so out of politeness, because he was right. "Most people know you were honest and straightforward. More importantly, Avery knows." I sighed. "Try not to worry about him. Deep down, I think he knows that a scandal would be out of his control. They only thing he can control is himself, right? And he's been a great candidate. People *really* like him. He's got brains and good ideas and a charming girlfriend." I smiled again. "If something did happen, if we had to weather something similar to what you went through, you'd be right there for him."

"So would you," Johnson said. "I'll be honest. I would have had to love you no matter who you were, as long as my son loved you. But I'm proud that he managed to get you to fall for him, because of who he's been since. I couldn't have chose better for him myself."

A lump rose in my throat and my eyes stung at the retired politician's ringing endorsement of me, the one who could potentially wreck everything although I was trying so hard not to.

On TV, the leadoff batter stepped up to the plate, and we both fell silent, letting the awkwardly sweet moment pass by. But too quickly, my thoughts veered back to Clayton.

Well, I couldn't destroy his lab. Not only would I be putting other people in his building at risk, but it would be useless because production of his toothpaste wasn't restricted to that room anymore. Clayton was right—I was too late for that. Smile Wide was out there already, cases and cases of it waiting to be sold and shipped.

I could try to appeal to TV-Spree, but by the time I got through all the red tape that must block the important people at the network, it would probably be too late. I could stage some kind of boycott outside TV-Spree's offices, but I was sure Clayton would cross my picket line with a glamour-filled grin and that would be that. Besides, a high-profile stunt by me wouldn't help Avery's campaign in the slightest.

I exhaled hard through my mouth and the hair on my forehead blew up and down. While I was considering every possible thing I could do to stop Clayton, the fact still remained that Mahoney wouldn't let go either. I had a feeling that his phone call wouldn't be the last.

"Oh, no," Johnson said, as the second Mets batter sent one up and up, and the center fielder gave up seconds before the ball sailed over the bleachers.

If only there was a way that I could knock both Mahoney and Clayton out of the park at the same time.

Wait.

Mahoney wanted me to give him a story.

Clayton was a local dentist about to sell thousands of tubes of tainted toothpaste to kids.

Johnson had just said it himself: If you want to ruin someone, go to the media with an allegation. Public opinion counts more than facts.

"I'm home!" Avery called. "What did I miss?"

"Mets homer," Johnson said, getting up to join his groaning son in the kitchen.

The D.C. Digger's talent was getting information out there, and getting it out there fast. He was a popular blogger whom Washington insiders hated *and* respected, and he was on the radar of the large networks. If he broke an interesting story that held even the smallest grain of truth, people would take it seriously. Clayton's story had more than a grain of truth. I had scientists who could confirm it—albeit anonymously.

And regarding Clayton, I was positive that as soon as it was publicly suggested that his toothpaste was eating away at teeth, his TV-Spree contract would sink, and sink deep. A huge television shopping network would never want to be liable for selling a questionable product. The possibility for massive recalls and class-action suits would be enormous.

Besides, everybody went nuts when they thought children were at risk. Would his product ever survive? My guess was no.

"Gemma," Avery said, coming into the room with a plate of pizza and nudging my butt with his foot. "Aren't you hungry?"

"Yes," I said, grinning widely. *I'm going to save kids' innocence. I'm going to save the Olde Way. I'm going to save you.* "I definitely am."

Was it ethical to make a deal with devil two if it meant bringing down devil one?

Kind of hard to say, but as I stretched and watched inning three end with a strikeout, I knew I was ready to try it.

The Mets had won last night and Avery and Johnson pretended to be glum, but they had a carefree, fun night together and I knew the final score wasn't important. I'd slipped away to make a quick phone call during a commercial break, whispering into my cell phone in the bathroom. I'd suggested meeting at the Tidal Basin at midnight, but he'd scoffed at my amateur effort at clandestine activity. The most effective place for a secret meeting, he'd informed me, was in the middle of a crowd.

After last night's loss by two, the Nationals were out for revenge. My ticket was waiting for me at the window and I'd gotten here early enough to watch the players lie supine on the field, stretching their quads, then throwing the ball around the outfield. At the top of the fourth, my nose was definitely sunburned, there was no score, and the seat next to me was still empty.

The pitcher threw a strike. As I clapped, a shadow fell over me. I looked up as he handed me a plastic cup of foamy beer, then he sat, wedging an open box of Cracker Jack between us. He took a sip and leaned back, surveying the field. "Nothing like a cold beer and a ballgame."

I nodded as the pitcher hurled another strike. "Well, Mahoney, that's the first thing you and I have found that we can agree on."

He pushed up his glasses with his middle finger and squinted at me. "Your nose is pretty red."

"I know. I can feel it."

He reached into a small duffel bag at his feet and pulled out a tube of sunblock. He screwed off the top and handed it to me. I rubbed the coconutty cream on my nose as the fans cheered at something I missed. Then I leaned across my knee and Mahoney leaned across his.

"There's a dentist, Riley Clayton," I said. "His office is at 14th and K. He's invented a toothpaste for kids called Smile Wide, and he's debuting it on TV-Spree Monday night. But I have it on good authority that it's tainted, and kids shouldn't be using it."

He didn't say anything for a moment, and just watched the field. A batter walked to first, and the crowd groaned. "How do you know?"

"Some scientists have run tests. I just know about it. But you *can't* name their names, and you *certainly* can't name mine."

"I won't need to. Didn't it get FDA approval?"

"Yes, but—" I thought of Denise and Rebecca rendered speechless and senseless by Clayton's gaze "—he's very good at getting his way."

"Did he bribe someone?"

"Listen," I told him, "I don't know. I'm giving you this, and now you'll have to do your job. I'll put a couple of lab geeks in contact with you. You can break the story and start the investigation rolling before Monday so TV-Spree can yank it. This toothpaste can't go on the market. It's dangerous for kids."

The runner got picked off at second, the catcher's throw hitting the second baseman's glove so hard, everyone in the park could hear the *thwump*. The crowd cheered around us, but Mahoney looked disappointed and bemused. "Is this all you've got for me?"

"What more do you want?" I asked him. "You said at the fundraiser that you're a hack, but that you want to write more important, bigger things. Well, here it is, pal. Write this one, expose this guy, and you can make an important contribution to society and help kids. Unless you were lying to me, and you really are satisfied with just making politicians cry themselves to sleep because you told everyone about their affairs with the nannies. In which case, quit wasting my time."

"Toothpaste," he said, and we sat in silence, watching the inning until the final out. Then he said, "I know there's more."

"Sure there's more," I told him. "But you threatened to mess with Avery. I don't trust you. You're lucky you're getting this much."

He frowned, and I continued. "You said you're willing to work together. Well, there is no partnership when one person's doing things out of fear of retribution. Do this, and do this *today*, and maybe our relationship will change a little bit."

He leaned back and considered for a moment. "You're afraid of me?" he asked.

"No," I said, "and wipe that smirk off your face. I have dirt on you, too, remember. I know your identity. What makes you so certain I'm not going to go blabbing that to media people?"

"Because no one cares," Mahoney said. "Seriously, who cares who I am? My phantom identity is a good gimmick, but the jig will be up sooner or later, and it won't affect my work."

So much for upper hand. "Do we have a deal?" I asked.

"I'm not sure. Is the deal that I get this toothpaste thing out in the open today, and then you and I have a little more of an honest give-and-take?"

I swallowed my pride and forced myself to really look at Mahoney—not as a mudslinger, but as a person who'd seen a fae and that after a lifetime of keeping only one secret, he just wanted to know he was right. I might be able to work something out where he didn't necessarily have to expose the fae. Maybe there was a way he could work with us. I couldn't figure it all out today, but today I had to accept that I could make a deal.

"Yes, that's the deal," I told him. "But I'm making this promise to Greg Mahoney and not to the D.C. Digger. The Digger and I have nothing more to say to each other after today. Do you understand?"

He thought for one moment more, searching my face, and then put out his hand. "I understand," he said, and shook much more firmly than I would have expected. Then he let go, reached his hand into the Cracker Jacks box, and turned his attention to the field. "Come on, Nats!" he yelled. Then, to me, "We're going to win this one. I can feel it."

"You know what?" I said. "So can I."

"I'm only going to be gone one night," Avery said. "You don't need to look so forlorn."

"I'm not," I said, watching cross-legged on the bed as he folded a tie and dropped it in his small suitcase. He hesitated, then folded a second tie and dropped it in also.

"I'm not sure which one I want," he said before I could ask. "I'll decide tomorrow. I don't know which would show better on TV."

"Either," I said, "as long as you're the one wearing it."

His smile was tight and I said, "You're really nervous about this, aren't you?"

"A lot of people watch *Late Night with Wright,*" he said. "He's political, but he's a comedian, and plenty of his viewers don't necessarily follow politics. It's the people who are ambivalent about or hate politics that I want to impress." He sighed. "That's hard."

"So what about just relaxing? You've seen Wright's show. You know he's going to do some funny stuff with you as the straight guy in the joke, so just go with it."

"That's the thing," he said, folding a pair of suit pants along the crease. "I usually go into speaking engagements and appearances more prepared because I know what to generally expect. Tomorrow night, I don't know." He dropped the pants in. "Hey, do you want to go? I didn't ask because it's only one night and we won't have much time, but you can tool around New York a little. I'm sure you can get a seat on my flight tomorrow morning."

"Nah," I said. "Unless you really need me there, I'd rather sit here and watch you on TV while I'm in my pajamas. I can fantasize that you're a famous person I have a crush on."

"Instead of?"

"Instead of the famous person I have a crush on who shares the rent."

"The former scenario is more appealing, eh?"

"It's the fantasy thing."

"This isn't a fantasy?"

I reached down to the floor beside the bed and lifted one black, dusty sock. "This," I said, holding it up with two fingers, "isn't a fantasy."

"My socks are never on the floor," he protested. "In fact, I think you planted that there, like a bloody glove at the crime scene, so you could make a convenient point at a moment like this one."

"Maybe," I admitted, and flung the sock at him. It hit his shoulder. "Do you really need me to go with you?"

"No, it's okay. I'll be back Sunday morning."

I was relieved, because I needed to stay here to monitor the Clayton situation. Until I knew for sure Mahoney had held up his end of the deal, I didn't want to go anywhere. Luckily, if I'd played my cards right—and I was confident I did—Clayton would cease to be a Olde Way threat this very weekend and would be hiring a lawyer, and I could tune in to TV-Spree Monday night and buy lipsticks or mops or casserole dishes—anything but toothpaste.

"Hopefully when I'm back," Avery was saying, "I won't be bummed because I managed to look like an idiot on national television."

"How could you?"

"The last time a McCormack was on television," Avery pointed out, "it was Dad, and they were crucifying him. Outside of Virginia and D.C., that's all the public remembers about my family."

"God damn it, already," I said. I hopped off the bed and wedged myself between him and his suitcase. "Look at me. Look *at* me. That is the past. You're the new McCormack in town. Quit looking over your shoulder. There's nothing back there for you. You're you and today is today and that's the end of it."

He furrowed his brow and took a step back as if to get a better look at me. "Wow."

"Wow, what?"

"Wow, that's exactly what I've said to you about your past, about your father."

I crawled back onto the bed and leaned into the pillows. "Obviously, that's not the same thing."

"No, of course not, but the advice is still sound. Would you take your own advice, then?"

Would I? "Yes," I said, nodding my head once as punctuation. "Yes, I would. I'm not still living with the consequences of what he did."

Avery lifted a brow.

"I'm not," I insisted. "Not anymore. I've gotten out from under that, and it's been recently."

"What brought on that transformation?" Avery asked.

"I've been transformed in ways even I can't get over." I dropped my head on the pillow and reached my arms over my head.

"You've gotten a sunburn, at any rate," Avery noted.

I had to admit, I was feeling pretty good. I was tempted to call Svein and gloat about my simple solution to Clayton's huge problem, but I decided to wait it out. Let him hear about it himself. With any luck, it would be news tomorrow.

Avery slipped a pair of black dress shoes into the sides of the suitcase. "Let's practice," I said to him.

"Practice what?"

"Practice what you're going to say on Wright's show tomorrow night."

"How can I do that?"

"I'll pretend to be Wright and throw a few things at you, and you practice reacting off the cuff."

"This is silly," he said, but he'd stopped packing and I was certain the perfectionist in him loved the idea.

"It can't possibly hurt, and maybe it will even help." I scooted over on my knees, lifted his wheeled bag and placed it on the floor. "Have a seat, Avery McCormack. Let the studio audience get a good look at you. You're a handsome man, you know that?"

"He won't say that."

"Believe me," I said, "he very well could." I deepened my voice. "Great to have you on the show."

"Glad to be here, Graham."

"I understand you're looking to represent Virginia in the House of Representatives."

"That's right."

"What do you think Virginia can bring to the table? Anything? I mean, they couldn't even hang on to West Virginia."

"Gemma, I'm pretty sure Graham isn't going to make me talk about secession."

"You really never know. That's why we're practicing." I deepened my voice again. "So, Virginia. As in, Virginia is for Lovers."

"That it is."

"I'll bet. I understand you and your girlfriend are living in sin."

Avery laughed. "I wouldn't exactly call it that, Graham."

"Well, then, what would you call it?"

"I call it spending the most intimate part of my life with the most intimate person in my life, a woman who I very much plan on convincing to change her last name at some point in the near future. Maybe even a nearer future than she thinks."

I lost my voice.

"Graham," he said, "I seem to have astonished you with that response."

I shook my head. "No," I said in my normal voice and then remembered my role. "No, I just can't believe you managed to weasel out of that line of questioning so, ah, so nicely."

Avery's eyes sparkled.

"I love you," I said.

"If Graham Wright said that to me," Avery said, "I'm pretty sure it would be one of the most famous interviews ever."

"Sorry. What I mean is, um, er…" I struggled to get back into interviewer mode. "Where was I? Right, Virginia. As in, 'Yes, Virginia, There Is a Santa Claus.' Are you familiar with that piece of literature?"

"Yes, Graham, that was a newspaper editorial written in the nineteenth century in which the writer sought to convince a little girl that it was very much worth it to believe in Santa Claus, and fairies, and other magical things that can't be seen, because just because you haven't seen them, it doesn't mean they don't, in fact, exist."

I was astonished for the second time. I had just been free-associating when I came up with that article, and I would have never remembered that the article had mentioned fairies. But while we were on the topic: "So, then, you're saying you believe in Santa Claus?"

Avery shifted. "I do believe in Santa Claus, on a certain level. I believe in the meaning of Santa Claus, the generosity of Christmas and the wonder of children."

"So what about fae?"

"What?"

"*Faeries,*" I said, wincing.

"What about them?"

"Do you believe they exist?"

"I'm—I'm going to have to say no." Avery smiled a perfect politician smile, humoring and kind but, at the same time, just a bit detached.

"Why not?" I asked. "Didn't you just say that you believe in Santa Claus?"

"I believe in the spirit of the Santa Claus legend. I don't believe in an old man in a red velvet suit."

"Do you believe in the faerie legend?"

"I wasn't aware that there was a faerie legend. I mean, certainly not surrounding a major American tradition."

I swallowed, and smiled to hide every little thing I was thinking in that moment. "So you've never heard of the tooth faeries?"

"Tooth faeries? There are more than one?"

"Oh, so you do believe there is at least one."

"No, I don't think…"

"Careful, Avery," I said in my non-Graham voice. "There are always kids who are up too late watching television. This is why you need to practice."

"There are a lot of things Graham Wright could ask me," Avery said, standing, "but I think I'm pretty safe from the topic of the freaking tooth faerie."

"You're awfully quick to mock beliefs on my show tonight, Mr. McCormack," I said in Graham-speak. "What about people who worship a different God than you do? Would you be so quick to mock their beliefs?"

"Jesus, Gemma." He picked up his suitcase and tossed it back onto the bed, bouncing me a little.

"Jesus, Allah, whoever."

"I stand for the right for every American to believe—and not believe—in any way or in anything he or she chooses."

"Except for the 'freaking tooth faerie.'"

"The tooth faerie," Avery said, rolling up a pair of boxers and shoving them in the bag, "is not a religion. It's a story we tell children to ease the pain of coming into adulthood."

"So all these parents are telling lies to their kids?"

"Where are you going with this, Gemma?" Avery asked. "Because I've got enough on my mind as it is without you badgering me with complete and total lunacy."

"I'm not Gemma, I'm Graham," I said. A vein in my temple was throbbing now. Mom had said I needed to be honest with Avery. I had said I wouldn't tell him about me, but really, deep inside, I'd hoped that one day, I could. That the man I loved—and who apparently loved me enough to marry me someday, I now learned—would have the strength come around to something that practically no one else could.

But he was human after all. And it broke my heart, and I wanted to lash out. "What if your girlfriend, whom you just claimed you love so much, believed in the tooth faerie?"

Avery threw up his arms and went into our small bathroom. I followed him, and hung in the door frame as he packed his electric razor and a washcloth into a little black nylon pouch. I reached a hand over my shoulder to scratch at my itching, burning back. "I mean, what if Gemma really believed with all her heart and soul?" I asked. "If she said, 'I know for a living, breathing *fact* that the tooth faerie is real'?"

He turned to leave the bathroom, but I was blocking his way. "Back off with this craziness, Gemma," he said quietly, prying my hand off the wall and slipping past me. "Please. I don't know what we're doing here, but now is not a good time."

"I *have* to know," I demanded. "What would you say to her? To me?" My breathing was rapid and panting, and my shoulder blades quivered violently. "Would you love me enough to believe me?"

He stared at me, bewildered and angry. "All right, here's your answer," he said. "And I hope that after this, this insane subject is closed. I *would* love you enough—to make sure you got the psychological and pharmaceutical help you needed to get out of your delusional world and back into the real one."

I stepped back as if I'd been slapped. My two realities crashed together inside my chest and I couldn't choose, because I was both. I needed to be both, now, in my own home, with the man who loved me. But he would never believe me, and he would never fully understand me, and I wished I'd never known what I was, and I couldn't accept…

And I couldn't breathe…

My wings exploded out of my back, their power pushing me to my knees on the cold tile. I looked up, and Avery stood there, his eyes wide and filled with sheer terror.

"Avery," I said, trying to crawl on aching knees over to him but he scrambled back, sliding on the sock I'd thrown at him earlier and half-landing on the bed. "Oh, my God, Avery."

He pushed himself up and his frantic gaze darted around the room, as if expecting more terrible things to appear, or as if searching for an exit.

"It's me, Avery," I said, lifting myself to my feet, swaying as I adjusted to my new form. He cringed. I held out my hands, palm up. "I'm me. I'm the same me. I love you. Please. Let me explain."

For the briefest moment, his eyes met mine, and I tried as hard as I could to project all the love in my heart to him, shining it out of my gaze, my fingertips, every part of me.

But the next moment, his eyes rolled up in his head and he crashed to the floor, unconscious.

CHAPTER 20

Chaos raged inside me, which was why when Avery awoke a few minutes later, my wings hadn't retracted, and I was still a fearsome apparition.

Luckily his head had hit the fluffy rug. I sat on the floor beside him holding his hand in both of mine, willing the impossible to occur—for him to give me a chance to make him understand.

He blinked over and over, as if he could make the sight of me fall away like sleep dust from his eyes. But I remained, and he stared over my shoulders at my pale gossamer wings. "What," he rasped, "are you?"

"Fae," I said.

He shook his head, not comprehending.

"Fae, like faerie," I clarified for his human mind. "But only half. I'm half human. I didn't even know. I thought I was human until the other week when they found me and…"

"Don't tell me," he said, and rolled away from me. He stood, unsteady, and put out both arms for balance. "I don't want to know. I want to get out of here."

"I wanted to tell you," I said. Weakness spread throughout my body. My shoulders slumped, my hands lay inert in my lap, my head hung down. "But I knew it would sound—that you would think I'm…"

"Crazy?" Avery said, with clear hysteria. "Crazy, I could do. Crazy, I can cope with. But this? What the hell *is* this?"

"You know what faeries are," I said. "You've heard about them all your life. You just didn't know they were true. You didn't know that," I hesitated, "that I'm one. Everything else is the same. When I found this out, and I was scared, my mother told me to remember that I'm the same person I always was, that the only thing that changed was my self-awareness. And I eventually realized she was right. I'm still Gemma the boxer and Gemma the ex-pollster and Gemma, your girlfriend. There's just something extra that we have to get used to."

Sometime in the middle of my small speech, Avery had started shaking his head and he kept it up. "No. No. This is—I don't know what this is." He covered his face with his hands and rubbed. "I haven't been getting enough sleep. I'm overtired. I'm having a nightmare."

I stood and reached out a hand. "Avery, please."

He jerked away. "Don't touch me," he shouted. "Just—don't touch me."

Hot tears filled my eyes and I wouldn't blink them away, instead letting them slide tracks down my face so that he could see I was human too, that this was hurting me too.

But he turned away. He turned his back and grabbed two fistfuls of his hair, his shoulders folding in. He said nothing for several minutes.

I sat on the bed, pulled my legs cross-legged and I breathed. I breathed into my heart, and I breathed into the space between Avery and me, and I breathed into the place on my back where my wings connected to the rest of me, and then I felt them retract into me. I shivered through the torn back of my tank top.

Then I heard Avery mumbling. I leaned a little closer to him to hear. "This isn't real. This isn't real. I have a campaign to do. I have a show to do. I'm dreaming. I—"

"Avery?"

He spun around and startled, realizing my wings were gone. He opened his mouth, closed it again, and then said, "I'm really tired."

A tear rolled over my upper lip and I tasted the salt. "I know."

"I have to get out of here."

"No," I said, "you don't."

"I'm going to be on TV." His voice was eerie, hollow.

"You're not leaving until morning."

"I'm leaving right now." He rushed over to the suitcase, zipped it up and dragged it into the living room. I followed, trying not to get too close to him but desperate to make him stay.

"It's late," I babbled, "and you just said you're tired. Go to sleep. I'll stay down here. I can wake you up early for your flight."

He dropped the bag with a clatter and whirled around. "No," he said, "I can't wake up to this. I just woke up a moment ago and saw you…" He put up his trembling hands, opening and closing them. "I can't wake up to you like that. This—you, us—is what I counted on to get me through." His voice broke. "This is what I knew was true. *Us*. This is what *I* believed in. How can this be falling apart? How?"

"It's not," I begged. "It's not. We can get used to this, get past this. I have so much to tell you, so much I wanted to tell you and now I can…"

He stuffed his feet inside a pair of sneakers and stood there in his sweats, bedraggled and panicky, with only one plan—to leave.

"Don't go," I said, and fell to my knees. "Avery, don't go. I believe in us. It won't fall apart." I broke down, my sobs coming fast and hard and agonized.

"I have to go," he said, backing away from me to the front door. He pulled a hooded sweatshirt off the coat rack and tugged it on, reaching in for his cell phone. "I'll call a cab."

"You're coming home," I said between sobs. "You're coming home on Sunday."

"I don't know what I'm doing, Gemma," he said, and opened the door.

"Don't leave me," I said, crying harder. "I love you. I love you."

He looked at me, and I tried to catch my breath. He was the man I slept with, laughed with, made plans with. I knew everything about him. And now he knew everything about me.

I couldn't read his expression at all. Hate, pity, fear, love, remorse. It could have been all of them, or none of them, or a thousand other things. But I had no idea.

Then he left, closing the door gently behind him.

"Avery!" I screamed in a voice that wasn't mine. I pounded my fists on the floor, then collapsed onto my side, crying, curling into a fetal position, clutching at myself, mourning what I'd known all along I was destined to lose.

>=<

I didn't want to knock and risk no one answering. I was already alone, and I couldn't stand to be even more so. Instead, I intended and walked through the closed door.

He was there, sitting at the cramped desk. He took in my ragged hair, my sweatpants and ripped tank top, my untied sneakers. "What the hell happened to you?" Svein asked.

"He left," I said. My empty voice echoed in my own ears. It had been years since I'd cried over anything or anyone, and two straight hours of weeping had left me drained, hopeless and incoherent. "My wings came out. He ran away. He ran away from me and us."

Svein rose and came around to where I stood by the door. He encircled me with one arm and I leaned against him as he walked me around the Archives office's desk and settled me into the chair. I fell back and blinked my eyes very, very slowly.

Svein perched on the desk and regarded me. "Where did Avery go?" he asked softly.

I shrugged. "Don't know. He has a TV show in New York tomorrow night. Probably got an earlier flight to get as far away from me as he could."

"Is he coming back?"

I didn't want to say the words, give them validity. "I don't know."

He reached over and took my hands in his. "I'm sorry," he said. "But I have to ask. Is there a chance that he'll..."

I set my jaw. "You're going to ask, is there a chance that he'll tell the world that faeries are real and that he just realized his girlfriend is one?" I tasted the bitterness of my own laugh. "No. The last thing he wants to do is sink his campaign by appearing mentally unstable. No matter what he's thinking about me, what he's feeling, it's his secret, at least for now." I narrowed my eyes. "So don't worry. I haven't given us all up."

"I'm not worried," he said.

I let my head flop back. "Why did I do this?" I asked the ceiling. "Why?"

"You know why."

"I'm an idiot. When did I start being an idiot?" I closed my eyes, then raised my brows, smiling mirthlessly. "Oh, yes, that's it. The dream. The goddamn dream where all my teeth fall out. That was it. That's how it always starts. I should have left town that night, just gotten the hell away from my life so that fate wouldn't step in to fuck it all up the way it always does after the dream. But you know what? I fooled myself into thinking that it would be okay this time, and then Frederica showed up and my mother told me the truth and I transformed. Right here, in fact." I popped my eyes open and sat up straight, yanking my hands away from Svein's and staring poison daggers at him. "Then you. What's your *deal*, anyway? One minute you think I'm a screw-up who should have never been recruited, and the next minute you're shoving your tongue down my throat. You like me, you don't like me. Which is it, already? I'm sick of tap-dancing around innuendoes. Let's get this out in the open for a change."

Svein met my gaze, daggers notwithstanding. "It's not a matter of liking or not liking you. It's not on that level."

"Yes, please," I said. "Be enigmatic and obtuse. Because that's going to really help me right now."

In an instant, he was off the desktop and leaning over me, his face very, very close to mine. His breath whispered against my cheek. "Regardless of what you might think," he said softly, "my feelings where you're concerned are hardly black or white. Tonight is not the time to dissect them. Let it go."

I grabbed the back of his neck and crushed my lips to his. I twisted my fingers into his hair as I persuaded him with my lips to part his and I pushed my tongue inside his mouth, tasting him, trying to feel anything, anything, to make me forget. Forget about Avery.

But I couldn't.

I pulled away and dropped back into the chair, wiping my mouth with the back of my hand. "Sorry," I mumbled. "I just—sorry."

Svein searched my eyes with his. "I understand."

"How could you when I don't?"

"You're here," he said, resettling himself on the desktop, "because I'm the one man who knows what you are, both sides of you, and accepts you. I understand you, and that's what you need right now. You kissed me because you'd rather believe you deliberately drove Avery away than believe he left you because of who you are and what you can't control."

I sighed. "I didn't even think of going anywhere else. It's not like I couldn't go to my mother's. I didn't want to be at home all alone. I waited two hours and he's not coming back tonight. I just came straight here. I wasn't even thinking."

I rubbed my face. "You're my mentor. Mentor me. Give me some wise answers so I can fix this."

"You don't need a mentor anymore," he said with a small smile. "And all I want to give you right now is something that will complicate things a whole lot more."

He stood. "There's a sleep room down the hall. It's for shift-working fae who need to crash. I don't think anyone's in there tonight."

"Are you saying you want us to go in there and complicate things?"

He looked at me for a long moment. "I won't take advantage of you tonight. You deserve far better. I'm saying you should go in there and get some rest. I'm going to hang around for a little while to get some work done. I'm on call. You'll be okay. It's across the hall, third door down."

I stood but once at the door, I lingered.

"Go," he said. "I'm noble, and I'm strong. But you have a habit of pushing me to my limit. You need to sleep."

I nodded, and my neck was having a hard time holding my heavy head upright. I left the office, closed the door behind me and headed for a bed and a temporary respite from the quick mess my life had become.

>=<

Grab the teeth, don't lose them, you have to get them…

"No," I said, my tongue thick. "No." I crouched among freshly lost, bloody teeth, and they cracked under my shoes.

Don't lose them, don't lose them…

"Shut up!" I yelled at the laughing voices, melodic voices...

"Gemma…"

"Shut up! I can't do it!"

"Gemma."

I awakened with a gasp, and Reese pulled her small hand away from me as she stepped back, startled. "Gemma, I'm sorry."

The room was pure white—walls, sheets, pillowcases, small wooden dresser that held a bunch of thin wooden reeds in a watery glass bottle. The bedspread was fluffiness that was six inches high. A small nightlight burned a rosy glow. My rapid breathing seemed out of place in the tranquil fae room, and I slowed it down, bit by bit. I knew I had been dreaming, but I touched my mouth anyway, pushing my teeth a little to make sure they were intact.

"Svein said you were sleeping in here," Reese said.

Svein. Oh God, Avery.

I flopped back on a pillow so buoyant it rebounded me nearly all the way back up. My head ached, and my eyes felt twice their normal size and very dry. It took me a moment to realize they were the side effects of a long cry, something I wasn't accustomed to.

"I'm really sorry," Reese repeated. "I should have just let you sleep."

"No," I told her. "It's okay. I *was* having a nightmare, but you had no way of knowing that I've awakened to an even bigger one."

Reese's face was full of sympathy, and I wondered how much she'd figured out on her own, merely because I was spending the night at The Root. She had never been anything but friendly and helpful to me, and I felt bad that she was now standing in the line of my emotional fire.

But despite my grim demeanor, she sat down on the bed beside me, and her diminutive weight barely made a dent on the blanket. "I brought you something," she said, and held out a little pink velvet pouch, tied with a drawstring. She watched my face, and though I didn't reach out to take it, I summoned up a small polite smile for her, and she took it as permission to continue. "Vikings believed that anything belonging to children was powerful and lucky. Of course," she added, "we know that their teeth are, and we know why. Maybe it was a Viking fae collector who started the tradition, but men heading into battle would often wear or carry a child's tooth, for strength."

She dropped her hands into her lap and watched her own tiny fingers turn the pouch over and over. "I'm sure you don't need luck, but I thought a little extra power couldn't hurt." She grinned into her lap. "I collected yesterday from two kids right next door to each other. One kid's tooth fell out, and the other one had his own loose tooth and was jealous or something, and they tied a string around it and yanked it out so they could both have a tooth faerie visit. This is the one that fell out naturally. I told Research and Retrieval I lost it, but I kept it for you."

She sighed, and her expression sobered. "I don't know the exact reason why you slept here last night, but I can tell this has all been very hard on you. I feel so awful about that, and responsible, because I'm one of the ones you're fighting for. And in case no one's told you, we do appreciate it." She looked at me, and her eyes were bright. "*I* appreciate it. The idea that I can help you means everything to me. That night, when you called me from Watergate, I was—I was *honored* to help you."

I reached out my hand, and Reese deposited the pouch into my palm. My skin tingled and my nose tickled at the nearness of the essence. "Thank you." My voice was raspy, and I cleared my throat. "But I think I may have already won the battle with Dr. Clayton."

Wistfulness played around the edges of her smile. "Then you might want to have it for another battle. Sometimes the most difficult wars to win are the ones we wage within ourselves. A little help can go a long way."

I closed my hand around the tooth. "I promised myself I wouldn't let the fae down," I said. "You've put your trust in me. But why? What makes anyone so sure I can take on such a monumental role when all I ever manage to do, even now, is screw up?"

"Because you're not taking on the role," she said. "You *are* the role. There's no thinking about it. It just is. You just are. Isn't it a relief to know that you only have to be you and you'll be perfect?"

"Is that what you do? You go around every day assured that you're perfect?"

Reese thought a second, then burst out laughing. "No, I guess I don't. I feel like I'm screwing up every minute too. It's easier advice to give than to live, I suppose."

"Well, how about this?" I suggested. "Every now and then, I'll remind you you're perfect. But you have to do the same for me."

"Will do," she said. "I promise. And I'm going to give you a hug." She leaned over and wrapped her thin, warm arms around me, and I couldn't stop a few tears from appearing and dripping onto her shoulder. I wanted to apologize but I thought that would make me cry harder. I clutched my little tooth pouch.

"Don't worry, Gemma," Reese said, giving me an extra squeeze. "Faerie tales can have really happy endings."

"Not faerie," I mumbled into her shirt. "Fae."

>=<

It was early for most people on a Saturday morning at Smiley's Gym. At 9:20 a.m., most of the regulars were still sleeping it off. In fact, that's what I usually did. I nodded now at one of the two unfamiliar morning guys lingering by the ropes. I wrapped my hands, got my gloves on, and got down on the floor for knuckle pushups.

After thirty-six of them, a shadow fell over me. I didn't glance up. "Thought I told you not to come back until next week," Smiley said.

I said nothing until I hit sixty. Then I rolled back to sit on my knees. He raised his brows to acknowledge my turn to speak, and to imply I'd better have something good to say.

"I don't bring my problems here," I said. "But"—I swallowed hard—"Avery walked out on me last night. I can't be at home right now. I need to work it out. Please, Smiley. I do remember I'm not supposed to be here. I won't stay long."

What I didn't add was that Avery's flight was at noon, and I hoped that if he hadn't left last night, if he'd just gotten a room or stayed with a friend, he might seek me out, and he'd know I'd be here. At *my* safe house.

Smiley looked me over and nodded once. "Do what you need to do," he said. He bent down and patted my shoulder gruffly. "If, uh, if you need anything."

"I don't," I assured him, because I knew that love wasn't something he wanted to give advice about.

"Bag's free," he said, and I got up.

"Thanks," I said. "You won't even know I'm here."

"It's okay. Here's where you belong."

He turned abruptly and I watched him go into his office. Strange that even though I was family here at the gym, and I'd recently acquired a magical extended family, I felt as though my heart had been abducted and dropped alone onto an uncharted island in the middle of Nowhere Ocean.

The heavy bag hung steady and unmoving. That was another thing about being here so early in the morning. Usually when I got my turn at the bag, it was still swaying and dented from the last boxer's go. But today it was yet unbruised and untested, and it was mine. I needed the challenge and the comfort it offered.

I put up my gloves and bounced a little on my toes, trying to shake off the nightmares and the harsh morning light on the long walk here and the headache and the still-fuzzy vision. I rolled my neck one way, then the other way.

Avery, I thought. I pushed the thought away and it returned. *Avery.*

Fine. I brushed a lock of hair off my face with my forearm. I'd faced my fears in the ring before and fought through them. I could fight through this one too.

Avery.

I jabbed and landed hard. It wasn't smart to start like this, not when I was so weak inside, but at the same time, there was a wild thing inside me that demanded to be set free. I jabbed, and jabbed, and jabbed, feeling the jolt of each hit run up the length of my arm until strength coiled strong and hot into my shoulders, and I unleashed a jab-cross. One-two. One-two.

Instead of switching sides, I kept power-punching with my dominant right, harder and harder with each hit. I didn't want to properly condition. I had to release, and I had a lot to release. I hit and hit and hit until I had to scream and I did, packing weeks of agony and frustration and despair into one last punch, and my own shout reverberated around the dim room.

Breathing hard, I bent my knees and leaned over with my gloves on my thighs. My head hung and I watched one, two, three drops of my perspiration plunk to the floor. When I lifted my head, the two men I didn't know were alternately staring at me, then at each other, no doubt wondering what I was really fighting. I glanced over at Smiley in his office and caught him watching me as well. When I nodded and held up a glove, he nodded back. But he didn't go back to whatever he was doing. Instead, he looked at a spot behind me, and his expression grew cloudy and strange.

He saw something, or someone.

Avery?

"Gemma," I heard behind me.

"Avery," I said, and whirled.

No, not Avery.

Dad.

CHAPTER 21

We stood, silent and staring.

Behind the cracked glass of the wall clock, the second hand ticked with each movement. I heard the long space between each tick, and I wondered how many of those ticks there were in twenty-two years.

Twenty-two years.

He cleared his throat. "Might want to work your other side for a while. You worked the right pretty hard." He offered a smile, and my small triumph was the wariness in its corners. "It looks good," he said. "You look good."

"You look old."

He didn't, really. His hair, which I remembered as blond as mine, had faded and thinned. He wore a long-sleeved Henley top that was definitely a few sizes larger, but his eyeglasses were smaller. He carried a black leather jacket over his arm. I didn't want him to look like a nice person, to look like someone I'd smile at on the street. I wanted George Cross to look like the man I was supposed to hate.

He chuckled, softly and cautiously. "Fair enough. And anyway, I feel old."

This moment was the one I'd anticipated for almost my whole life, even when it became clear to me that it would probably never happen. I'd choreographed and scripted the encounter to perfection, from my indignant one-liners right down to my dramatic turning and stalking away, leaving him abandoned and hurting. I had played it over and over in my mind, making a few minor tweaks here and there over the years. I knew the role inside and out, but now, I just couldn't perform.

Instead, I was forced to ad lib, and it wasn't very original. "Why are you here?"

"I'm here," Dad said, "because I know what's going on with you."

A few more seconds ticked by. "Well?" I said finally. "You want to clue me in?"

"They've got you," he said. "You're working for them."

"Working for who?"

"The fae," he said.

I blinked. "How would you know that? How would *you* know *anything* about me?"

"Smiley told me."

"What?" I snapped my head around again, but Smiley had left his office for the ring, where the other two boxers shuffled around each other. I stepped closer to Dad to keep our conversation private, and I caught the scent of him, the scent of him tucking me in at night, a scent that I should never have remembered but I did.

I dropped an iron veil over my heart. "Smiley doesn't know anything about the fae," I said.

"No, he doesn't. But he does know plenty about you. And when I called him the day before yesterday, he filled me in."

"You called when?" But as the words left my lips, I suddenly realized that the check-in calls Smiley admitted to having with my Dad were not ancient history, that they were still a regular thing, that Dad was hovering on the edge of my life all this time.

"Smiley said you're not sleeping, that you're coming in here exhausted, you're not acting like yourself, you're picking fights and deliberately getting hurt, that strangers are coming in and out to see you. I knew," he said. "I knew right away the fae had tracked you down and put you to work nights. But it can't be more. Tell me you're just collecting, and that it's not more than that."

"I'm not obligated to tell you what I ate for breakfast today, much less anything else."

"If it had been left up to me," he said, "then even now, you'd have no idea you were anything other than full human. Your mother agreed. That's how I felt when you were born and that's how I still feel. They shouldn't be using you."

"They're not using me. I had a *choice*," I said. "A choice, and I made it, and I'm dealing with the consequences. Just like *you* made a choice, and now you have to deal with it. With me."

He didn't respond. Instead, he walked over to a pile of hand pads in the corner of the room, picked through them, and found a matching pair. He tucked them under his arm, then dropped his jacket on a folding chair. He came to stand in front of me again, slipped the pads onto his hands, and tapped them together with two muffled thumps. Then he looked at my face for a long moment, and held them up.

I hesitated only for a split second before slamming my left glove into his left hand. It should have toppled him, but his feet were boulders, and he didn't move, didn't blink. I punched again, this time with my right, and I connected hard. Then my left.

"Slow down a little," he said. Then, "It's true I had a choice all those years ago, and I made it. It wasn't what I wanted. But when you're a parent, your strongest instinct is to protect your child."

I bent my elbow and came in hard with a hook, and he stepped out of the way, but I stormed into his space. "Is this your game now?" I snarled through gritted teeth. "Telling me you ran out on me to *protect* me?"

"I did."

"Well, *Dad*, I can't wait to hear your bullshit rationalization."

He didn't back up, and he didn't back down, and a grudging part of me gave him credit for at least that.

"I left," he said, "because he said he knew what you were, and said he'd turn you over to the fae if I didn't leave my family for good. He said he'd deliberately create an Olde Way threat and force the fae to recruit you to fight him, then he'd win. He said he'd kill you."

"Who?"

"Gemma, he meant it. He hated me. You were only eight years old. I couldn't…"

"*Who*?"

"Guy named Riley Clayton."

A rush of lightheadedness caused me to stagger back. Clayton? *What*?

"He was a man who used to be in love with your mother. He blamed me for stealing her away, but that was crazy. Bethany had mentioned him to me when we first met and she said then that it was nothing serious."

"No," I said, and my ears felt cloggy, and my voice sounded like I was underwater.

"Then one day he turned up, out of the blue, and I didn't even know who he was. I was walking home from the corner store with English muffins for your mother. He approached me and introduced himself as Riley Clayton, the man ready to ruin my daughter's life if I didn't listen to what he had to say to me."

I tried to clear my mind and retain my power of logic. "What did he say?"

"He said he was a half-fae, like you."

Apparently, I'd gotten something right.

"He said he hated both sides of himself, said humans and fae were both inferior, and as a hybrid, it made him—and you—twice as flawed. I told him that you were only a child, that you thought you were human and that your mother and I had told you nothing. He said he lived in secret also. He asked me why we kept you away from the fae. He said, 'Is it because of what they might make her do for them?'" Dad met my gaze dead on. "I said yes."

"Then he said as a hybrid, not only did he have the power to protect the fae, he had the ability to bring them down, and he hadn't made up his mind about his own destiny yet. But there was one thing he knew for sure he wanted to do: Hurt Bethany for leaving him, hurt me for supposedly stealing her away, and hurt you for merely being born."

When I'd played the scene over and over in my head of this reunion with my father, I didn't expect this. I expected to hear apologies and excuses, sincere or otherwise, and I would sanctimoniously declare him dead to me.

I didn't expect this. I didn't expect to begin to feel *for* him, and I didn't expect to believe his abandoning us was anything other than a careless whim, and I didn't expect to want and need to hear the rest of the story.

"So he gave me a choice." Dad's lips stretched into a thin-lipped, grim smile. "He told me to pick up and leave my family, just go away without explanation and never return. If I did, he said, I'd be securing your safety. He said there hadn't been a serious threat to the Olde Way in decades, and that the only real threat was him, and if I appeased him with my leaving, he'd refrain from causing any trouble. But if I didn't leave, he said, my daughter would be as good as dead, because he'd make her—you—his archenemy."

I walked over to the row of folding chairs and lifted his jacket to sit down. Instead of draping it across the back of a seat, I laid it in my lap. It warmed my legs. Dad sat beside me. "The fact that you're sitting, and the fact that you haven't taken my head off," he said, "makes me hopeful that you believe me."

"I don't understand why you didn't just..." I stopped. What I'd been about to say—it was the same assumption Svein had made about me, and after defending the human race so vigorously, I was mortified that I had been about to ask, quite as a matter of fact, why my father hadn't just killed Clayton.

"He threatened you," he said. "I couldn't go to the police, because why would they believe a man who had no connection whatsoever to my family had threatened my little girl? It would have been my word against his. I couldn't kill him, and I wanted to. I wanted to. But more than I didn't want you to not have a daddy, I didn't want you to have a daddy in prison for the rest of his life."

He sighed. "Clayton knew too much about you, about the fae, about everything, and I knew he meant every word. And your mother, she…"

He stopped and looked away from me, looked at the two men in the ring who were taking a break with water bottles and conversation about the NFL draft.

"Don't tell me that part," I said. "I don't want you to tell me what it took to leave her. I think I know how it felt to leave her because I know how she felt when you did."

He nodded, and squeezed his eyes shut and open once. "Then I stayed away, because I didn't know how to come back. I didn't think I should, because I didn't know how long Clayton would be watching. But even if I found out he was gone forever, I wouldn't have known how to come back to you. For years, I sent money to your mother for the house, and for you."

"She didn't tell me that," I said.

"Her husband left her in the middle of the night because he couldn't tell her why, and he couldn't bear to say goodbye. That's something a person has to deal with in her own way. A marriage is not for a child to understand, so I'm sure she made her choices too." He shook his head slowly. "I lived without you and Bethany and I managed to do it because with every moment I spent alone, I had the assurance that you were safe, that I'd saved you."

He looked at me again, and something in me broke apart. It might have been my heart. "Gemma," he asked quietly, "why did your mother tell you who you are? Why are you working for them? Because now, all this time, I've been hurting our family for nothing."

"If that's how you feel now," I said, just as quietly, "I can't imagine how you're going to feel when I tell you that Clayton lied. He tried to contact me only months after you left, and tried several times throughout my life to get to me. I didn't know. Mom protected me, never told me. But I was recruited a few weeks ago to specifically stop Clayton's plan."

Dad's face changed without moving so much as a muscle. A fog fell over him, darkening his eyes, deepening the lines at his temples and between his brows. A blackness wrapped around his shoulders at the revelation that his justification for leaving us, the reason that kept him strong enough to do what he did, was gone and the years behind him were an empty, dry desert.

"I wasn't going to tell you this," he said flatly, "but I was there for some things. I went to your high school graduation. It was outdoors, and your hair was long, and when they called your name, damn if you didn't strut across that stage, like you didn't care who knew how proud you were of your own accomplishment."

I listened. I couldn't bear to hear, but I had to.

"I've seen you in the paper once or twice lately with your boyfriend. He seems like a smart guy, but the smartest thing he did, I think, was to find and hang on to you."

I tried to ignore the stab in my gut as I glanced around the room for Avery, even though he was probably at the airport by now.

"And," Dad said, "I went to a couple of your fights."

I wasn't sure what was on my face, but he added, "I was at the one where you lost in a decision to that girl—I forgot her name, an Italian name. Who was it?"

"Mancini. Geri Mancini." He'd been there?

"Yeah, she was good," he said. "She was tough, but you were better, and the crowd agreed very loudly. But you were gracious. You lost like a winner. I said to the guy next to me, 'That's my daughter,' and he said, 'So why are you sitting way back here?'" He paused. "And now you tell me Clayton's out there making trouble for the fae and for you, despite our agreement, and now I wish more than anything that I'd been sitting ringside that night, that I could have told you how proud you made me—how proud you make me."

Watching the hurt take harsh hold of him, the scared, sad, abandoned little girl in me was finally satisfied.

And suddenly, the adult me knew that I would forgive him. Maybe not this second, maybe not this week, but I would forgive him.

I wouldn't be forgiving him because Clayton wouldn't want me to. I would forgive him because *I* wanted to.

It seemed I wasn't aware of the rock that had been sitting on my chest for more than two decades until it rolled off and I could breathe again. Freedom and lightness filled me.

Oh, I was angry. I had a feeling that if Svein handed that gun to me right now, I wouldn't be so quick to defend humanity's honor. I believed I still wouldn't kill Clayton, although right now, I really, really had the motivation.

But the inner rage that defined me, that guided me through every day from the moment I swung my legs out of bed to the moment I slipped back under the blankets had dissolved. I wasn't familiar with the Gemma it left behind. One thing was clear: The Gemma I was now had a father.

"I'm sorry," Dad said.

"Are you going to see Mom?" I asked.

"I hadn't planned on it. I thought I could come here, talk you out of working for the fae, duck your angry shouts and fists, and go home. I had no idea he was still out there doing… doing whatever. I had no idea he reneged on our deal."

"Listen," I said. "I took care of him. Keep an eye on the news today. If I succeeded, you'll hear Clayton's name. But you have to go see Mom. You have to."

He twisted his hands in his lap. "What am I going to say to her?" he mumbled. "What is she going to say to me?"

"Tell her what you told me. Tell her the truth," I said. "Then, well, my advice ends there. What comes after that has nothing to do with me." I looked down at my feet. "For what it's worth, I'm in your corner."

He put an awkward hand on my shoulder, and I let him. I let myself feel close to him again. "It's worth everything," he said.

>=<

I spent most of the day in front of Avery's computer. Usually I wouldn't spend more than ten minutes there. My polling job had required constant monitoring of the Internet and I couldn't stand being at a keyboard when I wasn't being paid.

But being online was marginally better than the only thing I really felt like doing—crying all day because I didn't know whether my boyfriend was ever coming home.

As it turned out, I had plenty of reading to keep me busy. Greg Mahoney had been efficient, breaking the story late last night on the D.C. Digger blog that Dr. Riley Clayton, local dentist, had created a toothpaste that was potentially dangerous for kids. My Root sources must have supplied him with the sample of Smile Wide, because he now had new, named sources who had tested the toothpaste and discovered some kind of calcium compound plus another ingredient not listed on the tube. They said daily use could eat away at teeth, raising a risk of infection. Riley Clayton refused comment.

The Digger stopped short of recommending action, but he didn't have to.

Several online news outlets picked up the story, with headlines like, "Could brushing teeth be *bad* for your kids?" All the reporters credited the Digger for breaking the story, and many ran the photo of Clayton from his practice's Web site. The picture was professionally done but I was certain the photographer hadn't had to touch up one bit of his flawless face.

Late in the afternoon, I was gratified to see CNN reporting on the headline-making dentist, and confirming that TV-Spree did cancel Clayton's scheduled appearance, citing their commitment to selling safe, high-quality products.

Luckily for both the Digger and myself, it was otherwise a slow news day, which was why a couple of children's health advocates and dental experts earned their day in the broadcast sun, speculating how the toothpaste got past the FDA and what toothpaste brands they personally recommended for healthy teeth.

No one charged the dentist with criminal negligence, but several parents whose children had been using Smile Wide from patient goody bags expressed interest in taking legal action. Even still, Riley Clayton refused comment. Though by this time, he had retained a lawyer who, blinking behind thick glasses, said, "Dr. Clayton stands by his integrity in creating Smile Wide."

I wondered about Clayton's glamour, and why he didn't pull off a press conference that would leave viewers reeling at his beauty, but then it hit me the way it must have occurred to him as well: If there was only one power stronger than fae glamour, it was a mother's protective instinct. There wasn't one mother out there who would fall under his spell about anything concerning her child's safety.

So, was I victorious? Yes, indeed. Smile Wide would never be sold, and if it was, it wouldn't be until after the most careful public scrutiny, and I doubted Clayton would bother trying to slip something under the radar again. I was certain that every last one of his young patients would be finding new dentists. His career was over within twenty-four hours, because of one tip to one blogger. Speaking from unfortunate experience, Johnson McCormack had been right—armed with the smallest piece of unsavory information, the media could break you in one day.

As evening approached, I finally snapped off the TV and shut down the computer. I stretched out on the sofa. Victorious, yes. But was I satisfied?

Not by a long shot.

That bastard had destroyed my family for a little bit of fun, then—driven by his apparent hatred of both races—didn't hold up his end of the bargain with Dad. He forced me out of hiding to transform and take him on. Then my transformation shattered my relationship with the man I loved.

He slowed progress to the Olde Way by stealing human children's innocence, and I didn't doubt we could shake that off and catch up. But I had no idea how many children he'd gotten to or for how long, or—

Riley Clayton had said he wasn't working with the midnight fae, but that they could very well pick up where he left off.

I put two fingers to each of my temples and tried to press the inevitable conclusion out of my head, but I couldn't do it. The midnight fae could have slipped into the psyches of the most affected, most vulnerable children, and expanded their hate and hurt until their still-growing bodies couldn't contain it anymore and it exploded out of them in fists and screams and guns.

Until it turned them into demons.

Those kids, those hate-infected newly psycho kids, they could influence other kids. There were plenty of kids who never tasted Smile Wide who were just sad, hurt, lonely kids out of circumstance. They could be easily influenced by their midnight fae-puppeted peers.

This was out there now, out there in my city, in Washington. The corrupt politics of this city wouldn't be able to compete with the corruption inside these kids, a dark manifestation of something I didn't know yet.

I hoped I wasn't right. I hoped he wasn't right. But I knew we were.

I hated Clayton all over again. It was easy to hate him. I'd succeeded in beating him down, but I *needed* him to suffer for hurting me, and for opening the door—however unwittingly—for a different evil to take root and grow. I wanted him to live in torment, to crawl on bloody knees and shake his fist in the air, screaming my name. I wanted him to cry at night at his failure. I wanted him to never experience a moment of happiness or peace.

But it was over now, and I'd beaten him. Clayton had to know the only thing he could do for himself was to fade into obscurity. My job was done, and my next task was to pick up the pieces of the things Clayton had broken and glue them back together.

Superhero movies never showed this part, did they? The bad guy lost and the good guy won, and the good guy was satisfied. You never saw him wondering, *well, that's done, but now am I supposed to do with the mess he left me with*? You never saw him wrestling with the unresolved rage and conflict within himself. It was all neatly wrapped up into a happy ending.

I fell asleep on the sofa wondering what it would take to secure my happy ending, and I knew I'd settle for Avery walking in the door and telling me he was ready to try.

>=<

When I woke up, I was alone and my back hurt. I glanced at the time on the cable box and slammed my knee on the ground as I scrambled to grab the remote and turn the TV on, skimming through channels until I landed on Avery.

He'd decided on the red tie. He and Graham Wright were laughing about something I'd missed completely, but I could tell even before either of them spoke again that the interview was going well.

I piled a few pillows behind me and sank my aching back into them as I watched Avery, the famous man I had a crush on, finish his interview.

"So," Graham said, "looks like there's some interesting stuff happening in D.C. today. A dentist," he said to the studio audience with his trademark snaggle-toothed grin, "created toothpaste that is so bad for kids, they're yanking it from the market."

Oh, no.

"That's right, Graham. In fact," Avery said, leaning forward,

"I'm taking the lead on this issue because I find it profoundly disturbing that this might have been routinely rubber-stamped by the FDA. As district attorney, I'm seeing to it that this case is investigated thoroughly."

Oh, no. Avery just couldn't get mixed up in this now.

"You think this Doctor"—Graham consulted a blue index card—"Doctor Riley Clayton set out to hurt kids on purpose?"

"I'm not saying that," Avery said. "I don't know that to be or not be the issue. What I am saying is that the public deserves assurance that the products they buy and rely on to take care of their kids' health are safe. We're going to get to the bottom of this toothpaste situation, and hopefully get measures in place to avoid another near-crisis."

"Tell us the truth," Graham said. "Do you floss every day?"

"Well," Avery said with a sheepish smile.

"Because," Graham told him, "you look exactly like the kind of person who does. The kind of person the rest of us pretend to be."

While the audience laughed, I groaned. Just when I had kicked Riley Clayton to the curb, Avery was going to pick him up and shake him until he rattled. As much as I'd just been thinking Clayton should have gotten more grief, I didn't want Avery to be the one to give it to him. As long as Avery was involved, I was still involved. Shit.

Graham thanked Avery for coming on to the show and as they stood to shake hands, I watched my boyfriend, along with millions of faceless viewers. I wondered when I would see him again. Even though I hoped with all my heart it would be tomorrow, I had a terrible feeling that it wouldn't, that our relationship was done.

And I had a more terrible feeling that Clayton *wasn't* done.

CHAPTER 22

"I need to see you."

As much as I'd wanted to hear those words, I was hearing them from the wrong person. "Mahoney," I said into the phone, "It'll have to wait. I've got some stuff to take care of here."

I hoped he wouldn't ask what stuff, because I didn't want to confess I was committed to camping out under the blankets in bed all day with the phone, waiting for Avery to come home or call. I'd gotten zero sleep last night, scripting what I'd say if he walked in the door today, and planning how I'd try to find him and change his mind if he didn't. "Listen," I said to the Digger, "if this is about our deal, we can talk another time." That is, after I'd consulted Frederica, et al., for advice on how much I could tell Mahoney about the fae.

"It's not about that," he said. "It's Clayton."

"What about him?" I sat up partway, and my hair rubbed against the sheet, crackling with static and zapping my earlobe. "Ow. Did he contact you?"

I heard a loud muffle, as if he'd covered the phone with his hand, then the line cleared again. "Gemma," he said. "It's really important that you meet me now."

"Just tell me what's up," I said.

"I can't," he said, and I sat up straighter, pulling the sheets away from me. His voice was as flat as a floorboard, with no trace of his trademark cockiness. No bragging about breaking the biggest story of his blogging career, no coaxing me to give him the information I'd promised, no teasing banter with a glaringly obvious ulterior motive. Nothing.

That's how I knew things had gone very wrong.

"Is he there?" I asked. "Is he with you right now?"

Say no, I begged silently. At a keyboard, Mahoney was a force of nature. But he'd be no match for a scorned and shamed half-fae.

He cleared his throat. "Yeah. Can you meet me at your boxing gym?"

I glanced at the clock. Quarter after noon. "I'm leaving now on my bike. But it's still going to take me a little while."

"I'm there now," he said. "I'm out front. Just—you have to get here." A note of panic broke through his monotone. "I'm sorry. He made me—"

He was cut off and I heard scuffling. I stumbled out of bed, scooped up the same pair of jeans I'd worn yesterday, and held the phone with my shoulder as I jammed one leg in. "I'm on my way," I said. "Don't worry. I'll take care of everything. Can you hang on?"

He didn't answer. I fell onto the bed to shove my other leg into my pants. "Hang on," I said, my own voice cracking. "Greg, hang on!"

The only response was a disconnection.

I threw on a T-shirt over my sports bra and pushed my feet into sneakers. I rushed over to the dresser, grabbed a fistful of my belongings—house keys, loose change, Fae Phone and cell phone, the tooth pouch from Reese—and stuffed it all into my hip pockets.

As I bolted from the condo, I tripped over one of Avery's running sneakers, keeping myself upright by slamming my arm into the door frame. Dreading I might be too late, I prayed to whatever fae gods existed that my screw-ups wouldn't hurt anyone else but me. I banged the door shut behind me and ran.

:>=<

My bike brakes screeched in protest when I got to Smiley's. I hopped off the bike before it came to a full stop and shoved it against the front wall. Panting from the exertion of riding here at top speed and trying to stay on my wobbly, sore legs, I looked around. No Mahoney.

"Mahoney!" I yelled. The only other person on the street, a man in a dirty denim jacket walking a Chihuahua, eyed me and hurried around the corner, his dog clicking frantically after him. "Greg!"

I was about to head inside when I heard it: a soft moan. I slipped into the narrow space between Smiley's and a Chinese take-out place and pushed around a bundle of white trash bags until I uncovered a man's foot in a flip-flop. I threw off a few more bags to find Mahoney in a T-shirt and long shorts, his eyes half-closed. His blood everywhere.

"Greg!" I yelled into his face. "Wake up! Wake up. Stay with me. I'll get you help."

"Gem—" he said, and his right hand curled, clutching at air. "No," he breathed. "Don't help—me. He has him. Clayton…" He coughed and the blood ran harder down his white shirt. "Clayton has him."

"Who?" I asked, gently guiding him upright and laying him against my shoulder as I stood.

He flopped against me as I half pushed him over my back. His voice hissed against my sweaty shirt. "He has—McCormack."

Avery. Oh, God. Oh, God.

I staggered under his weight and dragged us both to the front door, where Shirley and Not-Rocky were now chatting. Shirley was locking the door. Smiley didn't work on Sundays, and the regulars took the responsibility of closing up early.

"What the hell?" Not-Rocky asked, dropping his gym bag to help me with Mahoney. Shirley twisted back around and unlocked the door, kicking it open, and the three of us managed to get Mahoney in and lying on the floor.

Even fully occupied, the gym was a dim cave. It was even darker now, with no lights and the blinds on the two tiny windows drawn. Mid-afternoon sunlight squeezed in between two broken blinds, and dust danced in its wake.

"Are you okay?" Not-Rocky asked me, cupping the back of my head and glancing down at my blood-stained shirt.

"I'm fine. It's all him." I looked down at Mahoney, who had shut his eyes again. His chest rose up and down and his breath rasped through his parted lips. The blood came from his nose—and his ears.

"Oh, no," I whispered. "It's all me. This is all me."

"Who is this guy?" Not-Rocky asked.

Mahoney groaned and his arm twitched. I grabbed his wrist. "Where's Clayton?" I demanded. "Where's Avery?"

He shook his head back and forth, back and forth, his eyes still closed to the world he was leaving. "Don't know," he mumbled. "You have to—you have to find them. He killed me. He'll kill him."

My heart iced over.

"S-s-sorry," he said, his body convulsing with shivers.

"It's okay," I whispered, even though it really, really wasn't. I let go of his wrist.

Shirley pulled off his black track jacket, rolled it up and put it under Mahoney's head as Not-Rocky grabbed the first-aid kit off the wall and pulled out rolls of gauze. "I'm calling 911," Shirley said as I pulled out my own phone and speed-dialed Svein.

"No one is calling anyone."

We all turned.

Clayton stepped out from behind the ring, from the darkest corner of the room.

"Who are you?" Shirley demanded, just as Not-Rocky said, "How'd you get in here?"

Clayton moved a little closer, and Shirley broadened his chest and stared him down. Not-Rocky, crouching beside Mahoney on the floor, stood up.

"You did this?" Not-Rocky asked, pointing at Mahoney. "You beat the crap out of this guy? He needs an ambulance."

"You need to shut up and get out," Clayton said, and despite his words, his tone was affable. He smiled at me. "Gemma, tell them."

"Guys," I said, and dropped my phone. First Greg, then Avery. I couldn't let two more people I cared about walk into this fire. "Guys, I've got this."

"Yeah, guys, she's got this," Clayton echoed. "Go on home. Gemma and I have some unfinished business to take care of." He cut his eyes to me, and it became clear to all of us how he intended to finish it.

"Not goin' anywhere," Shirley said, moving to stand in front of me. "And right now, your business isn't with her. It's with me."

I laid a restraining hand on Shirley's cement block of a shoulder, and he gently lifted my fingers and pushed me further back behind him.

"Then why don't you come on over here?" Clayton said, smirking. "And we'll get down to that business."

"Surely," said Shirley.

If this was my first encounter with Shirley, and if he was coming at me the way he was coming at Clayton now, I'd be praying for a quick end. In one motion, Shirley cracked the knuckles of his right hand and pulled his elbow back to deliver his championship punch.

But all he hit was air, because Clayton vanished.

Shirley's back was to me, and I couldn't see his face, but I'm sure he was blinking in confusion. He turned his head to the right and the left, then pulled his arm back in to his body, raising both fists in front of his face to defend.

But even Shirley couldn't stop what he couldn't see coming.

The heavyweight champ's right knee suddenly buckled. He struggled to stay upright, but then he clutched at his stomach with a cry of anger before an invisible force slammed into his skull. He spun and crashed to the floor like a solid slab of granite.

Clayton materialized, looked down at the unconscious Shirley and laughed out loud. "Riley Clayton in a KO!" he shouted, throwing one arm up in the air.

Before I could do anything, Not-Rocky bull rushed Clayton, breaking up his celebration. "No!" I cried as Clayton once again blinked out of view. Not-Rocky stumbled, flailing his arms to stay on his feet as his target disappeared and moved out of the way. Before he could turn, his arm jerked up against his back and twisted, his fingers scratching nothing, reaching in vain for his assailant. I winced at the loud crack of breaking bone and gasped at Not-Rocky's scream of pain before he went down face first.

I ran in his direction but a now-visible Clayton stepped into my path. Eye to eye, we stared at each other until he looked away to where Mahoney lay unmoving. "Reporters," he mused aloud, and shrugged. "They always say they'll do anything to protect a source, but kick them in the head a few times and they'll give up their own mother's name and address."

He looked back at me, smiling again. "I knew you were behind my media scandal, but I just wanted to make him say your name before he called you to come here. Then I had him call Avery McCormack, and tell him he had some extra information about my case. Too bad I wasn't mollified by Greg's eventual obedience. He really needed to learn more of a lesson, so I taught him one."

"Where's Avery?" I said through a clenched jaw.

He smiled as I tightened my fists at my side. "He's safe and sound."

I stepped even closer, and noticed a dark bruise on his jaw where I'd caught him in his office. My eyelashes nearly swept against his as I said, slowly and with danger in every syllable, "Where is Avery?"

He stepped away and flicked a wall switch, and Smiley's office lit up. "Right in there, all along."

Avery. I could see him through the glass window. He struggled against ropes that wrapped around his chest, and his lower jaw worked against a hand towel stuffed into his mouth. His eyes met mine, and he stopped moving.

I'd been home waiting for him, and he'd been here.

I ran to the window. "Hang on," I mouthed, and he drew his brows together, the only response he could give.

Looking at him, helpless and vulnerable, rage surged through me. I pulled it out of the ground through my legs and drew it up my torso, electrifying every muscle in my body. A blinding, black rush spun through my mind and clogged my ears. Every inch of me was hyper alert, on the offense, and when my wings burst out through my back, I barely felt it.

"This didn't have to go so far," Clayton said behind me. "But you decided to make this public, and now I have to get rid of him too. Such a shame for the voters of Virginia. Oh, and for you. But you won't be around long enough to miss him."

I grasped the front of my T-shirt, tore the remains of it off me and threw it to the ground. My wings, pushing out either side of my racer-back bra, pulsed with the powerful force that had risen in me. It was the urge to defend myself and to protect Avery and the friends who had rushed to help me without a second thought. It was the urge to avenge my broken family and a fae-seeking journalist.

I was ready to kill.

I whirled around but Clayton had advanced on me while my back was turned. He sucker-punched me in the gut. Already sore from his attack on me in his office, I lost my breath for a moment, but homicidal adrenaline pumped through me—and my fae form strengthened me. I sprang and surprised the now-winged Clayton with a left hook to the jaw and a strong right to his stomach.

His lower body caved in, rounding his back, and he shook his head, a trickle of blood seeping from the corner of his mouth. I barely registered the pain in my newly split knuckles as I bounced on my toes, back and forth, feinted in, hopped out and landed a jab hard into his sternum.

My half-human nemesis exhaled sharply but the half-fae in him recovered quickly. He grinned. "Finally," he said. "Gemma Fae Cross unleashes some fight." He ducked into me, and I pummeled his stomach once, twice, until he pushed away. He retaliated with a hard, sloppy cross, but I saw it coming and I blocked it.

"Unfortunately for those who paid to see this headline bout," he said, "I'm not much of a boxer." He jabbed again and I sidestepped it. "I'm more of a do-what-you-have-to-do-to-win kind of fighter." His right side twisted and I raised my arms to block a punch, but he lifted his leg and kicked my shoulder, pushing me back a few feet. I righted myself and he spun 360 degrees, cracking me on the temple with a backfist, and I dropped, lights sparkling across my vision.

This wasn't my kind of fight. I boxed for sport, controlled by rules and by limitations. Despite my desperation to make him hurt, I had no experience in fighting dirty.

He raised his leg to kick me again and I rolled out of the way. I scrambled to my feet and put the hanging heavy bag between us, but Clayton punched straight through the bag, the molecules of his fist splitting and reassembling inches from my face. I leaned back, stepping on a free weight plate near the dumbbell rack. I picked up the five-pounder as he walked around the bag and pushed the weight with both hands into his chest, knocking him onto his back. I crushed the plate into him, gritting my teeth, trying to suffocate him, but he lifted his lower body, hooked his feet over my shoulders and flipped me back. I threw my hands out to the floor as he reversed our positions. He squeezed my sides with his thighs and hovered over me. I reached for his throat but he held the plate six inches over my nose.

"Move a muscle," he said. "Just twitch. Anything. And I'll smash your face into a million pieces with your boyfriend watching through the window."

I stilled.

"Actually," he whispered, "I think I'll do it anyway." He lifted the plate up and I squeezed my eyes shut.

"Riley!" I heard. "You know you're not supposed to show anger! Hold it inside! They can't find out what you really are!"

Clayton froze, and I opened one eye. "Dad?" he asked and snapped his head around.

"No," Svein said.

The overhead lighting switched on. I tried to raise my body onto my elbows, but Clayton threatened with the disc again, and I sank down. He stayed silent, but the ugly, amused smile he'd worn since I arrived was gone. He wasn't looking at me anymore, but at something in front of him. When Svein spoke again, I realized he'd come around behind me and it was him Clayton was looking at.

"I talked to Carl," Svein said. "Your dad. He said when he returned to the morning fae after your mother died, he was afraid for you. He didn't want to lose someone else."

Like my mother, I thought. Clayton's dad tried to keep his warrior child safe. This murderous bastard who held a blunt weapon over the fragile bones of my face once had someone who loved him.

"Said one day he caught you shoving a kid in the playground. Remember that? So he had to teach you how to control your human emotions so the fae wouldn't sniff you out. How was that?" Svein asked. "Couldn't have been easy. You can't bind your human side in any Butterfly Room. All those emotions, bubbling under the surface, so many years. How did you live with it? How did you…"

"Shut up!" Clayton exploded. "You don't know shit."

I risked speaking from under the heavy plate. "They ripped you in half," I said, echoing his last letter to me, one he'd written so many years ago. Did he feel anything anymore? "Your human side died. Your mother's side."

I thought of his first letter to little me, saying I might need a friend. But he did.

My father had left us, and because of that, I'd embraced my true self and finally took up my warrior role.

Clayton's mother had died, taking his true self to her grave, and because of that, he'd taken revenge on everyone.

Svein surged on, words his only possible weapon. "I hadn't realized your father worked in the Butterfly Room," he said. "Interesting. A Butterfly agent could bound your sense of essence, off the record, because you wanted to be a dentist, so you could help the fae."

"Good one," I said.

"And here you are," Svein said, "about to kill your fellow half-fae whose parents hid her too. Why the hell would you do that when she's the only one like you?"

"I *gave* her a chance," Clayton said.

"To stop you," I said. "You wanted me to stop you."

"I wanted you to *know* me," he said. "With someone like me, I could have—we could have doubled our strength. In fact," he said, "we still can."

"You've got to be fucking kidding me," I said.

He took the plate away from my face, placed it beside me, and dropped to his hands, close to me. "I tried to warn you, Gemma," he whispered. "My father was right, after all. Your parents were right. At birth, we were drafted into a war we didn't start. Now you're fighting for the Olde Way. Why? Don't you realize," he said, dropping his voice to an intimate whisper, "that they've sold you a bill of goods?" He poked his knee hard into my ribs. "Don't you see that the Olde Way is not for me, *or* you?"

"What are you talking about?"

"We have no place there. You're breaking your neck for a club that won't let you in. If the Olde Way is ever recreated, the fae will live in everlasting harmony and peace, and you, the great warrior—you'll be the underpaid security guard at the gate."

"No," I said. But I paused. I'd lost and sacrificed and now I was staring death in the face. That was my destiny?

"Think about it," he said. "You and I, together, we can make a new reality. The Olde Way is gone, and the human world has so much wrong with it, I don't even know where to begin. But you and I can start a lineage of mixed breeds."

"*What?*"

"Imagine," he said, hooking a finger underneath the bottom of my sports bra, "what we can do together."

The smash of glass made us both jump, and Clayton's head snapped around to look at Smiley's office, where Avery had kicked through the window with his bound feet. It was only a moment of distraction, but it was enough. As Clayton turned back to me, I swept my arm around, whipping the back of my right hand hard across his mouth. He fell to the side, and I jumped up as he spit out a tooth.

I laughed bitterly. "Good thing you know a thing or two about cosmetic dentistry," I said.

Clayton got up but his head still hung and he wiped his mouth. "I assume this means you don't want to work together," he said, "and that you'd rather just die here."

"What makes you think you can do this, anyway?" I asked. "Are you stupid? The political candidate who promised on television to investigate you, his girlfriend, and the D.C. Digger. You think the police won't figure that one out?"

"Who cares?" He straightened all the way up but he didn't come after me. "They won't see me to arrest me when I blink. Or maybe I'll get careless and they will arrest me. And what happens then? Do you think there's one woman on the jury who I can't convince, with glamour, that I'm perfectly innocent? Do you think, if I end up in jail, that I can't convince a guard to let me out, or convince an entire floor of inmates to do my bidding? I'll be fine, and I'll have a new plan by then, but this time, you won't be around to stop me."

"Pretty sure of yourself," I commented, still smiling. "I guess you'd have to be, because you never had anything else. If you weren't someone I was about to kill, I'd feel sorrier for you. If your father was trying to squelch your emotions, you've never been to a gathering, have you?"

"Who cares?"

"Don't you think that if you'd ever seen the Olde Way, just for a second—really seen it yourself, and not heard morning fae romanticize it—you might have had a much different goal?"

"I told you, Gemma," he said, advancing slowly, putting one foot deliberately in front of the other, "it's not for us."

"But, see," I said, refusing to back up, letting him get closer and closer, "that's where you're wrong. I've *seen* it. And it's calling me home."

He narrowed his eyes.

"Svein was wrong," I said, gesturing to where Svein now knelt beside Mahoney. "And you're wrong. I'm not like you. Here's the difference." I stepped forward and met him once again eye to eye. "I belong to both humans and fae. But you belong to *no one*."

I anticipated the punch before he let it loose. I heard the swish of air as I dropped to the ground and rolled away. I popped back up to my feet but he rose also, and I mean *rose*—suddenly he was in the air, his wings holding him aloft with no effort and barely a flap. Shocked at the vision of him floating before me, he caught me off guard and was inches from me in an instant, pulling both his knees into his chest and slamming both feet into my sternum, sending me sprawling back against a weight bench before I slid to the floor.

Again, I never saw him move, and he was upon me. His wings were warp-speed. I scrambled but whacked the top of my head on the chair, and in the moment between pain and movement, Clayton fell back to earth with all his might, on top of my left ankle.

Whether it was the white-hot knifing pain or the sickening crack of splintering bone, I didn't know, but I screamed. I screamed out the raw, searing, intolerable realization that I was about to lose everything I'd done this for and everyone I cared about.

When my scream was only an echo reverberating around the dusty room, Clayton smiled that disturbed smile and said, "Good job. You certainly did make this interesting. I'll be with you shortly."

He headed to Smiley's office.

"No!" I yelled, but he'd turned deaf to me. I looked at Avery, twisting frantically against the ropes that held him as Clayton approached the room.

Think, *think*. I gritted my teeth with the effort to force logic to break through the pain and the fear.

I wasn't going anywhere on this foot. How else could I move? Crawl? Hop?

My right wing twitched.

I breathed in sharply, the oxygen shooting straight to my brain.

Bracing himself on a chair against the back wall of the tiny office, Avery used his feet to push the large metal desk in the direction of the closed door. It moved a half-inch every two or three pushes. Clayton paused at the window to watch, chuckling.

Svein was looking at me. My wings opened and closed. He nodded once. Yes.

I tried to communicate with my face, widening my eyes, furrowing my brow. *How?*

He mouthed something, and I squinted to see. He mouthed it again, exaggerating the words: *Just intend. Just fly.*

I intended, and swooped backward and up like I was on a swing set. My arms and legs flailed, and the whooshing air burned through my wounded and swollen ankle. Just before I hit the ceiling, I intended to hover, and I did.

I'd expected the skin on my back to pull, that I'd have a feeling of my body weight hanging by a thread, but it was as though I was standing still—ground unnecessary. I didn't have to think about moving my wings any more than I thought about moving my arms and legs. They were my body, and they did what I needed them to do. My hovering was shaky, like a car that could stall at any moment, but I was doing it.

Clayton kicked the office door off its hinges and shoved the desk against Avery, pinning him to the wall.

I swooped crookedly down to the pile of jump ropes near the ring, grasping the wooden handles. Clayton didn't see me. His full concentration was Avery, who was squirming and angry, but not frightened. I knew he wouldn't be, and that was my only comfort in the nanosecond it took me to get up on Clayton from behind and wrap the jump rope around his neck.

He clutched at the rope—literally his last rope—gasping and trying to breathe, trying to cough.

I pulled tighter.

I had a life in my hands, and remembered what I said to Svein. *When you fae finally do bring back the Olde Way, I am going to be worthy of it.*

The Olde Way needed me to fight its battles, but I couldn't win its war. The problem was that the morning fae assumed they needed violence to win the war. And maybe—maybe they didn't.

"Svein!"

He ran to my side as I loosened the rope and, still floating just above his twitching wings, instead wrapped my arm around Clayton's neck. He took the reprieve to cough, tears of pain streaming down his face. "My pocket," I said. "A little bag."

Svein reached into my front pocket, the warmth of his hand sliding down flat against my inner thigh, grasping a handful of trinkets. He threw my keys on the floor and opened the pink pouch. I held out my free hand, and he dropped the tooth into my palm. I closed my fingers around it.

The sticky, sweet scent ran up my nostrils and into my brain, coating my mind like molasses. White light radiated from the crown of my head and dissolved into a rainbow that slid down the length of my body, branching out into my fingers and toes, pulsing warmth into my injured ankle. The chorus of otherworldly voices faded in and wrapped itself around me like a lace blanket, humming in and out of the surface of my skin. *We all came from here, this place of purity. The light moves in and out of all of us. It's eternity. It's not gone…*

"You can't even kill me," Clayton managed in a hoarse whisper. "The legendary warrior can't finish the fight."

As at peace as I would have been had I just been tucked into bed, I stretched my legs out behind me and put my mouth close to his ear. "The Olde Way," I whispered, "is that we all exist in each other. If I kill you, I kill us, and then I fail." I squeezed my elbow tighter, and he scratched at my forearm. "You opened my eyes," I said. "Because I understand now that to win, we don't need violence. We only need what we already have. We only need to share the memory with those who can't remember. Or won't remember."

Still weak from his near-strangling, he struggled, pushing back at me, but I held fast. "In the end," I said, "you poisoned yourself with your toothpaste. And to beat you, I need to save you. Innocence is stronger than me, and it's much stronger than you."

With the hand wrapped around him, I reached up and pinched his nose shut, and he opened his mouth, his gulps for oxygen hissing over his tongue and through the gap where I'd smashed away his perfect grin. Blood slid from the corner of his mouth.

Fae blood. Our shared blood.

"For the record, I wish I didn't have to do this, because I don't forgive you," I said. "But this is my destiny. Now, smile wide."

I jammed the tooth, shimmering and scented with innocence, into the empty hole in his gum.

He howled long and hard and convulsed, tugging at his own face and lips, but still I held him until he abruptly silenced and closed his eyes. He softened completely, and when I slipped my arm away and backed up, he nearly tumbled backwards, so I eased him to the ground before my underused wings gave out and I fell against the wall next to him. He curled up, trembling, and hugged his arms around himself. Then he smiled.

It wasn't the killer smile of Dr. Clayton. It was the smile of Riley, a child skipping downstairs to find a pile of colorful gifts under a Christmas tree.

He tilted his head back, and I knew he was hearing the song. His breathing slowed, and I knew he was breathing in the freshness and purity. His eyes rolled back and forth under his lids, and I knew he was seeing the rainbow light. The Olde Way pulsed through his blood again, surrounded him with love.

Then he opened his eyes, bright and wet. "I saw it." he murmured. "I saw it. I saw it."

Svein, lingering in the doorway, and Avery, silent and restrained, watched. Then Svein went to Avery, removed the towel from his mouth, and began working through the ropes.

I tried to limp, but had to drop to a painful crawl on my forearms, dragging my battered foot, to get to Greg Mahoney.

For a moment, I thought I was too late. Then his eyelids fluttered strangely and opened into slits. "Mahoney, you bastard," I said. "Don't die."

"I think," he rasped, "I already did."

My wings opened and closed behind me. "No, it's me," I said. "I'm what you've been searching for."

"You're real," he whispered. "I knew. I *knew* I saw her. I was a kid." He swallowed with tremendous effort. "No one believed me."

"Well, hotshot," I said, and my words caught in my throat, thick with emotion. "I hope you're finally satisfied."

"Biggest story of my career," he said without moving his lips, and closed his eyes. His breath rattled funny, and I shook his shoulders. He didn't move. "Greg," I pleaded, laying my head on his chest. Then I yelled. "Svein! 9-1-1, *now*!"

Phone in hand, he was at my side in an instant, his face sober. I looked up at him, hot tears falling fast down my face. "Hurry up!"

"Gemma," Svein said quietly. "It's too late."

I stared, numbed. Svein knelt beside Greg's body.

I felt a hand on my shoulder. I didn't turn around, just bowed my head. "Bricks," I heard in my ear. "I'm glad you're okay." I turned to see Not-Rocky cradling his broken arm with the other. He leaned into me for an improvised hug. "Shirley's all right. He's lying down. He didn't see nothing. And me—well, I didn't see nothing either. Understand?"

I nodded my gratitude. He nudged my arm with affection, warily eyed my wings, and moved away.

Svein took my hand, but I lifted my head, and Avery was in front of me.

There was nothing I could say. As it turned out, I didn't have to.

I let go of Svein.

Avery knelt and opened his arms, and I crawled to him. He wrapped one arm around my shoulders and one around my waist as I sobbed. As I pressed my chest to his, I felt him sobbing too. I cupped the back of his neck and drew him down. His kiss was as strong and forgiving as mine. My wings shivered and folded into my back.

CHAPTER 23

One week later, I was still in bed. Sorrow, exhaustion, relief, and my broken ankle were four good reasons not to get up. Avery, as often as he could, was the fifth.

Staying in bed also meant staying out of the news, for the most part. As far as the public was concerned, my story wasn't the compelling one, anyway—I was just a bit player that night. This is what the world understood: the dentist whose career was ruined had killed the journalist who'd broken the story and tried to kill the politician who had it in for him, as well as the politician's girlfriend and a couple of local fighters who'd tried to help us. A rambling confession by Clayton made the paperwork a whole lot easier. Avery was comfortable in the spotlight, so he spoke for both of us.

There were a few things he didn't need to say, however, because no one knew to ask.

That night, while Clayton rocked and babbled in the corner and I cried in Avery's arms, Svein had called in several people from The Root, a team wearing jackets emblazoned on the back with a large purple butterfly. They arrived swiftly and closed themselves in the office with Clayton to bind his fae abilities, effectively turning him into a masqueraded human. After they left, the police arrived. As the cuffs were slapped on him, the little baby tooth fell out of his mouth, and his nonsensical chattering immediately ceased. When they led him out to the squad car, he passed by me, and I tore the blood drop chain off my neck and dropped it in his pocket. A token of respectful acknowledgment of his sad story.

He looked over his shoulder at me, and although I'd never know what he felt in that moment, I understood that it wasn't hate.

Before we'd all parted ways that night, I'd asked Svein one last question. Would Riley Clayton tell the police, tell the world, about the fae? "No," he'd said. "Because now that you've shown him the Olde Way, he knows that he risks losing it too. He's become one of us."

I had a lot of time since that night to think about everything, including the kids that Clayton had already gotten to—the sunken-cheeked, hollow-eyed kids in his waiting room, and little Brian's foul-mouthed apathy. I wished the poison effect would wear off, that their parents would be able to get their children back, but I knew firsthand—as did Clayton himself—that once innocence is taken away, it's gone forever.

In the last week, Mom came to visit me a few times and we mainly talked about my father. Dad came to visit me a few times, and we talked about Mom. They had yet to visit me together, but I knew they would. Soon.

In the meantime, Mom told me, she planned to attend the next fae moon gathering. She offered to bring me but I declined, remembering my difficult journey last time. I did ask her, though, how she could have stayed away for so long. I felt responsible, I said, that I was the one that kept her away.

"I did miss the company of other fae," she'd said. "But I kept two of your baby teeth in a box. If I needed to remember, I poured the box into my hand and let my little girl take me there."

Today, Avery was at Greg Mahoney's funeral. Though my broken ankle was a convenient excuse, it wasn't the reason I couldn't go. I just—couldn't go.

When Avery returned, it was noisily. The door opened and there was scrambling and shuffling and I thought I heard something heavy fall in the kitchen. "Avery?" I called. When he didn't answer, I hauled myself out of bed and balanced on one foot as the clatter neared, ready to spring if I had to.

Avery threw the door open, and a bomb hit me. A furry beagle bomb. I fell back onto the bed, and the dog landed on top of me, licking my face, barking once with happiness.

"Down, boy," I managed to say, and we wrestled some more. "Down, Canine!"

"Have you two met?" Avery asked. "I wasn't aware."

"We go way back," I said, then sat up the best I could. "Is he here to stay?"

"Yeah," Avery confirmed. "He needs a home, and you need an excuse to be out walking late at night."

I looked at him.

"In case anyone sees you," he clarified. "When you're collecting."

"Thank you," I said, and meant it in a million ways.

>=<

A few months later, standing in front of an unfamiliar front door at night, I closed my eyes, concentrating on detecting movement on the other side. A dark shadow moved, and I realized someone was not only awake, but right behind the door. I popped my eyes open and turned to tiptoe down the walk in my bare feet, and the door opened behind me. I intended my molecules to evaporate and blink.

"I have to say, Gemma," I heard, "you're getting a lot better at this."

Sighing, I dropped the blink and whirled to face Svein. "You live here? Nice one," I said, "sending me your address on my Fae Phone for a tooth collection." I dropped my black slingback shoes on the ground and slid my cold toes into them. "I'll have you know I left a *party* to come here because I thought it was a legitimate call."

"Yeah, I know," he said, his eyes sweeping over me. Because the moment commanded it and because, frankly, he deserved it for tricking me, I spun dramatically around in my royal blue dress, showing straps that rose over my shoulders and crisscrossed in the back and a side slit that exposed several inches of my right thigh. He cleared his throat and I stood still again, satisfied.

"I wanted to see you in person," he said, "to offer my congratulations on U.S. Representative Avery McCormack's victory. I voted for him myself, but I guess it wasn't all that important, considering his landslide."

"Every vote counts," I said automatically, and grinned. "We're celebrating all those votes tonight. Haven't seen you in a while, by the way."

"Is that your fault or mine?"

I twisted my mouth. "Maybe both."

Truth is I had been avoiding Svein. I didn't know why.

Well, yes, I did.

"I'm sorry," I said now. "I decided to lie low for a few months. Avery and I needed some time to heal and to understand each other the way we are now."

Svein looked me in the eye. "Did that happen?"

I smiled, and maybe it was a little apologetic. "Yes."

He nodded.

"We weren't the only ones," I added. "My parents are—well, they're taking things slow with one another. They're working it all out. A lot was taken from them, and they had to start from scratch. But they never fell out of love."

"And you have a father again."

"Turns out I always did. Anyway," I said, "enough of all that. I'm back on the collection rotation."

"I heard."

I took a deep breath. "We need to talk about things."

"Like?"

"It's not over," I said. "With these kids. This city. It's not over. They're getting older. Something got to them." I stopped. "You read about that kid yesterday who held up the drugstore in Georgetown? Got what he wanted and he still stabbed the pharmacist. The kid's *twelve* years old."

"Humans are violent."

I blinked. "Sorry?"

"Our job's done," he said, his eyes not leaving mine. "We caught the Olde Way threat. It's over. It's human nature to turn against each other. Let it play out the way it always has. Our job's done."

It took me a moment to find my voice, buried as it was under a layer of shock and indignation. "But… but the fae caused this. They caused this to happen. If they didn't depend on the half-fae to be their warriors, Riley's dad would have been able tell the truth about his half-fae son. Riley would have been safe and wouldn't have had to live in that festering fear and shame that caused this whole mess. Instead, he became the perfect conduit for midnight fae, to weaken kids until they could be transformed into demons."

"You don't know that."

"I am making an unsubstantiated but educated guess."

He never broke eye contact, and his expression didn't change.

"Our job isn't done," I said. "The fae caused this. We have a responsibility."

"We bear no responsibility to a species that nearly wiped us out."

"But it's okay to feed off humans' teeth to help us get what we want? Humans don't even know fae truly exist, so displacing the fae on Earth wasn't intentional. But the fae have the advantage of knowledge. They know better. Right now, you and I both know we're at fault."

Svein didn't move.

"We need to act like morning fae should," I said. "You need to. Or am I supposed to save everyone myself?"

I'd moved closer to him without realizing it, and I noticed it now as I felt his tiny resigned exhale blow against my cheek.

"We'll revisit this," he told me.

I didn't want to push. I understood the magnitude of his concession and what it would mean for the fae to step in now. So I forced my happiness of the evening to push this aside for just a few hours. This was all going to haunt me for a very long time, so I'd grab this one night of peace.

Svein closed the front door behind him and leaned against it. The streetlamp directly in front of his building was buzzing, the bulb failing, and it played light over his hair.

Svein was adept at using his glamour, but he would never truly need it.

"You and I," he said, "we never resolved things."

"I'm sorry," I said, looking at my pointy-toed shoes. "When you tried to give me the gun, I got very—well, sanctimonious. That wasn't necessary. You were trying to help."

"I'm sorry," he responded, "because even after you gave me a tongue-lashing about my assumption that your human side could be so easily violent, I didn't believe you. I didn't believe you until I saw you defeat Clayton without killing him. I'm sorry that the moment I met you, I was positive you wouldn't be any kind of hero."

He tilted my chin up to look at him. "Well done," he said.

We stayed there for a long moment. "Are we resolved?" I finally asked.

"Not quite yet," he said quietly. "It's hard to put an end to your constant presence in my mind. But I'll get there."

He dropped his hand and I turned to go, but when I heard him open the door to go inside, I turned back. "Do you want to come back to the party?" I asked. "I did call to invite you but I guess you didn't get the message. Frederica's there, and Reese, and my parents and Avery's dad, and Smiley and the guys. We're having a great time. This part's a happy ending."

He smiled and shook his head. "Not quite yet," he repeated, and closed the door between us.

>=<

I woke up in the middle of the night, and in that space between conscious and unconscious, I tried to retrieve my dream. I couldn't. I remembered shedding my black shoes in the living room, my blue dress in the bedroom, and my underwear in bed, but I didn't remember anything after closing my eyes. Rolling over, I curled into Avery, all of his skin warm against all of mine, his arm around my waist.

When I drifted to sleep again, it was deep and dreamless.

ACKNOWLEDGMENTS

It takes team effort to win, and I would like to thank my talented, dedicated team:

Colleen Lindsay, the offensive coordinator with the extensive playbook.

My agent Louise Fury, who received the punt and ran the ball back up the length of the field for a touchdown.

Roberta Lerman, the head coach who yelled at refs who penalized me—and yelled at me in the locker room at halftime when it looked as if my mistakes could cost me the game.

Chris Cheney, the reliable running back who marched the ball up the field in a long drive.

Mike Downes, the medic who carted me off on a stretcher, bandaged me up, and sent me back on the field.

My sister, Elizabeth Markman, who provided colorful sidelines commentary.

My mother, the cheerleading squad captain.

My father, the season ticket holder.

My cat Shaq, who sleeps through most of the games but insists the kitchen concession stand be well stocked with 9 Lives.

My New York Jets, who inspired this long analogy.

Football comparisons aside…

I am grateful for all the students at Emerald Yoga Studio. Yoga, more than anything else, changed my life. Every single one of you is my teacher. Namaste.

ABOUT THE AUTHOR

Jennifer Safrey is an award-winning author of four romance novels. *Tooth & Nail* is her first foray into urban fantasy. Jennifer is the co-owner of Emerald Yoga Studio in Pembroke, Mass., and teaches vinyasa flow yoga. She holds a black belt in taekwondo. She grew up just outside New York City and is a graduate of Boston University.